Stephanie—
Sometimes
Happily Ever After
takes a bit more
work.

gorgeous

chaos

T.K. Leigh

GORGEOUS CHAOS

Published by Tracy Kellam, 25852 McBean Parkway # 612, Santa Clarita, CA 91355

Edited by Kim Young, Kim's Editing Services

Cover Design: Cat Head Biscuit, Inc., Santa Clarita, CA

Front Cover Image Copyright Stokkete 2014

Used under license from Shutterstock.com

Back Cover Image Copyright Tatiana Morozova 2014

Used under license from Shutterstock.com

ISBN: 1499198825
ISBN-13: 978-1499198829

Books by T.K. Leigh

The Beautiful Mess Series

A Beautiful Mess
A Tragic Wreck
Gorgeous Chaos

Heart of Light (Coming November 2014)

To Stan... My Always and Forever.

A NOTE FROM THE AUTHOR

Gorgeous Chaos is the third and final installment in my *Beautiful Mess* series. As with the first two books of the series, this book contains explicit sexual situations and strong language. In addition, there will be several scenes that contain graphic violence. I have spent hours making sure that I painted some of the violent situations that these characters face in the book in a certain light without sacrificing the integrity of the story, and I hope that I was able to reach a respectful balance. In particular, there are two scenes in which rape is alluded to, but not described in any detail at all, as I refuse to glorify a horrific crime in that manner. That being said, if you are particularly sensitive to arguably violent situations, proceed with caution.

Approximately every two minutes, another woman is sexually assaulted in this country. If you have been a victim, there are resources available to you so that you do not have to go through the healing and recovery process alone. The Rape, Abuse & Incest National Network is one of the leading services out there today. If you ever need someone to talk to, you can always call them at 1.800.656.HOPE or find them online at www.rainn.org.

As always, thank you for your loyalty and for supporting me.

CHAPTER ONE

THANK YOU, MAMA

SUN FILTERED INTO THE elegant master bedroom, waking up Sarah Olivia Adler on a bright Saturday in March. She stretched, a smile spreading across her face as she recalled the events of the previous night.

Alexander loved her, and she loved him. She was able to say those three words that had scared her most of her life. Her heart felt as if it would explode when the image flashed through her mind of Alexander dropping down on one knee, asking her to be his wife. It all made perfect sense. The dream she had all those months ago in Newport that scared her to death, causing her to flee, was suddenly clear. She firmly believed that her mama was sending her a message, from wherever she was, with that dream. Once Alexander sang that song, the song Olivia remembered so well from her childhood, the song her mama was singing in her dream as she danced with the green-eyed boy, she knew it was meant to be. She knew it was useless to fight it anymore.

"Thank you, Mama," she whispered, glancing at the large diamond on her ring finger. Turning over, she reached her arm across the mattress, surprised when all she felt was the cold of the bed. Alexander wasn't there.

She looked at the clock on the nightstand and sat straight up. It was almost noon! Olivia couldn't remember the last time she had slept the entire night and woken up so late. She grabbed Alexander's white suit shirt that he had been wearing the night before and threw it on, remembering the first

1

weekend she stayed with him and how turned on he got when she walked around wearing his clothes. She barely recognized the girl she was all those months ago, and she knew that she had Alexander to thank for finally breaking down her walls.

After pulling her wavy brown hair into a messy bun, she made her way downstairs, searching for her fiancé. An infectious smile crossed her face when she spotted him sitting at the breakfast bar, drinking his coffee and reading the newspaper. She sauntered up to him and kissed him full on the lips as he slinked his arm around her slender waist.

Alexander closed his eyes and moaned, pulling her against his body, and slipped his hand under the shirt she wore. "I love the feel of your skin, Olivia," he said quietly.

Her eyes became aglow at his affectionate words and she curved toward him, her lips poised on his. "And I love it when you feel my skin, Alexander," she replied, kissing him once more.

"You look hot," he commented, his voice raspy and sexy. "I like you in my clothes. Coffee?" He ran a finger up and down Olivia's spine, causing her to shiver before pulling back.

"I can get it. You sit," she replied, giving him a quick kiss on his neck and walking around the kitchen island. She grabbed a mug and made herself a cup of coffee before returning to the breakfast bar and sitting next to him.

"So, there are a few things we should probably discuss." His voice was firm as he turned to her with an austere expression on his face.

"What's that?" Olivia asked, raising her coffee mug to her lips.

"Have you spoken to my sister?" He lifted his eyebrows, already knowing what her response would most likely be.

She hid her eyes from him, recalling how she had spent the past several days since running out on Alexander after he declared his love for her. "No, I'm sorry. I just kind of ignored life this week."

He exhaled loudly. "I figured as much." He took a sip of coffee. When he put his mug down, a stern look crossed his face, his vibrant green eyes intense.

Crap, Olivia thought to herself.

"Well, Simon was released from prison yesterday."

"So, let me guess," she said loudly, standing up from her barstool. "Now you're going to assign an army to watch me? Is that what this is about, Alex?" She glared at him, her hands on her hips in irritation.

"Hey. Relax," he responded, caressing her arm. "That's not what this is about at all." His eyes pleaded with her not to be upset.

She stared at him for several long moments before a small smile crossed her expression. How could she stay mad at that adorable face? Her aggravation waning, she sat back down and waited for him to continue.

He raised his hand and pushed an errant curl that had fallen out of her bun behind her ear, gently brushing her forehead where her scar was. "I know I can be overbearing at times…"

"Ya' think?" Olivia interrupted with a sarcastic tone.

"Don't get fresh with me," he growled into her ear. "Or I'll teach that mouth of yours a lesson."

His words sent a primal desire through her body. All she could do was stare at him with her mouth open, thinking how much she wanted him to teach her a lesson. Moisture pooled between her legs at the thought.

"I'm just trying to keep you safe, Olivia. That's all," he said, immediately switching from the passionate lover to the concerned fiancé. "I protect the people I care about who are important to me. That's why I need to be in control…to keep everyone close to me safe. You're the most important person in my life." Grabbing her chin, he forced her to look him in the eyes to see the truth in his words. "So if I'm overbearing at times, I apologize. I just want to make sure that nothing bad happens to you."

"I'm sorry," she responded, her voice husky. She wondered if Alexander would always have that effect on her. She loved how caring and compassionate he was. Guilt spread through her conscience for jumping down his throat about protecting her when all he was trying to do was keep her safe from someone who had a history of attacking her. She knew he had issues with control. She guessed it went back to his childhood when he lost his friend all those years ago. He had admitted how helpless he felt after her death.

"So, back to Simon." He cleared his throat, releasing his grasp on Olivia's chin. She took a sip of her coffee and listened. "Like I said, he's out of prison. You probably have a notice sitting in your mailbox about all of this. Anyway, the protective order has been lifted. He is free to contact you if he wants."

Olivia glanced at Alexander, his face weary.

"Do you understand what that means, love?"

"It's just a piece of paper anyway, Alexander. Even if it hadn't been lifted, it wouldn't change anything. If he really wanted to see me, that protective order wasn't going to stop him," she said, withholding from him that Simon had already violated the protective order not even a week after he was arrested for attacking her back in August.

"You're absolutely right. But I just wanted to warn you to be careful. We know this Mark Kiddish, or Donovan O'Laughlin, paid Simon's attorney fees, but we have no idea if there's more to the connection than that. We still don't know what Kiddish could possibly want from you," he lied.

"Should I be worried?" Olivia stared into his eyes, searching for the truth.

He debated telling her everything. He wanted to, but her father's warning lay heavy on his heart…and his mind. What if Jack was right? What if her lack of memory was the only thing that had kept her alive those past twenty-plus years? "Let me worry about Simon. You just worry about planning a wedding." He winked.

"Holy shit! I totally forgot about that."

Alexander looked at her, aghast.

"Don't give me that look. I'm still trying to get my head around the fact that I'm getting married!" She bounced up and down on her barstool, excitement oozing from her infectious grin.

Alexander couldn't help but smile at her in return. "I can't wait until you have my last name, Olivia," he said softly, grabbing her hand and gently kissing her knuckles.

4

She was instantly reminded of the night that she met him. An awareness of complete euphoria washed over her from Alexander's sensual words and presence, and she truly believed that running into him outside her office building was the best thing to ever happen to her.

Alexander's cell phone started to ring, breaking their moment. He glanced down at the caller ID. "Sorry, love. It's my mom. I should probably tell her that I'm getting married, if she doesn't already know." He slid off the barstool and answered the phone. "Good morning, Ma."

"Is it true?" Colleen Burnham asked excitedly. "I was watching the news this morning and they're reporting that you're rumored to be engaged, darling."

Alexander laughed. "Yes, Ma. I asked Olivia to marry me last night."

She squealed out in joy. "Oh, Alex. I'm so happy for you. Gosh, after all these years. Who would have thought? Is she there? Can I speak with her?"

"Mom…"

"Alex. Don't worry. I won't say anything, I promise. But you need to before it's too late and you lose her again," she scolded before softening her voice. "I just want to talk to her about the wedding…girl stuff."

"Fine." Alexander handed the phone to Olivia. "It's my mom. She wants to speak with you."

Olivia sent him a questioning look.

Don't worry, he mouthed.

She smiled, taking the phone. "Mrs. Burnham?"

"Good morning, Olivia, dear. And please, call me Colleen."

"Sorry. Colleen."

"I just wanted to offer you my congratulations on your engagement, darling."

"Thank you. It still hasn't really sunk in."

"I'm sure it will take a bit. Anyway, I wanted to invite you and Alex over to the house this evening for a little family get together. The reason I'm asking *you* is because he'll shoot me down right away. He likes to keep you for himself. Selfish bastard."

Olivia laughed. That sounded like Alexander.

"You're going to become a member of our family," Colleen continued. "And I'd like to introduce you to everyone."

"I'd love to, Colleen. That sounds wonderful." Olivia couldn't believe the words that came out of her mouth. Just a week ago, she was scared to meet Alexander's mother. Now, she was agreeing to a family gathering.

Alexander looked at Olivia, raising his eyebrows in an inquisitive manner. *Family dinner at your mom's*, she mouthed. He held out his hand for the phone. She responded by raising her finger, indicating that he would have to hold on.

"I'm looking forward to seeing you and the rock I heard about on television this morning."

Olivia held her hand in front of her and admired her new piece of jewelry. "Your son *does* have excellent taste."

"I taught him well. Please put Alex back on and I'll see you this evening."

"I look forward to it," she replied before returning the phone to Alexander.

"Mother, what do you think you're doing?" he seethed, his teeth clenched.

"Oh, nothing, dear. Just having a little family get together this evening at the house. Don't worry. Mrs. Carlson is helping me prepare it and rid it of anything 'Olivia-related'."

Alexander sighed, worried that being back in Mystic could trigger memories about her past...a past that could kill her. "I'm not going to win this fight with you, am I?"

"Not a chance. See you tonight," Colleen said before hanging up.

Alexander shook his head in defeat, turning to face Olivia. "Well, you better pack a bag, love. We're heading to Connecticut for the evening."

She gasped. "Oh, I'm sorry. I didn't realize your mother lived in Connecticut! I would have spoken with you first if I had known. She made it sound as if she was close by, or maybe I just assumed she was."

Alexander laughed. "She can be a bit deceiving at times. I think that's where I get it from."

CHAPTER TWO

THE DEATH OF ME

THE AIR WAS THICK with tension as Alexander drove with Olivia from Boston toward Connecticut that afternoon. Glancing at the man she was going to marry, Olivia couldn't help but notice his rigid and taut stature, as if he was uptight about the party that evening. "I'm looking forward to seeing where you grew up," she said, breaking the strained silence.

"Are you sure that you're okay with this? We can go back if you want to." Alexander met her eyes briefly, a nervous expression permanently drawn on his face at the thought of being back in his childhood home with Olivia.

She reached across the car and grabbed his hand. "I'm fine with it," she reassured him. "Are you going to be okay being there? I know it's difficult for you…" She trailed off, looking out the window at the rolling green hills. She should have known that it would be painful for him to be in a place where he would be surrounded by constant reminders of the friend he lost when he was just a young child.

"It's okay. I'm fine with it. Ever since I met you, it's been much easier for me to deal with the memories." He squeezed her hand and gave her a comforting look before returning his eyes to the road.

Over the last several months, he had been able to confront his memories but, in turn, was constantly forced to hide information from the girl sitting next to him. He had to remind himself that it was necessary to keep those secrets from her. It was the only way he could protect his Olivia.

Before long, he maneuvered his Maserati off the freeway and onto the main road through Mystic. Olivia took in her surroundings as they made their way toward the downtown area, driving past the train station. She furrowed her brow.

"Penny for your thoughts?" he asked with a hint of apprehension upon noticing her expression.

"This place looks familiar," she replied as they drove over the drawbridge, passing Alexander's favorite ice cream shop.

"It's a fairly popular place in Connecticut and New England, really. There's a lot of maritime history here. In fact, at one time, the house I grew up in belonged to a sea captain. I was obsessed with boats and ships when I was younger. Maybe that's why I wanted to go into the Navy so badly."

"No. I don't ever remember visiting here," she said quietly, her eyes still glued to all the old buildings. "But it just seems familiar." Olivia stared as they drove down Main Street, searching her brain for a memory that wouldn't come.

Within a few minutes, Alexander pulled his car into the long driveway of his house overlooking the Mystic River, worried that being back inside his home would stir even stronger memories. He wanted to throttle his mother for her hair-brained notion that it was a good idea to bring Olivia back here.

"This is where you grew up?" Olivia asked, astonished at the breathtaking large white house with a wrap-around porch. "It's beautiful, Alexander." She got out of the car, gazing over the river at a tall ship docked on the opposite side of the bank. "What a view."

Alexander stared at her, relieved that perhaps she truly had no memory of her childhood. She grew up just a few houses down from him and had the same view. She practically *lived* at Alexander's house most of the time, and yet she acted as if it was the first time she had ever laid eyes on the river...and the house.

Starting to relax, he walked up to her and pulled her into his embrace. "If you're good, I'll take you down the street and buy you some ice cream later." He swatted her ass, making her jump, before leading her up the driveway and into the house.

She followed him down a long hallway, past several formal living rooms and an ornate dining room, and into the kitchen.

"Olivia, darling," Colleen said, embracing her as she entered the open, modern room. "It's wonderful to see you. I'm so glad that you dragged my son here." She pulled back, winking. "Alex, please take your things upstairs while your fiancée and I have a little chat."

"Mom…"

"Hush. I don't bite, dear."

Alexander rolled his eyes and carried their bags up the stairs to his room.

"Now, dear, let me see the ring," Colleen said, turning back to Olivia.

She held out her hand.

"Oh, my," she exhaled, holding Olivia's hand up to her eyes for a closer inspection. "That is beautiful. I wonder if he picked it out himself."

"Based on his closet at home, I'd guess so. He does have fantastic taste in clothes."

Colleen laughed. "He absolutely does. I guess that's what happens when you grow up with mostly women as influences."

"Stop talking about me, you two," Alexander joked, making his way back downstairs after scanning the walls to ensure that his mother had done a thorough enough job of ridding the house of anything 'Olivia-related'.

"Well, listen. Why don't you both relax for a while? People won't start to arrive until seven, so you've got plenty of time to go for a walk or whatever you want. It's finally supposed to be such a nice evening so I had everything set up out back."

"Ma, who all is coming?" Alexander glared at his mother. She loved to throw a party.

"Oh, you know. Family."

Alexander walked toward the back door, gazing at their expansive backyard to see that it was set up for roughly a hundred guests.

"Mom, this is *not* a small little get together."

"We have a large family. Now out with you two so I can finish getting everything ready."

Alexander looked over at Olivia, a look of panic across her face. "Come with me, gorgeous." He pulled her hand and led her out of the house. "Want to go for a walk?"

Olivia nodded, needing a minute to calm her nerves.

"I'm sorry about all of this," Alexander said, clutching her hand as they walked along the river toward downtown Mystic on the warm early spring day.

"It's okay," she replied nervously, letting out the breath that she had been holding. "I know that I need to get used to it. I just grew up with no family. My uncle was the only family I really had." She looked down at her hand enclosed in his as she savored the warmth of his skin on hers, feeling comfort in the innocent contact.

"Were you close to him?" He was desperate for more information about his father's secret life.

"It's hard to say." Olivia hadn't thought about her younger years in quite a long time. "He was my legal guardian, but I really only saw him during summers. He had a house on Folly Beach right outside of Charleston, and we would spend our summers there. But he always seemed somewhat distant. Mom died leaving me a fortune, as you know, and when I was younger, he hired a nanny to take care of me."

"Sorry…"

"It's okay," Olivia said, shrugging. "I guess I was better off than a lot of girls I was in school with. Most of them were sent to the boarding school so that their parents could travel and not be saddled with dealing with their kids. At least I had no parents. I guess the hardest part was around the holidays."

"How so?"

"Well, even though all the other girls' parents dumped them at some school so they didn't have to actually care for them, at least they got presents and cards. I was the only one who never got anything. My nanny would sometimes send me a small little something, but when you're a little kid and you see everyone else around you opening gifts and you don't have anything to open, it's difficult. You start to think that nobody loves you enough to remember to send you a gift for Christmas or even your birthday."

"Fuck…" Alexander said under his breath, wondering why his father would agree to look after the girl and then practically ignore her.

Olivia glanced at him as they strolled along the riverbank past rows of historic homes. "Tell me about it."

They walked in silence for a moment. "I had some pretty good friends there, especially in middle school and high school." Her mouth turned slightly upwards, thinking about the girls she used to hang around with. "We used to get in so much trouble together."

Alexander listened as she recalled her younger years, wishing he had known her during that time in her life. Maybe both of their lives would have turned out differently. Then again, if she hadn't been taken from him, maybe they would have eventually grown apart, as childhood friends often do. He shuddered at the thought of not having her in his life.

"As the years went on, I spent more and more time at the school," Olivia said, bringing him back from his thoughts. "My uncle was hesitant at first. He could be overbearing at times." She tilted her head to look at Alexander with a playful expression. "You probably would have gotten along wonderfully. You remind me of him a little bit."

His breath caught and his eyes met hers, silently questioning her.

"You know. You're both rather protective of me," she explained. "It's cute and all, but you do realize that I'm an adult, right, Alex?"

"Of course I do," he responded, bringing her hand to his mouth and placing a gentle kiss on her knuckles. "But I just have this deep-seeded need to look out for you and keep you safe."

She opened her mouth to say something and then closed it, not wanting to argue after they were getting along so well. "Anyway, my uncle finally relented and allowed me to stay at school during the holidays so I could participate in sports and theater and other stuff. Of course, before he agreed to that, he made sure the security in place during regular sessions was exactly the same. He was just as paranoid as you." She winked.

There was more silence as they turned onto Main Street. Olivia took in the narrow street with the drawbridge, everything seeming eerily familiar to her. "There's an oyster place over the bridge, isn't there?"

Alexander stopped in his tracks, causing several tourists to almost bump into him before they maneuvered around him, cursing underneath their breath. "How do you know that?" He met her gaze, his heart racing in his chest.

"I have no idea," she blanched. "That seems to be happening a lot lately...as if I had been to certain places before, you know, the accident."

He continued walking with Olivia by his side, hoping her surroundings didn't stir any more memories. "Do you recall anything about your life before the accident?"

"Not really. I guess my brain just forgot everything. My uncle told me that I couldn't even remember my name due to the head injury I had suffered. The doctors hoped that I would get my memory back once I returned to my regular life and went home, but I guess Charleston didn't hold any memories for me because nothing ever came back."

"That's kind of depressing."

"Well, I've got the cure for that," Olivia said, eyeing the ice cream shop adjacent to the drawbridge. "Ice cream!"

Alexander laughed. "Okay. You got it, love." He pulled her along, skirting by tourists exploring the shops in downtown Mystic.

They walked through the front door of the relatively empty shop, making their way to the counter to order. "What'll it be, Olivia?" Alexander asked.

She took in her surroundings. The store looked familiar, just like the rest of the town. "Scoop of strawberry, scoop of rocky road with pineapples on top," she replied without even thinking about it.

"Are you serious?" Alexander asked with a blank expression.

Olivia laughed. "Yeah. I don't know why I'm ordering that. I don't think I've ever had it, but something about this place makes it seem like the right decision."

"Okay. You got it." He placed their order and handed her

the bowl full of ice cream.

"Is that a park across the street?" she asked, sticking a spoon in her frozen treat.

"Yes. Do you want to go sit over there?"

Her eyes widened. "Yes, please," she responded excitedly. "We can watch the boats come by."

Alexander stilled again, thinking that bringing Olivia to Mystic was probably the worst idea his mother had ever come up with. He remembered doing the same exact thing with her when they were growing up. It didn't help that he had ordered what he always did when he and Olivia were kids – vanilla with cherries on top.

"Are you coming?" Olivia asked, holding the door open for him.

He snapped out of it. "Yes. Sorry. I'm coming." He walked behind her, checking out her tall, slender body from behind as they made their way across the drawbridge.

She glimpsed over her shoulder and shivered from the primal stare Alexander gave her. "See something you like, Mr. Burnham?" She winked.

"I see something I *love*, Miss Adler." He slinked his arm around her waist and planted an affectionate kiss on her temple as they walked across the street to the park and sat down on a bench, looking out over the river.

"It's so peaceful here," Olivia remarked, enjoying the feeling of the light breeze on her skin. "I think I would have enjoyed living here as a child. There must have been so much to do."

"It was a good place to grow up." Alexander recalled spending nearly every day with Olivia. He remembered how she cried when he got to start school, but she was still too young. He smiled, thinking how her eyes lit up when he stopped by her house after that first day and told her all about it.

She had been coloring with her mother and she excitedly ran into her playroom, handing him a piece of construction paper with a drawing on it. It was supposed to be of the two of them sitting on a bench at the park eating ice cream. He wondered if he still had that somewhere at his house.

"And, I mean, what kid wouldn't love living right down the street from an ice cream shop!" Olivia brought him back from his memories as she took another bite, moaning with pleasure.

Alexander glanced at her, leaning into her neck. "You better stop with that or I'm going to throw you on the ground and have my way with you, and I don't care who's around to watch," he growled, his voice husky.

Olivia's spine straightened, her eyes growing wide. She met Alexander's gaze, the heat emanating from it palpable. She swallowed hard. "That's pretty fucking hot." She grabbed another spoonful of ice cream, brought it to her lips, opened her mouth slightly, and took a bite while Alexander watched her, his expression intense. She closed her eyes, moaning as she slowly slid the spoon out of her mouth.

"Do you want me to fuck you, Olivia?" he whispered in her ear.

She opened her eyes to see Alexander looking at her with a hooded stare. "Yes," she exhaled.

He grabbed her hair, tilting her head back to expose her neck. "Yes, what?"

Olivia's blood spiked. She loved playing his little game. "Yes, Mr. Burnham."

"That's better." He stood up, grabbing her hand. "Let's get home." He pulled her down Main Street. The short walk back home seemed to take an eternity.

"Oh, you're back," Colleen said, spotting Alexander and Olivia as they practically ran through the front door.

"Yes. We're back. Olivia wants to lie down. See you soon, Ma," Alexander said quickly, rushing through the living room in the direction of the staircase.

"Okay. Go easy, kids. That bed isn't nearly as sturdy as it used to be."

Olivia stopped dead in her tracks on the stairs and turned to look at Alexander, her face bright red. A wicked grin spread across his face and he couldn't help but laugh.

"I used to be your age once, too, ya' know!" she explained.

Olivia gawked at Colleen, speechless.

"Come on, love," Alexander said, still laughing. Picking her up, he slung her over his shoulder, making her squeal with excitement when he playfully smacked her ass.

He opened the door to his childhood bedroom, thankful his mother and Mrs. Carlson had taken down all the photos he had of him when he was a boy. Placing Olivia on her feet, he sat on the edge of the bed, glaring at her with a lustful expression. "Strip," he ordered.

Fuck, this is hot, she thought to herself as her eyes roamed his beautiful body. She met Alexander's stare and slowly unbuttoned her jeans, taking her time lowering them to the floor, her eyes never leaving his.

"Are you trying to be a tease, Olivia?" he asked sternly. "I am not a patient man. I said strip. Now."

The tone of his voice made her heart race even faster. She lifted her shirt over her head before quickly removing her bra and panties.

"That's better," he said, crossing his arms in front of his chest.

Olivia gaped at the muscular biceps threatening to bust the seams of his t-shirt.

"Now, getting back to our conversation in the park," he said, bringing her back from her thoughts about his gorgeous frame. "Do you want me to fuck you?" He surveyed Olivia's naked body as she stood in front of him, her engagement ring the only item she wore. He felt a twitch in his pants.

"Yes, Mr. Burnham," she replied quietly.

"Ask me, then," he ordered, his voice full of hunger and yearning. Reaching out, he grabbed her hips, pulling her closer to him. He planted kisses across her stomach before lowering his head, licking between her legs.

"Fuck," Olivia breathed out when Alexander stopped a few seconds later.

"I said ask me, Olivia." He looked up at her, gently plunging a finger inside of her.

She squirmed in response. "Will you fuck me, Mr. Burnham?" she exhaled, the sensation of just one finger inside of her too much.

Standing up, Alexander rid himself of his clothes in a hurry.

He walked up behind her, brushed her hair to one side, and kissed her exposed neck. "Hold on to the bedpost and lean over, love." His voice was gentle and soft.

Olivia still marveled at the dichotomy of the man she had fallen in love with. Sex was always different, no matter how many times they did it. She walked over to the bedpost and placed her hands on it, bending over, using the frame to support her body.

"You should see the view I have right now," he commented, curving toward her, his lips warm against her neck. Olivia looked over her shoulder as he softly caressed her ass, setting her body on fire from the anticipation. "It's hot." He gently eased himself into her, filling her completely.

She moaned out, the sensation of Alexander slowly pushing into her from behind overwhelming her once more.

"You like that, Olivia?" he asked, withdrawing before entering her again.

She closed her eyes, reveling in the electricity coursing through her veins from Alexander's gentle motion.

"I asked you a question, Olivia." He grabbed on to her hips and leaned down once more. "And I expect an answer," he growled into her ear.

"Yes," she exhaled as he continued his deliberate movements.

"I know that I always say this, but you feel so damn good," he grunted. She met his rhythm thrust for thrust, her breathing becoming erratic as she fought against her orgasm.

"Do you like it slow like this, or do you want it fast?"

She moaned, not wanting to answer. She was ready to fall apart from the gentle pace Alexander was maintaining. She couldn't even imagine what would happen if he picked up the tempo. She thought she would explode. "Slow, Alexander. Please," she begged.

A grin spread across his face as he continued filling her. "And why's that, Olivia? Are you ready to come already?" he asked, dragging his tongue across her shoulder blade. "Is my cock too much for you to handle?" he whispered against her skin.

She closed her eyes, convinced that Alexander could make her come from his words alone.

"Well, Olivia," Alexander said, his voice demanding. "Is it?"

"No," she responded.

"No, what?" he growled, pulling her hair back and slowly increasing the pace.

"No, Mr. Burnham," she exhaled, her voice barely above a whisper. She knew her orgasm was imminent. She felt as if she was wound tighter than she could remember in all her years, and she didn't know why or how that could even be possible.

"We'll see about that. I have a feeling my cock is more than you can handle, Olivia. You always come so quickly when I start driving into you. Don't you?" he commented.

She could hear the smile in the tone of his voice. Her heart began to race, not wanting to respond to him. She knew it was absolutely true. Alexander completed her in more ways than one.

"Well, if you're not going to answer, we'll just have to test my theory." He immediately began plunging into her at a punishing pace.

"FUCK!" Olivia screamed out, her body trembling as her orgasm overtook her entire being, waves of ecstasy rolling through her core.

"Holy shit!" Alexander said, thrusting into her faster, turned on by her shaking body underneath him. He soon found his own release, screaming out Olivia's name, forgetting that his mother was just down the stairs and could probably hear everything that they were doing.

Once their breathing began to slow, he placed his hand over her stomach, helping to lower her onto the bed. She lay on her back, utterly spent. She turned her head to see Alexander in the same position. "Sex with you is always fucking fantastic," she said, smiling, her body still tingling from her orgasm.

Alexander was still breathing heavy as a sly grin crept across his face. "It absolutely is." They both stared at the ceiling for several long minutes, trying to get their breathing under control.

"Hey, Olivia?" Alexander said, breaking the silence.

17

"Yeah?" She turned her head to look at him.

"Have I told you today how much I love you?"

She dragged her finger up and down his sculpted chest. "Yeah. But you can say it again." She repositioned herself so she was lying on her side, propping herself up with her elbow. Alexander followed suit.

"I love you, Sarah Olivia Adler." He ran his hand up and down the length of her body.

"I love you, too, Alexander Thomas Burnham," she replied, pushing him onto his back and climbing on top of him.

Alexander growled, loving the feeling of her soft flesh on his body. She placed her legs on either side of him and he could feel the warmth emanating from between them. He raised his eyebrows.

Olivia nodded before slowly lowering herself onto him, his erection hard again.

"You're going to be the death of me, Olivia," he exhaled as she started moving up and down, moaning.

Chapter Three

Letting Him In

OLIVIA AWOKE FROM AN afternoon nap, admiring the beautiful man sleeping peacefully next to her. She glanced around the large bedroom, the duvet and several pillows thrown on the floor. A grin spread across her face, thinking about the amazing sex she had with Alexander just a few hours earlier. She pried herself out of his arms and went in search of a much-needed bathroom.

Grabbing her jeans and sweater, she threw them on before quietly walking over to the door, thankful when it didn't creak and wake up Alexander. After finding a bathroom, she went to see if his mother needed any help getting things ready for that evening.

The house was eerily quiet as she walked down the stairs searching for Colleen. "They must all be outside," she said to herself. She headed in the direction of the back door, when a room off the hallway caught her eye. She stopped dead in her tracks, a memory rushing back. Her fifth birthday. Her mama had made her a cake in the shape of a Care Bear. She could have sworn she remembered her mama and the green-eyed boy from the dream sitting beside her in that very room, singing to her as she blew out the candles on that cake.

Turning, she headed toward the ornate dining room, the table and chairs all covered with sheets. Walking around the room, she felt as if she had been there before, but that was impossible. She hadn't even known Alexander for a year and this was the first time he invited her home with him. Still, the smell and sounds in that room were strangely familiar.

She scanned the walls and her eyes settled on a large picture frame covered with a white sheet. The other portraits weren't hidden. Curious, she slowly made her way to the center of the room where the enormous frame hung. She gingerly began to raise the sheet, wondering what was underneath.

"Olivia, dear! There you are!" Colleen called out, startling her.

She jumped, placing her hand over her chest. "Colleen. I'm sorry. I came downstairs to see if you needed any help, and I guess I got a little sidetracked." She shrugged her shoulders, feeling guilty that she was caught snooping around.

Colleen walked over to Olivia and placed her hands on her shoulders, trying to lead her out of the room and away from the large family portrait of Alexander and Olivia as children. "I understand. It happens to the best of us."

"Colleen," Olivia said, raising her voice. "Why is that portrait covered up?"

She stopped, turning to look at her. She hated having to lie to the poor girl, particularly when her son should have simply told her the truth by now. He swore he would tell her, and she didn't want to interfere...not yet, anyway. "I'm sorry, Olivia. It's just that whenever Alexander comes home, I try to rid the house of any memories of..."

"Oh," she said, understanding. "I should have known." She turned to head back upstairs, her shoulders slightly dropping.

"Olivia, dear!" Colleen called out.

She stopped and faced her.

"He loves you very much. I've never seen him so happy in all his life, even when he was a little boy." She smiled before retreating back outside, leaving Olivia alone with her thoughts about Alexander and why the dining room in that house brought back memories of her fifth birthday.

~~~~~~~~~~

"LIBBY, LIBBY, LIBBY!" KIERA shouted, running up to her friend as she stood underneath a string of Chinese lanterns in

Alexander's large backyard.

Olivia couldn't believe her eyes when she walked outside that evening. The transformation was remarkable, particularly after such short notice. White party lights were strung all across the lawn, casting a subtle glow on the backyard. Tables and chairs were set up, but most of the guests milled about socializing with each other as servers walked through with trays of hors d'oeuvres. Olivia was shocked that Alexander's mother could pull something like that off in a few short hours. But she was even more surprised to see Kiera walk in with Mo and the rest of the guys in the band, followed by Melanie and Bridget.

"Oh, my god! What are you guys doing here?!" She looked at her friends and then at Alexander.

"I called Kiera while you were in the shower before we left Boston," he explained. "I figured it would be nice for you to have a few familiar faces here."

Olivia leaned over and kissed him on the cheek. "Thank you. You're the best boyfriend ever!"

"He's not your boyfriend anymore, slut!" Kiera exclaimed, her green eyes brimming with enthusiasm.

She laughed. "That's right! I'm never going to get used to that."

"Guys," Alexander interrupted, talking to Mo and the rest of the band. "You can set up your gear over on the stage. You can play for five minutes or five hours. Doesn't matter to me. Just enjoy yourselves."

Olivia looked at Alexander again, noticing a make-shift stage set up that she hadn't seen earlier.

"They asked if they could play at the party tonight. My mother was thrilled that I was able to find a band at the last minute." He winked.

Over the next hour, more and more people started arriving. Alexander introduced Olivia to his relatives, as well as several family friends. A few people seemed to look at her awkwardly, almost as if they were silently questioning Alexander. Olivia couldn't help but feel that he wasn't being entirely truthful about something. She thought they were past that but, now, she wasn't too sure.

"Come on, Libby," Kiera said, waking Olivia from her unsettled thoughts. "Let's go dance. I'm stealing your girl, Alex."

"Enjoy it while you can, Kiera!" Alexander said, brushing his lips against Olivia's temple before Kiera dragged her away.

They made their way through the party guests mingling on the enormous lawn, soon finding Melanie and Bridget. Kiera pulled her deep red hair back and started to move to the rhythm of an Allen Stone tune the guys were playing, the rest of the girls soon joining in.

"So, I'm thinking bachelorette in Vegas. You game?" Kiera asked above the music.

"We haven't even set a date yet. It still hasn't sunk in that I'm getting married."

"Oh!" Melanie squealed. "I'm just so excited!" The tall, skinny blonde jumped up and down animatedly.

"And don't even say you're picking someone else for your Maid of Honor because I'll make a scene right here in front of everyone," Kiera joked.

"Of course I want you to be my Maid of Honor," she responded. "I think I'm going to keep the wedding party small, though. Just you, Bridget, and Melanie." She smiled affectionately at her other two best friends who were brimming with enthusiasm. "I'm not really close to anyone else. Well, not close enough that I'd want them standing by my side on the most important day of my life."

"Awww, Libby," Kiera exclaimed, hugging her and nearly spilling both of their drinks. "I love you, too, bitch."

"So, what's the deal with you and Tyler?" Olivia asked Melanie, wanting to change the subject. She nodded toward the younger version of Alexander as he stood by the bar, discreetly checking out Melanie.

"Oh, when they're together, he can't keep his eyes off her," Bridget explained, grinning. "But neither one of them will make the first move and ask the other one out."

"Shut up, guys! He's just so flippin' hot!" Melanie exclaimed.

"Mel!" Kiera shouted. "So are you. He's probably

intimidated. Make the first move. Sometimes you have to. I had to make the first move with Jack!"

Bridget looked at Kiera, a questioning look on her face.

"Oh, I mean Mo, but Libby's the only one who calls him Mo. Well, I guess now you guys, too." Kiera rolled her eyes.

"Come on, Mel. Go talk to him," Olivia said, nudging her friend toward the bar.

"If you don't, I'll drag him over here so you *have* to talk to him," Kiera said. She almost felt guilty, forcing her. She remembered how she felt talking to guys when she was only twenty-one.

"Fine. Fine. I'm going." She stormed off and the girls giggled a little as they watched their friend nervously interact with Tyler.

They continued to dance the night away, Olivia thinking how drastically different her life seemed from just twenty-four hours ago. Every so often, she would find Alexander in deep conversation with an old friend or neighbor, but their eyes would always meet. No matter who he was talking to, he always seemed to keep an eye on her. For once, she was happy about that. She felt truly loved.

"Thanks everyone," Mo said into the microphone after playing for a few hours. "Can I just get your attention, please?"

Olivia looked around at the party guests as servers walked through the backyard carrying trays of champagne and distributing them to everyone. Alexander walked up next to her, snaking his arm around her waist.

"Miss me, love?" he asked with a twinkle in his eye.

"Of course," she responded, planting a gentle kiss on his lips. "How did your mother put this together today?"

"You have no idea how easy it is to do something like this if you're willing to throw money at people," he laughed. "And my darling mother can be *very* persuasive."

"I see that."

Alexander grabbed two glasses of champagne, handing one to her before they turned their attention back to the stage.

"We're all here to celebrate the engagement of my good friend, Olivia Adler, to Alexander Burnham," Mo continued.

"I've known Livvy since she was a freshman at Boston College and, to be honest, I never thought I would see this day. Livvy's not the easiest person to get along with."

Olivia pinched Kiera, her face turning red as she listened to the crowd roar with laughter. "He better not think this is a fucking roast," she hissed quietly.

"He wouldn't. Don't worry." She gave her a reassuring look.

"Olivia was always sort of an enigma when she was in college," Mo reminisced. "She worked as a bartender at this bar called Scotch, where we all had the pleasure of meeting her. Guys would fawn over her and she would send them packing with their proverbial tails between their legs, never letting anyone get close to her.

"But, eventually, she let me and Kiera in and, of course, the rest of the band here. Although we may all have had our disagreements in the past, that doesn't mean we love each other any less."

Olivia listened to his words and didn't cringe when he said the word "love". She finally realized that she *had* begun to love people again. She loved Kiera and Mo, and she loved Alexander more than she thought her heart was capable of. Love no longer scared her.

Mo looked over at Olivia as she stood in Alexander's embrace. A smile spread across his face, reaching his dark eyes, and he thought back to all the drama of the past several months. "Something changed in Olivia after she met Alex. She lost some of her edge, in a good way. She slowly began to let him into her life, and she finally realized how truly special it is when you find your soul mate." He raised his champagne glass. "I'm so happy for you, baby girl." He faced the audience. "To Alexander and Olivia!"

Everyone raised their glasses, toasting the couple.

Alexander looked down at Olivia. "Thank you for letting me in, Olivia." His lips met hers, coaxing her mouth open, the taste of champagne making her tongue taste sweet.

"I love you, Mr. Burnham," she said, surprised at how easy it was to say those three words over and over again. She never wanted to stop telling Alexander how much she loved him.

"Looks like you're empty. Refill?"

Olivia looked down at her glass, noticing that she had finished all her champagne. "Yes, please."

"You got it. Be back in a second." He kissed her neck before heading across the lawn, surprised to be met with jealous eyes as he approached the bar.

"Adele. What are you doing here?" he asked nervously.

"Your mother invited my parents. I found out about your little engagement and left Boston to get here to celebrate with you, Alex, dear," she responded, placing her hand on his arm.

He took a step back, cringing from her touch. "Why are you *really* here?" he demanded.

"No reason," she replied rather nonchalantly. "Just wanted to offer my congratulations to you and your bride-to-be."

"Well, you've done it. So please leave," Alexander growled, his eyes frantically searching for Olivia, relieved when he felt someone come up next to him.

Olivia slinked her arm around his waist and planted a kiss on his cheek before turning her eyes to the tall blonde. "Hello, Adele. What are you doing here?" she asked, her voice sweet.

"Just came to offer my congratulations to the happy couple," she replied with a smug expression.

"Well, thank you, Adele. That's very kind of you." Olivia faced Alexander. "Excuse me, darling. Nature calls." She retreated toward the house.

"If you'd rather I'd left, I understand, Alex," Adele said once Olivia was out of earshot.

"Adele, I appreciate you coming, but there's too much bad blood between you and Olivia, and I'm here to look out for her," he said softly.

She shot daggers at him and took a step closer. "Making up for lost time, Alex?"

"What are you talking about, Adele?" His mind raced.

"Oh, nothing. Imagine how little Olivia will react when she finds out that you've been keeping secrets from her."

He stared at her, the tension building.

"I *know*, Alexander," she spat out, answering the question that was so clearly written on his face. "I know she's *your* Olivia and that you've been keeping that secret from her. Do you think you can keep it from her forever?"

Alexander looked at her in complete shock. Closing his eyes, he took a deep breath. "How did you find out?" he asked quietly.

Adele's voice softened. "Alex, I knew she looked familiar. Granted, it's been over twenty-one years, but the similarities were too much," she lied, placing her hand on his arm. A compassionate look crossing her face, she continued, "Do the right thing before it's too late. I'll keep it to myself for now, but I can't guarantee that I'll remain quiet forever."

He hung his head low. "I know, Adele. Just give me some time. She needs to know."

She walked away, smiling. She knew him well. He would keep his secret from Olivia as long as he could. He couldn't bear to lose her, and telling her would make her run. Hell, it would make any woman furious to know that they had been lied to, and that's what Adele was counting on.

When she received that phone call earlier in the day, she thought the man on the other end was full of shit when he said that the woman Alexander was now engaged to was Olivia DeLuca. But he had just confirmed that it was true and that he was aware of her real identity. Adele had no idea why the man on the other end of the phone was concerned with Olivia's true identity and she didn't really care. As long as she got her money once Olivia found out about her past, she was fine with whatever was going on.

CHAPTER FOUR

STARTING NOW

"DO YOU EVER THINK you'll move all your things into my place?" Alexander asked one warm evening in early May as they enjoyed a relaxing dinner out on his balcony. Since their engagement party several weeks ago, Olivia and Alexander attempted to adjust to the change in their relationship. There were quite a few arguments. Both had been so fiercely independent for the majority of their adult lives that it took time to acclimate to their new living arrangement...an arrangement Olivia was still having trouble with.

"Alexander, we've already discussed this. Every day. It's just taking me some time to adjust." She looked down at her plate, slowly losing her appetite.

"I know, love, and I'm trying to be patient. I know this isn't easy for you, but we've been engaged for over a month and you've refused to agree on a date or move the rest of your stuff over here. What's really going on?" He looked into her eyes, a soft expression on his face. "Are you having second thoughts?"

"No!" she said forcefully. "Of course not." She lowered her voice. "I love you, Alexander, and I want to spend the rest of my life with you."

"Damn it, Olivia. Then why don't we start the rest of our lives now? Please?" He stood up and walked the short distance to the other side of the table, kneeling in front of her and grabbing her hands. "I want to wake up to your beautiful smile every morning. I want to feel your body next to me as I fall asleep every night. I want to finally experience all those little quirks of yours. The way you take one last look in the mirror when you're getting ready. You simply sigh and shrug your shoulders, and it's the cutest thing I've ever seen. And I want to see that every single day for the rest of my life, Olivia. I know you like your space and that you've been on your own nearly your entire life. I know this is going to take some adjusting, on both our parts, but we'll work through those things. Together."

Olivia looked down at the man kneeling in front of her, a sincere expression etched on his strong face. At that moment, he looked so vulnerable and she immediately felt guilty for making him doubt her devotion to him. "Fine." Her lips turned into a crooked smile. "But where am I going to fit all of my shoes?"

Alexander laughed, pulling her into his arms. "I'll have a closet built just for your shoes, love."

She giggled, butterflies swimming around her stomach. After all this time, she was surprised that he could still give her those butterflies. She recalled her mama's words when she was just a small child, telling her that she'd know when she was in love by the constant butterflies. That's how she knew he was the only man for her. "I love you so much, Alexander." She planted a soft kiss on his lips.

"I will never tire of hearing you say that," he remarked before standing up and returning to his seat to finish his meal.

"About a date…" Olivia took a sip of her chardonnay, nervous to be discussing plans for her upcoming wedding.

"Yes? Have you given any thought to what I suggested?" he asked.

"Actually, I have and, well… I just want to make sure that this is something you want to do. Get married then, I mean."

"Of course it is. I wouldn't have suggested it if I wasn't serious about it," he said firmly.

"It's just…" She trailed off, looking down at her fingers fidgeting in her lap. "I know how difficult that day is for you, and I want to make sure that you only have happy memories of our wedding day."

"Olivia, look at me." His voice was forceful and demanding.

She quickly raised her head to see Alexander smiling at her.

"Darling, that's exactly why I want to do this. I didn't realize it, but my life didn't truly begin until I met you. Marrying you on that day will erase any bad memories from early on. I need to close this chapter in my life, and start a new one." He reached across the table and grabbed her hand. "With you."

His words sent Olivia's heart soaring. She loved how passionate he could be at times. She still couldn't believe how far they had come from their first meeting when he whispered in her ear, *"People only call me Mr. Burnham in the bedroom."*

"So what do you think?" he asked, interrupting her thoughts of Alexander in the bedroom.

"Okay. August twenty-fourth it is then." She smiled. Up until that moment, it hadn't sunk in that she was going to marry Alexander. Now, with a date, it all began to feel real, and she couldn't be happier.

"Good." He thought it was fitting, marrying the girl who was taken from him on the exact date twenty-two years later. It was romantic.

"That's less than four months away," Olivia said, staring out over the boats on the waterfront as a gentle breeze blew. "I guess I better find a dress." She dreaded the thought of going to bridal shops with the hopes of finding the perfect wedding dress. She immediately considered asking Alexander to elope.

"You could show up naked and I wouldn't care." He raised his eyebrows and gave her a devilish grin.

"Of course you wouldn't." She giggled.

"God, angel, all these months and I still love the sound of your laughter," he said, making her blush. "Now, where would you like to get married? Any idea?"

"At a casino in Vegas," she muttered under her breath, looking toward the sliding glass door. She laughed at the sight of Runner standing there, begging for table scraps from the other side of the glass.

Alexander grabbed her hand across the table again, getting her attention. "Olivia, if that's what you want, I'll support it. I just want to marry you. I don't care if it's in a crappy Vegas casino or an ornate cathedral. All I care about is you saying those two words to me."

"I do?" Olivia asked, smirking.

Alexander rushed to the opposite side of the table and swooped her in his arms.

"No, Olivia," he said quietly, kissing her neck. "I will. Always. I will."

Olivia's heart raced at his gentle voice whispering those two words in her ear. "Alex," she exhaled as he ran his tongue down her collarbone. "Don't start anything you have no intention of finishing."

She felt Alexander's mouth turn up into a smile. "When have you ever not finished?"

"I can think of a few times that some dominating prick wouldn't let me come," she joked.

He pulled back and stood up, planting a chaste kiss on her cheek. "Sometimes, Miss Adler, delayed gratification is worth it." He turned and walked back to his seat.

She closed her eyes, trying to regain her composure.

"So, tell me. Where would you like to get married?" he asked, his voice serious once more.

"Well, I've always imagined getting married on the beach somewhere," she responded, opening her eyes, trying to ignore the desire flooding through her entire body. "I'd like to keep it casual, you know?"

Alexander thought about her words. He immediately recalled the beach house where he spent nearly every summer with her all those years ago. It was a massive estate with its own stretch of private beach. After finding the storage room beneath his office containing all the documents pertaining to his father's cover-up, he found that Olivia still owned that property, although she did not know it. The beach house had been maintained beautifully over the years, ready to be handed over to her when it was safe to do so.

"I think I have the perfect place."

CHAPTER FIVE

SOLITUDE

THE FOLLOWING DAY, OLIVIA woke up early, pried herself from Alexander's arms, and quickly changed into her running clothes before descending twenty-five stories to the lobby.

"Miss Adler," Carter said, intercepting her on the street as she exited the tall building.

She looked up and saw Carter standing next to Marshall outside of the SUV parked in its usual spot. "Where to this morning?" he asked, scanning the sidewalks.

"I'm just going for a run and then back to my place. I'll be fine by myself." She began to walk away.

"Miss Adler, please wait for a moment!" Marshall called out nervously.

Olivia exhaled loudly before turning around, her irritation evident by the scowl on her face.

"I'm sorry, ma'am, but Mr. Burnham is our boss." Carter surveyed her demeanor, debating how to proceed.

"Fine. Go ahead and call him to tell on me. All I want is one fucking day where I can go for a run by myself. Is that too much to ask for?" she huffed as she plopped down on a bench, glaring at her protection detail. Is this what her life would be like once she married Alexander? Would he always have one of his agents following her, protecting her from some invisible threat that he made up in his head? All because he lost his best friend when he was young?

Agent Marshall stared at her, an appearance of sympathy about her. "Just one moment, ma'am. I'll see if I can convince him that you'll be okay on your own."

Olivia glanced up, a smile creeping across her face. "Thank you."

~~~~~~~~~~

ALEXANDER WOKE UP TO his cell phone ringing. Opening his eyes, he noticed that Olivia wasn't in bed next to him. He became alarmed when he saw the name flash on his caller ID. "Marshall. Is everything okay?" he asked frantically.

"Yes. Sorry to disturb you, sir. Miss Adler is out in front of the building and wants to go for a run."

"Well, what's the problem? Send someone with her."

She exhaled loudly before lowering her voice, and walked out of Olivia's earshot, still keeping her eyes trained on her. "Sir, with all due respect, she feels smothered. Let her have this one run unaccompanied. It might make her feel better."

"What?!" Alexander shouted, jumping out of bed. "Are you out of your fucking mind?!"

"Sir, please. We've been keeping an eye on her the past several months and haven't come across any threats to her safety."

"Of course you haven't!" he fumed. "That's because you've been around her! Once there's a window, someone will take the opportunity!" He found a pair of shorts and quickly threw them on before grabbing a running shirt, socks, and a pair of sneakers, dashing down the stairs and into the foyer, anxiously pressing the elevator call button as he dressed himself.

"I'm not second-guessing your decisions, sir," she continued calmly. "But perhaps if you clue me and Carter in so that we're aware of the threat you seem to think exists, maybe we could have a better understanding of what's going on."

The elevator dinged, announcing its arrival. Alexander lowered his voice. "I can't do that. I wish I could, but the less anyone knows about this, the better. I trust you. You're one of my most valuable agents. That's why I assigned you this job."

"You're going to lose her for good if you don't give her some breathing room," Marshall explained cautiously.

Alexander stepped back and the elevator doors closed, letting it leave without him. He stared at the wall in front of him and contemplated Marshall's words. He knew she was right and that he was smothering Olivia. Perhaps one run unaccompanied would go a long way. "Okay. Let her go for a run." He sighed in resignation. "But keep an eye on her from a safe distance," he warned.

"Yes, sir. Thank you, sir." She glanced at Olivia, giving her a thumbs up sign.

"And, Marshall?"

"Yes, sir."

"I want constant updates. Do you understand?"

"Yes, sir. I can do that." She hung up and walked back toward Olivia. "Okay. Off you go. Don't make me regret sticking my neck out for you. Be safe."

Carter walked over to the SUV idling on the side of the street and opened the passenger side door, grabbing something out of the glove box. Turning back to Olivia, he handed her a small can of pepper spray. "Take this with you."

"Oh! Thank you! Thank you! Thank you!!" Olivia squealed, wrapping her arms around Carter's neck and planting a quick kiss on his cheek. "You guys are the best!" She put the pepper spray in her pocket before heading off on her run.

"Um, Miss Adler?" Carter interrupted.

Olivia turned around, removing her ear buds. "Yes?"

"Keep that in your hand. If you're attacked, you won't have time to reach into your pocket. Sometimes one second can be the difference between life and death."

She glared at him, her irritation returning.

"Or...I can call Mr. Burnham back and have him accompany you," Marshall threatened.

"Fine," she spat out, dramatically grabbing the can of pepper spray out of her pocket. "Happy now?"

"Very. Enjoy your run," Marshall said, grabbing her cell phone and searching her contact list. She watched as Olivia ran off down the streets of Boston. "Excuse me for a moment. I need to return a phone call."

"You got it, Cheryl."

~~~~~~~~~~

SIMON WAS SITTING AT the counter of a diner, drinking a cup of coffee early on a Sunday morning when his cell phone began to ring. "Hello?"

"It's me, Simon. She's out for a run. You know what to do. I was able to give you a wide berth so don't fuck it up. I'll text you the location."

"Okay, okay. I got it." He hung up and glanced at a text that had just come in. It appeared as though Olivia was heading toward Boston Common Park. *Perfect*. He threw some money on the counter and ran out of the diner, hailing a cab.

~~~~~~~~~~

OLIVIA TURNED ONTO TREMONT Street, crossing over to Boston Common Park past the old Granary Burying Ground, enjoying her momentary solitude. She would finally be able to stretch her legs a bit and really push her pace. It was always difficult running through city streets, having to stop every few seconds at another crosswalk.

She entered the park and opened up her stride, basking in the morning sun. She had finally gotten her legs back after running in the Boston Marathon. The week following the marathon had been a tense and scary time in the city. Olivia was one of the lucky ones who had crossed the finish line before the bombs ruined the event for thousands. She had just returned to Alexander's place when she turned on the news to see what had happened at the finish line. Her heart sank, wondering why someone would possibly do something so hateful at an event that inspired millions. It still broke her heart to think about it, but what those cowards didn't count on was the spirit of runners and the city of Boston. She had a new drive to run, desperate to continue on for all those who no longer could.

That's what she thought about as she made her way through Boston Common. Every time her legs started to feel tired, she reminded herself that at least she still had the ability to run. She still had legs. Dozens of people who were injured on that tragic day would do anything to be in her position right now so she ran on.

Running past the swan boats, a wide smile crawled across her face as she thought about the day she bumped into Alexander at that very spot. She came to a stop and gazed out over the crystal lake, replaying that fateful day in her mind.

"Olivia? Is that you?" a voice called out from across the path.

She turned, her brows furrowed. "Simon?" She took a few steps toward him. "Wow. I hate to say it, but it looks like prison was good to you," she remarked, taking in his appearance. He looked like an entirely different person. He was skinnier, but more built than he was before. His usual attire of dirty jeans, t-shirt, and work boots was replaced with a crisp white polo shirt, dress khakis, and loafers. His hair was much shorter and he was clean shaven. For the first time in his life, he looked like someone you would be proud to take home to meet your parents.

"Yeah, about that," he said softly, turning his eyes down, a shy look covering his face. "I've been wanting to talk to you, but I didn't know how you would react to seeing me again. And, well, I understand if you want to walk away right now, but I'd really appreciate it if you would listen to what I have to say."

Olivia met his eyes, a look of sincerity on his face. But there was something else there, too. A troubled look. He appeared as if he was in pain, and Olivia's heart went out to him.

She walked over to a bench and sat down, motioning for him to do the same. "Okay. I'll listen, Simon." It seemed as though Simon had turned over a new leaf and the least she could do was hear him out. Plus, she had the pepper spray that Carter had given her clutched in her hand so she didn't feel threatened.

"I just wanted to apologize for my behavior all those months ago," he started, his eyes trained straight ahead on the swan boats. "I never wanted to hurt you, Olivia." He faced her, beseeching her to believe the words that he spoke. "I don't know what came over me, and I regret agreeing to help those people…"

"Wait," Olivia interrupted. "What are you talking about, Simon?" She scrunched her eyebrows, confused at what was coming out of his mouth. "What people?"

"I don't know all the details, but this guy paid me the equivalent of two years' salary to get close to you and see if you remembered something from your childhood," he explained, almost avoiding her eyes.

Olivia sat there in shock.

"I know it was stupid now," he continued when she remained silent. "You have to believe I would *never* do anything to hurt you again." He lifted his head, meeting her eyes once more. "I had a lot of time in prison to reflect on my behavior, and I want to be honest with you, Olivia." He took a deep breath before continuing, "You're in danger." His voice was firm as he warned her. "I don't know what these people want. Hell, I don't even know who's behind any of it. Some guy bailed me out of jail and paid for my attorney, but I have no idea what his connection is to this whole mess. All I know is that they think that your dad…"

"My dad died years ago, Simon," she interrupted, dropping her voice to barely a whisper. "Both of my parents did." She turned her head, not wanting to talk about losing her family at such a young age. She fought back the tears as a gentle breeze rustled through the trees, making her shiver despite the warm spring air.

"I know. This guy said that they died in an accident, but was it really an accident?"

Olivia's mind began to race, recalling her dreams. Her head spun around quickly and she glowered at him. "I was in the car, Simon," she said, swallowing hard. "I survived. I relive that day in my dreams every night of my fucking existence. Yes. It really was an accident."

He noticed her reaction and proceeded with caution. "I'm sorry, Olivia. I'm not trying to upset you. The last thing I want to do is hurt you. I just want you to be safe."

She stared at him, her eyes intense. Why was Simon being so nice to her now? It didn't make any sense. Then again, maybe he was able to gain some clarity and insight into his life while he was in prison.

"I heard you're engaged to Alexander Burnham," Simon said quietly, hoping she would keep talking to him if he changed the subject.

She avoided his eyes, blushing. "I am."

"Good. He's a good man, Olivia. He can protect you."

"Why are you telling me all of this, Simon?" She tilted her head and eyed him suspiciously. "What's your goal here? What do you hope to get out of it?"

He exhaled loudly, running his hands through his hair, exasperated. It reminded her of Alexander. "I don't know," he said quietly. "I just want to make amends for my past behavior, and maybe telling you what I know will mean the difference between life and death. These people are very dangerous so please be careful. I guess that's what I wanted to say... And that I'm sorry." His eyes met hers. "I'm scared for you." He got up and began to walk away.

Olivia watched as he strolled along the path, dodging other runners out for their morning exercise. Could she trust him? He knew so much. "Simon! Wait!" she shouted, running to catch up to him.

A grin crept across his face. He paused and readjusted his expression into a solemn look before turning around. "Yes, Olivia?"

"I just wanted to say..." Her voice trailed off.

"Yes?"

She took a deep breath. "I forgive you," she said, knowing how difficult it must have been for him to tell her everything. The least she could do was forgive him for what had happened in the past. Maybe it would help him continue to grow. "You scared me back in August, but I'm not going to hold that grudge anymore. I hope you can move on from this and that my forgiveness gives you some peace. You did the right thing telling me what's going on. I value your honesty." She took his hands in hers, their eyes locking, thankful that one person in her life was finally being truthful with her.

"All I ever wanted was to get to know you, Olivia," he said sweetly. "You just made it so damn hard. You kept everyone away, and it nearly broke my heart," he explained, his voice shaking. "I wanted you so badly, but all you were looking for was a fuck buddy. Then when this guy found out that I was sleeping with you, he came to me with a proposition and…well, I wasn't born into money like you were. I've had to struggle my entire life to make ends meet. But, in the end, I know it wasn't worth it. I ruined whatever we had going between us…"

"Simon, please…" she said, releasing his hands, glancing down at the cobblestone path.

"I just need to get this off my chest." His unyielding tone made Olivia look back into his eyes. "The day I walked into your studio to work on that construction project, I thought you were the most beautiful woman I had ever laid eyes on, and I still believe that to this very day. I'll always be here for you, no matter what you need. I will never hurt you again. I wouldn't be able to live with myself if I did. That's why I need your forgiveness. I know there's no future for us, and I'm glad that you've found someone who makes you happy. I just wish that you had let me in all those months ago. Maybe things would have turned out differently." Simon turned to walk away, leaving Olivia speechless.

As soon as he walked onto Charles Street and looked over his shoulder to make sure that she hadn't followed him, he picked up his cell phone. "Donovan. It's Simon. I think she bought it. You're a fucking genius, man."

"No. I just know people."

Chapter Six

Our Place

OLIVIA CIRCLED OUT OF Boston Common Park, her conversation with Simon replaying in her mind for the remainder of her short run. It was unmistakable that he had changed quite a bit since August when he came at her with a knife. He now seemed like an entirely different person. Maybe being in prison gave him some perspective about where his life was headed if he didn't get his act together. The pain on his face when he confessed his feelings for her was heartbreaking, and she felt bad for the way she treated him during their brief "relationship".

Still, Simon's warning lay heavy on her mind. She always thought that Alexander was simply being overprotective, but maybe he knew something, too. He had mentioned the possibility of Simon having a connection to Mark Kiddish. That must have been the guy who wanted to get to Olivia. Regardless, she was certain that Simon's apology was genuine. He looked desperate and distraught as he begged for forgiveness. She couldn't imagine what he had gone through those past several months sitting in prison, having to live with his stupid mistake.

Olivia ran down Commonwealth Avenue, slowing to a stop in front of her house. She looked up at the brownstone that she had grown to love over the years. The three-story brick building was her first home when she moved back to Boston. It was symbolic to her of finally putting down roots, but now she would put down new roots with Alexander on the other side of the city.

They had discussed what she should do with her house. After a few heated arguments, she decided to hold on to the property for a while and perhaps rent it out. The housing market had started to turn back up, but she wasn't ready to part with her home just yet.

She punched the code into the door and ran upstairs to start packing her things. She was sweaty from her run so she hopped in the shower, rinsing off the salt that had settled on her skin. Once she felt refreshed, she put on a change of clothes and set about boxing up her life.

After several hours of going through her belongings, she heard her phone buzzing. She glanced at the caller ID and saw Alexander's photo flashing on the screen. *Crap*. She had forgotten to turn the ringer back on. Hesitantly, she answered his call.

"Olivia…?"

"Yes?" she breathed.

"Where are you?" He knew perfectly well where she was, but he had no intention of telling her that he had been sitting in his office, tracking her every movement as if he didn't have anything better to do on a Sunday morning.

"I'm at my house packing up some boxes."

"Would you like some help?" he asked, his voice softening. "I can see if I can get some movers to come and take care of that for you."

"No. That's okay," she responded, glancing around her bedroom at all her belongings, starting to feel overwhelmed by the enormity of the job ahead of her. "Some of this stuff is kind of personal. I'd rather do it all myself."

"Do you want me to come and lend a hand, or would you rather be alone?"

She could hear the hurt in his voice. "I'm sorry about this morning, Alexander. I just feel a little smothered sometimes. I know you're just trying to keep me safe, and I really do appreciate that but, sometimes, it's just a little overwhelming."

"I know, Olivia," he sighed. If she only knew what he was trying to protect her from. "I'm sorry. I don't want to scare you off. You just have to tell me how you feel. I can't read your mind. I promise I'll try to not be as much of an overbearing asshole."

Olivia giggled. "Okay. I'll try to do better, too."

"So, want me to come over?" His voice was brimming with hope.

"It would be a shame to waste this opportunity to put you to work."

He chuckled. "Okay. I'll be there in a bit. Carter and Marshall are out front of your house should you need anything in the meantime."

"You knew where I was, didn't you?"

"You'll have to torture me if you want me to answer that." There was a pause. "Until then… I love you. Always."

His words made her want to melt into the hardwood flooring. "I love you, too, Alexander," she replied before hanging up.

Olivia returned her attention to the task at hand and began sorting through the bookshelf in her study, boxing up books and other trinkets. Occasionally, she stopped to look at various photos from her college years, memories flooding back from all the trouble she and Kiera used to cause. She paused when an old photo album fell off the middle shelf, pictures scattering across the room. Chasing one of the photos all the way to the doorway, she was met with a jean-clad leg.

Her eyes followed the leg upward, meeting Alexander's brilliant smile.

"Afternoon, beautiful. I brought sushi."

Olivia straightened up and kissed him gently on the lips. "Thank god. I'm starving and there's no food in this joint except for cat food." She leaned down to pick up the photo that had escaped. Her breath caught in her throat and she spun around to hide her face from Alexander.

"What is it? Are you okay?"

She stared at the image in front of her. It was one of the few photos she had from before the accident. She was standing on a bunch of rocks on a large beach, her father behind her, holding her up beneath her arms. They were both smiling at

41

the camera. Her hair was in two braids on either side of her head and she was wearing a long Harvard sweatshirt over her bathing suit. She caressed the photo, her finger lingering over her father's face.

Alexander walked up behind Olivia and peered over her shoulder. "Is that your father?" he asked.

"Yes," she replied quietly.

"It looks like he loved you very much."

A tear fell down Olivia's face. "I think he did. I just wish I could have remembered more about him, ya' know?"

"I know. I get it." He wrapped his arms around her shoulders, bringing her back flush with his body. Guilt overwhelmed his conscience for keeping so many secrets from her, especially for not telling her that her father was still alive. He could end her pain right now if he just told her everything. He wanted to, but her father's warning sounded in his head, reminding him that he could lose the woman he loved if she remembered her past.

"We should probably go eat before Nepenthe gets into the sushi," she said, wiping the tears that had fallen down her face. "He's got a thing for raw fish."

Alexander released her, kissing her on the cheek. "Well, let's go eat then."

After finishing all the sushi Alexander had brought over and downing a few beers, they drudged back up the stairs to continue packing her belongings, deciding to start in the bedroom.

"I'm going to miss this room most of all," Alexander said after over an hour of boxing up Olivia's shoes, barely even putting a dent in her enormous collection of footwear.

She looked up from the dresser. "Oh, yeah? Any particular reason for that?" she asked, her eyebrows raised.

He stood up and strode across the room toward her, pulling her to her feet and pressing her body into his. "If I remember correctly, Miss Adler, you gave me the most amazing, earth-shattering blow job in that bed," he commented.

His words sent a warmth through her body, her heart racing.

"The first of many incredible blow jobs, I might add." He pulled back, winking.

"Perhaps one more for the road, Mr. Burnham?" Olivia asked, brushing her lips against his neck, planting soft kisses across his collarbone. She slowly lowered herself, running her hand down his chest before kneeling in front of him and unbuckling his belt.

"Olivia," Alexander exhaled, staring down at her. "You drive me crazy. Do you know that?"

She nodded her head slowly as she unbuttoned his jeans, sliding them down his muscular legs, his erection springing free. Even after months of being intimate with Alexander, she still got incredibly excited every time she saw him. Grabbing on to his arousal, she took him into her mouth and sensually dragged her tongue across his length.

He closed his eyes for a moment, enjoying the sensation of Olivia's tongue on the most intimate part of his body. He immediately hardened even more in her mouth.

She moaned, loving that she turned him on like that. Continuing her slow motion, she looked up at him, his eyes now open and trained on her. Her heart stopped when she saw the primal stare he gave her. It made her burn for him even more. She was completely unable to break her gaze from his.

"That's right, baby. I love it when you look at me with my cock in your mouth."

She moaned again, not breaking eye contact with him because that's what he liked. That's what made him happy and, for the first time in her life, she was with someone who she wanted to make happy.

Alexander reached down, gently placing his hand on her head, helping to guide her motions as she continued torturing him with her mouth and tongue. Nothing turned him on more than looking down at Olivia, her eyes wide as she took him into her mouth.

"Faster, Olivia," he said softly. "I'm close, baby." Slowly exhaling, he closed his eyes and tried to fight against his impending orgasm. He wanted it to last longer, but he knew that nothing was going to stop him from exploding in a matter of seconds. "Damn, you give amazing head." He thrust into her mouth, signaling with his body the rhythm he wanted Olivia to maintain.

She picked up the pace in response, meeting his motion, gently licking and sucking as she continued to drive him crazy. She loved that she could make him fall apart so quickly from such a simple act. She felt him tighten his grasp on her head and knew he was about to release.

She slowly bared her teeth, pushing him to his breaking point, and he came in her mouth, shouting her name. She slid her tongue against his length until the aftershocks of his orgasm subsided. Meeting his eyes, she smiled, a feeling of complete satisfaction enveloping her. A year ago, she would never do that for anyone. Now, she loved pleasing him that way, and she didn't even want anything in return.

"Damn, Olivia. I love your lips," he said, helping her to her feet.

She giggled at his compliment, sending Alexander's heart soaring. Placing a hand on the small of her back, he carefully dipped her back, kissing her full on the mouth, his tongue invading where his erection had been seconds beforehand.

"That's the most beautiful sound in the world," he murmured against her neck. "Now, back to packing." She yelped when he smacked her ass, causing an infectious grin to spread across her face.

They spent the remainder of the afternoon going through her things while she decided what she wanted to keep and what she would donate or throw out. By early evening, they had boxed up most of her bedroom and study.

"Moving is more of a pain in the ass than I remember," Olivia joked.

"Let me hire some movers to deal with the rest of it. I get not wanting people sorting through your personal stuff, but I think we tackled most of that already."

Olivia looked around the kitchen, not thrilled with the idea of having to pack up the cabinets. "That's fine. But what are we going to do about all my furniture? You already have everything we need."

"Well, is there anything you can't live without? Anything you like better than what I have?"

She surveyed her living room. "I'll have to think about it. Maybe I'll just keep the rest of the house like it is and rent it out fully-furnished or something instead of bringing it all over to your place."

"Great. And stop calling it my place. It's *our* place."

Olivia smiled, snuggling against his chest. "I like the sound of that."

Alexander kissed the top of her head. "I do, too, love."

CHAPTER SEVEN

PLANNING

OVER THE COURSE OF the following week, movers transported all of Olivia's personal belongings from her house over to her new home, while Alexander was out of town on a training exercise with a group of his latest "mercenaries-in-training", as Olivia liked to call them.

After returning from her appointment with Dr. Greenstein on Thursday, she decided to open a bottle of wine and enjoy a glass out on the enormous balcony overlooking the waterfront. The sun was shining and there were only a few clouds in the sky as a light breeze blew through the city.

It was the type of day Olivia loved. Normally, she would go for a walk through the city, take her e-reader, and read in the park. But lately, after Simon's warning, she took Alexander's security detail a little bit more seriously. Before bumping into Simon, she thought Alexander was overreacting. Now, she knew he had every reason to overreact. Someone wanted to hurt her. Simon inferred that the accident that had taken her parents from her was not an accident at all. If that was the case, maybe she was supposed to die in the crash, too. She wondered why anyone could possibly think that she was worth hurting…or worse.

Her phone rang as she sat on the balcony thinking about Simon and what it could all mean. She smiled when she saw Kiera's face pop up on her screen.

"Libby. God, I have spring fever something fierce today," her friend said before Olivia even had a chance to say hello.

"Yeah. It's beautiful out, isn't it?" She took a sip of her wine.

"You got that right. Are you heading to the gym this afternoon?"

"No. I got up early this morning and went before going to see my therapist. I knew it would be a nice day and I'd hate to waste the afternoon sweating inside the gym."

"What are you up to?"

"Not much. Just relaxing on the lanai, drinking a glass of wine, enjoying the view from my castle in the sky," Olivia responded somewhat jokingly. She had a good life.

"Well, my afternoon meeting was cancelled. I was thinking of ditching work early."

"Great. Why don't you come over here? I could use some girl time."

"It's been too long, and we have to start planning your wedding!"

"Yeah. There's that pesky detail, too, isn't there?" Olivia didn't even know where to begin when it came to organizing the wedding. It was still rather overwhelming. Unlike so many other girls, she never saw herself as the type to actually get married, and she was at a loss of what to do. Thankfully, she had Kiera.

"Okay. I'll be there in twenty."

"Sounds good," Olivia responded. "I'll call down to the concierge and alert them that I'm expecting you."

"Aren't you all 'Miss High and Mighty'?" Kiera huffed.

"You know it. My minions prefer to screen my visitors for potential security threats. It's tough to be the queen." Her voice was heavy with sarcasm.

"Yeah. Yeah. Be there soon. Love you, bitch."

"Love you, too."

Olivia opened the sliding glass door and stepped back into her new home, making her way to the enormous wine cellar just beyond the kitchen. She scanned the aisles of Alexander's impressive collection for a good, crisp white wine. Her eyes settled on a nice Sancerre and she grabbed it before heading back to the kitchen.

Searching the refrigerator for some snacks, she grabbed a

block of brie and gouda, and set about preparing a cheese and fruit plate for her visitor. There was something about Alexander's museum-like home that made her feel as though she should actually attempt to entertain Kiera as she would a guest. She hadn't been to his place yet so she was eager to show her friend around.

A short while later, she heard the buzzer sound. Sliding back the door, Kiera stood in the foyer with her mouth agape. "Holy shit! This place is incredible, Libs," she said in awe.

"I know. For a straight guy, he has fantastic style."

Kiera nodded in response. Olivia was surprised that her friend was completely speechless. Kiera was never one to have nothing to say.

"Let's go enjoy this weather," Olivia said, grabbing Kiera's hand and leading her through the open floor-plan of the penthouse's main level. "I'll give you a tour later." She led her toward the windows, sliding back the glass door that opened to the balcony.

"This view is amazing." Kiera looked out over all the boats below on the glistening water. "I would never leave. Well...I probably would when it snows."

"Thank you." Olivia sat down at the bistro table and gestured at the cheese and wine she had set out earlier. "Help yourself."

"Aren't you the best little host?" She took a seat opposite Olivia, grabbed the bottle, and poured herself a glass. "So, you've set a date then?"

Olivia grinned, her heart racing at the thought of marrying Alexander in just a few short months. "Yes. August twenty-fourth."

Kiera's eyes grew wide. "Really? Even though it's the same day as...?" She trailed off, gauging Olivia's reaction.

"I'm okay with it," she said, giving Kiera a convincing look. "It actually never even crossed my mind that it would be the same day that my parents died. I guess being with Alexander is more important than dwelling on something that I can't change."

"Okay then. That doesn't really give us a lot of time. I'll call around and see what we can do about getting you an appointment to go look at some dresses."

Olivia flushed, not realizing how little time she actually had. Her excitement quickly turned to nerves when she was met with the reality that she had absolutely no clue where to begin with wedding plans.

"Any idea what kind of dress you're looking for?" Kiera grabbed a cracker and sliced a piece of brie.

"Not really. I haven't even looked."

Kiera reached down and grabbed her commuter bag, unzipping it. "Well, it's a good thing I'm your friend. Here." She shoved several large bridal magazines at her. "Just start looking through these so you can get an idea of what you may want. The good thing is, between the two of you, you have more money than sense, so you'll be able to get whatever you want, whenever you want."

Olivia took a drink from her glass of wine, starting to feel like she was about to break out in hives from discussing her future wedding.

"Have you gone over any details with Alex?" Kiera asked, all business.

"Not really. I think we're going to do it on the beach. Cape Cod."

"Kinky…" she said with a smile on her face.

Olivia picked up a cracker and chucked it at her friend. "His company owns this huge beach house with a massive private beach."

"I love the idea of a beach wedding. It's very 'you'." Kiera grabbed a legal pad out of her bag and started to take notes.

"We're going to try to keep it small, though. I know it will be hard. He has a huge extended family but…I don't know," she lamented. "I have no family and I think he feels bad that the majority of the guests will be there for him and not for me." Olivia looked down, thinking about how difficult that day would be for her with no family there to watch her marry the love of her life.

"Hey." Kiera reached out and grabbed her friend's hand. "It doesn't matter how many people you have there supporting you. That's the problem with weddings. People feel like they need to put on a big show. Most people only go to weddings for the free booze and couldn't give a shit about celebrating the actual day. So fuck 'em. Do what you want and what makes you happy."

Olivia met Kiera's gaze and gave her a grateful smile. "Thanks, Care Bear." She loved her friend's perspective.

"Okay. Back to important shit," she said, releasing Olivia's hand. "Pick a weekend for Vegas!"

She laughed, relieved to be discussing a lighter topic.

The friends spent the next several hours enjoying the weather and each other's company, as well as a few bottles of wine. As the sun began to go down, a chill set in and the girls retreated indoors.

"Shit," Olivia said upon noticing the time. "I should probably call Alexander before he freaks out."

"Yeah. You're probably right. Jack's expecting me, as well."

Olivia raised her eyebrows.

"Yup. That's right, Libby. Kiera's getting laid tonight."

"Jesus, Kiera," she responded, her face turning bright red. "I don't want to hear the details about you and Mo."

Kiera laughed. "Okay, Libs. Thanks for the fun afternoon. Dress shopping this Saturday."

Olivia hugged her friend and said good-bye. When she was all alone, she grabbed her cell phone and walked up to the bedroom, eager to hear Alexander's voice. She hated when he had to leave town for work.

"Burnham here," he barked angrily into the phone, picking up on the third ring.

"Hi. It's me," she said quietly.

"Olivia, angel." His voice relaxed. "How are you?"

"Good. Everything okay?"

"Yes. As good as it can be. I miss you terribly."

"I miss you, too. How much longer will you be gone?"

Alexander exhaled loudly. "It's hard to say. This mission isn't going as well as I had hoped. I wanted to be home by tomorrow to see you sing with the band but, at this rate, it will probably be after the weekend before I can get back."

"Oh," Olivia replied, clearly disappointed.

"I'm so sorry, love, but I have to make sure these guys are properly trained."

"It's okay, Alexander. I understand. I just miss you." She sat on the bed, lying down. "I don't like being apart from you."

"I don't like it, either. I miss falling asleep next to you, listening to your gentle breathing. I miss the feel of your skin on mine."

She moaned, thinking about his body moving on top of her.

"I miss the taste of your sweet pussy," he breathed out, his voice turning husky.

"Fuck, Alex," she said quietly. "I need you here, inside me."

"Touch yourself," he ordered.

She obeyed, slipping her hand into her panties.

"Are you wet for me, Olivia?"

"I'm always wet when I'm thinking about you," she replied coyly.

He groaned. "Tease your clit for me. Gently."

She followed his instructions, her breathing becoming heavy with longing. Alexander was over a thousand miles away, but he still had her bundled up in knots, the desire for him building with every stroke.

"How's that feel, Olivia?"

"Good," she whimpered, feeling overwhelmed with sensation as she fondled herself, listening to Alexander's sultry voice over the phone.

"Good. Now I want you to put two fingers inside. Slowly."

She bit her bottom lip as she complied with his request, the pleasure starting to overtake her body.

"Now, picture me on top of you, Olivia. Picture me fucking you senseless. Are you doing that?"

"God, yes, Alex. I need you."

"Pretend I'm there, slamming into you, filling that delicious little pussy," he growled into the phone, his breathing heavy. "Sliding in and out as I bite your perfect nipples. You like it when I do that, don't you?"

Olivia moaned, thinking about his teeth on her breast, loving when he was gentle and rough with her at the same time. Her heart rate increased and she felt that familiar tingling feeling from her stomach down to her toes.

Alexander must have sensed it as well. "Come for me, Olivia. Give me your pleasure."

She rubbed harder, screaming Alexander's name as she felt herself spasm around her fingers, her orgasm ravaging her body for several long moments. Her breathing began to slow down, neither person saying anything for a while.

"Did you enjoy that, love?" Alexander asked, finally breaking the silence.

She giggled. "I would have enjoyed it better if it was your hand, but I guess beggars can't be choosers."

"I'll let you beg when I get back," he replied. She could almost hear the smile on his face. "Till then... I love you."

"I love you, too."

"Hey, Olivia?"

"Yes?"

"Thank you."

Olivia scrunched her eyebrows. "For what?"

"For letting me love you. For letting me in. For letting me beneath your skin...your beautiful, perfect skin."

Olivia's heart swelled at his words. She loved how one minute he could be telling her how much he loved fucking her, and then the next, he could say the most sweet and sentimental things. "Thanks for not giving up on me, Alexander."

"Olivia, I'll never give up on you. No matter what this life throws at us, no matter what obstacles we face, I will always stand by your side, looking out for you, protecting you. I love you. I'll hurry home."

"I love you, too, Alexander," she replied quietly, a lump forming in her throat from his sweet words. Placing the phone on the nightstand, she curled up on the bed, feeling completely satisfied. Not from the orgasm she just gave herself, but from Alexander's loving words.

Chapter Eight

Fix Or Ruin

OLIVIA SAT IN HER office Friday afternoon, thinking about Alexander. She longed for his arms to be wrapped around her, for his body to be next to hers as she drifted off to sleep. Instead, she woke up that morning in an empty and cold bed. She was rather disappointed that he would be unable to make her gig that night, but understood he had obligations and couldn't be expected to blow off his job just to see her sing with a band in a bar.

She began to think about how much her life had changed since she met him. Just a year ago, she would shudder at the thought of having an actual relationship with anyone, and now she was planning a wedding. Maybe Alexander was exactly what she needed in her life. She still worried about losing him, but she no longer let that fear control her.

As she gazed out her window at the bustling city streets below, her brain rewound to the phone conversation she had with Alexander the previous night, a smile creeping across her face. Her body warmed when she recalled his sweet words, amazed at how his sensual tone could send her over the edge so quickly.

She was so engrossed in her daydreaming that she had lost track of the time. "Shit!" she exclaimed when she looked at the clock, finally snapping out of her thoughts, realizing that she was late for a circuit training class she was supposed to teach. "Crap. Crap. Crap," she muttered under her breath as she ran down the hall and into the studio.

"Sorry I'm late, y'all." She smiled at her waiting class, making her way over to the sound system. "Okay. Let's get to work." She returned to the center of the room once the music began blaring. "Warm up time. Let's start with some arm crosses." She exhaled deeply as she began to lead her class, clearing her mind of everything as best she could...everything except for Alexander Burnham.

Over the next half-hour, she worked her class pretty hard, leading them through three circuits. As she began the last exercise in the third circuit, she heard the door to the studio open and close. She ignored it and focused on finishing her class.

"Just five more, guys. Almost there. Do *not* quit on me." The class began to groan as she pushed on through bicycle crunches, doing them alongside everyone. "Last one...and done!"

She laughed when she heard sighs of relief from all around her. "Great job. Now let's cool down. Everyone go to sitting position." She sat up and pulled her legs wide, looking up. Her heart skipped a beat when she saw Alexander standing in the back of her studio, wearing an olive green t-shirt with camouflage cargo pants and boots.

She blushed, having trouble concealing her smile and excitement. He looked hot. She had never seen him in his fatigues before and she was so incredibly turned on.

She finally snapped back to the present when she realized she had her class in the same stretch position for far too long. Hiding her distraction, she finished leading her students through their cool down stretch rather quickly. "Thanks, guys. Keep it up." She dismissed her class and grabbed a towel, dabbing the sweat off her body. She felt rather exposed wearing only her sports bra and a pair of gym shorts. She silently wished that she had grabbed a t-shirt to throw on.

"Olivia, love. I've missed you." Alexander pulled her into his arms.

She tried to push him away. "Stop. I stink. I'm all hot and sweaty."

"I like it when you're hot and sweaty." He leaned down,

kissing her neck.

She stopped trying to fight him and relaxed in his arms, breathing in the heavenly aroma she had missed the past few days. "You smell delicious. Like rugged man." Their eyes met. "I like this look on you. It's fucking hot."

"Come, let's get you all cleaned up." Alexander grabbed her hand, leading her out of the studio and into her office. "Do you have any more classes to teach today?" he asked, walking over to her refrigerator and grabbing a water bottle. He loosened the cap and handed it to her.

She sat down at her desk and glanced at her daily schedule. "Nope. Free and clear for the rest of the day. We have a lot of new staff so, thankfully, I'm not needed as much. I have a wedding to plan after all." She winked, taking a sip from the bottle.

Alexander stared down at her, his eyes hooded.

"You're back sooner than expected," she said, breaking the growing tension in the room. His proximity still overwhelmed her on occasion, her heart racing with the look he was giving her, almost like an animal stalking his prey...prey that anxiously wanted to be caught. "Not that I mind. I'm thrilled but, when we spoke last night, it sounded like you wouldn't be home for a while," she rambled.

"Yes." He softened his gaze slightly. "The training exercise is still going on right now, but I'd hate for you to think that I don't value our time together. I will not be one of those husbands that puts their work ahead of their wives. You have a gig tonight so I came home. I do need to fly back out tomorrow morning, though."

Olivia shot out of her chair and rushed through her office, packing up all of her things.

"What are you doing?" His voice had a hint of amusement in it.

"I want you to take me home, Alex. I haven't felt your body on mine since Sunday. I need to feel you inside me before I have to meet the girls at MacFadden's."

A sly grin spread across his face as he watched her bend over and kneel on the floor to unplug her laptop charger. She glanced over her shoulder, feeling his eyes surveying her body. "See something you like?" She smirked, their eyes meeting.

His smile grew wider and he nodded slowly.

"Good." She quickly raised herself off the ground and placed her things in her commuter bag. Alexander took the bag from her and practically ran down the hallway and out of the wellness center, dragging Olivia behind him. He punched the elevator call button repeatedly, praying for the car to arrive as soon as humanly possible.

He pulled her body against his, her back to his front. "Do you feel me?" He brushed her hair to the side, exposing her neck. He traced his tongue across her smooth skin. "Even after a workout, you smell amazing, love."

The sensation of Alexander's mouth on her skin after being absent for so long made Olivia's body tingle with anticipation. "Alex," she exhaled breathlessly.

"Yes, Olivia." He gently nibbled on her earlobe.

"Take me to your office."

She felt a smile creep across his face as he leaned forward and pressed the up elevator call button.

"And what do you want to do there?" he asked coyly as his hands roamed her body.

She spun around, her eyes blazing into his. "I'm pretty sure you know what I want to do, Alex," she said, leaning in and whispering against his neck, "But in case you want to know in greater detail, I want you to fuck me. I want it fast. And I want it hard." She pulled back. His eyes were wide. "Are you game?"

He grabbed her hair, tilting her head back. "Olivia, I love your dirty mouth."

The elevator finally sounded, announcing its arrival and they were whisked nine stories up to Alexander's office. When the doors opened, he grabbed her hand, practically running through the reception area.

"Mr. Burnham." His secretary jumped, apparently nervous that her boss had unexpectedly shown up. "I didn't think you would be here today."

Alexander punched his code into the door. "Pretend I'm not

even here. I won't be long," he snapped just as the door opened, pulling Olivia through a hallway she had become so accustomed to walking down over the past several months.

"Do you think she knows?" Olivia asked.

Alexander turned to face her, punching his code into the office door. "I think we made it pretty obvious when we ran down the hallway like a couple of horny teenagers." His eyes sparkled with amusement.

Olivia blushed as the door buzzed, allowing them access to his office. She rushed to his enormous bathroom and turned on the shower.

"In the shower, Miss Adler?" Alexander asked.

"Yes. I stink." She began stripping out of her gym clothes.

Alexander's breath caught at the sight of Olivia standing naked in front of him.

"Olivia," he growled, pulling her body into his. "I don't care if you just finished teaching your class. I plan on fucking you right now. The shower can wait."

Her body came alive with hunger as she watched him lean down and turn off the water.

"I've been dreaming about the day I could see you sprawled out beneath me on my desk. Now, go stand there. Face the windows. Don't you dare turn around."

She stared into his deep green eyes, unable to make a sound.

"Olivia, love, did you hear me?"

She simply nodded, her mind a daze as she walked out of the bathroom toward his desk, the room bright from the sunlight streaming in. She faced the windows, looking at the bustling city all those stories below. Her breathing increased as she continued standing there, waiting. The anticipation was killing her. It always did, and he knew that.

After what seemed like an eternity, she sensed him behind her. "It's about fucking time, Alex," she said. "I'm going crazy over here."

He wrapped his arm around her stomach and pulled her against his naked body. She gasped at the feel of his erection on her back.

"Do you feel what you do to me, love?" he asked softly. "All week, all I could think of was the next time I could be balls deep in that perfect pussy of yours." His hand traveled down her stomach, slowly making its way to her clit. "Did you miss my cock as much as I missed your pussy, Olivia?" he asked as he slowly began rubbing her.

She threw her head back against his chest, moaning with pleasure. "Yes," she exhaled. "Please. I need to feel you inside me, Alexander."

He quickly spun her around to face him. She reached up and ran her fingers through his hair, pulling his face down to hers. "I missed you so much, so will you please fuck me already?" she breathed into his mouth before pressing her lips against his.

He groaned, running his hands all over her body. He tore his lips away from her mouth, panting after the sudden invasion of her sweet tongue. "I will never tire of kissing you. Every kiss feels like our first kiss. Do you remember that?"

She stood up on her tiptoes and planted a gentle kiss on his lips. "How could I forget? You pinned me against my door."

He brushed his fingers against her lips. She closed her eyes in response, remembering their first kiss. He was right. Every kiss felt the same. Every kiss forced the same reaction from her body. Every kiss ignited sparks deep within.

"Olivia," he whispered.

"Yes," she exhaled.

"I want to watch."

She flung her eyes open, not understanding what he was talking about. His hands roamed her body again as he feathered kisses against her soft skin. "Last night, angel. On the phone. I want to watch you touch yourself." She closed her eyes, relishing in the feeling of his hands on her body. "Please, love. For me."

Her heart melted at his gentle plea. She would do anything for him if it made him happy. Pulling back, she smiled. "Okay."

Alexander's eyes grew wide in surprise before he crushed his lips to hers once more, moaning into her mouth as he slowly walked her back to the desk, carefully lowering her on top of it.

He hovered over her, kissing her neck before exploring the rest of her body with his tongue. Grabbing her hand in his, he slowly moved it down her stomach, spreading her legs as she lay on the dark mahogany.

He guided her hand over her clit, rubbing with her, his hand on top of hers. Nuzzling against her, he dragged his tongue across her neck. "I'm going to remove my hand now, Olivia," he said rather calmly. "I'm going to sit in the chair in the corner and watch as you make yourself come. Okay?"

Olivia moaned, entirely lost in the moment. She never thought she could be so turned on from her hand alone, but the fact that Alexander was watching as she pleasured herself set her body on fire with each stroke.

Alexander slowly walked away, sitting down in a chair a few feet away from the desk, never taking his eyes off her. "Spread your legs wider, Olivia," he ordered. "I want to see how wet you are."

She immediately obeyed his command, forcing her legs further apart as she continued toying with her clit. Why did it feel so good?

"Alex, I don't know how much longer I can do this," she said, her breathing becoming ragged.

"Does it turn you on that I'm sitting over here watching you, Olivia?" he asked.

"Yes," she answered quickly.

"Good. Look at me," he said. She opened her eyes and glanced at him over her legs. He was stroking himself. A smile spread across her face. "Well, I couldn't let you have all the fun," he explained. "Now, don't you dare stop. I want to see you come."

"Damn it, Alex!" Olivia shouted, lying back down on the desk. "I just want to feel you inside of me," she exhaled. "Stop teasing me like this."

"I'm not the one teasing, Olivia. You're doing that all by yourself," he replied. "And it's the hottest thing I've ever seen in my entire fucking life so don't you even think about stopping."

Olivia moaned as she returned her fingers to her clit.

"That's my girl," Alexander murmured, watching the woman he loved touch herself as he continued stroking his own erection. He was ready to explode and was trying to hold back, not wanting to come before she did. Standing up, he walked over to the desk and watched as she continued rubbing. "Olivia," he said quietly. "I'm going to come soon. Are you?"

She pulled her bottom lip between her teeth, nodding fervently. "Yes." She couldn't believe that she was ready to fall apart so quickly from her own fingers.

"Good. I want you to come and then I'm going to fuck you. Okay?" He ran his hand across her stomach, stopping at her nipple, and squeezed.

His words and hands on her body sent her over the top. She screamed out his name as she shuddered from the satisfaction that her own fingers gave her.

Alexander grabbed her legs and brought her to the edge of the desk, slamming into her.

Olivia moaned out, the orgasm still coursing through her, making her entire body tremble around him.

"God, love. You feel so fucking good." He thrust into her as he stood against his desk. "I'll never get enough of this beautiful pussy of yours. Tell me you like it when I fuck you hard like this," he exhaled, his breathing labored.

"Yes," Olivia said, her mind a blur. "I like it hard like this." Her voice was husky as she spasmed beneath him, her orgasm never seeming to end.

"Olivia!" he moaned out, leaning over the desk and biting her nipple as his orgasm ravaged his own body.

She gently caressed his sweat-laden forehead while their breathing slowed. He turned his face to look at her. "Can I just say that may have been the hottest thing ever." A boyish grin spread across his face.

Olivia grabbed his face and brought it to hers, kissing him full and deep. "I missed you, Mr. Burnham."

"And I missed you, Miss Adler. Now, shower time."

~~~~~~~~~~

"LIBBY!" MELANIE SHOUTED FROM the opposite side of MacFadden's when Olivia walked through the door with Alexander several hours later. She ran up to them as they made their way past the bar, hugging Olivia with a mischievous smile plastered on her face. "Don't be mad."

Olivia raised her eyebrows. "What are you talking about, Mel?"

"I kind of told a few friends how friggin' awesome you are, singing and all that, and I invited them to come out tonight."

"It's okay. I'm used to performing in front of several hundred people. I don't mind." She gave her a reassuring look.

"Good. I was worried you'd go off the deep end. Don't worry. I'll be good tonight. Early morning tomorrow and all."

"Are you working?" Olivia asked, a confused look on her face. Melanie usually didn't work on the weekends.

"No. Kiera invited me to come dress shopping with you!" she exclaimed excitedly. "Bridget is coming, too, I think. Kiera figured you'd never ask anyone else to join you, and we all think that having a few different opinions would be beneficial."

"What's this?" Alexander asked, his interest piqued.

Olivia turned to face him. "Apparently, I'm going shopping for a wedding dress tomorrow. Kiera is hell bent on making sure I actually marry you, for some reason."

He slung his arm around her waist. "Good. Remind me to keep her on my good side then."

Melanie smiled at Olivia and Alexander, sighing. "You guys are too freakin' cute together." She looked over at the couches, her eyes meeting Tyler's, a dreamy expression spreading across her face before she snapped back to reality. "Come. We're all over there."

She led the way through the bar toward a large section of couches where quite a few people Olivia had never met sat enjoying some drinks and having a good time. And amongst all of them sat Tyler, looking just as nervous as Olivia felt.

"Is Kiera here yet?" Olivia asked Melanie.

"No. Not yet. But she should be here soon, I think."

Olivia tensed up when she saw everyone in the group eye her and Alexander as they sat down in the seats Melanie had pointed to. She still grew somewhat uneasy in social situations like this, hating how everyone stared at her because of whom she was there with.

"This is Olivia, one of my bestest friends in the whole wide world," she said. "And this is her fiancé, Alexander Burnham. And, yes. It's *the* Alexander Burnham. He's Tyler's big brother." Melanie sat down, visibly bouncing in her seat, grabbing Tyler's hand in hers.

Alexander leaned over to Olivia. "Are you okay with all of this?" he whispered in her ear.

"It's fine, Alexander," she said quietly, giving him a reassuring smile. "Don't worry about me."

He sighed, brushing that errant curl out of her eye. "It's my job to worry about you, love."

"Hey! Who brought the party?" a voice called out seconds later.

Olivia breathed a sigh of relief when she heard her friend's voice. She got up and wrapped her arms around Kiera, winking at Mo over her shoulder.

"Happy to see me, huh, Libby?"

"You have no idea," she replied under her breath.

Mo and Alexander exchanged a handshake as a server came by to take some drink orders. Melanie introduced everyone, but Olivia knew she would never remember all their names. She laughed a little at the look on Tyler's face as he spoke with his brother, keeping his eyes trained on Melanie and smiling affectionately at the bubbly blonde, while she enthusiastically spoke with all of her friends. Olivia had seen that look before. Tyler was in deep.

She thought that maybe this was a good thing for Melanie. She had never seen her out with anyone and knew that she was lonely and desperate to feel a deeper connection with someone. She was incredibly sweet but got her heart stomped on more times than anyone should. Although she had just turned twenty-two, Melanie was wise beyond her years, and she wanted something more than a quick hook-up...something like what Olivia and Alexander had. Maybe Tyler could give that to her.

"Well, we should probably go set up," Mo said after a few drinks. Olivia nodded and they said their farewells to Melanie and her crowd of friends, Kiera and Alexander joining them as they made their way through the bustling bar.

"So, we need to start planning for Vegas," Kiera said as she and Olivia walked up the stairs behind Alexander and Mo.

"What's this?" Alexander asked, stopping abruptly on the stairs and turning around to look at Olivia. "When are you going to Vegas? And why?" He crossed his arms in front of his chest, a concerned look covering his face.

"Chill. It's for the bachelorette party," Kiera responded, trying to brush him off.

"When were you going to tell me about this, Olivia?" He glared at her, his tone accusatory.

"Relax, Alexander," she said, not wanting to fight about something as insignificant as going to Vegas with a few of her friends. "Kiera just threw it out there. We haven't made any plans just yet. No need to get all bent out of shape over this." Olivia noticed that Kiera and Mo had disappeared. *Cowards*, she thought to herself, making a mental note to murder Kiera for opening up this can of worms.

"Olivia, I protect what's mine," he said sternly, his eyes intense. "Something could happen to you while you're in Vegas and I'd be nowhere to be found!"

"For crying out loud, Alex! You're being ridiculous!" She attempted to walk past him up the stairs. He blocked her way. She glared at him, her eyes full of venom. "And stop talking about me like I'm a piece of fucking property or someone you need to protect! I'm not a child. You need to stop trying to control every little thing about my life!" Alexander stared at her, her voice becoming louder. "You have to let me make my own decisions and stop being so fucking suffocating!" She pushed against his chest and stormed past him. He let her go, still in shock over her words.

"Am I suffocating?" he asked under his breath to no one in particular.

"Yeah. You can be." He hadn't noticed Kiera standing at the top of the stairs. She appeared sorry for saying anything about the Vegas trip. "You need to remember that Olivia's been on her own her entire life," she explained. "She's taken care of herself for as long as she can remember. So you need to ease up on your controlling tendencies. I know you love her and you just want to keep her safe, but you've got to let her do what she wants to do or you'll lose her again." Kiera sent him a pleading look, hoping that his overbearing behavior wouldn't tear them apart.

"But I worry about her," he said quietly.

"That's no excuse. I worry about her, too, and I still let her date you." She winked. "If I were you, I'd get your ass up there and apologize to that girl." Kiera glared at him for several long moments before softening her gaze. "I know you mean well, but sometimes you need to be more compassionate. Stop looking at her as someone who needs protection or saving. Okay?"

Alexander sighed. "I get it. I'll try."

Kiera smiled, returning back to her normal cheery self. "Good. Now get back in there and apologize to my best friend because, so help me god, if I have to call and cancel all the dress shopping appointments I booked for tomorrow, I will rip your balls off." She turned and bounced across the empty room toward the stage where Mo was setting up.

Alexander scanned the dance floor and saw Olivia standing at the bar getting a drink with a few of the band members.

"Olivia," he said quietly as he walked up behind her. She grabbed a shot off the bar and slammed back the small glass filled with the silver tequila she needed. After swallowing the liquid, she spun around, her eyes shooting daggers through him. She was pissed.

The rest of the band members grabbed their drinks and left quickly, the tension between Olivia and Alexander obvious.

"Olivia, I'm sorry. I don't know what came over me. I just get so jealous sometimes. I want all your time. I know it's selfish of me to want that, but it drives me crazy to think that something could happen to you and I won't be able to do anything about it." His eyes pleaded with her.

She took a sip of her beer as she absorbed Alexander's

words. "Alex, you have to trust me to make my own decisions. I'm an adult, for crying out loud! You can't always be by my side. I need my own space, and I need time with my friends."

"I know. I know. And I'm so sorry." He grabbed her hands in his, gently caressing her skin. Leaning down, he planted a soft kiss on her neck, lingering several seconds as he breathed against her skin.

Shivers ran down Olivia's spine, loving the feeling of Alexander's lips on her neck...or any part of her body, for that matter. "Okay," she exhaled. "Apology accepted." She wrapped her arms around him and ran her fingers up and down his muscular back, thinking how it was nearly impossible for her to stay angry at him for too long. "I hate fighting with you."

He grabbed Olivia's chin, forcing her to look into his sincere eyes before placing a gentle kiss on her lips. "Why do we seem to argue all the time?" he asked as he brought her head back into his chest, holding her close to his body.

"Because you are the most frustrating man I've ever known." She smiled and listened to his heartbeat, feeling safe as his warmth surrounded her. "You're the only one who can fix or ruin everything in the blink of an eye," she said quietly.

He pulled back, staring down at her, unsure of how to respond to that. He didn't know what to think of her revelation. Was that true?

She noticed the forlorn look on Alexander's face after muttering those words and it broke her heart. "And that's one of the many reasons I'm madly in love with you, Alexander," she said, smiling. "There's never a dull moment with you around." She winked, walking away.

Alexander watched her hips sway as she bounded up the stage, guilt overwhelming his conscience for constantly keeping her in the dark about her past. Olivia was right. He could ruin everything. Maybe he already *had* ruined everything and she just didn't know it yet.

But he couldn't tell her. What if her father was right and her lack of knowledge was the only thing keeping her alive? Until he knew more, she needed to stay in the dark. It was the only way.

CHAPTER NINE

JUST A COINCIDENCE

TWO SMALL CHILDREN RAN around the beach, chasing each other, the end of a game of hide-and-seek.

"I found you, Olibia! Fair and square!"

"I know. But maybe I want you to chase me for a little bit, Alex!" Olivia continued to run up and down the beach, hoping that the tall, dark-haired, green-eyed boy would keep following her.

He stopped running and placed his hands on his knees, trying to catch his breath. "I'll never stop chasing you, Olibia. We're best friends, and we'll be together always. Forever and ever." He walked toward the rocks leading up to the enormous beach house.

~~~~~~~~~~

OLIVIA'S EYES FLUNG OPEN. She looked over at Alexander as he slept next to her, his breathing rhythmic. What did her dream mean? The same green-eyed boy that pulled her out of the car in her nightmares was there, and she had called him Alex. It had to just be a coincidence.

Wanting to forget about the dream and everything it inferred, she drew her body closer to Alexander's and listened to the rain fall outside.

A devilish smile spread across his face and he groaned, the sensation of Olivia's delicate flesh so close to his waking him up in more ways than one. "Good morning, love," he murmured groggily. "I can certainly get used to being woken up like this." He raised his hips to meet hers. His eyes grew wide when she pushed him onto his back and placed her legs around his waist.

"Mmmmm…" he moaned as she began a slow circling motion, teasing his already hard erection. "God, I've missed you…"

Olivia leaned down, not wanting to look into those same green eyes she always saw in her dream, and kissed Alexander deep on the mouth, their tongues entwining softly at first. Her kiss became more needy, her hips beginning a more torturous rhythm. She needed to forget it all, and Alexander was the only one who could help her.

"Damn, baby," he breathed, flipping her onto her back. "What's gotten into you this morning?" He admired the beautiful woman panting below him. "Do you want me inside of you?" he asked, his eyes narrowed.

She nodded her head, bringing her hips up, pleading with her body for Alexander's touch.

"Oh no, Olivia," he said coyly, shaking his head. "I need to hear you say it." He gently trailed kisses down her neckline, taking his time so he could savor each intoxicating minute. "I love the taste of your skin," he whispered in her ear.

His voice sent electric currents through her veins, igniting her body with passion. Olivia wondered if she would always have that reaction to him. She hoped so.

Pulling back, he returned his intense green eyes to hers. An evil grin spread across his face as he teased her, pressing his pelvis rhythmically between her legs.

"Alex, please. I need to feel you." She reached up and forced his mouth against hers, kissing him full on the lips, telling him with her tongue how desperately she wanted him.

He groaned and Olivia felt him harden even more against her, surprised that was possible. He positioned himself between her legs and traced circles with his tongue on her nipple. "Say it, love." He teased her clit with his erection, nibbling on her ear. "Tell me you want me inside you, Olivia," he whispered, his voice husky. "That you want to feel me slowly moving inside you over and over again, pushing you higher and higher with each motion until you can't think from the amazing sensations you feel from my love."

"Alexander," Olivia exhaled, her breathing ragged from his words alone. "I want you inside me," she panted, running her fingers through his dark hair. "I want you to make love to me."

Alexander crushed his lips to hers, his hands traveling up and down her naked body before he pulled back and gazed into her eyes. "Do you have any idea how much I love you?" he asked sweetly.

She nodded, biting her bottom lip as she stared at his chiseled body moving slowly on top of her. He wasn't even inside her yet, but she was ready to explode from the love she felt for him at that moment. Grabbing his head, she brought his mouth just a mere breath from hers. "I love you, Alexander Burnham. Forever. You're the only man for me," she whispered sweetly against his lips as he slowly entered her, her eyes growing wide from the total euphoria enveloping her body. It was the same feeling she felt every time she was with him, and she never wanted it to stop.

"God, love. There is nothing like being inside you. I never want this moment to end." He looked down at her in admiration, still in shock that he had found his Olivia after all these years. His life was finally complete. She made him complete. "I don't think I'll ever get my fill of you, Olivia."

"Alex..." she moaned out, wondering how one man could cause a thousand different emotions to run through her body from one simple act.

"Do I make you feel good, Olivia?" He buried his face in her neck, nibbling gently on her soft skin.

Not wanting any more space between them, she wrapped her legs around his waist and moved with the gentle pace he set. "Yes, Alex." Her breathing became erratic as she fought against her impending orgasm. "You do." No one she had ever met in her life made her feel as good and complete as that man. She had fallen head over heels in love with him, never expecting to fall for anyone. He was perfect for her. He anticipated all her wants and desires.

Alexander picked up the pace to a quick but gentle rhythm. "I love that I can bring you so much pleasure so quickly, angel. I love that I alone can do this for you."

Olivia closed her eyes, getting lost in the moment.

"Look at me, love," Alexander said softly. "Please. I want to see those gorgeous brown eyes of yours."

She opened her eyes and stared at him as he continued moving inside her, ready to explode and fall over the edge.

"I've looked for you my entire life, Olivia. I love you so much," he said, the love he felt at that moment causing him to release inside her. He pressed his lips to hers, delicately caressing her tongue with his. He pushed into her once more before her body began convulsing around him, her own orgasm taking hold. He continued his slow gentle movement until the aftershocks finally subsided.

"Promise me something, Olivia." He looked down at her, his heart overwhelmed with the love he had for her.

"What's that?" she whispered as she ran her hands up and down his back, trying to regulate her breathing.

"That you'll never run again, no matter what. That we'll be together always."

Olivia inhaled quickly, her dream rushing back to her memory. She tensed up, her heart thumping in her chest as her chin quivered from what it could all mean.

"What?" Alexander pulled back and stared at her in confusion. "What's wrong?"

She searched his eyes…those same green eyes she saw in her dreams. But what was she going to tell him? That she was starting to think that he was the green-eyed boy that pulled her from the car accident? That was absurd. They grew up in two entirely different places. Realizing how ridiculous it all sounded, she softened her expression. It was all just a coincidence.

"Nothing's wrong," she said sweetly. "Just another déjà vu moment."

A smile replaced the concerned look on Alexander's face and he leaned down, kissing her softly on the nose. "Come on. Shower with me." He pulled her to her feet.

She cringed as she felt the aftereffects of their lovemaking trickle down her leg. "Gross," she said, laughing.

Alexander glanced down and smiled when he saw his semen

dripping from her. "That's hot. You're a marked woman now, Miss Adler." He grabbed her hand and pulled her into the bathroom, turning on the shower.

~~~~~~~~~~

AFTER OLIVIA FINISHED GETTING ready for the day, she made her way downstairs, smiling at the sight that greeted her. Alexander was hard at work in front of the stove making her breakfast. It warmed her heart that he had no problem cooking for her.

"Eggs okay, love?" he asked, feeling Olivia's presence behind him.

"Of course, *love*."

He turned around. "Are you mocking my term of endearment for you? I could change it and start calling you my wench instead."

Playfully, she punched him in the arm. Alexander faked being hurt as she walked past him over to the coffee brewer and made herself a cup. "Of course not, Alexander. I love your term of endearment for me. It sends shivers up my spine every time you say it."

Alexander looked up from where he was sautéing potatoes. "Good."

CHAPTER TEN

HIM

"MIRANDA, WHO'S ON THE phone?" Donovan shouted from his office into the reception area.

"He wouldn't say. He said *you'll know*."

Donovan stilled. *Fuck. It's him.* He took a deep breath and picked up the phone. "Donovan here."

"Hi, Mark," the voice said. "How are things going?"

Donovan had heard that voice only a few times over the past several decades and, every time, it sent chills up his spine. It was a cold, calculating voice. He could only imagine the person attached to it. He never wanted to meet him in person. "Pretty good, sir," he replied. "We're getting closer every day." His voice was audibly nervous.

"Really? Are you now?" he sneered. "Why do I feel like I've had to do everything for you? I found the girl for you back in July, and you still haven't gotten me the information I'm paying you to find. That I've *been* paying you to find for years now."

"I understand that, sir, but patience is something all of my clients need to have. If we rush things, it could blow up in all of our faces. The way I can ensure that nothing will get back to you, or me, or anyone else is to take our time and make sure things are done right. I'll admit that we've run into a few complications, but everything is back on track, I assure you."

"Convince me, Mark. Convince me that everything is okay."

Donovan glanced around the room before getting up from

behind his desk and closing the door. He hated to divulge his plans to anyone, but this guy was not someone to be trifled with.

"Well, the girl is engaged to a hot shot here in Boston. He runs his own private security company and noticed a few threats to her safety so he made sure she had a protection detail assigned to her. We were able to spook him enough to add to that detail and include one of our own people on that job to try and get close to her. It hasn't been fruitful yet, but we're still hopeful it will all work out. In the meantime, we're working another angle."

"Which is?" the man on the phone growled. "I'm quickly losing my patience and you do not want to be around when that happens."

"We have everything in place to drive a wedge between the girl and this man she's planning on marrying. We have information that will shatter her fucking world. Apparently, they were friends as children. He knows and he's keeping that from her. We plan on using that to tear them apart. And when that happens, we already have someone in place to pick up the pieces."

"And then what?"

"Then we'll hope that this Alexander fellow tells Olivia everything, which he probably will, and then she'll start to remember things about her past, leading one of our people to the information you're looking for. An expert we've hired is quite certain that she could very well be able to remember her past once she realizes who Burnham really is."

The man on the phone thought about what he had just told him. It could work. "Fine. Keep it up, but so help me God, if you don't get a move on, you will regret it."

Donovan hung up, trembling with anxiety. Why did he have to get into the family business?

~~~~~~~~~~

"OLIVIA, LOVE, I NEED to get back to Texas," Alexander said, walking down the hall from his office. His heart warmed when he spotted her curled up on the couch, her laptop in front of her.

She looked up, her face sad at the thought of Alexander leaving her again. Getting up from the couch, she strolled over to him and wrapped her arms around his shoulders. "When will you be back?" she whispered against his neck.

"Hopefully no later than tomorrow night. Now, you have fun with the girls today. Marshall is out front and will drive you wherever you need to go. Understand?"

Olivia exhaled, her frustration evident as she turned away from him. "Yes, Alexander."

"Hey, Olivia, look at me." He reached out and grabbed her arm, spinning her around to face him. "It's for your own good. I don't like it any more than you do, but I need to know that no harm will come to you while I'm gone."

His voice was sincere and full of worry. Simon's warning sounded in her head and she knew Alexander's concerns were valid. Olivia couldn't help but throw her arms around him again, kissing him fully on the mouth. "I love you, Alexander."

"I love you, too. Now, enjoy your day. I'll hurry home to you, angel," he said sweetly, planting one last kiss on her temple.

~~~~~~~~~~

"GOOD MORNING, MISS ADLER," Marshall greeted Olivia, opening the door to the waiting SUV. "Where to first?"

"Starbucks, please. The one by Alexander's office building." She climbed into the car and was soon on her way to go meet the girls at their usual Starbucks before starting their day of dress shopping.

After a short car ride, Marshall pulled up outside the coffee shop. Walking into the bustling store, Olivia wasn't surprised to find that she was the first to arrive. Her friends were notoriously late. She ordered four coffees and found a table to wait for the rest of the girls. Sipping her coffee, she was thankful to have the extra caffeine to get through the day. She hadn't slept much and, even then, it wasn't a restful sleep.

"Well, if it isn't Olivia Adler?" she heard a snide voice say a few minutes later.

She looked up from her e-reader, her heart racing as she stared into Adele's cold eyes. "Nice to see you, as well, Adele," she replied coldly before returning her eyes to her book, hoping she would get the hint and move on.

Adele stared down at Olivia. She was told to be smart about what she was supposed to do today. Plant a seed of doubt, but don't drop the bomb...not yet, anyway. "You know it won't last between you two, don't you?" she sneered.

Olivia looked up again, sighing. She had hoped that Adele would finally be past all that juvenile bullshit. No such luck, apparently. "Adele, you need to get over this. We're getting married, and there's nothing you can do to stop it from happening."

Adele's eyes softened. "Are you sure that's a smart idea? I mean, do you really even *know* him? He has a tendency to keep secrets, and I just want to make sure that you know what you're getting into, Olivia. Once you say 'I do', there's no going back. Well, except through a rather lengthy and public divorce."

"What are you getting at? Alexander doesn't keep anything from me. He's an open book." Olivia's voice wavered slightly at the lies coming out of her mouth. She knew Alexander kept things from her. A lot of things.

"Oh, really? Have you ever been in his office at home?"

Olivia looked at her, wondering why that even mattered. She never *had* been in his home office, and he was diligent in ensuring that he kept it locked at all times, even when he was in there. "Adele, the nature of Alexander's business is such that he has to keep his work classified," she explained, all the while wondering what he was keeping in that room.

"It's not his work he's trying to keep from you, Olivia. It's something much bigger than that."

Olivia eyed her cautiously, her heart beating nervously in her chest as her brain ran through hundreds of different scenarios. Did Adele know something? She *was* childhood friends with Alexander, after all. Maybe she knew more than

Olivia thought. What *was* he hiding from her? She hated that she was beginning to doubt the man she loved.

"Olivia, is this woman bothering you?" a deep voice broke through her thoughts. She breathed a sigh of relief when she saw Simon standing next to her table, glaring at Adele with venom in his eyes. Olivia was surprised to find that, for once, she was actually thankful to see him.

A smile spread across Adele's face when she heard that voice. *All part of the master plan*, she remembered. "No," she said sweetly, her eyes not breaking from Olivia's. "I was just wishing Olivia good luck on her upcoming nuptials." Adele turned to leave before muttering loud enough for everyone to hear, "She's going to need it."

Simon continued to shoot daggers at Adele as she walked through the front door of the store. Once she was gone, Olivia visibly relaxed, exhaling a breath that she didn't even realize she had been holding.

Simon turned to face her and pulled out a chair, eyeing Olivia before he sat down, almost as if he was asking if it was okay for him to do so. She nodded.

"Are you sure you're okay? You look a little shaken up. Who was that bitch?"

"Just someone who is jealous that I'm marrying the man she was hoping to. But she's only interested in his bank account."

Simon smiled. "Money grabber."

"Totally." She returned his smile, finally feeling better about what had just happened.

"Well, as long as you're okay, I'm going to get out of here. It looks like you're meeting someone, and I can only assume Kiera will be one of them. I'm pretty sure that she'll cut off my dick if she sees me speaking with you," he joked.

Olivia looked at the four coffee cups on her table before returning her eyes to meet Simon's. There was a slight twinkle in his gaze that she had never noticed before. *I like the new Simon*, she thought to herself. "Yeah, you're probably right." They both snapped their heads toward the door when they heard it open, thankful that it wasn't any of her friends just yet. Simon was right. Kiera would absolutely castrate him if she saw him standing there talking to her. And she wouldn't even ask for an explanation until afterwards.

"Here. Take this." Simon reached into his pocket and pulled out a business card. "In case you need anything. I'm always just a phone call away and willing to help out or listen. I'm a real good listener. I promise." He noticed that Olivia still seemed to be thinking about whatever Adele had said to her. *Good*, he thought. *It's all coming together.*

Olivia took the business card and studied it. *Simon MacKenzie, General Contractor*. He must be doing pretty well for himself if he had begun to work as a general contractor. "I'll keep that in mind."

Simon waved as he walked out the front door of the shop. Olivia wondered why he hadn't grabbed a coffee. It *was* a Starbucks after all. She didn't worry about that for long as, just moments after Simon's departure, Kiera showed up.

"Libby, you are a goddess!" Kiera exclaimed, grabbing one of the cups of coffee off the table. "I barely slept last night." She winked.

Olivia smiled. "Join the club," she mumbled, her dream rushing back to her brain. Was Alexander the boy from her dreams? And was that what Adele inferred that he was keeping from her?

CHAPTER ELEVEN

ENOUGH

"I DON'T THINK I can try on one more dress," Olivia pouted. She slumped into a chair in the sitting area of an upscale boutique on Newbury Street. Her bridal consultant gave her an irritated, yet contrite look.

"Come on, Libby," Melanie said, trying to comfort her. "We just need to re-focus our efforts. That's all. I get that it must be frustrating having tried on dress after dress all morning, but you need to have a little bit of patience. The perfect dress is out there somewhere."

"She's right." Bridget walked over to Olivia's chair and sat on the arm, hugging her friend. "We'll find it, even if it means we have to spend every Saturday from now until August helping you sort through racks of hideous white gowns." She gestured to an atrocious white concoction that the consultant had carried into their sitting area.

Olivia laughed. "Thanks, girls. I just don't really know what I'm looking for. I didn't grow up dreaming about the day of my wedding. Hell, just a year ago, I would have rather been thrown into a pit of poisonous snakes before agreeing to marry anyone."

"EEK!" Kiera exclaimed, breaking her gaze from her smartphone. It was obvious that she had been texting Mo by the lovestruck expression on her face. "That's a little extreme, don't you think, Libby?"

Sighing, she got out of her chair and started to head back to the dressing room. "No. I don't, and I'm starting to re-think my position on that."

Kiera gave her a swift kick in the ass. Olivia turned around and grinned at the girls, thankful that she had three good friends there to help her with everything. "Okay," she groaned. "I'll get back in there and keep going with dresses."

Once inside the fitting room, she stared in resentment at all the gowns in front of her that she still had to try on. Not one of them appeared to be anything she would wear. They were too big and extravagant. She didn't want anything like that. She liked simple. She wanted to get married on a beach, for crying out loud. None of these screamed beach wedding.

There's no way in hell I'm wearing this piece of shit, she thought, picking up the next dress just as Kiera opened the door, peeking in.

"Kiera! I could be naked!"

"Whatever. Not like I haven't seen you naked before. Anyway, here." She shoved another dress into Olivia's hands. "This is the one. Trust me." She winked and returned to sit next to Melanie and Bridget.

Olivia looked over the dress in her hands. "Oh my," she said under her breath. At times, it felt as if Kiera could read her mind. The dress was gorgeous. It was exactly what Olivia would have chosen herself.

She carefully put it on and stared into the mirror. "Holy crap." She couldn't believe her eyes. The sumptuous light champagne-hued dress had a low halter and clung to all her curves in the right way. The back of the silk gown was open, going down into a subtle V right above the beaded appliqué waist with a small chapel train trailing just slightly on the floor.

"It's perfect," Olivia said as she opened the door.

"You look absolutely ravishing, Libby!" Melanie squealed, jumping up from her seat. "You look like a movie star from the 1920s in that dress. It's very *Gatsby*."

"Let's just hope that Alexander doesn't meet the same fate as Jay Gatsby," Kiera said as she adjusted the dress a bit.

"He used to be a Navy SEAL. I'm fairly certain he can handle a pool just fine. He can hold his breath underwater for five minutes or something like that," Olivia remarked.

"Okay. Buy the dress and let's go celebrate with some drinks!" Bridget clapped her hands in excitement.

Olivia nodded and the bridal consultant took down the necessary information she needed to fit the dress for her. It was finally starting to feel real. She was going to marry Alexander in just a few short months.

After enduring the tedious process of having every inch of her measured, Olivia and the rest of her entourage emerged from the boutique and clambered into the back of the large SUV.

"Did you find a dress, Miss Adler?" Marshall asked once all the girls were situated in the car.

"I did!" Olivia replied, rather excited.

"Where to now, ma'am?"

"Take us to the Green Dragon, please."

The girls cheered. "This is going to be a fun afternoon!" Melanie exclaimed, oozing with enthusiasm as she bounced in her seat.

"I need a girl's day with all of you!" Olivia admitted, finally feeling relaxed for the first time all day. Now that the pressure of finding a dress no longer hung over her head, she was looking forward to enjoying the afternoon with her friends.

After the short car ride toward the North End of Boston, Marshall pulled over on Congress Street, running to open the door for the girls, allowing them to exit onto the busy Boston street. "Go ahead," Marshall said. "Carter is already inside, keeping an eye on things. I'll be in after I park."

Olivia nodded, thankful to actually have Carter and Marshall looking out for her after recalling Simon's warning. The girls entered the old historic pub, nodding a greeting to Carter, who was sitting on a barstool near the entrance. They grabbed a high top table close to the bar and sat down to enjoy their afternoon of alcohol consumption. "You sit. Nature calls."

Olivia began walking toward the back of the bar, not paying too much attention to where she was going, and slammed into a tall, hard body. "OH! I'm so sorry. Excuse me." She didn't look up and side-stepped the man, heading for the back hallway.

"Olivia? Is that you?" a soft voice said.

She spun around and her mouth dropped open in surprise. "Cam?! What are you doing here?!" She walked over to him and hugged him enthusiastically.

"Wow. You look so much better than you did..." He trailed off.

"It's okay, Cam," she assured him, placing her hand on his arm. "Things are much better than they were."

"I've been wanting to get in touch with you and find out if everything was okay. I assumed that you worked things out with Alexander and that's why I didn't hear from you again."

Olivia looked down at her feet, guilty that she didn't at least get to thank the guy who pretty much saved her life. "I'm sorry. Alexander and I stopped at your house on our way out of town about a week later, but you weren't there."

Cam ran his fingers through his wayward sandy hair. "Yeah. I just needed to get out of town for a little bit," he explained with a hint of sadness in his voice. "You know how that goes." He raised his eyebrows.

Olivia nodded, remembering Cam telling her that he loved her just days before she was reunited with Alexander. "What are you doing here anyway?" she asked, wanting to change the subject.

"I'm here on a conference. The American Psychotherapy Association's convention is here starting Monday. A few of us decided to come early to roam around the city. I've never been to Boston before. And the concierge at our hotel told us we couldn't leave town without stopping here for a pint, although it seems like a tourist bar. What are you doing here?"

Olivia shrugged. "Even though I live here, I never really do the tourist thing. It's nice to do it once in a while, especially on the weekends. It's great for people watching."

There was an awkward silence, neither one of them knowing how to act.

Cam cleared his throat. "I guess congratulations are in order." He nodded his head toward her ring. "Elsie had mentioned something to that effect a few months back."

She beamed. "Yes. I will be Mrs. Alexander Burnham come late August."

"I'm happy for you, Olivia." He wrapped his arms around her, struggling to maintain his composure. It felt as if his heart was just ripped from his chest. It was nice to see her happy, but he wished that he could be the one to put that spark back into her eyes. He knew he wasn't what Olivia needed, but that didn't make it hurt any less.

"Hey! Who's this?" Kiera asked, sidling up next to where Cam stood.

"Kiera, this is Cam."

She looked at Olivia, confused.

"You know... *Dr. Cam.*" She raised her eyebrows in a knowing manner.

"Oh!!! You're so my new BFF!" Kiera exclaimed, nearly toppling him over and hugging him with all her strength.

Cam looked at Olivia, a surprised expression on his face from Kiera's forwardness. Olivia simply shrugged. There was nothing she could do about Kiera.

"We're so happy that you were able to knock some sense into this girl and make her come back home," Kiera said when she finally released him. "She didn't realize how much everyone back here would miss her after her little disappearing act. At least it didn't take her four years to return this time!"

"Kiera," Olivia said under her breath. "Enough."

"What?" she asked.

Olivia gave her *the look*, and she knew she'd better shut her mouth.

"Sorry, Libs."

Cam gave Olivia a concerned look. "You've done that before?"

"Yeah, but you are not my therapist so we're not discussing it. So there..." she responded playfully, Cam's uneasy expression waning.

"Well, I should probably get back to my friends," he said, knowing that the longer he was in Olivia's presence, the harder it would be to forget about her again.

"How long are you in town for?" Kiera asked. "You should

come to MacFadden's Friday night to see Miss Olivia sing! Libby is a motherfucking rock star. The band was always popular, but since Olivia returned, you should see the crowd they attract now."

Cam turned toward Olivia, raising his eyebrows in a questioning manner. She glanced down, hiding her eyes from him, blushing.

"Is this true? Are you a motherfucking rock star?" he asked quietly, his voice husky.

Olivia raised her head and looked deep into Cam's kind silver eyes, remembering all the times he whispered the things he wanted to do to her. But those days were over. Things were better now. "Fuck yes, I am!" she exclaimed. "Okay. Nature calls. Come see me before you leave, okay?"

Cam nodded and watched her beautiful body walk toward the back of the bar, exhaling loudly. Running into Olivia again was the last thing he needed. He knew that she lived in Boston, but when he decided to attend the convention, never in a million years did he think he would run into her. Seeing her again re-opened old wounds that he thought had healed over the past few months. Now he wasn't too sure.

"So, she fucked you, huh?" Kiera asked him rather nonchalantly.

He broke out of his trance and turned to face her, shocked at her question. "What?"

"Oh, come on. I've known Libby for a long time, and I've seen the look on the face of every man she's left in her wake. You've got the same exact look."

He started to walk away, uncomfortable with the conversation. "It's not what you think, Kiera."

She followed him, surprising him with her relentless spirit. "Well, humor me then. What is it? I saw the way you were looking at her. I'd say you've got it bad for that girl."

"I *did* have it bad for her," he admitted, his expression turning from soft and wistful to intense. "But she was so broken when she was in Florida. I just wanted to make her smile. Then I realized I would never be the one to make her happy...not truly happy. Not like *him*. In Olivia's mind, I'll never compare to him, and I'm okay with that. All I care about is her happiness, and if it means sacrificing my own, it's worth it. There's a girl out there for me somewhere."

Kiera's expression softened. "You're a good guy, Cam. I like you. You can stay."

Cam nodded. "It was nice to meet you, Kiera."

"You, too. Thanks for being there for Libby. She's like a sister to me. I couldn't imagine life without her in it."

"I know the feeling," he said sadly.

~~~~~~~~~~

"SO, LET'S TALK BACHELORETTE," Kiera said once Olivia returned from the ladies' room and a server dropped off a round of beers.

"OOH! Yes! Let's!" Melanie said. "I know you haven't really talked plans yet, but Bridge and I would love it if we could crash your party."

"Yes!" Bridget said. "I could so use a weekend away in Vegas with my three favorite girls. It'll be so much fun!"

"Okay, but this can absolutely not turn into *The Hangover*," Olivia joked. Her friends had a tendency to get slightly out of control at times. And that was why she got along with them so well.

"And if it does, there's nothing your bitch ass can do about it," Kiera responded. "But we won't be stupid enough to go the week before the big wedding. Now, here's the thing. You're going to be swamped with plans and shit the closer you get to the big day. And you don't have much time as it is, so how about the last weekend in June? It will work for everyone's schedule. I already checked with Alexander and he said he'd be out of town that weekend for a meeting with a big client."

Olivia thought about Kiera's proposition. She hated being in that big penthouse apartment all by herself. Runner and Nepenthe were good company, but it always seemed so empty without him. Not to mention it didn't feel like home to her yet. She wondered if it ever would.

"Okay. Last weekend in June it is!" Olivia said. "But there's one catch. You aren't paying a dime for that weekend. I can't ask you all to spend your hard-earned money on this trip."

"Whatever," Kiera interrupted. "Alexander told me this morning that he already booked everything anyway. He's paying for it." She winked.

What a bastard, Olivia thought.

"He's a sneaky one, isn't he?" Melanie asked.

"That he is."

"I think he felt bad about overreacting last night," Kiera explained.

Olivia smiled as she raised her beer glass and clinked with her friends, wanting to forget about Alexander's overbearing tendencies for a minute. "To Vegas, bitches!"

"Vegas!"

Olivia turned her head to see Cam staring at her with a sad look in his eyes. She knew how difficult it must be for him to watch her and realize how happy she finally was. She cared for him, but her feelings for him were no match for how much she loved Alexander. Even so, that still didn't make her heart break any less looking at the forlorn expression on his face.

Throughout the afternoon, the small tavern became more and more crowded. The sun finally came out to play after the rainy morning and Boston was swarming with tourists. The bar was located on the Freedom Trail in a rather popular section of the city. Many out-of-towners began to fill up the pub, wanting to grab a beer at the historic tavern in the city that was at the heart of the American Revolution.

The beers continued to flow hours into the evening as the girls planned their Vegas trip, although there wasn't too much planning to do. Alexander had already done most of it.

"He probably had his secretary plan most of it," Olivia slurred, finishing another beer. She wondered what number that was as she looked around the table at her friends. All of their faces were flushed from the liquor they had been consuming.

"It doesn't matter," Bridget said. "Whoever planned everything for us did a badass job. We're in a presidential suite that sleeps, like, a gazillion people. We're all having a spa day.

And he's arranged for bottle service at a bunch of the clubs in the area. It's going to be a rockin' good time!" She sounded rather excited. "And I'm *so* getting laid."

The entire table erupted in laughter.

"I'm glad he's pulling out all the stops for this one," Olivia said, thinking how busy Alexander must have been arranging everything that morning. "And I'm glad none of us have to do the planning. I wouldn't even know where to begin."

"Libby," a soft voice called out. All of the girls' heads turned to look in Cam's direction as he stood by their table. "I'm heading out. It was great to see you again."

Olivia glanced at her friends. "I'll be right back, girls." She slid off her barstool and walked with Cam toward the front door, the silence deafening as she tried to figure out what to say to him after everything they had been through.

"Well, listen, here's my business card," he said, breaking the awkward tension and pulling a card out of his wallet. Olivia was immediately reminded of Simon...and Adele. "My cell number is on there so if you ever need anything, anything at all, you know you can count on me."

She met his eyes and could see the pain that she caused him. But he was the one who pushed her back to Alexander. If it hadn't been for him, she wouldn't be where she was right now -- physically and emotionally. How could she ever repay him?

Olivia took the card from him and placed it in her pocket, not able to say a word as her appreciation for everything he had ever done for her came rushing forward. No words could adequately convey what she needed to say to him.

"It was great to see you again. Good luck with everything, Libby." Cam began to walk toward the front of the bar.

"Cam! Wait!" Olivia shouted, finally finding her voice.

He turned his head, his feet unable to walk any further. His heart wanted her to confess her undying love for him, but his head knew that would never happen.

"Thank you," she said. "For everything. I mean, helping me get my shit back together. I just... I don't..."

Cam's legs finally listened to his brain and closed the distance, cutting her off. He took her soft hand in his, savoring the contact once more from the only girl he knew he would ever love.

"You don't need to thank me, Libby. I was just doing what any friend would do." He stared into her eyes one last time before turning to leave the bar. She was a friend and that was all she could ever be. Nothing more. He regretted pushing her into the car all those months ago, and then making her confront Alexander when he showed up after he left his bride-to-be at the altar. But she would never have found her happiness unless she did so. Olivia was happy, at last.

He walked the few short blocks up the street to his hotel and flopped on the bed. After tossing and turning for hours, he couldn't shake the feeling that the walls were closing in on him. He got up and grabbed his laptop. He needed to leave the city. He couldn't stay there. It was something Olivia would do, but it had to happen. He now understood why she had done what she did.

He found his return flight information and called the airline to change his reservation to the next available flight. The customer service representative told him he could get on a flight leaving Logan Airport at six in the morning, less than five hours away.

"I'll take it," Cam said into the phone as he hurried to pack all of his things into his suitcase.

A few hours later, as he watched the city of Boston disappear beneath him cloaked in a pink-and-orange hue from the rising sun, he knew he made the right decision. He needed to try to forget about Olivia, and he couldn't be in the same city as her. "Enough," he said to himself, more as a request than anything.

CHAPTER TWELVE

MAKE UP

"I HAVE SOME INFORMATION, Donovan."

"Yes, Cheryl. What is it?" he spat into the phone. He needed some good news, and soon, before everything fell apart.

"I have information about Olivia going to Las Vegas. Apparently, it's her bachelorette party, and Burnham has agreed to allow her to go without normal protection, thanks to my prodding."

Donovan brought his hand to his chin, thinking about what that meant.

"Do we deviate from the plan and take a chance at this opportunity?" Cheryl inquired.

"No," Donovan said after much thought. "The plan remains the same. But we'll use this opportunity to our advantage. Send me the details that you know."

"Yes, sir."

Donovan pressed the receiver on his phone and dialed another number. "Lucas, would you and your brother be interested in taking a little trip to Vegas?"

~~~~~~~~~~

THE NEXT SEVERAL WEEKS seemed to fly by while Olivia continued to prepare for the wedding at the end of August. As she sat at a sidewalk table at a Newbury Street restaurant on a warm Thursday in late June, she couldn't help but smile at the thought of getting on the plane the following day and spending a long weekend in Las Vegas. She perused the menu while she waited for Kiera to show up, thankful that Alexander had agreed to allow her to go without her protection detail that coming weekend...thanks to much convincing by Agent Marshall.

"Good afternoon," Olivia heard a shrill voice say.

She glanced up from her menu and was met with Adele's smirking face. She put on the best fake smile she could muster on such short notice. "Afternoon, Adele. It's a beautiful day, isn't it?"

"Ugh," she groaned. "I hate this humidity. I should have never left California."

"Well, feel free to return at any time. I don't think anyone here in Boston would miss you very much." Olivia gave herself a mental fist bump before returning her eyes to the menu, hoping Adele would take the hint and leave.

"Whatever," she said, clearly irritated with Olivia's lackluster response. "Have you thought at all about what I said during our last conversation?"

"No, Adele. I haven't thought about you one bit, but it's rather apparent that you've been thinking about *me*. Why else would you feel the need to pester me? Next time you see me, feel free to continue walking."

Olivia looked across the street and met Marshall's eyes as she kept watch in the parked SUV. She gave her a thumbs up, indicating that she was fine and did not need any help. Marshall simply nodded. Olivia was grateful that she had begun to ease up on the ropes a bit. Any of her other assigned agents would have been out of the SUV immediately, making a scene. At least Marshall treated her like an adult and let her fight her own battles on occasion.

"Olivia," Adele said softly, her voice changing from harsh and trite to warm and sympathetic. "I'm just trying to warn you before you get in too deep. Alexander is keeping secrets from you."

"What the fuck are you doing here, bitch?" Kiera said rather loudly as she approached Olivia's table. Several restaurant patrons raised their heads, aghast at hearing such language, and gaped at her.

"Kiera, please. People are staring," Olivia said quietly, her expression wide as she scanned the other tables to see them gawking in her direction.

"Whatever," she said, her green eyes wild with fury. "When have I ever cared what someone thought of me?" She turned to Adele. "We have a lunch date, so if you would please excuse us."

"Okay. I'm sorry for interrupting." Adele's eyes met Olivia's gaze. "Olivia, please. I just want to talk to you about something important. Can we get together for a coffee, say, next Tuesday? Then I'll never bother you again. I promise."

"Libby," Kiera hissed, glaring at Adele. "Why the fuck would you listen to anything she has to say? She's been nothing but a pain in the ass from the beginning."

Olivia faced Kiera. "I understand that," she admitted, trying to figure out what game Adele was playing. The promise of never having to see or listen to her again was rather tempting. "Okay, Adele. I'll listen to what you have to say," she reluctantly agreed. "Starbucks by Alexander's building. Tuesday. Four o'clock."

"Perfect," Adele replied, clapping her hands. "I do appreciate it. Have a wonderful lunch, ladies." She walked down the street and hailed a cab, taking the burner phone out of her purse.

"Hi. It's Adele. It's going down on Tuesday."

"Wonderful. We'll be ready."

~~~~~~~~~~

"ALEXANDER?" OLIVIA CALLED OUT when she arrived at her place several hours later after a fun lunch and shopping outing with Kiera.

There was no answer.

Wondering if he was home from work yet, she walked down the hall toward his office, thinking he may be in there. It was after seven and he never worked that late. As she approached the door, her run-in with Adele came rushing back to her mind. Was he keeping secrets from her? Olivia knocked gently. "Alex? Are you in there?"

Still no answer.

She tried the handle even though she knew that it was useless. She could see the numbered keypad on the door. If there was one thing Olivia had learned over the past several months, it was that Alexander was diligent with ensuring everything was locked and secured. He would never leave without re-securing that room, or any room for that matter.

Defeated, she tried the handle one more time before turning around to head back into the kitchen, thinking about what to cook for dinner.

"What the fuck do you think you're doing?" Alexander yelled, storming down the hall. He had just gotten home no more than a minute ago, planning to drop off a few files in his home office, when he saw Olivia standing at the door, attempting to get in.

Olivia looked at him, wide-eyed at the tone of his voice.

He closed the gap, glaring down at her, his eyes wild with fury. "Answer me, Olivia. NOW!" His face was red with rage.

"Nothing, Alex! I wasn't doing anything, alright?!" she shouted. "And, unless you've forgotten, this is my house now, too! If I want to go somewhere, I'm damn well going to do so! So if you'd please get out of my fucking way, I'd appreciate it!" She pushed him away, storming down the long corridor, seething with indignation.

Alexander closed his eyes and took a deep breath. He placed his head in his hands, angry at himself for having such a knee-jerk reaction to seeing Olivia at the door to his office. He knew there was a perfectly reasonable explanation. She was not a nosy person. Opening his eyes, he slowly followed her down the corridor, apprehensive about how to calm her down. He walked into the kitchen and found her standing in front of the refrigerator, perusing its contents.

He carefully placed his hands on her upper arms as she continued to stare into the refrigerator, keeping her back to him. The silence was deafening as both of them stood there, neither one saying anything.

Alexander sighed, breaking the tension-filled room. "Olivia, love. I'm sorry. I may have overreacted a bit before…"

She spun around quickly, slamming the refrigerator door shut. "Oh, ya' think, Alex?" She glared, her eyes shooting daggers. "You think that you may have overreacted when you nearly chopped my head off for standing in the hallway, knocking at your office door to see if you were home?" She was furious, partly because she did feel guilty for being somewhere that she knew was off-limits.

"I'm sorry, Olivia. It's just…"

She crossed her arms over her chest, her normal indication that she was waiting rather impatiently to hear a good explanation for his behavior. He had gotten quite used to seeing her in that pose over the past several months.

"What is it, Alex? Why do I always feel as if you're not being honest with me? Why does it always feel like you're keeping things from me?"

Alexander searched her eyes. With each passing day, it was becoming harder and harder for him to finally tell her the truth. He wanted to tell her all those months ago, but that was before her father reappeared out of nowhere, imploring him to keep her ignorant of her past. Could he really listen to a man who had ruined Olivia's life? What should he do? Is this the moment of truth? He smiled at the pun.

"What's so funny, Alex?" Olivia hissed, her anger growing with each passing minute.

"Olivia, I'm sorry," he said, his smile disappearing from his face. "I didn't mean to be a jerk. There's just a lot of work that I do that has to remain classified, even from you. I pride myself on our company's work ethic in maintaining the highest level of confidentiality. I only know how to work one way, and this is it."

Olivia surveyed Alexander's face. It was an entirely legitimate reason for his behavior. She had no clue about half of the operations his company was involved in, but she did know that a lot of it entailed dealing with other countries.

Her face softened as she gazed into his beautiful green eyes.

"Okay. Apology accepted, but next time, don't get your panties in a bunch." She pushed by him and started to head toward the staircase. "Aren't you coming?" she shouted when she was halfway up the stairs.

"What are you talking about?"

"Come on, Alexander! Make up sex!"

And with that, he shot up the stairs, chasing her toward their bedroom.

Olivia squealed when he caught up to her, picking her up in one swift move and cradling her in his arms, planting a deep kiss on her lips.

He threw open the bedroom door, startling Runner awake from his nap. "Come on, boy. Out," Alexander said. Runner begrudgingly obeyed his master.

Alexander closed the door and slowly lowered Olivia to her feet. His eyes searched hers, making sure her anger from before had actually subsided. The fury he saw earlier was nowhere to be found. All that was left was a look of admiration.

"Kiss me," she whispered, tugging his tie and pulling his body toward hers. She stood on her toes and their lips met. The kiss was soft, both of them eager to show the other that they were sorry for arguing about something that appeared to be so insignificant. They wanted to show their love.

Alexander pulled back, gazing down at Olivia, her eyes still closed. She moved a finger over her lips where his mouth had just been. "I still remember how I felt when you first kissed me," she whispered quietly, opening her eyes and dropping her hand from her mouth.

All Alexander could think about was how lucky and blessed he felt at that moment as his eyes remained locked on hers. He felt so fortunate for having finally found his childhood best friend after years of being told that she was dead. And she loved him. She was going to marry him, and they would live a happy life with no more worries.

Alexander refused to think about all the secrets he was keeping from her as he led her over to the bed they shared and made love to her.

Chapter Thirteen

What Happens In Vegas...

THE FOLLOWING MORNING, OLIVIA groaned when the alarm went off, waking her up. It had been a fitful night of sleep. She had woken up in a cold sweat after having strange dreams. First, the green-eyed boy was there, promising Olivia that nothing bad would ever happen to her. Then a young blonde girl appeared out of nowhere and she had Adele's voice. They were playing Barbie's together in Alexander's backyard in Mystic. The blonde girl had grabbed her Barbie out of her hand, and the green-eyed boy yelled at the blonde girl for being so mean. *"Stop causing problems, Adele. You're always so mean to Olivia."* She could still hear it. Then, almost as if a new dream, Cam was there, trying to soothe and calm her down.

"Penny for your thoughts, love?" Alexander asked as he handed Olivia her coffee mug, leaning down to kiss her good morning.

"Just thinking about my trip this weekend," she lied. "When will you be back from your meeting?" Olivia adjusted her legs, sitting up in the bed, and scratched Runner's head while Nepenthe glared at the dog.

"Tuesday afternoon, I hope."

"I'll miss you terribly."

"I'll miss you, too, but you better enjoy your time with your friends."

Olivia smiled. *Vegas!* She was going to Vegas with her three best friends. "Fuck!" she shrieked, looking at the time. "I need to pack or we'll miss the flight." She dashed out of the bed and ran toward her closet, practically downing her coffee in one gulp.

"Why didn't you pack last night?" Alexander asked, following her into the massive walk-in closet that housed all of her clothes and shoes.

"Well, I had planned on it, but someone kept putting his cock in me."

Alexander chuckled and wrapped his arms around her. "I didn't hear you complaining about it last night. If I remember correctly, I had you screaming my name quite a few times." He smacked her ass before strolling out of the closet, allowing her to pack in peace.

Olivia returned to her suitcase, an infectious grin on her face as she thought about all the sex they had the previous night. Her nightmares were now the furthest thing from her mind.

Later that day, Olivia sat in her first class seat next to Kiera, watching the Vegas strip appear in the distance as they prepared to land at McCarran Airport.

"I'm so excited!" Melanie said enthusiastically. Olivia glanced across the aisle and smiled at Melanie and Bridget, happy that the two girls were able to join them.

Once safely on the ground, the girls rushed off the plane, antsy to start their fun-filled weekend. "Where to first?" Olivia asked Kiera as they made their way through the bustling airport, the sound of slot machines chiming throughout.

"I figure we'll take it easy today," she replied as they walked through the gate area toward baggage claim. "We'll just check into the hotel and then relax by the pool. We have an evening filled with dancing tonight!"

"I love dancing!" Melanie said.

"Oh, this must be us." Bridget led the group toward a chauffeur holding a sign with *Adler Bachelorette Party* written on it.

"That's us!" Melanie beamed at the man clad in a black suit standing near a baggage carousel.

"Good afternoon, ladies," the chauffeur said, nodding at them.

Olivia surveyed the man, the buzz cut and muscular build of

him giving her a sinking feeling that he somehow worked for Alexander. She made a mental note to look into whether he had offices in Las Vegas.

"My name is Toby and I'll be at your disposal this weekend for any of your transportation needs around town."

After no time at all, the girls' bags appeared and they were soon on their way to the Vegas Strip and their luxurious hotel room for a relaxing afternoon of sunbathing without a care in the world.

~~~~~~~~~~

TWO MEN IN THEIR mid-twenties made their way out of their first class seats on a flight from Boston to Las Vegas. They maintained a discreet distance behind their targets, not wanting to arouse any suspicions. They were told to wait and make their approach when the girls were at their most vulnerable so they would wait until the club that night. Until then, they would simply keep an eye on them.

"Are you sure about this, Lucas? I mean, is it really worth it?" the taller one asked.

"Of course it is," Lucas growled. "That's a million fucking dollars going into each of our bank accounts, Dylan. It is so worth it. Oh, and just to sell it, I'm gay. Chicks never find a gay guy suspicious."

Dylan rolled his eyes. His younger brother was right. That money could go a long way, and they'd never gotten caught on a job for Donovan before. "So what's the plan then?"

"I have their itinerary. They'll be in the V.I.P. area at a club tonight. They're bound to do some dancing, and when they do, we'll pour on the charm, buddying up to her two little friends...the ones Donovan pointed out to us. I have all the background information we need on both of them. I'll take the blonde. She looks like an easy mark." He winked. "Just remember, this has to work. We need them to feel comfortable with us so that we can continue seeing them in Boston. That's the important part, so don't fuck it up."

Dylan was nervous about everything, but what was there to

be concerned about? All he had to do was play nice with the girls and make them feel comfortable. What's the worst that could happen?

~~~~~~~~~~

"WAKE UP, LIBBY!" KIERA shouted later that evening, jumping on Olivia's massive bed and waking her up from a far too short nap. The girls had spent the majority of the afternoon by the luxurious hotel pool, sipping too many cocktails to count as they basked in the warm desert sun.

"Go away," Olivia groaned.

"Nope. It's your bachelorette weekend, and we are *not* going to spend it sleeping. Get up, take a shower, and then we're going out!"

Olivia raised her head, squinting at her friend. "What time is it?"

"It's seven-thirty. Dinner is at nine at a five-star sushi restaurant here in the hotel so get moving."

"Fine, but do me a favor."

"What is it?"

"Call down and have a bottle of champagne brought up."

"That was so thirty minutes ago." Kiera handed Olivia a glass of champagne off the nightstand.

"I love you, Care Bear."

Kiera smiled as they clinked glasses.

Later that evening, after a relaxing sushi dinner, the girls filed out of the casino they were staying at and made their way toward Toby as he waited for them with the limo out front.

"I totally think he works for Alexander," Olivia whispered.

"Ah, who cares?" Melanie smiled. "I, for one, am happy that we have our own driver and don't have to stand in that cab line." She nodded her head at a line that snaked around the building.

"Good point." Olivia laughed as she stepped into the limo.

"I love all the stares we're getting, like we're celebrities or something," Bridget said as the limo pulled out of the valet area.

"We are," Kiera stated. "We're with Olivia, and she's about to marry one of the country's most eligible bachelors." Her face brimmed with excitement.

"You love those gossip mags, don't you?" Olivia asked, smiling at the fact that she was less than two months away from becoming Alexander's wife. She didn't care that he was one of the country's richest and most successful single men. She'd want to marry him even if he didn't have a penny to his name.

"Yes," Kiera admitted. "And be glad that you have someone keeping an eye on what they say about you. Some girls would kill to be in your shoes. Literally. I mean those heels are pretty bitching…"

Olivia laughed, the rest of the girls joining in.

After a short ride down the Vegas Strip, Toby pulled up in front of a rather impressive looking hotel and the girls made their way through another crowded casino toward a night club. As soon as the bouncers saw their entourage approach, they immediately pulled back the rope, allowing their party to enter ahead of the line. A hostess greeted them immediately.

"Miss Adler, it's wonderful to see you this evening," she said, leading them toward the back of a dark club that was decorated black and red throughout. The dance floor was already packed and people were lined up at the bar, anxious to grab a drink as loud music blared. Olivia couldn't wait to get onto that dance floor and let loose. "Your fiancé has arranged for anything you and your friends need this evening so I do hope you enjoy yourselves."

The hostess led them to a small V.I.P. area adjacent to the dance floor that was roped off from the general public, two bouncers standing guard. The noise level was slightly lower and Olivia secretly loved that Alexander made all the arrangements, ensuring that they had a private place to relax between shaking their booties.

After the hostess left, Melanie turned to Olivia. "I wonder how she knew it was you."

Olivia shrugged.

"It's because her face has been plastered all over the internet for months now," Kiera interjected, winking at the hot server that had just come to take their drink order. "Two bottles of Cristal, please."

The server nodded and returned in record time with their champagne.

"To Olivia!" Kiera shouted, raising her champagne flute. All the girls followed suit, clinking glasses. Olivia smiled at how different her life seemed from just a few short months ago. She still couldn't get over the fact that she was getting married.

"We've been sitting down all night," she said after pouring herself a second glass. "Let's dance!" She jumped up from their table and made her way to the dance floor, the rest of her party close behind. Olivia closed her eyes, getting lost in the rhythm of the music, mindful to not spill her champagne as she moved to the beat.

She felt someone nudge her and immediately opened her eyes, smiling when she saw Kiera grinding up next to her. "Look over there!" she shouted, nodding her head a few feet away. Olivia followed Kiera's gaze and saw Bridget dancing rather intimately with an attractive man, Melanie talking to another guy just a few feet beyond that. "Only been here for five minutes and she's already attracting the hotties! That girl's on a mission!" Kiera commented, referring to Bridget.

Olivia laughed. "That's fine! She can have them! We've got our own hotties back home!"

Kiera clinked her glass with Olivia. "Damn straight!"

They danced for a few minutes, enjoying their time together, knowing that it was probably one of their last outings before Olivia got married. Kiera couldn't be happier for her friend.

"Hey, guys!" Melanie shouted over the music. A rather imposing man stood next to her, making her tall, lean body look tiny. He had dark hair and olive-toned skin with a strong jaw and a dazzling smile. "This is Lucas! He lives in Boston, too!" she said, placing her hand on his thick bicep. "Isn't that funny? He goes to Northeastern with me! He's even a psych major, although we've never met each other. We have a class together this fall!"

Olivia looked at Melanie with a questioning look on her face.

"Oh, don't worry, Libby," she said. "I told him I'm not single. Plus, he's gay."

Olivia laughed, slightly relieved.

Bridget approached with the guy she had been dancing with. He had a rather strong resemblance to the young man standing at Melanie's side.

"Lucas, it's great to meet you." Olivia extended her hand to him. "Where in Boston…? Oh, fuck it. Come back to our table with us," she yelled, not wanting to shout over the music anymore.

The guys followed the girls back to their booth, Olivia letting the bouncers guarding their area know that it was okay to let them in.

After pouring champagne for everyone and ordering a few more bottles, Olivia turned back to Lucas. "Well, where in Boston do you live?"

"I live in Brighton. This is my brother, Dylan," he said, gesturing to the guy sitting next to Bridget.

"Dylan went to Harvard!" Bridget said, her dark eyes brimming with excitement.

"Oh, really?" Kiera asked. "What do you do now?"

Dylan smiled and his hand disappeared beneath the table. "Oh, a little bit of this. A little bit of that."

"Who's older?" Olivia asked, noticing Bridget's face flush red. She could only assume that Dylan had his hand on her leg.

"Dylan is," Lucas said. "He's twenty-seven. I'm twenty-five. I started college a little late, but I'll graduate this December."

"Me, too!" Melanie exclaimed. "I can't believe we haven't run into each other before!"

Lucas nervously shifted in his seat, obviously flustered with Melanie's beauty, even if he *was* gay. "Well, Northeastern's a big school, and there are a lot of psych majors."

Melanie rolled her eyes, an adorable look of mock irritation crossing her face. "You can say that again. We should totally form a study group for Professor Meecham's seminar next fall. I hear it's a bitch."

"Definitely. I could use all the help I can get."

100

"You both live in Brighton?" Olivia asked, interrupting Melanie's conversation.

"I live in Cambridge," Dylan explained, sharing a look with Bridget.

"You guys need to come to MacFadden's one of these nights and see Miss Olivia sing! She's a rock star!" Melanie said excitedly.

"Olivia?" Lucas said. "That's it! I thought you looked familiar. You're Olivia Adler, aren't you? You're about to marry Alexander Burnham! Man, if he was gay…" He flashed a dazzling white smile.

Olivia took a sip of her champagne, hiding her grin as the entire table erupted in laughter. She still got butterflies just thinking about marrying Alexander. She wanted it to be August twenty-fourth already. The past few months felt like a big waiting game and part of her wanted to just drag Alexander to Vegas that weekend and marry him there without all the bullshit of having a big wedding.

"Well, congratulations," Lucas said, raising his champagne glass. "I wish you the best of luck in your marriage." A strange look crossed his face. Olivia tried not to read too much into it, but something seemed off. Then again, maybe Alexander's paranoia was just rubbing off on her. These guys meant no harm. They were in Vegas on a guy's weekend, having a good time…just like she was.

They danced the rest of the night away, Bridget attached to Dylan's hip throughout the entire evening. Melanie seemed content to be her wingman, spending time with Lucas and talking about school.

"I gave him my number!" Bridget slurred on the limo ride back to their hotel. "And I got his, too!"

"That's great!" Kiera said excitedly.

"I know! He's so sweet, guys! I mean, like really, really sweet. He kept telling me that I was the most beautiful girl he had ever seen and that he felt like he had been waiting his entire life to meet me."

"You two make a really cute couple," Olivia said, watching Bridget brim with excitement.

"We already have plans to see each other on Tuesday. He wants to take me out to dinner! I have a date! I haven't had a real date in so long!"

Olivia smiled at her friend, hoping that everything worked out with Dylan and Bridget because she deserved someone who treated her like a princess.

CHAPTER FOURTEEN

No Choice

"I'LL JUST PARK THE car and be right up with your luggage, ma'am," Carter said late Monday night after picking up Olivia from the airport. She had a wonderful time with her friends, but was thankful to be home. At that moment, she finally realized that Alexander's penthouse was home.

"Thank you," she said quietly, climbing out of the car and making her way into the waterfront building. She ascended the twenty-five stories and quickly punched the code into the door, eager to see Runner. As the door to the penthouse slid open, the fifty-pound ball of energy wrapped in fur came bounding up to her, nearly toppling her over.

"Hey, boy. I sure did miss you!" She scratched his head before walking over to the couch, ready to collapse. Runner jumped up and snuggled next to her. Nepenthe stalked down the corridor, his keen eyes trained on the dog, debating whether or not he would allow him to live another day. He stretched and yawned before walking down the stairs to find another warm, dark spot to sleep in.

"Excuse me, ma'am," Carter said, interrupting Olivia's relaxing minute with the dog. "Where would you like your bags?"

"Up in the master bedroom is fine, Carter. Thank you."

"It's my pleasure, Miss Adler."

Olivia collapsed back into the couch, feeling absolutely exhausted from the weekend. She fell asleep before she even heard Carter leave the apartment, dreaming of beautiful green eyes once more.

Several hours later, she woke up with a start after hearing Cam's voice in her sleep. She had no idea what it all meant. Why, after all this time, was she dreaming of Cam? It wasn't as if she had feelings for him in any way other than him being a good friend who had helped her during her darkest time. But there was something about the dream that made it feel so real.

She raised herself off the couch and walked into the kitchen. Opening the refrigerator, she grabbed a bottle of water and glanced at the clock on the wall. It wasn't even midnight yet, but she felt completely exhausted. After rummaging through her purse, she found her cell phone, wondering why she hadn't heard from Alexander yet.

Shit, she said to herself once she found it. *Alexander is going to be pissed.* She had forgotten to turn it back on after she landed.

Letting out a long breath, she pressed the power button and waited for it to boot up. Once it found a signal, she was immediately bombarded with texts and voicemails from Alexander.

"Great," she muttered to herself. She hated the feeling she got when she didn't check in with him when he expected her to. He always overreacted, thinking that she wasn't safe for whatever reason he concocted in his head. She was starting to get tired of Alexander's hero complex. She loved him with every fiber of her being, but she still wondered whether he would love her when she no longer needed protection from whatever force he believed was threatening her.

She sat down at the kitchen island, savoring the coldness of the water as she stared at her phone. Memories of that day months ago came flooding back. She had just gotten back into town and went to Alexander's office, begging him to take her back. He had chased her through the streets of Boston to give her the coat she forgot. A strange man approached her and attempted to hit on her, rather poorly, Olivia thought. Alexander saw it and pummeled the guy to the ground.

She recalled how it always seemed like he was trying to protect or save her from one threat or another. But she couldn't shake the memory of his face when she told him exactly what she wanted from him while they stood on the snowy street that day: *"I don't want you to always feel like you have to come and help me, Alex. I just want you to stand by my side while I try to help myself."*

Olivia began to realize that, no matter what, he would never follow those words. He would always try to be the one to do the saving, and she wasn't sure how she felt about that.

Her phone interrupted her thoughts, Alexander's photo flashing on the screen. She became nervous and was hesitant to answer, not wanting to be yelled at as if she was an errant child. "Well, I either have to face this today or tomorrow."

She pushed the button on the screen and answered the call. "Hello, Alex."

"Olivia! What the fuck?! Where have you been?! Your phone was off! I've been worried sick about you! I'm in the middle of an important meeting and, instead being able to describe in detail what my company's doing over in Afghanistan, I'm worried about whether my wife-to-be is still fucking alive!"

"Jesus Christ, Alex. I'm fine. I fell asleep after getting back to the apartment tonight. You always go overboard where my safety is concerned and it's getting old. Not to mention that I'm pretty fucking sure the chauffeur you arranged for us was one of your trained mercenaries, even though you promised that I could have this weekend to myself!" she spat out, fuming as she paced the kitchen. "Plus, you could have just called Carter! You know he was picking me up from the airport and dropping me off at home!"

"I don't want to talk to Carter! I want to talk to you!" The line was silent for several long moments before Alexander spoke, softening his voice. "I'm sorry, Olivia. I'm working on my overbearing tendencies. I am. I just need to make sure that you're safe."

"Alex, how many times do we have to go through this? I don't want you to constantly go behind my back to try to keep me safe! I can do that on my own!" She exhaled loudly before lowering her voice. "Do you know what I was thinking about just before the phone rang?"

"What's that?" he asked quietly.

"That day in the snow back in January…"

The line went silent.

"Do you remember what I said to you?"

Alexander let out the breath he was holding. "I do, Olivia, but I just can't stand aside where your safety is concerned. I have control issues. You know that."

She walked over to the couch, flopping down on it. "But it's suffocating me, Alex. I love you, but sometimes I wish I could go back to how things were before you came into my life."

"What are you saying, love?" he asked, his voice full of hurt.

"No!" she yelled, shooting up into a sitting position. "I'm not saying that. I love you and I want to spend the rest of my life with you, but since I met you, you've been smothering me, making sure I have a protection detail with me at all times. I want my simple life back. I know I'll never truly have that now that I'm marrying you, but I don't always *need* protection, Alex, and you know that."

Alexander sat there, reeling from what Olivia was saying. If she only knew the threats to her life that he was aware of, maybe she would be singing a different song. He didn't know what to do. This conversation had been occurring more and more often, and he knew it was only a matter of time before she would figure it all out.

"Olivia, darling, there are things you should know," he sighed, resigning himself to do the right thing…although it went against her father's wishes. "I'll be home tomorrow evening and we'll discuss all of this then, face-to-face. We'll come up with a compromise. I never meant to suffocate you. I just need to make sure you're safe. Always."

"I know, Alex, but you need to start telling me what you're trying to keep me safe *from*."

"I know, and I will. Tomorrow. I love you, Olivia."

She smiled. "I love you, too, Alexander. Good night."

"Good night, love." Alexander hung up as he sat at a desk in his hotel room in San Francisco overlooking Union Square, thinking about what he had just promised. He would have to tell her, and he would have to do it the following day. He didn't know if he was quite ready for that but, suddenly, he no longer had a choice.

CHAPTER FIFTEEN

TRUTH AND CONSEQUENCES

"CAN YOU TAKE ME to the Starbucks by Alexander's office building?" Olivia asked Marshall as she exited her apartment building just before four o'clock the following day.

"Absolutely, ma'am," Marshall responded, opening the door for Olivia to climb into the back seat of the SUV.

Olivia was somewhat surprised that she made no move to contact Alexander to make sure he was okay with it. Then again, she met Kiera out for coffee quite often so it wasn't an unusual request. This time, however, she wasn't seeing Kiera. She had promised Adele that she would speak with her one last time and listen to what she had to say. Then, if Adele kept her word, she would never have to see her again.

After the short ride, Marshall pulled up outside of the coffee shop, the financial district bustling with activity on that warm summer day. Olivia grabbed two coffees and walked over to a table to wait for Adele, who walked through the doors a few minutes later. She spotted Olivia and began heading in her direction, the normal bitchy look on her face nowhere to be found. Instead, she looked forlorn and solemn. "Thank you for coming, Olivia," she said, taking a seat.

Olivia slid the extra coffee toward her.

She smiled in appreciation before bringing it to her mouth and taking a sip.

"So, Adele, what is it you want to say to me?"

She stared at Olivia, still in disbelief that she was sitting across from the girl she used to play Barbie's with when they were young. "What do you know about Alexander's childhood?" she asked cautiously.

"If this is about his friend who had the same name as me, I already know about that, and I don't think that it's weird. My real first name is Sarah anyway." She raised her voice, becoming a bit defensive. "Olivia is my middle name. He didn't fall in love with me just because I go by the same name as that little girl."

Adele lowered her eyes, hesitant to say what she was about to say, but it had to be done. She needed that money she had been promised. "Olivia, it's not that you go by the same name as that little girl. You *are* that little girl…"

Olivia looked at Adele as if she was crazy. "Adele, that little girl died. Alexander told me so. He goes there every year to visit her grave and…"

"Your parents were killed, weren't they?" she interrupted.

"Yeah. What does that have to do with anything?" Olivia's heart began to race.

"Isn't it a coincidence that they were killed the same day as Alexander's Olivia?"

She sat there in silence, unsure of how Adele even knew when her parents died, or what to think of her inferences. She had never proven herself to be trustworthy in the past so she was hesitant to believe a word that came out of her mouth at that point. Still, it was a *huge* coincidence. But that's what she always thought it was…just a coincidence.

"I grew up in Charleston, Adele," Olivia responded, snapping out of her unsettled thoughts. "That little girl lived near Alexander in Mystic." She started getting nervous. She couldn't remember anything about her life before being sent to that boarding school in Charleston. That's where she must have lived before the accident. Why would she be sent to Charleston if she didn't live there? It didn't make sense.

"Look at this, Olivia." Adele reached down and pulled a few old photos out of her purse. "I went home this weekend and searched my parents' house for my old photo albums. Here." She handed her a photo. "I couldn't find many of the two of us. We never really got along that well."

Olivia stared at the photo. It was of her when she was a little girl. Her hair was in two braids on the opposite sides of her head, and she was standing next to a small blonde-haired girl. They were both holding their Barbie dolls and smiling at the camera.

"All this proves, Adele, is that we knew each other when I was little. I don't remember much about my life before the accident that killed both of my parents," she said, trying to ignore the loud voice in her head telling her that her worst fears had become a reality.

Adele sighed. "Well, how do you explain this?" She pushed another photo across the table.

Olivia gasped when she saw it. It was probably taken the same day as the previous photo. Olivia sat on a swing set in a large backyard. She recognized the yard. It was where she had her engagement party. Alexander's house was visible in the distance.

"So, it's Alexander's backyard. I have no idea how I could have been there but, like I said, I don't remember anything. That doesn't mean that I knew Alexander or that I'm his Olivia," she said more for herself than anything. She didn't want it to be true, but knew she wasn't going to get her wish. It all made sense. All the puzzle pieces that she had ignored or excused away over the past several months were falling all too neatly into place.

"Here." Adele threw the final picture at Olivia. "I just don't want you to go on any more not knowing the truth," she explained compassionately.

Olivia looked at the picture, tears welling in her eyes. It was her. She was sitting on the same park bench across from the Mystic River where she recently sat with Alexander. In her hands was a bowl full of ice cream. She could faintly make out a few pieces of pineapple on her spoon.

And next to her was the boy with green eyes from her dream.

"He pulled me from the car. I remember that," Olivia said quietly.

"That little boy in the photo is Alex. You're his Olivia…the little girl he lost all those years ago. I grew up with him and he was beside himself after you died, but he never believed for a minute that you were actually dead. He was always suspicious for one reason or another…or maybe he just didn't want to say good-bye to you."

It all made perfect sense. That's why Olivia heard herself calling the green-eyed boy Alex in her dreams. Because Alexander *was* the green-eyed boy. "Does he realize who I am?"

Adele looked at her, unsure of how to respond. She wanted Olivia to trust her. She wanted her to leave Alexander, but she didn't want it to seem so apparent that it was her goal, given her history. "I don't know, Olivia. I truly don't, but Alexander is very good at keeping secrets."

Olivia stared at the three photos in her hand. She had so many questions. Why was she taken away from all her friends and family? Why didn't her uncle tell her any of this? Why couldn't she remember anything from before the accident?

But one question remained at the forefront of her mind. *Did Alexander know?* And if he did, how long has he known?

"I need to get out of here," Olivia said suddenly, quickly getting up from the table. She was almost out the door when she realized that she was still clutching the photos in her hand. Turning around, she met Adele's eyes again.

"Keep them, Olivia."

She looked down at the photo of the green-eyed boy, gently caressing the picture. "Thank you." She ran out of the shop and into the waiting SUV.

Within moments, Marshall was driving toward Atlantic Avenue and Olivia's home that no longer felt like a home.

She walked through the front doors of her penthouse and the place never seemed so small to her. She felt as if the walls were closing in, suffocating her. She glanced around, wondering if Alexander was back, seeing no sign that he had gotten home yet.

She grabbed her cell phone from her purse and saw a missed text he had sent less than twenty minutes beforehand.

Alexander: *Just landed. Be home in about thirty. I love you. XOXO*

She had maybe ten minutes before he would be getting home. Dropping her purse on the kitchen island, she walked down the long corridor toward his office. She tried the doorknob with no luck. It was locked. She punched a few different number combinations into the keypad with no success. Just when she was ready to give up, she tried one more…the date she supposedly died. The door beeped and she slowly turned the knob, pushing it open.

Her jaw dropped as she entered the room, looking at the walls covered with framed photos of his family and other important people. Her throat closed up when her eyes settled on a photo that must have been taken while Alexander was on leave from the Navy. He sat at a table, clearly in his family's enormous backyard, with a younger version of Tyler and Carol sitting on either side of him. Immediately behind Alexander stood his mother. And next to his mother stood someone she assumed was his father, but it couldn't be. It was her Uncle Charles. She backed up, trying to process everything, and bumped into the desk. A framed photo fell to the ground.

She picked it up and a memory came flooding back.

"Whatcha doing, Olibia?" a young Alexander asked, entering her play room.

"Nothing. Just playing house." Olivia had just received a toy stove and kitchen set for Christmas, and she was excited to finally play with it.

"Can I play, too?"

She looked up from her toys. "You can't play house with me, Alex. We're not married." She laughed, returning to baking her make-believe cake.

Alexander scratched his head. "Well, let's have a play wedding and then we'll be married and we can play house all we want."

Olivia thought about it for a minute. "Okay!" She ran to her dress-up chest and grabbed a long white veil and a top hat. She threw the hat on Alexander and grabbed his hand, dragging him down the hall.

"Mom! Dad! Alex and I are getting married!" she yelled joyfully.

"*Oh, look at you two!*" *her mom said, laughing. "Jack, go get the camera!*"

Olivia's father came running back with the camera and snapped a photo.

~~~~~~~~~~

ALEXANDER WAS UNEASY ABOUT returning home and talking to Olivia. He still wasn't sure how he was going to tell her everything. The information could ruin her. And put her in danger.

He walked through the foyer of his penthouse, anxiety coursing through his veins about their impending conversation. "Olivia," he called out. "Are you here?"

He listened for a few minutes. The house was eerily quiet, the only sound that of the dog snoring on his bed in the living room. Glancing at the kitchen island, he saw Olivia's purse sitting there. He wished she wasn't home. He had never been as scared about seeing her as he was at that moment. He wanted to tell her everything, but knew that she would never understand why he had kept that information from her. He couldn't bear the thought of losing her, but he had a feeling that it was already too late.

Alexander made his way toward the staircase when he noticed a light on in a room down the hall. He figured Olivia was in the den watching TV, which struck him as odd. She barely ever watched television.

Walking down the corridor, he followed the source of the light. But it wasn't coming from the den. It was coming from his office.

He quietly made his way down the rest of the long hallway, his breathing growing uneven. He turned the corner and looked into the room. His heart dropped to the pit of his stomach at the sight that greeted him.

Olivia stood there, holding the picture he kept framed on his desk. Tears were flowing down her face. "What is this, Alex?" she asked, her voice empty of all emotion as she stared at the picture in her hands.

"Olivia, please. I can explain." He took a step toward her, pleading with his eyes for her to understand why he had done what he did.

"You knew?" She looked up and Alexander could see the pain in her eyes.

"It's not what you think, Olivia. Please."

"How long?" she asked quietly.

Alexander remained silent, words escaping him.

"I said how long, Alex?!" she repeated through clenched teeth, her tone raised.

He ran his fingers through his hair, his voice full of resignation. "Since August."

"What?!" Olivia screeched, her eyes growing wide. "You've known who I am since August and didn't have the decency to say anything?!" She pushed past him, running toward the living room, still clutching the framed picture.

"Olivia, wait!" He chased after her, catching up to her in the kitchen. "I had no choice. Just let me explain."

"No, Alex!" She spun around to face him. "The time for explaining is so far past! You've known about this since August and you didn't say anything! Nothing! You kept me in the dark even when you watched me struggle with my past! You held me after I woke up screaming from my dreams! You listened to me talk about the green-eyed boy, wondering who he was or if he was even real! And it was you! You heard me talk about the man I thought was my uncle, Alexander! And you never thought it was important enough to mention that he was *your father*?!" She took a deep breath, her chest heaving through her heavy sobs. "You sat there holding all the answers and you kept them from me!"

She grabbed her purse and started toward the foyer, pushing the elevator call button repeatedly. Feeling Alexander approach behind her, she refused to face him, cursing the electricity that was still present.

"Give me a chance, Olivia. I beg you." He gripped her shoulders and spun her around, holding her in place as he stared into her tear-drenched eyes.

"I gave you more than enough chances, Alex. I did. You've

had so many opportunities to come clean. But, instead, you chose to keep this from me."

The elevator car dinged, announcing its arrival.

Olivia rid herself of Alexander's grasp and ran into the elevator, pressing the button for the lobby. "You know, Alex," she said, her lips trembling. "I thought you were a decent person. I thought I was important enough to you that you'd tell me the truth." Taking a deep breath, she raised her eyes to meet his. "I guess I wasn't worth it." The elevator doors closed and Olivia collapsed under the weight of everything she just learned.

~~~~~~~~~~

NATHAN ROBERTS WAS SITTING across from Alexander's waterfront penthouse, watching. A short while after following Olivia during her coffee meeting with a tall blonde that looked eerily familiar, he observed her running out of the Starbucks in tears. He followed her to the building she had been living in the past several months, surprised to see her storm out of the skyscraper a short time after Alexander returned. He immediately knew something was wrong.

He picked up his cell phone and dialed the one person who had the answers he needed. "What did you do to her?!" he barked into the phone.

"She knows, Jack. She figured it out," Alexander said, a lump forming in his throat as the realization sank in that he lost his Olivia.

"FUCK!" Nathan shouted, punching the steering wheel of his car. He took several deep breaths, trying to calm down. "What does she know?"

"All she knows is that we were childhood friends and that she is, in fact, the little girl who supposedly died all those years ago. And that the man she referred to as her Uncle Charles is actually my father. Other than that, I'm not sure."

Nathan breathed a sigh of relief. "Okay. Okay. We can work with that. This isn't as bad as I expected. Whatever you do, you cannot tell her everything. She mustn't know."

"What are you saying, Jack?!" Alexander exclaimed, fuming. "This is ridiculous! I just lost the best thing that's ever happened to me because I kept her true identity a secret. Hell! She doesn't even know her real name! She stormed out of here without me even getting a chance to explain *anything* to her!"

"Alex, I understand your position," he said calmly. "But she can't remember. The only thing keeping her alive is that she is the only one who knows where that evidence is hidden. If you tell her about her past, she may start to remember certain things. If she remembers, she'll be able to point some very bad people in the right direction. And at that point, she's no longer valuable."

Alexander's heart sank as the line went dead. Olivia's father was right.

~~~~~~~~~~

OLIVIA DIDN'T KNOW WHERE she could go. She needed to think. She needed time to clear her head so she did the only thing she could think of…she walked, clutching the photo of her and Alexander's play wedding in her hand.

The sun began to set over the city, the tall buildings casting shadows on the streets as she walked down Atlantic Avenue in the direction of Columbus Park. People on the street stared at her as she wailed, tears streaming down her face. She felt as if the ground had just been ripped from beneath her. She didn't know who to trust anymore. The one person she had learned to trust and opened her heart to had lied to her.

She needed someone to comfort her and tell her that everything was going to be okay, but the only person who ever did that was the one person she couldn't go to. He hurt her more than any person had. How could he be so selfish as to keep her past a secret from her?

Olivia reached into her purse and grabbed her phone, wanting someone to take the pain away. She collapsed on the park bench, desperately trying to clear her mind. All of a sudden, she realized who she needed at that moment. The one person who had helped her through her darkest time in the past.

She scrolled through the contacts in her phone and pushed the call button, a voice on the other end answering almost immediately.

"Cam…" she sobbed.

"Olivia. What's wrong? Are you okay? Has something happened?" He hadn't expected to hear from her again.

"I don't know who I can trust anymore. Please, Cam. I need you."

The pain in her voice was so raw and real. He immediately knew that she shouldn't be alone, not in her fragile state. He had seen and heard that pain on the day that she swallowed those pills, but this was far worse. "I'll be on the next flight out. Please, just hang tight for me. Okay?"

She nodded her head, sobbing.

"Olivia. Please say you'll be okay until I can get to you. Please," he begged.

"I don't think I'll ever be okay again," she cried, dropping her phone on the ground as tourists walked by, staring at the girl with brown eyes whose world was falling apart around her.

CHAPTER SIXTEEN

SLIPPING AWAY

"WHAT IS IT?" AN irritated Donovan shouted into the phone.

"It looks like your little plan worked, Kiddish."

Shit, he thought. *It's him*. He always made Donovan nervous.

Donovan cleared his throat as he straightened in his chair. "Of course it did. I was certain it would. No woman wants to be with a man who lies to her."

"It appears she has returned to her old house then?"

That was news to Donovan. He hadn't done any follow up just yet. But *he* couldn't know that, unless… "Yes. She has," he responded, not wanting to sound incompetent.

"But it also appears Burnham still has eyes on her."

"We're working on that as we speak, sir."

Shit. Where was Simon? He was supposed to be buddying up to Olivia now.

"Well, work faster!" The line went dead.

~~~~~~~~~~

AFTER WALKING AIMLESSLY AROUND the city, Olivia returned to her old home on Commonwealth Avenue. It all looked just as she had left it. Everything was still there except for most of her clothes and, of course, Nepenthe.

Just as she began to search her place for any remnants of a liquor bottle, her cell phone buzzed with a text.

Cam: *Libby, it's Cam. I'm on an 8 PM flight out tonight. I'll be landing at Logan at 10:48.*

Thank God, she thought. She needed him at that moment. He had always been honest with her, and that was what she craved right now.

Olivia: *What airline? I'll come and pick you up.*

Cam: *Don't worry about it. I'll come to you. If I know you, and I do, the last thing you should be doing right now is driving. Looking forward to seeing you. Hang tight for me. Please.*

For the first time all day, Olivia smiled as she texted him back with her address. Cam really did know her pretty well. She felt bad for not rushing to Kiera or Mo, but they wouldn't understand. They would just see this as another excuse to push Alexander away, but that wasn't the case anymore. She didn't want to push him away. She wanted nothing more than to marry him. Deep down, she wished that she had never found out who he really was. The green-eyed boy. Her childhood friend. The boy who saved her.

It all became so clear. She couldn't believe that she didn't see it earlier. That was why he felt like he had to constantly protect her. He thought he had failed her all those years ago. But Olivia still had plenty of unanswered questions, and she knew that the only person who had all the answers was the one person she did not want to talk to…the one person she didn't think she could ever look at again without feeling betrayed. Not wanting to think about that anymore, she grabbed the bottle of bourbon out of her cabinet, thankful that she hadn't thrown out her liquor during the move, and poured herself a glass.

By eleven that evening, she was well on her way to being rather drunk, wanting to numb everything. All she could think about was Alexander and how he had lied to her. She couldn't stop crying when she flashed back to the look on his face when he realized that he had been caught in the lie. It tore her apart that he had kept everything a secret from her since August. Why didn't he just tell her when he figured it out?

He had comforted her when she woke up screaming and crying nearly every night after seeing her parents die in the car crash. He had so many opportunities to tell her what really happened, but he didn't. He stayed silent, and that hurt more than anything.

She thought she felt pain when she walked out on him all those months ago and fled to Florida, and then the even more intense heartache when she thought he was going to marry Chelsea. But this new hurt was even worse. She didn't know how, or even if, she would ever survive the new wound that Alexander had caused her heart. She didn't know who she was anymore. Part of her guessed that she never really did.

Olivia was almost passed out from all the alcohol she had consumed when her doorbell rang. She immediately remembered that Cam said he was flying in to be with her. The guilt she felt for ripping him from his life washed over her as she stumbled from her couch.

She pulled back the door and couldn't keep her emotions in when she saw Cam standing there, concern plastered on his face. He wrapped his arms around her and she cried, her entire body shaking.

"Hey. It's going to be okay, Libby. I promise. We'll get you through this. You're stronger than this."

Olivia glanced over his shoulder and sobbed even harder, eyeing the tall silhouette across the street who ruined everything. "I don't think I'm strong enough to get through this one, Cam."

~~~~~~~~~~

ALEXANDER SAT IN THE SUV next to Martin all evening, keeping an eye on Olivia's house. He messed up. He knew it. His sister had warned him that something like this would happen. If he could turn back the clock, he would, if only to tell Olivia the truth from the beginning. The moment he found out, he should have told her. It was selfish of him to keep her past from her.

"Sir, it appears that Miss Adler has a visitor. Would you like me to intercept?"

Alexander snapped out of his daydream and re-focused his eyes on Olivia's front door. Cam. *Of course*, Alexander thought. *She* would *call him.*

He wanted to walk up to him and ask what the fuck he was doing there. He mustered enough courage to open the passenger side door with the intention of doing just that when he saw Olivia appear in the doorway.

He stood frozen in place when he saw how broken she looked, and he did that to her. He made her feel like that. He wanted to scream when he saw Cam drop his bags and wrap his arms around her, soothing her tears. *That's supposed to be* my job.

Alexander couldn't move, even though he knew he should. She shouldn't see that he was out there, watching her. His brain tried to tell his legs to move and get back in the SUV, but they wouldn't listen. He stood on the sidewalk, a deer in the headlights, when Olivia's eyes met his.

I'm sorry, he mouthed to her.

She shook her head and began to cry even harder before Cam helped her into the house.

Alexander's mind began to race. It had only been a few hours since she ran out on him, and she was already inviting another man into her home. And not just any man. A man she had been intimate with in the past. He started to feel Olivia slowly slipping through his fingertips and all he could see was red.

~~~~~~~~~~

"YOU'RE DRUNK, AREN'T YOU?" Cam asked after helping Olivia back inside her house.

"I couldn't help it, Cam. I needed to dull the pain. I just didn't want to feel anymore. I'm done feeling."

He followed Olivia into her living room, watching as she made her way toward a large collection of liquor bottles on the kitchen island, drinking from one.

"You should probably sleep it off, Libby. We can talk tomorrow about what's going on. Sleep is the best medicine for you right now, not that bottle."

"I can't sleep, Cam," she sobbed. "All I'll see when I close my eyes are his eyes staring back at me, betraying me, lying to me."

Cam didn't know what happened, but he guessed it had something to do with Alexander. "I know it hurts right now," he said, his tone soothing as he rubbed her back. "But you need to sleep." He looked down on her. "Where is your bedroom?"

Olivia glanced up the stairs. "Up there." She became dizzy from the sudden movement of her head and fell to the ground.

"Whoa. Easy there, sweetheart." He wrapped his arms around her, steadying her. "I'll help you upstairs. You need to lie down."

She exhaled loudly. "Fine. You're the expert," she slurred.

"Thank you," Cam replied quietly. Scooping her into his arms, he carried her up the stairs and into her bedroom. He placed her feet carefully on the ground before pulling back the covers and helping her into bed. Once she looked comfortable, he sat down next to her, pushing the hair out of her eyes, trying to calm her down.

When he was sure that her tears were done, he stood up. "Get some sleep, Libby. I'll be downstairs on the couch if you need me."

Olivia's hand shot out, grabbing his wrist. "Don't go. Please, stay. With me. I don't want to be alone when the nightmares come." Her eyes met his and he could see the fear in them.

Reluctantly, he agreed. He knew, deep down, that it was a bad idea to get into bed beside her, but she looked so scared and he wanted to help her any way he could. He peeled out of his clothes, leaving on his t-shirt and boxers, and crawled in next to her.

"Cam?" Olivia asked several minutes later as they both lay there in the dark.

"Yes, Libby?"

"I'm sorry I called you. I didn't know who else to turn to." She rolled over to face him.

Cam had been dreaming of the day that he would finally be able to fall asleep next to her again, but he didn't expect it to be like this. She was hurting, and he refused to take advantage of her vulnerability like he felt he did before. She appeared so much worse than she did that night all those months ago. This was something so much bigger.

"Hush, Libby," he said, reaching his hand out and caressing her arm. "I'm glad you called me. Now, get some sleep." He planted a gentle kiss on her forehead and she closed her eyes.

"Cam?"

"Yes?"

"Can you hold me, please? I just need to know that I'm not alone and this is the only way I know."

He was hesitant, but the pain in her voice was too intense for him to deny her that simple act. He wrapped his arms around her and pulled her into his body, savoring the smell of her hair as he listened to her gentle breathing.

~~~~~~~~~~

"SIMON, WHAT THE FUCK happened?!" Donovan shouted, glaring at him as he sat in his office late Tuesday night. "She was supposed to feel so goddamn comfortable with you that she would run into your arms after having her world ripped apart! Instead, she called some goddamn therapist she met in Florida?! What the fuck?!" He was pissed. Simon had assured him that Olivia was past everything that had happened between them. The entire plan rested on Simon being able to get that information. And that depended on him being there when she needed him most so she felt comfortable with him.

"I know, man. I'm sorry. I thought I had her eating out of the palm of my hand. I really did. I don't know how this happened."

"FUCK!" Donovan shouted at Simon, punching the wall of his office. He took several deep breaths.

"I have an idea that might fix this," Simon said quietly,

hoping to calm down the intimidating man pacing in front of him.

"I think I've listened to enough of your shitty ideas," Donovan growled.

"Just hear me out. I've been thinking about this one lately, and I really think it might work. The problem is she's never run into my arms when she's been scared."

Donovan was hesitant to trust Simon's idea, but what did he have to lose? The more he thought about it, the better the idea sounded. Of course, running into Simon's arms would be just one part of the plan. A sly smile crossed his face as he formulated the end-game in his head. *Finally*, Donovan thought.

Chapter Seventeen

Come Back To Me

"FEEL BETTER NOW?" CAM asked Olivia the following morning, handing her a cup of coffee and some water. He hated to admit it, but he had never been as happy as he was the night before, holding Olivia in his arms all night long. She woke up several times, screaming. It concerned him that she was still having those dreams. He wasn't sure that she had truly made any substantial progress over the past several months. He had a feeling she wasn't being entirely truthful with her therapist. He vowed to get to the bottom of everything so he could help her get back to where she needed to be, even if that place was in another man's arms.

"Much better. Thank you." Olivia took a sip of her coffee, savoring the warm liquid as it traveled through her body.

"So…what's going on, Libby?"

She eyed Cam suspiciously. "I wanted you to come here as a friend. Not as a therapist, okay?"

"I understand, and I'm here as a friend who just happens to be a therapist, so I may have a little more insight than, say, Kiera."

Olivia sighed. "I'm not ready to talk about it quite yet, Cam. It hurts too much right now." She looked away, trying to hide the tears that had re-formed in her eyes at the thought of the months of lies that she had endured because of Alexander.

He reached across the kitchen table and grabbed her hand. "You need to talk about it eventually. You know that, right?" he asked quietly.

She turned her head back toward him, meeting his eyes…his kind silver eyes that never lied to her. "I know."

Throughout the rest of the day, Cam tried to get Olivia to talk about what was going on. And all day, she refused, the pain of Alexander's lies and secrets all too fresh in her memory.

The more she thought about how much he kept from her, the more it hurt. Every time she thought about what Adele had said to her and the look on Alexander's face, she broke down. Who else was keeping secrets from her? She had no idea who she was. Alexander was the green-eyed boy in her dreams. He had known for so long, but he never said anything.

"I'm glad you're here, Cam," she said later that afternoon.

He smiled at her, putting his arm around her as they lounged on the couch, watching some vampire show that she seemed to like. "I'm glad I'm here, too. But, at some point, we need to talk."

She stared ahead, her expression blank. "I think there's something I need to do tomorrow night," she said flatly.

"What's that?" He turned his head to look at her. She seemed like an entirely different person than she was that day at the bar just a few weeks ago.

"I need to go to Open Mic. I think Alexander will be there and maybe I'll be able to move on and begin to talk about this if I go. It always seems to help…singing, that is." She turned her head, meeting Cam's eyes, tears trickling down her cheeks.

"If that's what you think you need so that you can begin to heal, then let's do that."

~~~~~~~~~~~

WHEN OLIVIA EMERGED FROM her house Thursday evening, she was surprised to see her Audi sitting out front. She had left it over at Alexander's when she ran out on him and never asked for him to return it, but she was glad he did.

She walked down her front steps toward her car and scrunched her eyebrows in confusion, wondering how she would get in without her keys.

"What's wrong?" Cam asked, noticing her hesitation.

"Nothing. It's just…I ran out on Alexander and all my stuff is still over there, including the keys to my car." Olivia glanced down at the driver's side door and noticed that there was a numbered keypad by the lock that hadn't been there before. Alexander had a keyless entry installed on it. "Smug bastard," she said under her breath before punching the code that he must have used…the date of her supposed death. The door unlocked. She found the key fob in the center console and the car started immediately.

"Come on! Get in!" Olivia yelled to Cam as he stood on the sidewalk, staring at the car suspiciously.

"Are you sure he didn't plant a bomb or anything?" he joked.

"Take a risk, okay?" she responded dryly. Cam got in the car and Olivia pulled into Boston traffic, ignoring the dark SUV that was following them from her house all the way to Davis Square.

~~~~~~~~~~

"LIBBY!" KIERA SHOUTED AFTER Olivia wrote her name down on the sign-up sheet for Open Mic. "What the fuck is going on? Alexander has been blowing up my phone these past few days. Mo's, too!" She spotted Cam at Olivia's side, her expression turning severe. "What the fuck is he doing here?" she sneered. "No offense."

"None taken," Cam said, a grin on his face before facing the olive-toned man standing at Kiera's side. "I'm Cam." He held out his hand in greeting.

"Mo, or Jack. Take your pick. Nice to finally put a face to the name."

"Likewise."

Mo returned his attention to Olivia, a look of concern crossing his face. "What's going on?"

Olivia took a deep breath. "I don't want to talk about it just yet. I don't think I can. So please, be the friends I know that you are and give me time to process everything I've learned the past few days."

Mo eyed her suspiciously. "Are you sure you're okay? I know he's bigger than I am but, so help me, if Alexander hurt you, I'll do my best to kick his ass."

She smiled for probably the first time in days. "I appreciate the sentiment, but I would never ask you to do that."

Mo grabbed two more chairs and Olivia and Cam joined their table.

"Are you doing anything tonight?" Kiera asked after they finally flagged down a server and placed their drink order.

"Yeah."

"What song are you going to do?" Mo asked.

"You'll just have to wait and find out," she spat.

Kiera looked at her friend. "Libby, don't do anything that you're going to regret later." She nodded her head toward where Alexander sat at the bar, a drink in his hand, keeping his eyes trained on Olivia.

"I'm not saying I won't regret it later, but I need him to understand how much his actions have fucked with my head."

"What did he do?" Mo asked, his voice rising in anger as the current performer finished his song. Olivia turned her eyes back toward the stage, unable to answer Mo's question just yet.

"Alright," the M.C. said into the microphone. "Next up, ladies and gentleman, is an old fan favorite. Miss Olivia Adler! Or, I guess, the soon to be Mrs. Alexander Burnham. Get your butt up here."

Olivia's eyes went wide at the introduction, almost unable to get up from her seat.

"You don't have to do this if you don't want to," Cam whispered.

She took a deep breath. "No. I have to." She slowly walked up to the stage and sat down at the baby grand piano, adjusting the chair and microphone stand.

"Hi, everyone." Olivia looked out over the audience and found Alexander's eyes. "I'm not going to talk much tonight. Just one quick song and I'm out of here. I just need to sing this to let someone know how much their inability to tell the truth has hurt me."

A lone tear fell from her eye. "This is *I Was Gonna Marry You* by Tristan Prettyman."

"WHAT?!" Alexander said loudly. Several people in the bar turned to look at him, including Kiera and Mo.

What the fuck? Kiera mouthed to Alexander as Olivia started to play the opening measures on the piano.

Alexander sat at the bar, listening to Olivia sing, trying to process the words coming out of her mouth. She looked like an empty shell sitting on that stage. There was only pain. And he caused that. Again.

Olivia knew the song was a bold choice, but she needed Alexander to feel her suffering...to know that locking away the secrets of her past destroyed her. And maybe he needed to think that she no longer wanted to spend the rest of her life with him. She didn't know if that was true, but maybe it could be. How could she still want to marry someone who had lied to her? That kept her true identity a secret from her? She had put her trust in him and he betrayed that. He held all the answers to the questions she had struggled with her entire life, and he kept them from her.

She almost didn't care about knowing the truth anymore. Did it really matter? Maybe the last thing she needed to do was talk to Alexander and get answers. He always had an uncanny ability to make her understand why he did certain things. She would run back into his arms like she always did. But, this time, he hurt her far worse than he ever had before.

Alexander listened to Olivia sing, her sweet voice ringing through the bar as she played the gentle melody on the piano. He knew that he had lost her, not just in the lyrics she sang, but in the way she stared at him. She was gone. He still had so much he wanted to say to her. He just didn't know if he could say the words she needed to hear, her father's warning constantly ringing in his ears.

Olivia finished the last verse, her chin trembling as she thought how empty her life would be without Alexander in it. Tears streaming down her face, she shook her head as the final chord sounded through the bar, the audience remaining oddly silent. She stood up and her eyes met Alexander's. She tore her gaze from his and looked down at her left hand, her breathing ragged from the heavy sobs overtaking her body. Grabbing the ring, she started to slide it off her finger, locking eyes with Alexander once more.

His chin quivered. "No. Please." His deep voice echoed through the bar. "Olivia, love. I beg you." He reached his hand toward her from across the large space, but his feet remained frozen in place.

The audience looked back and forth between Olivia and Alexander, watching the drama unfold.

"Please," he begged once more. "I can't lose you again."

Olivia wanted to take that ring off. It felt as if it was scorching her skin, constantly reminding her that their entire relationship was based on deception. "I'm not sure I was ever yours to lose," she whispered through her tears, staring at him as she slid her ring back into place, keeping it on. She bolted off the stage and ran to the table, grabbing her purse, not saying a word to anyone. Cam jumped up from his chair and followed her out of the bar.

She practically ran down the sidewalk, her sobs heavy, not caring how many people gave her strange looks. She entered the unlock code through her tear-stained eyes and got behind the wheel of her car, her cries making her entire body shake. She knew, at some point, she would take off the ring. She just wasn't ready for that yet.

Seeing Alexander again made her entire body ache. She hated looking into those green eyes that she saw every night. It hurt that she wasn't worth the truth to him, and she wanted nothing more than to leave and never return to Boston. The city that once held so many fond memories, now only held heartache and pain at every turn.

She looked over the steering wheel, almost hoping to see Alexander come running out of the bar to talk to her. To tell her how sorry he was. To say that he was a fool for destroying their relationship. To promise that he would make it up to her. But that never happened so Olivia cried even harder.

Cam walked up to the driver's side door and opened it, helping her out.

"Oh, Cam," she cried into his chest, hugging him with all

her strength as she trembled from her sobs.

"Come on, Libby. You're in no condition to be driving." He helped her over to the passenger side before getting behind the wheel and turning on the GPS, punching in Olivia's address. During the short drive back to her house, the crying didn't stop. It only got worse. Cam wondered if she would ever return from this, and what it would take to get her to bounce back.

As he held her that night after she finally drifted off to sleep, he pleaded with her, "Please, Libby. Come back to me."

CHAPTER EIGHTEEN

CONSTANT

"LIBBY, YOU NEED TO talk about it," Cam said in a feeble attempt to get Olivia to open up about what happened. "Especially considering the meltdown you had last night at Open Mic." He walked from the kitchen to where she sat in her reading nook by the bay windows overlooking the street. "I can help you work through this, and not as a therapist." He grasped her hands in his, kneeling in front of her. "As a friend, Libby. A friend who is so fucking worried about you right now." His face was awash with concern.

Olivia sighed, staring out the window and meeting Alexander's eyes. She was glad he looked exactly how she felt. Empty. Broken. Shattered. "Well, I guess I should start at the beginning." She got up and made her way to the couch, Cam joining her. She immediately lay down and placed her bare feet in his lap.

The familiarity he felt with her made him grin. "That's a pretty good place to start." He grabbed some lotion and began rubbing her feet, hoping that the comforting gesture would help her be forthcoming. It worked.

Over the next several hours, Olivia proceeded to tell Cam everything she could think of, even if he already knew some of it. How her parents were killed in a car accident when she was six. How she had nightmares about the crash nearly every night. How the dreams became more vivid once she met Alexander. How she dreamed that her father made it out of the car alive. How, in her dreams, she overheard a conversation between her father and uncle saying that they needed to fake both of their deaths. How she was raised by her uncle. How the man she thought was her uncle was really Alexander's father. How Alexander and she were childhood friends. And how Alexander knew her true identity back in August, but never told her. He had lied to her since then, in the guise of trying to protect her from some unknown threat.

"So, if most of your dreams were true, do you know if your father is still alive?"

That hadn't even crossed her mind. She was so upset with Alexander lying to her that she never even thought about anything else. "I don't know. It was just a dream."

"Was it, though?" he asked urgently. "Our brains try to protect us, Olivia. You were in an accident that, apparently, caused you to suffer from memory loss. Usually, after such an event, you'd be surrounded by people from your past and you'd eventually come to remember everything again, but that didn't happen. You were taken away from everyone and went to boarding school with sporadic contact from a family friend you were made to believe was your uncle. You never had the chance to regain your memory. But those memories were still there in your brain somewhere, desperately wanting to get out. Once you saw Alexander years later, your brain was trying to tell you something and help you remember."

"Do you think my father could still be alive?"

"I don't know. I don't want to get your hopes up, but it's a question you need to ask him."

She looked at Cam, wide-eyed at the suggestion that she speak to Alexander.

"Libby, I'm not stupid. As much as I would love for you to forget all about him, I know that won't ever happen. You'll never love anyone like you love him. I know that now."

Olivia processed his words before grabbing her iPad, searching through her music library.

"What are you doing?" Cam asked, a quizzical look on his face.

"That just reminds me of a song," she explained, finding the tune she was looking for and streaming it to her speakers.

"You're too much." He shook his head and listened to the soulful blues song reverberating throughout Olivia's home. "But seriously, Libby. You need to talk to him at some point. He holds all the answers to your questions. You need to give him a chance to explain everything. You need closure, and he's the only way you'll get it."

She sighed, her eyes still glued to the iPad in front of her while she looked up chord progressions online. "I just need time. I'm not ready yet. Part of me doesn't want to know because, if my dreams are true, then Alexander knew my life was in danger and he kept me in the dark about everything."

"I'll give you time. But you need to do this."

"I know," she agreed before looking into Cam's kind eyes…eyes that never lied to her. "Will you stay just a little longer? Please? I don't want you to leave me just yet." She reached across the couch and grabbed his hand. "You're the only person I feel I can talk to who will give me a straight answer."

"What about Kiera and Mo?"

"I love them both dearly, and they're good about calling my bullshit, but there's something about talking to you that I don't get when I talk to them."

A smile crossed Cam's face, his dimples popping. "I'll stay for as long as you want me to, Libby."

"Thank you." She squeezed his hand.

That night, as she lounged on the couch with Cam, she glanced outside, tears welling in her eyes when she noticed Alexander sitting in the driver's seat of the SUV. Slowly getting up from the couch, she grabbed her glass of wine and sat in the window. She stared at Alexander for nearly two hours, tears falling down both of their faces. She wanted him to come up to her door and say something…anything. But he didn't.

~~~~~~~~~~

"TAKE ME TO MISS Adler's," Alexander slurred after climbing into his SUV the following Wednesday evening. He had just had more than a few drinks with his brother, finally telling

Tyler the whole story about what happened between him and Olivia. Of course, he left out a few details, like her father still being alive. No one could know that.

"Yes, sir," Martin said.

As the SUV pulled up in front of the brownstone on Commonwealth Avenue, he saw Olivia and Cam through the window snuggled up on the couch together. He was infuriated to still see him there with her after over a week had passed. His blood spiked with anger at the thought of someone else being there to comfort his Olivia. Grabbing his cell phone in a moment of weakness, he dialed her number, knowing that it probably wasn't the best idea for him to call her in his inebriated state. He watched with furrowed brows to see if she would answer her cell phone.

Inside her house, Olivia heard her phone ring. She slowly raised herself off the couch and made her way over to the kitchen island, a sad expression on her face when she glanced down at her phone. Her lower lip began to tremble when she saw those green eyes staring back at her from the screen. Every night that he sat outside her house and simply stared at her, she felt her heart break a little bit more. She was shattered, and each day that passed was another reminder of his inability to tell her the truth.

Answering the phone, there was no response on the other end. She sat down in the bay window with the phone glued to her ear, willing Alexander to say something. Apart from his gentle breathing, the line was eerily quiet.

"I learned a new song today, Alex," she said, cutting through the thick silence. "It reminds me of you. And me. All songs seem to remind me of you in some way. Mama always said that music is the best solution to any problem." She lowered her voice. "But you probably already know that. Anyway, that's what I've been doing...locking myself away in my music room, playing music. Mostly blues because that's how I feel without you.

"I should be so angry with you. And I am, Alex. I'm so furious with you. I'm sitting here questioning everyone in my life. I don't know what's real and what's not. I've been lied to my entire life. Hell, I don't even know what my real name is." She took a deep breath and put her hand up to the glass in front of her. "But through it all, through all the soul searching and all the questions, I've realized that the one thing I do know is that I need more time to figure everything out."

Olivia heard Alexander let out a small cry. She locked eyes with the man sitting in the SUV, tears flowing freely from both their eyes. For the first time, she not only saw the Alexander she had gotten to know over the past several months, but she also saw the scared little boy who pulled her from the car when she was a young girl, saving her life. And she realized that he had continued to save her life on a daily basis. With everything going on, he was her constant...the one person she could depend on. The one person who had loved her throughout her entire life. Olivia dropped her voice, realizing that Alexander was family. The only family she had left. "I'll never love anyone as much I love you, Alexander."

"So you still love me?" he asked, his voice full of hope.

Olivia's heart fell to the pit of her stomach. It had been nearly a week since she had heard his voice...his gentle voice that had told her how he had searched for her his entire life. The voice that was the calm in the storm of her life. Letting out a soft cry, she met his eyes through the glass. "I don't think I'll ever stop loving you."

Alexander held the phone to his ear for a moment before realizing she had hung up. He looked at the window and met her tear-filled eyes. His face flashed red with anger when he saw Cam come up behind her and put his arms around her, leading her away from the window and toward the couch.

~~~~~~~~~~

"OKAY, ENOUGH OF THIS bullshit, Libby!" Cam exclaimed the following day as he worked at his laptop, watching her scroll through the Google image search results for Alexander. The gossip magazines had been speculating about a possible break-up for the past week and it was still a hot news story.

"Suck it, Cam," she hissed, rolling her eyes.

"I'm not going to put up with it anymore. What is it going to take to get you to stop feeling sorry for yourself and *talk* to me? You've turned Kiera and Mo away every time they've come to check on you. They care about you and are worried. You're wasting away again, and it's not good for you, Libby. You need to talk to them about what's going on. Let them in."

"What do I say to them?"

"Tell them the truth. They're your friends," he replied, walking over to the couch and grabbing her iPad out of her hands, forcing her to talk to him.

"Yeah, but they'll probably just say that I made everything up in my mind so I could push Alexander away. The last thing I was looking for was a reason to leave him. I was so looking forward to marrying him." She furrowed her brow, the vein in her forehead popping like it always did when she was nervous.

"Libby, don't underestimate your friends." He grabbed her hands, savoring the feel of her soft flesh on his. "They'll always be your biggest cheering section if they're worth it. And if they give you trouble, I'll be here for you, supporting you." He dropped his gaze from hers, staring at her small hands enclosed in his. "Just like I always will."

His eyes returned to hers, her breathing increasing as she listened to his affectionate words. The atmosphere in the room suddenly became heated. Cam could feel his heart rate pick up when he noticed Olivia's expression change from one of anxiety to almost one of desire, her eyes flaming with lust. He leaned in slowly and gently brushed his lips against hers, softly at first as if asking if she was okay with it.

Olivia was unsure about how to react. She had always found Cam attractive and, for the past week, he was the only one she felt that she could depend on. But she knew his feelings for her were stronger than hers were. She didn't want to lead him on, but it felt so good to be kissed and loved by someone. Getting lost in the moment, she closed her eyes and deepened the kiss, pulling Cam on top of her as their tongues tangled. Olivia wrapped her legs around his waist, reveling in the feeling of closeness she had missed the past week that she had been away from Alexander.

Snapping back to reality, Cam pulled out of the kiss, looking down at Olivia.

"Don't stop. Please," she begged.

"Libby…" He sat back up, running his hands through his hair. "We shouldn't…"

She closed her eyes and took a deep breath before looking into his eyes. "Oh, Cam," she exhaled, realizing what she was about to do and how much she would have regretted it afterwards. "You're right. I wish I could love you. I really do. You'd be so easy to love."

He sighed, shaking his head. "You can't say stuff like that to me, Libby. I wish you could love me, too, but I know that'll never happen." He was starting to think that he needed to get out of Boston before he became so attached to Olivia that he would never get over her.

"Well, I guess I'm going to talk to Kiera and Mo," she said, bringing Cam back from his thoughts.

Smiling, he handed Olivia her phone. "Invite them over."

"Fine," she huffed.

~~~~~~~~~~

"WHAT THE FUCKITY-FUCK, LIBBY?" Kiera asked when Olivia answered the door a few hours later.

"Nice to see you, too, Kiera." She stepped back and allowed Kiera and Mo inside. "You both remember Cam?"

"He's still here? Are you telling me that you left Alexander for Cam? I knew there was a reason he was with you at Open Mic!" Kiera fumed before turning to Cam. "What the fuck are you thinking? I know you have a thing for her, but she was supposed to get married!"

"KIERA!" Olivia yelled, everyone turning toward her. "Enough! Please," she begged, lowering her voice. "It's not what you think. I needed Cam and he came to help me work through some things. If you'll please stow your pitchfork, I'd like to tell you both what's been going on."

"Fine," Kiera said, flopping on the couch. She turned her eyes up to meet Cam's. "But I'm keeping my eyes on you, mister!"

Cam laughed and took a seat next to Olivia, grabbing her hand in a show of support. She smiled at him before proceeding to tell Mo and Kiera the story that Cam had heard so many times.

"So, he's known secrets about your past since August and refused to tell you?" Mo asked when Olivia had finished telling them everything that had happened between her and Alexander. It was obvious that he was quite irritated.

"Now you see why I stormed out on him."

"That bastard!" Kiera exclaimed, unable to process the fact that Alexander and Olivia were childhood best friends.

"But the problem is that he holds all the secrets to my past. I know I should want to find out more about everything, but part of me is scared to know. What if there's a good reason that his father changed my identity?"

"I'm sure there is," Mo said. "You said the guy was ex-CIA. He wouldn't do that unless it was necessary."

"Libby," Kiera said, bringing Olivia's attention back to her. "Nothing we say is going to tell you what you should do. This is your life and your past. Mo and I have the luxury of knowing our family. You never did. Whatever you decide to do, we'll support you. Always."

Olivia walked over to the couch and sat between her two friends, both of them hugging her. "Thanks, guys. I love you both so much."

"Just so you know," Kiera said. "If you want to have a retaliatory fuck with Cam, I'd totally support that."

Cam's eyes went wide and Olivia looked at him, shaking her head at her friend's offer. "Thanks, Kiera," she replied, grinning at Cam. "I'll keep that in mind."

"Good. Because that fucker deserves to be hurt after what he's put you through."

"Maybe you should tell him, Livvy," Mo said. "Tell him how much pain he's caused you."

"I have," she explained. "I just don't think he's listening."

"Well, make him listen."

CHAPTER NINETEEN

OPENING UP

"LIBBY!" MELANIE SHOUTED WHEN she saw her walk into MacFadden's the following Friday. "How have you been? Are you back playing with the guys again?" she asked, excited to finally see her friend.

"Hi, Mel. Bridge," Olivia said, nodding a greeting to her friends. She hadn't seen them since Vegas. That seemed like ages ago, even though only a few weeks had passed.

"Kiera told us about you and Alexander," Bridget said, placing her hand on Olivia's arm, a compassionate look across her face. "We're so sorry."

"There's definitely more to the story than just a simple break-up, but we'll get to that later. To answer your question -- yes, I'm singing with the guys again tonight. It's about time that I got my ass back in gear."

"Who's this?" Bridget asked, eyeing Cam up and down. "This is the same guy that you were talking to at the Green Dragon all those weeks ago, isn't it?"

"Yes. Mel, Bridget, this is my friend, Cam. He's kind of been helping me through my issues."

"Nice to meet you both," he said politely before turning his eyes back to Olivia. "Would you like a drink? The usual?"

"Yes, please. I need it tonight."

He nodded, walking toward the bar through the audience that had gathered to see the band.

"Damn. He's a hottie. You go from one hottie to another."

"Bridget!" Melanie exclaimed, smacking her friend. "You

came here with Dylan!"

"Dylan? You mean Vegas Dylan?" Olivia eyed Melanie and Bridget.

"Yeah," Bridget replied, blushing and looking around the dark bar. "He agreed to come with me tonight, although I'm not sure where he's run off to." She furrowed her brow. "We've gone out a few times over the past couple of weeks." She returned her attention to Olivia and Melanie. "And Mel's been tutoring Lucas in a psych class he's struggling with that she's already taken."

"At least he's gay so I don't have to worry about him stealing my girl," Tyler said, walking up to the girls and snaking his arm around Melanie's waist. Olivia stared at him as he kissed Melanie's neck affectionately. She hated how much he reminded her of his brother. She wondered if he had known about her all along, too.

"Hey. You almost ready?" Mo asked, surprising Olivia. She didn't even realize he was standing next to her. Turning her head toward him as he stood with his arm around Kiera, she noticed Alexander walk in.

"Yup. Let's do this." Olivia spun on her heel, not wanting to stare into Alexander's sad eyes any longer, torn about whether she should still want to be with a man who kept her past from her.

"Hey all! We're back!" Mo shouted into the microphone to enthusiastic applause once the band was set to begin. "And, thankfully, we have the whole band back as well. Miss Olivia Adler, everyone!"

The crowd cheered as Olivia scanned the audience, her eyes locking with Alexander's. Mo stepped aside from the microphone, bringing a barstool in front for her to sit on.

"How's everyone doing tonight?" She grabbed the microphone out of the stand and sat down on the stool. "I know many of you have already heard about my little break-up." The audience laughed politely as they kept their eyes glued on her. "All my life, I've had difficulties expressing my feelings, except through music," she explained. "Earlier this week, I went for a run and a song came on my iPod that I think does a pretty good job at saying exactly how I feel. So that's what I'd like to sing for you all tonight. And for Alexander." A tear fell down her cheek. "This is *Last Love Song* by Z.Z. Ward. Alexander, I need this to be the last love song I sing for you unless you can tell me the truth. Please."

Olivia nodded at Mo and he started playing the simple guitar line. Her chin trembled a bit as she began to sing about the wedding that would never be and the life with Alexander that was suddenly a distant dream.

Cam stood watching as Olivia sat on her barstool, her eyes trained on Alexander, singing every word for him and him alone. He finally realized that he was crazy for thinking that she would ever see him as anything other than a distraction from the pain. He wanted so much more from her...something he knew she would never be able to give him, no matter how things ended between her and Alexander.

"I need to get out of here," he said to Bridget.

She looked at him. "Where are you going?"

Cam glanced back at the stage, taking one last look at Olivia. "Home. Where I belong." He turned to leave the bar, stopping when he saw Alexander standing in the back of the room with his eyes fixed on Olivia.

"Alexander," he said, reaching his hand out toward him.

"Cam," Alexander replied curtly, shaking it.

"I just want to say this as a friend of Olivia's. She's hurting, but she's still madly in love with you. You need to do the right thing. Maybe if she knows about her past, she can move on from this and start living again. I don't think she'll ever be able to move past you if you don't."

Alexander looked at Cam, surprised at his candor. "What the *fuck* qualifies you for knowing what she needs?! You don't know her like I do!" he yelled before lowering his voice. "How can she move on? I love her."

Cam exhaled loudly, running his fingers through his hair. "Then prove it to her. Do the right thing."

Alexander simply stared as Cam turned abruptly and left the bar, knowing that he was right. Looking over at the still crowd, he listened to Olivia pour her heart out to complete strangers, the betrayal in her voice absolutely devastating. He wished that he wasn't the cause of that pain.

He had been a coward back in August when he kept the truth from her. Every day since then, he had let his fears get the better of him. Cam was right. She deserved to know everything, regardless of her father's wishes, and that's what he resolved to do. It was time to come clean and tell her everything.

Remorse overwhelmed him as he watched Olivia close her eyes, her chin quivering with unshed tears. She belted out the last few lines of the song, a hollow look on her face. The audience erupted in cheers and whistles as the final note rang through the bar.

Taking a small bow, she turned to Mo, tears streaming down her face. "I'm sorry, Mo. I have to go. Can you…?"

"Don't worry, kid. I'll break down your gear." He embraced her, squeezing her tight. "I love you, Livvy."

"Oh, Mo. I love you, too."

"And Alexander loves you," he whispered. "I'm sure of that."

She pulled back, meeting Mo's eyes. "But I'm not sure if I should keep loving him." She walked away, running into Melanie and Bridget. "Where's Cam?" she asked, wiping the tears off her cheeks.

"He said he went home. He looked so sad, though."

"Home?" Olivia asked. "What do you mean?"

"He said it was where he belonged," Bridget explained.

"I need to go," she said quickly, knowing that Cam was probably already on his way to the airport. "Where's Kiera?"

"She left right after you went on. She said she wasn't feeling too well and that she would probably just go home. She looked pretty pale."

"I hope she's okay," Olivia said, her voice full of concern.

"She said she hadn't been feeling well all day and just needed to lie down for a bit. She said not to worry about her and that she'd call you tomorrow sometime when she was feeling better."

"Okay. I'll see you later!" Olivia shouted, heading down the stairs and out the front door to try to catch Cam before he left.

"Olivia?" a quiet voice called out.

She stilled, her breath catching. Slowly, she turned around to face Alexander. It was the first time she had been that close to him since the day she left him. The day she found out who he was. He looked so sad. The normal confidence he exuded was nowhere to be found. He was broken.

"What is it, Alexander?"

"I just wanted to say how sorry I am about everything that's happened between us," he said quietly, his eyes pleading with her. "I wanted to tell you for so long, but the longer I kept it from you, the harder it was to say anything."

Olivia kept her fierce brown eyes glued to his, wanting him to continue talking. Taking a step forward, he brushed a stray piece of hair behind her ear. She closed her eyes, reveling in the contact she had ached for since leaving him.

Alexander chuckled a little as his thumb brushed over the scar at her hairline. "I remember when you got this. You were screaming bloody murder after slipping on these rocks in front of your family's beach estate. You cut your head wide open and I had to run and find your mom and explain how you got hurt. We weren't supposed to be on the rocks."

Olivia's bottom lip started to quiver as she listened to him recall the memory. She wanted to know more. She wanted to know everything about her past, but then again, she didn't. She felt so weak at that moment. She wanted to walk away from Alexander and never see him again. But, at the same time, she wanted to stay close to him, to hear everything he had to say, to feel his body next to hers.

"You were such a pain in the ass when you were little. A spoiled little brat. But I loved you so much, Olivia, even when you always cheated at the games we used to play. The day of the accident, I was beside myself. I'll never forget sitting through your funeral. Your casket was so small." A tear escaped from his eye as he recalled the painful memory. "I couldn't help but think how truly horrible it was to watch them lower you into the ground."

Olivia listened to Alexander's words as she tried to fight

back her tears, the entire time wondering what he went through when he was a little boy. Losing your best friend at such a young age is something no child should have to go through.

"My parents put me in therapy after that," he explained. "I never snapped out of it. By that time, Dad had begun his mysterious disappearing act. I hated him for that. I hated him for thinking that one of his stupid protection details was more important than his own son. Until recently, I had no idea it was *you* that he was looking out for." He gently brushed a tear away from her eye before continuing his story.

"My therapist suggested that I find some way to honor your memory." He looked down and reached for her, a warmth spreading through his body from the chaste contact of her delicate hand enclosed in his. "That's when I started going to the cemetery every year on the date of your death. I think she suggested it so that I would finally stop looking for you everywhere." He returned his eyes to hers, his expression intense. "But I never stopped, Olivia. I just didn't want to believe that you were dead.

"I think I had such a hard time believing it because I knew you made it out of that car. I was the one who saved you. I'm the boy with green eyes that you see in your dreams. I should have told you the first time you mentioned the dream, but I was selfish and I didn't, and I know I'll have to live with that decision for the rest of my life."

"In my dream, when I saw the green-eyed boy, or you, get hit over the head..."

"That did happen."

"I dreamed that my dad was still alive. Do you think...?"

"Olivia, listen to me, please." He clasped both of her hands between his. "I promised that I would keep everything quiet, but I've made that promise in the past, and I've lost you because of it."

Olivia stared into Alexander's eyes, searching them for the answer she yearned to hear.

"Yes. Your father is still alive."

She gasped, fighting for air as her legs gave out from the

shock of his words. Alexander reacted quickly, wrapping his arms around her to steady her.

"I just don't understand!" she cried out. "Why didn't anyone ever tell me?! Where is he?!"

He looked down at her, tears flowing down her cheeks as he contemplated what he should tell her. Technically, her father was still under protection so he couldn't divulge any information to her about his whereabouts or his name, but she needed something.

"I'm right here, Livvy," a voice said.

Alexander and Olivia both snapped their heads in the direction of the voice.

Olivia stared at the man in front of her, unable to believe her eyes. She would recognize his face anywhere, even if it had aged a bit since she had seen him last. The face belonged to her father.

"Daddy?!" Olivia cried out, pushing away from Alexander's embrace. "Is it really you? Please tell me this isn't just another dream and I'm about to wake up screaming."

Jack DeLuca wrapped his arms around her, comforting her tears. "It's really me, Livvy. I'm not going anywhere ever again, but we have to be careful. You can't call me by my real name. You have to call me Nathan."

"I don't care what I have to call you. As long as you're alive, that's all I care about," Olivia sobbed.

"Oh, Livvy. I made such a huge mistake letting Alex's dad take you away from me after your mom was killed. I've spent every minute of my life looking for you since that awful day. I've been waiting for this moment for over twenty years."

Olivia couldn't control her tears any longer. She had experienced such extreme emotions over the past several weeks and she was tired of trying to keep it all together.

"It's okay, baby girl. Let it all out," he soothed, rubbing his daughter's back.

Alexander met Jack's eyes and he knew that Olivia was in good hands. He quietly walked away, knowing he still needed to tell her everything. However, right now, she needed her father more than him.

CHAPTER TWENTY

THE POINT OF NO RETURN

"DONOVAN, IT'S GRANT. I did what you asked me to do."

"Excellent."

"What's next?"

"Proceed as planned, and let me know as soon as you make contact with the girl."

"Yes, sir."

Donovan clicked the receiver before dialing, thankful that something was finally going right. "Cheryl, it's me. Get ready, and tell Simon to get ready, as well."

"Yes, sir."

~~~~~~~~~~

THE FOLLOWING DAY, OLIVIA was still reeling from the revelation that her father was alive and in the same city. He drove her home the previous night and they sat on her couch talking for hours. By the time he left, promising that he would be in touch, she had all but forgotten about Cam and wanting to find him. When she finally remembered, he was long gone. Maybe it was for the best that he left without saying good-bye. That seemed to be how it was with them.

As she paced her living room, ready to burst from wanting to share her good news with someone, she glanced at the time and decided to give Kiera a call, hoping that she would be awake and feeling better than the night before.

"Libby," Kiera croaked into the phone, picking up right

before the call went to voicemail.

"Hey, Kiera. Are you okay? You don't sound too good."

There was a brief pause. "Sorry. I'm fine. Just feeling a little under the weather."

"Do you want me to bring you something?"

"NO!" Kiera screeched.

"Are you sure you're okay?" she asked hesitantly. "You don't sound like yourself."

Olivia heard Kiera take a deep breath. "Yes. I'm fine. Mo and I just had a little argument. That's all." She let out a small cry.

"Oh. I'll be there in an hour."

"Libby, no!"

But Olivia didn't hear her protest. She had already hung up the phone.

Tears streamed down Kiera's face as the large man took the phone away from her ear.

"Now, what did I tell you would happen if you did something stupid?" Grant raised his gun, pointing it at Kiera's chest.

"Please, no. Don't kill me," she sobbed out.

"I love a girl who begs." A smile crept across his face. "Well, it would be horrible to waste an hour doing nothing." He pushed Kiera over on the couch and quickly untied her legs. "Oh, wait. A little insurance that you won't run away."

Grant picked up his gun and shot her in the knee.

"AAAGGGGHHHHH!" Kiera screamed out in agony.

"That's better."

~~~~~~~~~~

OLIVIA EMERGED FROM HER house less than an hour later. She couldn't wait to tell Kiera all about her father being alive, but it sounded like she was upset. She had always been a good friend to Olivia, constantly listening about her problems. It was time for her to return the favor.

As she walked onto Commonwealth Avenue and into her car, she noticed that a dark SUV was no longer parked out front. Maybe Alexander finally realized that she didn't always need protecting. As she drove through the city streets, she was confused about her feelings. She had grown accustomed to sitting in her bay window, staring into his eyes. Would she ever see him again?

Olivia arrived at Kiera's house in a matter of minutes. She locked the car, thinking how useful the keyless entry Alexander had installed was. Walking up the front steps, alarm bells began going off when she noticed that the front door was slightly ajar. "Kiera? Are you in here?" she called out, slowly pushing open the door. She wasn't prepared for the scene that met her eyes.

"OH, MY GOD! KIERA!" She ran over to her friend as she lay unconscious, covered in her own blood. She checked her breathing and her pulse, thankful when she was able to find one, although it was rather weak. She took in Kiera's appearance, bile forming in her throat when she noticed that her skirt was pushed up around her waist.

With shaky hands, Olivia grabbed a blanket and immediately tried to cover her up, her heart racing. A loud bang sounded from down the hall, startling her and making her almost jump out of her skin.

She knew what she was about to do was probably one of the most idiotic things she had ever done in her twenty-eight years, but her legs were on autopilot. She followed the noise, stopping dead in her tracks when the bathroom door swung open. The large man standing in front of her looked familiar, but he lunged at her before she had time to search her brain for how she knew him.

"Must be my lucky day. Two girls in one morning."

Olivia screamed at the top of her lungs, kicking the intruder in the balls and taking off down the hallway.

"Fuck. You're a feisty one." Grant was relatively unaffected by Olivia's assault to his groin. He grabbed her by the waist and slammed her against the wall, reminding himself to not go overboard with her. His job was to scare her off so she would run.

Olivia's head hit the wall fairly hard. It wasn't the worst pain she had ever felt, but she knew that the monstrous man in front of her would overpower her at some point. It was fight or flight, and it was no longer the time to fight. The best thing she could do was get to her car and call for help. She gave him one more kick in the balls and made her escape out the front door.

Running frantically up to her Audi, she attempted to punch her unlock code into the car door. The large man appeared in the doorway and Olivia became anxious, unable to get the code correct. The man started down the steps toward her. "Damn it!" she cried, running away from the house.

"Finally," Grant said under his breath when she bolted down the street.

He picked up his cell phone and punched in a number. "It's Grant. Your turn. She's heading north toward Columbus."

~~~~~~~~~~

OLIVIA FELT COMPLETELY HELPLESS as she ran up toward Columbus Street. Every few seconds, she turned around to see if she was still being followed. She didn't see anyone chasing her, but she couldn't risk it.

She needed to call 911, but her purse and phone were locked in her car which was still sitting in front of Kiera's house. Then she saw someone she recognized. He appeared to be out for a morning run.

"SIMON!" she screamed.

Simon turned his head to see Olivia running toward him, obviously panicked about something. "Olivia? Are you okay? Oh, my god. What is it?"

She slammed into his arms, clutching on to him, her breathing labored and tears streaming down her cheeks. A grin crept across his face before he replaced it with the look he had spent so much time practicing.

"You're shaking. What's going on?"

She pulled out of his arms, looking up into his eyes. "It's Kiera, Simon. Someone was in her house. They shot her. They attacked me, too, but I was able to get away. My phone and everything is in my car in front of her house. I need to call for help."

He looked at Olivia with a confused look on his face. *He shot her?* He didn't think anyone was going to get hurt. Not like that. They were just supposed to scare them a little.

"Here. Use mine," he offered, snapping out of his thoughts. "Let's go back there. You need to get your car and phone. I'll go with you to make sure you're okay."

"Simon, no…"

"Olivia. Listen to me. If Kiera's hurt, she needs help, and you need to be there to answer any questions the police may have, okay? For Kiera."

She nodded. *Of course. For Kiera.* He handed her his phone and walked with her while she made the call to 911. In a stupor, she followed him around the block, arriving at Kiera's house within a few minutes.

"Wait here." Simon protectively pushed Olivia back before walking up the steps.

"Simon, no. Don't go in there," she begged, grasping on to his arm.

"Olivia," he said, turning to look into her huge, frightened eyes. He immediately felt a strange feeling for his part in all of this. It was something new… Remorse, maybe? He brushed a curl out of her face before pulling her into his body, comforting her. "I'll take care of this. If the intruder is gone, Kiera needs help and the EMTs aren't here yet. I can help her."

"But if he's still in there…" she sobbed into his chest.

He pulled back, looking down into her water-filled eyes, and dried her cheeks with his fingers. "I can handle him, Olivia." He leaned down and placed a chaste kiss on her forehead before walking up the rest of the front steps into the house.

"Well, it's about fucking time."

"What the hell…?" He looked over at Kiera, a look of horror crossing his face.

"Don't worry about her. Bitch is unconscious. Even half-dead, she was a good lay."

"You're an asshole." Simon punched Grant in the face, and he deserved it. Although it was all part of the plan, the scene laid out in front of him was more than his stomach could handle. Kiera looked like she was on the cusp of death and he couldn't believe he had a part in it. But, he knew that if he didn't follow through, he'd be as good as dead, too, so he did what he had to do. He punched Grant again. "You motherfucker! She's a friend!" he shouted loud enough for Olivia to hear as regret overwhelmed his conscience.

Opening the basement door, Grant looked at Simon. "I can't look. Just push me. Make it quick."

Simon grinned, driving into his body with all of his strength. A feeling of vindication washed over him as he watched Grant tumble down the stairs before getting up and winking at Simon. Closing the basement door, he ran down the hallway and out the front door, his breathing heavy.

"It's okay, Olivia. He's unconscious at the bottom of her basement stairs. I need to go before the police get here. I can't get arrested again."

Olivia immediately felt guilty for dragging him into her mess. "Okay. I get it."

"Are you going to be alright?"

She stared blankly ahead, trying to process everything. "I don't know how to answer that question, Simon."

"I'll call you later to check on you, okay?" He gently squeezed her arm.

Olivia nodded, thankful to have a friend to help her with what she was going through, even if it was Simon. "I'd like that."

He walked away just as he heard an ambulance round the corner.

CHAPTER TWENTY-ONE

BECAUSE OF OLIVIA

AFTER TALKING WITH THE police and telling the officer what she knew, Olivia left Kiera's house, racing toward the hospital. She grabbed her cell out of her purse and dialed Mo's number. He didn't answer. She tried again. Still nothing.

"Damn it!" she screamed, throwing her phone on the seat next to her as she pulled a U-turn and drove out to Arlington to find Mo. Twenty minutes later, she pounded on his door.

Mo answered the door wearing a pair of cargo shorts and a t-shirt. His face paled when he saw the panicked look on Olivia's face, her eyes red from crying. He knew that something had to be wrong and he immediately thought about Kiera. She had left the bar the previous night without saying good-bye, giving Melanie some story about how she wasn't feeling well. He tried calling her, but she didn't pick up. At the time, he just thought that she was sleeping off whatever sickness she had. Now that he thought about it, none of it made any sense.

"Olivia..." he said, cautiously opening the screen door. "What's wrong?"

"Mo, it's Kiera," she quivered.

"No..." he cried out under his breath.

~~~~~~~~~~

OLIVIA DROVE MO TO the hospital. He was in complete shock

when she told him what had happened. She didn't give him all the details because she was quite uncertain of them herself. She didn't want him to worry any more than he already was so she kept the information she gave him to a minimum. She felt guilty for doing so, but she saw the fragile state that he was in and didn't want to add to it.

She immediately began to sympathize with Alexander's reasons for keeping her true identity a secret. He said he did it to protect her, and she started to see why. Wasn't she doing the same thing to Mo? It still didn't make what Alexander did to her right, but she started to understand his reasoning.

After an excruciatingly long drive, Olivia pulled up outside the emergency room, allowing Mo to run inside and find out what he could while she searched for a parking spot.

Once she finally found a spot in the garage, she ran toward the emergency room. The sliding doors opened and she was surrounded by so many familiar faces standing in the stark white waiting area. There was one face she wasn't expecting to see.

She immediately broke down in tears when Carol pulled her into her arms. "Oh, Olivia. I'm so sorry. I know how close you are to Kiera."

"How did you find out about what happened?" she sobbed.

"I was working when I heard the call come in. The name sounded familiar so I wanted to make sure that I was here for you. I called Tyler and he let everyone else know."

"I'm so glad you're here. I don't know what to do or think. We're all a mess right now." She glanced over at Mo. His face was still blank, obviously unable to come to terms with what was going on. Melanie and Bridget were hugging each other and crying, Tyler trying to comfort both girls. Kiera's parents sat in the corner of the room, sobbing uncontrollably.

"There's something else," Carol said gravely. "Walk with me for a minute, please."

Concern washed over Olivia as she followed her out of the waiting room and down a long corridor. Once they found a quiet corner, Carol turned to face her. She reached into her purse and pulled out her cell phone, handing it to Olivia.

She glanced at the photo on the screen. It was of a small bag marked EVIDENCE that contained a piece of notebook paper.

"The crime scene techs found it at Kiera's house," Carol explained quietly, looking around to make sure no one was walking nearby. "The lead on this case is going to contact you about it eventually, but I convinced him to let me talk to you first."

Olivia looked closer and was able to make out what was written on the piece of paper.

We know who you are. Your loved ones are no longer safe unless you give us what we want. Consider yourself warned, Olivia.

"Have you told Alexander about what's going on?" she asked Carol with a hesitant look on her face.

"No. I haven't. Not yet. At some point, I will have to. He may know more than what he's letting on." Carol looked at Olivia as she stared off into the distance, deep in thought, the sound of heart monitors echoing through the empty hallway. "What do you know, Olivia?" Carol gave her a questioning look.

"Probably no more than you do," she sighed, handing the phone back to Carol. "I know that I was a child with Alexander and that my mother was killed in a car accident. Your father faked my and my father's deaths."

"Wait. What?" Carol looked at her, surprised by her revelation. "Your father is alive?"

"Yes. You didn't know that?" she asked with her eyebrows raised. How many more secrets was Alexander keeping? And from his own sister?

"No. Alexander never told me," she responded quietly.

It was silent while both women contemplated what it all meant.

"Do you think he's keeping even more information from me? Do you think my dad knows something more?" Olivia asked.

Carol exhaled loudly. "It's possible. If my dad did change

both of your identities to hide you, I'm assuming your father is still under protection so I can't officially talk to him. He needs to stay protected...and a secret. These people obviously know about you. We don't want them to find out about your father, too. Unfortunately, that means that you need to stay as far away from him as you can until we can figure everything out and make sure it's safe. For both of you."

"But I just found out he was alive last night!" Olivia protested.

"Libby, it's for your own good. And his. Look at what happened to Kiera. Beaten, assaulted, and shot. She's barely hanging on to life. Please. Listen to whatever Alexander thinks is best for once. He's only ever had your best interests at heart. You may disagree with how everything went down in the end, and I'm right there with you, but he's very good at what he does. He's the only one in the world I would trust with my life, and you should do the same." Carol walked away, leaving her completely speechless.

Olivia sighed as she reached into her purse and grabbed her cell phone. She dialed a number that she hadn't in weeks.

"Burnham here," Alexander answered curtly.

She didn't know what to say.

"Olivia, love. Is that you?" His voice softened.

She melted when she heard his term of endearment. She had heard him call her that in her dreams, but hearing it for real was so much better. Tears took over and she broke down, the weight of that morning crashing down on her.

"Olivia, is everything okay?"

After several long moments of crying and fighting to breathe, she finally spoke, "No, Alexander. Everything is not okay. I need you. Please."

"Where are you?" he asked with panic in his voice.

"M.G.H!" she cried out. "Oh, Alex! It's Kiera!"

"Shit!" he shouted. "I'm on my way. Hang tight, love."

She slid down the wall and sat on the floor, burying her head in her knees as she cried for her best friend who was fighting for her life at that very moment. All because of Olivia.

~~~~~~~~~~

"ALEX!" MELANIE EXCLAIMED WHEN he ran into the emergency room, searching for a familiar face...the face he missed so much since she had run out on him. "Oh, it's so horrible!" she cried out. "I don't know what do to!"

"What happened?" Alexander asked as he surveyed the group of people huddled in the waiting room. Olivia was not among them.

"I have no idea, and no one is telling us anything! Mo is in shock over there. We're all falling apart. Please, Alex. Figure this out because none of us are strong enough to deal with it." Melanie cried into her tissue as Tyler rubbed her back.

"Okay, Melanie. I'll get some answers." He looked around the corridor. "Where's Olivia?"

Melanie burst into tears, unable to hold back at the thought of one of her best friends fighting for her life at that very moment.

"I'm not sure," Bridget said, comforting Melanie. "She went to go talk to a detective and never came back."

"A detective?"

"Yeah. Carol's here, bro," Tyler explained.

"Of course," he said under his breath. "I'll be back."

He strolled down the halls, not having to search for long before finding the girl he was looking for. She was sitting with her back against the wall, her arms wrapped around her legs and her head on her knees. She was visibly shaking, her quiet sobs echoing through the vacant hallway.

He approached her slowly and gently placed a hand on her shoulder. "Olivia, love..."

She snapped her head up quickly upon hearing those words. It was exactly what she needed at that moment. She jumped into Alexander's embrace, savoring the warmth of his arms. She inhaled deeply, basking in the smell and feel of him. This was home. "I've missed this," she said softly.

"Oh, Olivia. So have I." He placed a gentle kiss on her head.

157

She looked up, their eyes meeting. "I'm sorry for the way I've behaved, Alexander." She began to cry again.

He pulled her head back against his chest. "Hey. It's okay, Olivia. I'm sorry, too. Sorrier than you know. I knew you'd come around eventually. This isn't the type of love that happens all the time. This is the real thing. I never gave up hope that you'd return to me all those years ago. I certainly wasn't about to give up after we had a little hiccup."

She laughed through her tears. "You call *that* a little hiccup?"

"In the grand scheme of things...yes, I do."

She ran her fingers up and down his back, suddenly feeling calm considering everything she had been through that morning. "I've never stopped loving you, you know?" She pulled her head out of his chest and looked deep into his eyes. The affection he had for her was evident.

"I know, Olivia, and I will never stop loving you. I've loved you since the day you were born, and I'll love you until the day you die. And I plan on making it up to you every day in between."

Reaching up, she grabbed his face with both her hands, bringing his mouth to hers. As their lips touched for the first time in weeks, tremors ran through her body. She had grown accustomed to his kisses over the course of their relationship, but that kiss felt so much more meaningful now that she knew who he really was...the boy that saved her when she was little. And he was the boy that saved her again less than a year ago. And he would always be there to save her. Finally, Olivia was happy with that.

Their tongues met briefly before Alexander realized where he was and what he was there for. While he was happy to finally be reunited with his Olivia, he wasn't sure making out in the corridor of the emergency room at Mass General was appropriate, given the circumstances.

Slowly, Alexander pulled back. "To be continued later, love." He winked and grabbed her hand before stopping abruptly. He lifted her left hand, examining her delicate finger. "You're still wearing it...?"

"I never stopped wanting to be your wife, Alexander, aside from what I may have wanted you to think. Like you said, we had a little hiccup." She shrugged.

He embraced her again, groaning. "I didn't think it was possible, but I just fell a little bit more in love with you."

She smiled briefly before focusing her attention toward the waiting room. "I need to go check on Mo. He's in a bad way."

"Come," Alexander said, placing his hand on the small of her back and leading her down the hallway.

Melanie smiled when she saw them return together.

"I'll be right back. I'm going to see if I can find out what's going on." He kissed Olivia on the cheek.

"Well, finally some good news today!" Melanie said once he was out of earshot.

Olivia blushed, avoiding her eyes.

"We'll talk later." Melanie winked.

Olivia glanced to the corner of the waiting room, her eyes welling up with tears as she made her way over to speak with Kiera's mom and dad. "Mr. and Mrs. Murphy," she said softly.

They raised their heads simultaneously. "Oh, Olivia, dear." Catherine Murphy stood up and embraced her. "Our poor Kiera."

Olivia willed herself to not break down. Everyone seemed so sad and dejected. She needed to stay strong for them.

"I'm so sorry, Mrs. Murphy. I…" She trailed off, not able to form the words that said that everything was all her fault.

"Hush, dear. You have nothing to apologize for. The only one who should be here apologizing is that monster who did this to my girl."

"Excuse me…" an authoritative voice rang out, grabbing everyone's attention.

Olivia turned and saw Alexander standing next to a doctor. *Damn. He can be persuasive, can't he?* she thought to herself.

"I'm Dr. Rosenblatt. I'd like to speak to Miss Murphy's parents privately for a moment please." He looked toward where Olivia stood next to Kiera's mom and dad.

"*All* these people are Kiera's family," Catherine Murphy

told him very matter-of-factly. "Anything you need to tell us, you can say to them."

Dr. Rosenblatt sighed before he continued, "Kiera is in stable, but critical, condition. She's lost a lot of blood. She was shot in the leg, chest, and head. We've been operating on her for the past several hours and were able to successfully remove all the bullets. Thankfully, they missed hitting all vital organs. The shot to the head appeared to just graze her. We induced a coma as a precaution to operate and remove bullet fragments."

"Is she going to be okay?" Bridget asked.

"It's touch-and-go at the moment. She still has quite a bit of swelling in her head so we need to keep her in a coma until that has reduced. Once the swelling begins to subside, I'll know more, but until then, that's all I can really tell you."

"Can I see her?"

Everyone turned to the source of the voice. Mo sat there with a blank look still on his face, staring ahead at nothing in particular, his eyes glassed over.

The doctor looked at Kiera's parents, silently asking permission if it was okay that he be allowed to see her.

"Like I said, Dr. Rosenblatt, this is Kiera's family. Anyone here is allowed to see her as long as the hospital is okay with her having visitors."

"Follow me, please," Dr. Rosenblatt said to Mo. "No more than two people at a time."

"Libby, dear, why don't you go with him? He looks like he could use a friend."

Olivia looked at Kiera's mother. "Are you sure? You can go first, if you want to."

"You go. James and I will go after you return."

Olivia wrapped her arms around her, pulling her in tight. "Thank you. We'll make it quick." She turned, following the doctor and Mo down a long corridor past double doors marked ICU. They continued through what seemed like a maze of hallways before stopping outside the door to a private room.

Mo sobbed quietly when he entered the room and saw Kiera's lifeless body lying on a stark white hospital bed. He sat down next to her and held her hand, his cries making his entire body shake.

Olivia walked in and closed the door, giving them some privacy. She placed her hand on Mo's shoulder, still determined to remain strong, even though she wanted to break down and scream and cry. She had to keep it all together…for Mo.

Everything was her fault. She knew it. The letter Carol had shown her proved it. She had something these people wanted and they weren't going to stop until they had it. But what was it? Was Alexander still keeping information from her? Carol's words kept repeating through Olivia's head: *"Listen to whatever Alexander thinks is best. He's only ever had your best interests at heart."*

After looking down at Kiera's swollen and badly beaten body, Olivia couldn't take it anymore. "Come on, Mo. Let's give her parents a chance to see her."

He slowly nodded. "You're right. Sorry," he said, his voice void of emotion. He raised himself from his chair and leaned over, planting a kiss on Kiera's lips. "I love you, K."

Walking over to the bed, a tear fell down Olivia's cheek. She placed her hand over her friend's, noticing how cold and lifeless it was. "I'm so sorry, Kiera," she whispered. "I'll make it up to you. I promise."

She turned and left the small room, closing the door behind her. Olivia resolved to do whatever it took so that none of her other friends met with the same fate as Kiera…even if it meant putting herself in danger.

Chapter Twenty-Two

Home

How's she doing?" Alexander asked as soon as they returned to the waiting room.

"Oh, Alex," Olivia cried out, unable to muster any more strength after seeing Kiera's lifeless body.

His arms were around her instantly and he soothed her tears, trying to comfort her.

"It's so horrible. She looks like she's dead. I just…"

"What is it, love? What do you need? Name it and I'll do it for you."

Her chin quivered as she listened to his heart beating in his chest. "Take me home, Alexander. Please. Get me out of here. I can't be here anymore, and if that makes me a weak person, I don't care," she sobbed, clutching on to his back, wanting him to take the pain away.

"Olivia, look at me."

She slowly tilted her head up, staring into his beautiful green eyes.

"Don't ever think that you're a weak person." He brushed the tears from her face. "You're not. You've just been trying for too long to stay strong. Let me be the strong one for a little bit. Okay?"

She nodded, wiping her tear-stained cheeks.

"Good," he smiled. "Now, you said you wanted to go home. Do you want me to give you a ride to your place or did you bring your car?"

"I have my car, but I was referring to *our* home, Alex."

His smile widened and he grabbed Olivia's hand, pulling her through the sliding glass doors and out of the emergency room.

He led her toward the parking garage, grabbing his cell phone as he walked. "Martin, it's me. Miss Adler's Audi is in the garage at M.G.H. Coordinate with Carter to retrieve it and bring it to my place." He hung up just as they reached his Maserati. He opened the door for her and she smiled, happy that things were starting to feel somewhat normal again.

He glanced over at her as he pulled out of the parking garage and onto Storrow Drive, heading back to the waterfront. "Olivia, darling, I know you probably have a lot of questions right now, and I promise…"

"Alexander," she said, interrupting him. "I don't want to think about any of that right now because I'm pretty sure I'm going to get pissed off at you again. Please. Let's forget about all of that for now. I just want to sit here and hold your hand. I've missed feeling your skin on mine."

He opened his mouth to say something, quickly realizing that she was right. She would get more than just pissed off when she found out how much he had kept from her. Instead, he smiled at her, happy to have her at his side once more, even if it was fleeting. "Okay, love. Whatever you want." He grabbed her hand and clutched it in his, not letting go as he made his way through the busy Boston streets and parked his car in the garage beneath his building.

After a tension-filled elevator ride to the penthouse, they finally exited into the foyer. Olivia inhaled deeply, thankful to be back where she belonged. She missed everything about Alexander, including the smell of his home.

"What would you like to do, Olivia? Name it." He turned to face her once inside their living room.

She gazed into his brilliant green eyes. The eyes that once haunted her dreams. The eyes that had loved her since the day she was born. "Alexander, I want you to make love to me."

He bowed his head. He wanted nothing more than to feel Olivia's skin against his, but there were still unresolved issues.

Olivia noticed his hesitation and reached for his hand, clutching it in her own. "Alexander, please. I need to feel you.

I need to feel the love you have for me. It's what I need right now," she pleaded with him before turning her lips into a smirk. "Don't make me beg," she said coyly, pulling his body into hers.

Alexander lost any willpower he had left. Leaning toward her, his lips brushed hers very gently. "But I like it when you beg," he whispered.

Olivia could feel a smile creep across his mouth. "Please, Mr. Burnham. Make love to me." Her voice was sweet as she softly kissed his lips, sliding her tongue between them. Her kiss was warm and passionate as she explored his mouth like it was the first time.

Bending down, he scooped her into his arms and carried her up the stairs into the bedroom. "Are you sure about this, Olivia?" he asked, placing her feet on the floor next to the bed.

"Do you not want to have sex with me, Alex?" she asked, her voice brimming with hurt.

"Olivia, I would love nothing more than to be inside of you every waking moment of every day, but I know we still have things you probably want to talk about."

She lifted her finger up to his lips, hushing him. "Stop talking, Alexander. All I want is to feel your lips on every inch of my body. I need you inside of me. I feel like an addict that hasn't gotten a fix so, please, make love to me."

Alexander crushed his lips to hers, gently lowering her onto the bed. His hands roamed all over her body, never staying in one place for too long.

"Take off my shirt, Alex," she said, her voice husky with desire.

He made short work of her blouse, unbuttoning it and throwing it on the floor as he stared down at her lacy black bra. She could feel him get hard as he knelt between her legs, admiring her.

"Kiss me, Alex."

She was bossy. Alexander liked this side of her. He lowered his head to her neck. "Where?"

His breath was hot on her skin, sending shivers up and down her spine. She panted greedily, basking in the closeness of his

164

body to hers once more.

"Tell me where, love," he said quietly.

"My neck." She tilted her head, giving him better access.

He planted gentle kisses from her earlobe, down one side of neck and up the other. "God, I missed the feel of your skin, Olivia. You have the softest skin known to man."

She moaned, arching her back.

"Where else do you want me to kiss you?"

"My chest."

He lowered his lips to her collarbone and proceeded to delicately nip at her skin, circling her chest with his tongue, leaving her squirming from the anticipation.

"My nipples, Alexander. I want them in your mouth."

He looked down at her, an evil grin across his face. "Your wish is my command, princess." He pulled back the material on her bra, exposing both of her nipples. Groaning, he lowered his mouth, tugging and licking on one before moving to the other one and giving it the same treatment. He glanced up, smiling when he saw her slowly becoming unhinged.

"Where else, love?"

"My stomach."

"Is that all?"

Olivia slowly shook her head, pulling her bottom lip between her teeth.

"Then where else, Olivia? Tell me…"

"I want you to kiss me down there," she said, raising her eyebrows.

"Where? Down here?" Alexander asked, mischievously grabbing her knee.

"No," she replied, smirking.

"Then, tell me, Olivia. I want you to tell me exactly where you want my tongue," he said, tracing circles around her stomach.

She moaned out, her breathing increasing. "I want you to kiss me on my clit."

Glancing up, a wide smile spread across his face. "That's my girl," he said quietly, reaching down and sliding off her skirt, followed quickly by her panties. Their eyes met as he buried his tongue between her legs.

Throwing her head back, she closed her eyes, trying to control the amazing feeling from the contact of Alexander's tongue on her most sensitive spot. It had been far too long since she had felt his mouth on her. Over the past few weeks, she had often thought of him while touching herself, but nothing compared to the sensation of his tongue swirling around and teasing her.

"God, I missed the taste of you, Olivia," he said, sliding one finger inside of her. "You're so tight. I need to stretch you out a bit."

"A little cocky, aren't we?" she asked with a hint of amusement in her voice as Alexander continued pleasuring her with his fingers and tongue at the same time.

He smiled. "Not exactly. That's why I need to stretch you."

She moaned when he returned his mouth to her, sucking gently. "Fuck, Alex," she exhaled, starting to feel her entire body tremble around his rather talented tongue. She was surprised how quickly she was ready to fall apart from his delicate touch.

"That's it, Olivia," he said against her soft flesh. "Just remember how good I make you feel. How I'm the only one who can make you come within seconds of licking your clit."

She closed her eyes, desperately trying to fight back her orgasm. She didn't want to come yet. She wanted it to last, but she knew there was no controlling how he affected her.

"Don't deny your body. I want you to come for me. I want to see that beautiful body shake because of what I do to you." He returned his tongue to her clit and continued circling her, sending her over the edge.

She screamed out his name as she shook in his enormous bed, her entire world a haze as she slowly came down from her orgasm. When the aftershocks died down, Olivia grabbed his face and brought it to her own. "I've sure missed that, Mr. Burnham." She pressed her lips to him, invading his mouth with her tongue, tasting herself.

"I've missed it, too," he admitted as she ran her fingers up and down his back, bringing his shirt over his head. "Know what else I've missed?"

Olivia looked up at him sweetly, admiring his naked chest.

"Being inside of you."

"Then what are you waiting for?" she asked in a deep, throaty voice.

He quickly stripped out of the rest of his clothes and positioned himself between her legs, easing into her in one slow move.

She moaned out as he flexed back and forth slowly, making sure her body was re-acclimated to him before he picked up his pace.

"I love you so much, Olivia." He kissed her as he moved inside of her.

"I love you, too, Alexander." She felt so full and overwhelmed at that moment. She thought the first time that they made love was special, but that moment, right then, was even more so.

She wrapped her legs around his waist, not wanting to feel any space between them as she pulled his mouth back to hers, kissing him again. She caressed his back, running her fingers up and down his body.

"Fuck, Olivia," he exhaled. "I love being inside you. There's nothing like it." He kissed her passionately, moaning into her mouth. "I just knew you were still alive. I never gave up hope that I would find you, Olibia."

A tear fell down her face at the mention of his childhood nickname for her. "Oh, Alex," she exhaled, bucking him with her hips. "I love you. I'm so sorry. I never should have left you."

He leaned down, gently nibbling on her neck, tracing his tongue across her soft flesh. "I've never stopped loving you. You're the only one for me."

Olivia threw her head back, reveling in the feeling of Alexander's mouth on her body as he moved delicately inside her. It was all becoming so overwhelming. She thought she loved him with all her heart before, but this was so much more. The simple act of him moving inside her was so much bigger than anything she had ever experienced before. She was climbing higher and higher, the love she felt for Alexander making her tears flow even harder.

"Don't cry, Olibia. I'll always be here for you."

Tears continued to stream down her face as she processed everything that she had been through over the past several months.

Alexander slowed his rhythm, looking down at the beautiful woman beneath him. "Please don't cry, angel. I need to know you're alright. I need to know I'm not hurting you." He brought his hand to Olivia's face, gently wiping her tear-stained cheeks. He planted soft kisses all over her face where her tears once were. Pulling back, he beamed his brilliant smile at her. "That's my girl."

Olivia grinned in response, giggling through her tears, moving beneath Alexander once again. He met her rhythm, burying his face against her neck.

"Faster, Alex," Olivia breathed out, starting to feel that familiar clenching feeling.

"Are you going to go again?" he asked, pulling back to stare into her eyes.

"I think so."

He began to move at a quicker pace on top of her.

"Alex, wait. I haven't taken my birth control pills lately. I forgot them when I went to Vegas and never started a new pack."

He continued moving quickly, his own orgasm imminent. "What do you want me to do, Olivia? I'm about to come. I can't stop now. Are you worried about getting pregnant? If it happens, I'm okay with it."

Olivia stared deep into Alexander's eyes, unable to focus as she took in those green eyes and felt her body begin to tremble.

"Olivia, answer me. What do you want me to do?"

"Fuck, Alex. Don't pull out!" she cried out as her orgasm took over her body.

He pumped faster, leaning down and gently tugging on her nipple with his teeth as he found his own release, muttering her name against her skin before collapsing on top of her.

"That was pretty fucking intense," she commented while

they both attempted to get their breathing under control.

Alexander rolled over, pulling her body against his, wrapping his arms and legs around her as he gently caressed her skin for several long moments. "Olivia, darling, do you want to talk about what happened to Kiera?" he asked sweetly.

She sighed. She didn't even want to think about it, but she knew she couldn't avoid it forever. Turning to face him, she ran her fingers through his messy hair, his green eyes intense and desperate for information.

"I called her earlier this morning," she started. "I wanted to tell her about my father."

Alexander scowled.

"Hey. You never said I had to keep it quiet."

"Okay, okay. Sorry. Continue."

"She didn't sound too good. She said something about a fight with Mo, so I told her I'd be over there soon. I grabbed my car and drove over."

"Wait a second. Where the fuck was your protection detail?" His eyes grew wild with anger.

She glared at him.

"Okay, okay. I'll worry about that later. Go on."

She continued to run Alexander through the events of that morning, leaving out the part about running into Simon. She knew he would overreact to that piece of information so it would be best to just keep that from him.

"Back up a second, Olivia. You said the guy looked familiar?"

"He did, but I can't remember where I've seen him before."

"What did he look like?"

His face was now ingrained in her brain. "He was big. Tall and built. He had evil eyes and his breath stunk. His voice..." She trailed off, her mind racing.

"What is it? Do you remember something?"

"It was the guy from that day in the snow..." Olivia shot up, covering her chest with the blanket. "I *knew* he looked familiar."

Alexander had a feeling that there was more going on than she probably knew. His heart sank as he came to the realization that the attack wasn't about hurting Kiera. It was about hurting Olivia. "Listen to me, Olivia. This is not your fault." He pulled her back down next to him, staring into her eyes. "Nothing you could have done would have stopped it. We don't even know who that guy is or what he wants. It could all just be a coincidence that he attacked Kiera."

Olivia buried her face in Alexander's chest, relishing in the warmth of his body, not wanting to tell him about the letter Carol showed her. "I don't want to talk about it anymore, Alex. I'm exhausted. Every time I close my eyes, all I see is Kiera's blood-covered body, and I just want to forget it, even if just for a minute."

"Okay, but we need to talk about it at some point, about what it all means." He gently kissed the top of her head.

"We will, but right now, I need you to help me forget." She pushed him on his back and crawled on top of him, desperate to feel him inside her again.

CHAPTER TWENTY-THREE

MORE SECRETS

OLIVIA CROUCHED IN THE corner of her family's large estate on the beach, playing hide-and-seek with her best friend, Alex. She was a great hider.

"What is this, Jack?" her mama asked, her voice concerned.

"Marilyn, you weren't supposed to find that." Her father sounded angry.

"Jack, this is some serious stuff. Please tell me that you're not involved."

"What do you take me for? Some criminal? I would never betray my country like that!"

"Then explain to me what this is. Please. I beg you."

"This is classified stuff. Something I'm working on. A bit of a side project. There's a lot of big brass involved here, Mary. I don't know who I can trust. This runs so deep, even up to the top of the CIA. I had to bring all the evidence home so that they don't find out that I know. To keep me safe… To keep you safe…"

Olivia's mother let out the breath she was holding. "Thank god. You had me worried for a minute," she said, running her hand against his face. "I need to go. I'll be back by dinner."

"Marilyn, wait. Where are you going?"

"Out with Colleen. She's heading back home later this week to get ready to deliver the baby. I want to spend some time with her before I don't see her again for the rest of the summer."

"Okay. I love you, sweet girl."

Olivia saw her mother turn and smile at her father. "I know."

She heard the door close. Her father strode over to the phone in the kitchen and dialed. "Hey. It's me. I need your help."

~~~~~~~~~~

"OLIVIA, WAKE UP, PLEASE. You're scaring me. Come on, baby," Alexander pleaded, trying to shake her awake. He had been trying to wake her up for the past several minutes. He had hoped the nightmares would subside once she knew who she was. Apparently, that wasn't the case.

"Olivia, please…" He watched as she shook and screamed, unable to do anything. "Please…"

Suddenly, her eyes flung open and she gasped for air.

"Oh, thank god. You had me worried, love." Alexander pulled her head flush with his chest. "That must have been some nightmare."

Olivia couldn't speak. Her tongue felt as if it was caught in her throat. She had never had that dream before and she didn't know what to make of it. It didn't make any sense. Nothing did anymore.

At first, Olivia thought that the only thing Alexander had kept from her was that they were childhood friends. There had to be something more…something that had to do with the reason his father had to fake her and her father's deaths. She had a feeling Alexander had all the answers, and she wanted those answers. But, at the same time, she kept hearing Carol's words in her head, pleading with her to trust his judgment.

Alexander held Olivia tight and soothed her tears as her shaking began to subside, desperate to calm her down. He didn't want to ask, but he needed to know what had her so shaken up. "Do you want to talk about it?"

"Just another stupid dream, Alex. Go back to sleep. Don't worry about me." She took a deep breath, inhaling his scent.

"But I *do* worry about you, Olivia."

"I know you do. I just don't want to talk about it. Okay?"

He held her tight, scared that he would lose her again if he pushed her any further. "Okay."

~~~~~~~~~~

THE FOLLOWING MORNING, ALEXANDER'S phone began ringing, waking him and Olivia up. "Alex, don't answer it. Please," she begged sleepily. "I don't want you to leave this nice warm bed."

Reaching for the cell, he looked at the caller ID. "It's Carol. She may have some information about Kiera's case."

Olivia exhaled. "Fine. But you owe me."

He answered the phone, grinning at the beautiful brunette in his bed. "Hey, sis."

"So, thanks for telling me Jack DeLuca is still alive."

Shit. Alexander got out of the bed and walked down the hall to a spare room for a little bit of privacy.

"I'm sorry. I didn't mean for anyone to know. I didn't even want *Olivia* to know."

"What?!" she shouted, enraged by Alexander's admission. "That's her father, for crying out loud! You really wanted to keep that information from her?! After everything she's been through?! Haven't you kept enough secrets from that poor girl?!"

"I know, I know. But there was a reason that Dad put them both under protection. There was a reason their lives were better off if the people they were before the accident were thought to be dead."

"I trust you, Alex. I always have. But you need to start looking at the bigger picture here. Some serious shit must have gone down back then for Dad to do what he did."

Alexander walked over to the window and stared down at the waterfront, sunlight shimmering on the ocean below him. "What I'm about to tell you cannot be repeated to another soul."

"Alex, come on. I'm a detective, in case you've forgotten. I know all about classified information. I deal with it on an almost daily basis."

He took a deep breath. "Several months ago, I confronted Jack outside of Olivia's home. He was sitting out there, keeping watch over her. I have no idea how or when he found her, but he did. I had just read Dad's letter that told me what happened all those years ago…or, at least, a rough idea of what did.

"Anyway, I had been seeing the same rental sedan everywhere Olivia was so I wanted to find out who the hell it was. As I approached the car, I thought my eyes were betraying me. It was him. Jack. But an older version of him."

"Wow," Carol exhaled.

"I made him get out of the car so that we could have a little talk. I still had no idea why Kiddish and his goons were after Olivia again after all these years. She was just a little girl back when everything went down."

"I've always wondered the same thing. None of it made any sense."

"I know. Come to find out, Jack had collected evidence on certain higher-ups in the government, including the CIA, who had been brokering deals with known terror organizations. It became clear that the entire family was in trouble so he reached out to Dad for help. After the crash, Jack was concerned that both his and Olivia's lives were still in danger."

"But that doesn't explain why these people hired Kiddish again. I mean, Olivia was…"

"Just a little girl. Well, here's the kicker. When we were little, we used to play this game with her father. Olivia loved it. Treasure Map. Her father would take a box and bury it somewhere and would then draw a map with clues as to where it was hidden. But, that time, Olivia apparently grabbed the chest with all that evidence, saying she would hide it and, when she was finished, would draw *him* a map. Her father had locked the documents in a chest for safe-keeping. You remember the great room at their beach house? Olivia's mother had it decorated in a nautical theme with lots of fake treasure chests? Olivia loved it. Anyway, her father didn't realize she had grabbed *that* chest until it was too late, and then the accident happened."

"So, the only person who knows where that evidence is hidden is Olivia."

"Exactly, and Kiddish knows that."

"Fuck."

AFTER SPEAKING FOR SEVERAL more minutes about what everything meant, Alexander hung up. He didn't even *know* what it all meant yet, but he was determined to find out. When he re-entered the master bedroom, a smile crept across his face as he stared down at Olivia's sleeping form.

Hearing the door creak open, Olivia stirred, turning her body to face Alexander's frame in the doorway. "Come back to bed," she said groggily.

He stood there, admiring her naked silhouette from afar. "You're so cute in the morning when you're all tired."

She yawned. "You tired me out last night, Alex. You were like a machine."

He strode over to the bed, getting back under the covers and wrapping his arms around her. "You have that effect on me, love. I just can't get enough of you."

She smiled, pushing him onto his back and slowly climbing on top of him. "Good," she said breathlessly, leaning down and dragging her tongue across his chest. "Because I want you. Now." She leaned back, gazing at the boy who saved her. Her hips circled his waist, waking up his erection. "There's my boy…"

"Olivia," he exhaled, pulling her toward him, their lips almost touching. "Don't ever leave me again." Carefully, he slid inside her.

She moaned out in pleasure, closing her eyes as she basked in the amazing sensation of him filling her. "Never, Alexander. Never again."

"Good." He gently moved inside her, slowly picking up his pace as he held her hips, guiding her on top of him. "Because I plan on spending the rest of my life fucking you senseless."

"Fuck." Olivia never thought she could come by hearing words alone, but she knew that with Alexander, anything was possible.

"I plan on putting lots of babies right in here," he said, his breathing ragged as he gently caressed her stomach.

Olivia leaned down, pressing her lips to his as her movements became even more hurried, searching desperately for her release. Alexander lowered his hands, cupping her ass gently before bringing one palm back and spanking her cheek.

She screamed out in surprise.

"You like that, don't you?"

She couldn't put a coherent thought together, the sensation overwhelming her.

"Answer me, Olivia," he growled.

"Yes!" she screamed.

"Yes, what?!" he shouted, spanking her again, harder.

"Yes, Mr. Burnham! YES!" she screamed out, coming undone. Waves of pleasure flooded through her body, her entire core shuddering from the intense feeling before she began spiraling down.

Alexander flipped her onto her back and hovered over her, rubbing his erection against her clit while she continued to spasm beneath him from the aftershocks of her orgasm.

She began panting, moaning out. "Alex. Please," she begged. "Stop being a tease."

He leaned down and took one of her nipples in his mouth, tugging it with his teeth. "Am I really a tease?" he asked coyly, his voice heavy with amusement.

"Of course you are, and you know it." She grabbed his head, bringing it inches from her own. "Please, Alexander. I want you to come inside me."

He groaned, slamming into her. His rhythm was fast and relentless. "I love when you talk like that, Olivia. It's such a turn on."

She closed her eyes, meeting his pace thrust for thrust. "I love you, Alexander," she murmured.

He leaned down, pulling on her earlobe. "And I love you. Always," he grunted before he emptied inside her, gently biting her neck and savoring the taste of her soft skin.

"I missed this," Olivia said quietly as she ran her hands up and down his back. "My fingers just weren't cutting it," she joked.

"Lucky fingers." Rolling onto his side, he pulled her into his arms.

She snuggled up against him, clutching his hand in her own, placing a chaste kiss on his knuckles before glancing over at the nightstand. "Holy crap. Is that the time?!" she exclaimed, shooting up from the bed.

Alexander looked over at the clock. "I guess so."

"Shit. I have to get back to the hospital. I can't believe we stayed in bed until almost noon!" She jumped out of bed and ran into the shower.

He laughed, watching her beautiful naked body run into the bathroom, frantic. It was good to have Olivia back home…where she belonged.

CHAPTER TWENTY-FOUR

TRUST

"ARE YOU SURE YOU'LL be okay without me?" Alexander asked as he opened the front door of their apartment building.

"I'll be fine," she said, the irritation showing in her voice. "Mo needs me right now. I promise I'll call you if anything comes up."

He searched her eyes, nervous about letting her out of his sight.

"Alexander, please. It's a hospital, for crying out loud. There's security every two feet in there. What could possibly happen to me? I'll be surrounded by everyone. Carter will be with me anyway." She gestured with her head toward one of the two idling SUVs.

He sighed, not wanting to argue with her now that they had finally reconciled. "Okay, love. I'll be at the office getting some work done if you need me. Remember, if you want to leave the hospital for any reason, Carter will accompany you. Or you can call me and I'll come right away."

"I will." She cocked her head toward him and their lips met. "Oysters tonight?"

He grinned, loving the taste of Olivia's lips. "And do we want to practice making babies before or after that?" he asked, his voice barely above a whisper.

Something had certainly changed in Alexander over the past few weeks that they had been apart. Olivia had never heard him mention wanting kids before. She was excited about the prospect of starting a family with him, but there were still some unresolved issues between them…issues that she had no desire to address at the moment. "How about both?"

"That's my girl."

Alexander watched Olivia walk away from the building and into the SUV, his heart racing as her hips swayed in that way that always turned him on. Then he climbed into the backseat of the second SUV.

A few minutes later, he entered the vacant reception area of his company's headquarters, making his way down the corridor and into his office. Once he was sure the door was locked behind him, he returned to the bathroom and was soon down in the large safe room once more.

He began digging through the boxes again, knowing that he would eventually have to give Olivia some information about her past. He was also secretly hoping that he would find the infamous evidence box. He knew it was a long shot, but maybe it was there and his father never found it.

As he sorted through box after box, he came across items from Olivia's childhood…and his own. Family photos. Stuffed animals. Toys. Some boxes were full of documents…deeds to various property holdings, bank statements. As he dug through everything, he stumbled upon his father's handwriting on a piece of paper amongst years' worth of financial records. Numbers and letters were scratched on several sheets of legal paper. It was obvious that he was onto something, but what was it?

Alexander grabbed the box and brought it to a desk to sort through, on a mission to determine what it was that his father had figured out. None of the records made any sense. All the numbers seemed to run together. He recalled his mother saying that his father had grown rather paranoid during the last few months of his life. Maybe this was just a result of that paranoia. Still, he needed some advice and he knew there was only one person he could turn to.

"Hey, sis. It's me," he said into his cell phone. "Are you working today?"

"No. I'm off. I was about to go to the hospital to see how Kiera was doing. Why? What's up?"

"Think you could swing by my office on the way? There's something I need to show you."

~~~~~~~~~~

"WHAT ARE YOU TALKING about, Simon?!" Donovan shouted into the phone, unable to even believe what he was saying. "You better not be having second thoughts. This whole plan rests on you following through!"

"I just didn't think anyone would get seriously hurt," Simon explained. "That bastard raped her. It was horrific."

"Hey. Buck the fuck up. I hope you're not getting soft on me now. You wanted to pull the trigger anyway. We're giving you your goddamn wish. Need I remind you that if you fail, we'll kill both you and the girl? Either way, the girl will die. It's just a matter of whether you go down the same path."

Simon began to shake with apprehension. What else could he do? He was in too deep and the only way to save his own life was to throw Olivia to the proverbial wolves. "I got it. I won't let you down. I promise."

Fuming, Donovan slammed his phone,

"Trouble in paradise?" a voice called out, walking into his office.

Donovan looked up. He recognized that voice, but had never actually met the man before. All of their business was conducted solely over the phone. After looking into the man's cold hard stare, Donovan finally answered, rather confused, "Nothing I can't handle, sir. This is why you pay me."

"I understand that, but it seems like your golden boy, Simon, has grown a bit of a heart. Are you sure he'll follow through when the time comes? Can you be sure the girl will even lead him to those documents?"

"It's a risk we all have to take. That's the reason we left that note at her friend's house…to draw her out, hoping that she'll come forward in order to prevent further harm to anybody else she's close to. That is, unless you have a better plan."

"I pay *you* to come up with the plan. Now, the second you know where the box is, you better fucking call me."

"Yes, sir."

~~~~~~~~~~

"LIVVY, I'M SO GLAD that you're here," Mo said when he saw her walk through the sliding glass doors of the hospital and into the waiting area, Carter close behind her.

She made her way over to him and gave him a hug. "Of course. How's she doing today?"

"Good, actually," he responded with a hopeful look on his face. "The doctors say the swelling in her brain is going down and if she stays on track, they may be able to bring her out of the coma tomorrow."

"That's fantastic news, Mo! Thank god." Olivia looked around the empty waiting room. "Is anyone else here?"

"Her parents are sitting with her right now."

"Good."

"Can I ask you a question?" His eyes narrowed and suddenly became rather serious.

She had a feeling what that question would be, and she wasn't sure how she should answer it. "Sure, Mo. Anything," she replied nervously.

Carter took a few steps back, giving the two friends a bit of privacy.

Mo took Olivia's hand and walked her over to a lounge chair, never releasing his hold on her as they both sat down. "I need to know, Livvy. No one is telling me anything and that leads me to suspect something more than just a physical attack occurred yesterday."

Olivia stared at him, swallowing hard at what she knew was about to come.

"What did you see when you got to her house yesterday?" he asked with a shaky voice.

She looked down at her hand as Mo ran his fingers over it.

"Please, Livvy. I need to know," he pleaded with her. "Was she…?"

His voice trailed off and Olivia's eyes met his. All she could see was Kiera's lifeless body covered in blood, her skirt hiked up around her waist with more blood trailing down her thighs. She briefly closed her eyes, trying to muster the strength to say the words. He seemed so much stronger than he had been the day before, and telling him may send him back to the dark place he had just returned from.

But if she withheld all that from him, she would be no better than Alexander keeping all those secrets from her, and she knew how badly that hurt. She couldn't do that to her friend, as well. Making her decision, Olivia slowly opened her eyes, meeting Mo's gaze.

"Was she?"

She nodded slowly. "Yes. From what I could gather about everything, she was. And when I spoke with Carol yesterday, she had inferred that there was evidence that she was…"

Mo let out a small cry and bowed his head, unable to process what Olivia had just confirmed for him. "No one would be straight with me here because she's unconscious…" He took several deep breaths. "I'm going to kill that motherfucker."

"Mo, please. I ran into a friend while I was trying to escape, and it sounded like he did a number on the guy. I'm pretty sure the police have him in custody."

"No, Livvy," he said urgently. "They don't. They never found anyone in the house."

Olivia's mind started to race. "What are you talking about?" she asked.

"Who is this friend?" He eyed her suspiciously.

She looked down at her lap, unsure of whether to tell him about her run-in with Simon.

"Livvy, damn it! Who was it?!" he shouted, standing up and hovering over her as he glared down at her.

Glimpsing to where Carter stood, she hoped that he couldn't overhear their conversation. "Simon," she replied quietly, avoiding his gaze.

Mo's eyes went wide. "Are you fucking *crazy*, Olivia? After all the shit he did to you?!" He began to pace back and forth, unable to comprehend how a woman as intelligent as Olivia could even think about speaking to Simon again.

"Calm down, Mo," she pleaded, trying to get him to lower his voice. "He's one of the good guys. He had me stand outside while he went back into the house to see if the guy who attacked Kiera was still there. I heard the fight. Then I heard someone fall down the basement stairs. I guess he must not have been as unconscious as Simon originally thought. There is that back door in the basement. He could have escaped that way."

"Livvy, don't you think it's a little strange that you just so *happened* to run into the same guy who attacked you?"

"No, Mo. I don't," Olivia replied loudly, becoming irritated with his questions. Did he not realize that if Simon wasn't there, Kiera may not be alive at all? "He let me use his phone to call the police and he went into that house, when he didn't have to, in order to make sure it was safe. To make sure I wasn't attacked again. To help Kiera. He's one of the good guys. I promise. I've spoken to him a few times since he got out of prison and he's really changed, Mo. He's turned his life around. I'm not about to jump back into bed with him or anything, but he's proven to be someone I can count on, especially yesterday. If it wasn't for him, Kiera may be dead right now."

Mo's eyes searched Olivia's for a clue as to how he should react to what she just told him. He exhaled loudly. "I trust you, Livvy, and if you trust him, then I guess that's going to have to be good enough for me."

"I do trust him, Mo. He has yet to lie to me. That's more than I can say for Alexander."

"Speaking of which, I saw you leave with him yesterday..." He raised his eyebrows at her. "Are you guys back together?"

Olivia sighed. "I guess so. He wants to talk about everything, but I'm torn. I'm scared to find out how much he's been keeping from me, but we eventually need to address the elephant in the room, ya' know?"

He nodded, sitting back down next to her, and wrapped his arms around her.

"But right now, I'm enjoying the hell out of getting laid again."

Mo laughed, bringing a smile to Olivia's face.

Chapter Twenty-Five

Guilt

"WHAT IS THIS PLACE, Alex?" Carol asked after being led to an enormous room in Alexander's office building that she had never seen before.

"It's a safe room Dad had built years ago for security reasons, I guess."

"But what is all this stuff?" She gazed around at the piles and piles of boxes stacked on metal racks placed against the walls. It reminded her of the evidence storage locker at work.

"Files, photos, stuff like that." Alexander shrugged.

"About what?" Carol asked, interested in what her father hid from them during his lifetime.

"Olivia," he replied, gauging his sister's reaction.

Carol surveyed the room, astonished. "Holy shit."

"Yeah. I found out about it after I read Dad's letter. Then I found this today." He handed her the legal sheet with numbers and letters scratched on it, almost as if written in his own unique code.

She read it, trying to figure out what it could mean. "I don't understand, Alex."

"Neither do I. I was hoping that you might be able to shed some light on it."

"I wish I could help. I really do, but this doesn't mean anything to me." She handed the notepad back. "Maybe the answer is somewhere in here." She motioned to the hundreds upon hundreds of boxes filled with potential clues.

His eyes grew wide at the prospect of having to dig through

each box, looking for a needle in the haystack.

Carol noticed his apprehension at the enormity of the project. "Well, I guess we better start digging then." She grabbed a box off one of the shelves and brought it over to a desk.

He looked at her, disbelief written on his face. "You're going to help?"

"Of course I am. I'm probably the only person you can actually trust with this shit."

Alexander shook his head. "You're right about that."

"Well, get your ass to work then." Carol began to sort through the box, wondering if Olivia had mentioned anything about the letter the techs had found at the crime scene.

~~~~~~~~~~

OLIVIA WALKED THROUGH THE bustling hospital corridors before stopping outside of Kiera's room, taking a deep breath and entering. As she sat by her friend's side throughout the afternoon, she thought about Alexander and how silly she felt for staying angry at him for so long when he was only trying to protect her. There were people out there who wanted to harm her. Yes, it was painful to know that he kept her identity from her for so long, even when he watched her struggle with her past, but Carol was right. He only ever had her best interests at heart.

She clutched Kiera's cold hand and stared at her lifeless body, trying to find the words to tell her that everything would be okay, even though she couldn't hear her. Her eyes welled with tears every time she looked at her swollen head, bandaged from where they had to extract the bullet. "I'm so sorry, Care Bear," she cried softly. "I never meant for this to happen to you."

She stayed by her side for what seemed like hours, her thoughts consumed with revenge. As the sky streaked with lightening, a summer thunderstorm rolling in and drenching the city, her cell phone rang. She didn't recognize the number, but answered anyway.

"Hey, Olivia. It's Simon. I just wanted to check in and see how you're doing after everything that happened yesterday."

"Oh...hi, Simon. I'm glad you called." She released Kiera's hand and stood up, walking toward the windows.

"Really?" he asked, noticeably surprised by her response.

"Of course. We're friends after all, aren't we?"

He was silent, unsure about how to respond. His guilt started to overwhelm him. At first he wanted Olivia to pay for having him arrested, but things had begun to spin out of control. In the end, he wasn't so sure he could follow through with what he was supposed to do. "You really want to be friends with me? Even after everything that's happened?"

"I do, Simon. You're one of the few people I know who has never lied to me. I could really use someone like that in my life right now."

He cringed at her words. "How's Kiera?" he asked after several long, silent moments.

"As good as can be expected." She turned and walked back to stand next to her friend's still body. "She was shot in her head, chest, and leg..."

"Bastard..." Simon muttered under his breath.

"I know. They had to induce a coma in order to remove the bullet from her head. Surgery went well and they were able to remove all the bullets and stop the excess bleeding. The swelling in her brain has gone down and they say that they may be able to bring her back from the coma within the next few days, if not sooner."

"That's a relief. She's going to make it then?"

"It appears so."

"That's great news."

Olivia heard her phone beep, indicating she had another call coming in. She ignored it and continued speaking with Simon. "I just want to thank you for everything you did for me yesterday. If you weren't out for a run when and where you were, I don't know what would have happened. You saved Kiera's life. I don't think I can ever repay you. She was lucky that none of the bullets hit any vital organs."

"I don't know if I'd call what happened to her lucky," he

said.

"I know." She brushed her friend's forehead. "But she was totally helpless. All that guy needed to do was put one more bullet in her and she'd be dead," she said with a quiver in her voice just as she heard her phone beep again. She continued to ignore the incoming call.

"Well, I'm glad I was able to help." He felt incredibly guilty for deceiving her. What was happening to him? Just a few months ago, he was itching to get his revenge. But there was something so different about Olivia. It was as if she was a completely new person than the girl he dated the previous summer. This new Olivia was kind, caring, compassionate…a huge change from the cold-hearted bitch he knew all those months ago. He hated what he had agreed to do to her.

"I just wish they were able to catch the guy. Apparently, he got out of the house before the police were able to detain him."

Simon lowered his voice. "I'm sorry to hear that."

"Yeah. I'm sure I'll have to go and give a description of him, especially once Kiera wakes up."

"Listen, Olivia, talk to Alexander. Make sure he assigns a couple of guys to watch Kiera's hospital room."

She scrunched her eyebrows, curious as to why Simon was suddenly more concerned. "Why? She's in a hospital. I don't think anyone would be stupid enough to try anything here."

"Libby, I doubt this guy, whoever he is, intended to leave her as a witness. In fact, both of us should probably be careful. We've seen his face." He didn't know what else Grant and Donovan had planned. The least he could do was warn her. "You remember what I told you a few months ago about those guys who were after you for some reason, don't you?"

"I know. I already can't go anywhere without my protection detail. I can't remember the last time I didn't have one of Alexander's security people keeping an eye on me. I know he's just trying to keep me safe and I appreciate it, but sometimes I feel like I have no privacy."

"Alexander cares about you, that's all. I'd do the same if you were mine…" His voice became quiet, trailing off.

"Simon, I'm sorry. I wasn't into the whole relationship thing when I met you."

"Listen, I should get going," he said, remorse overwhelming him. He couldn't listen to her voice anymore without breaking down and telling her exactly what was going to happen. And he couldn't do that or he'd end up dead, too.

"Good-bye, Simon, and thank you for everything."

He hung up, not wanting to feel any more guilt than he already did.

~~~~~~~~~~

"DO YOU THINK SHE'LL be okay?" Alexander asked later that afternoon, breaking the silence that had permeated the storage room. Neither one had been able to figure out their father's code, nor how it related to the financial statements the papers were found with. "I mean, after walking in on Kiera and seeing…" He trailed off before composing himself. "Will it be enough to know that they were able to catch the guy?"

"What are you talking about, Alex?" Carol asked, looking at him with her eyebrows scrunched in confusion. "They *didn't* catch the guy."

"Olivia said she ran for help, and a stranger walked back to the house with her. She said that this guy attacked the intruder after he saw he was still in there," he said urgently. "She said he pushed him down the basement stairs and that he was knocked unconscious."

"Nobody was ever found, although the exterior basement door was open."

"So this guy is still out there?" he asked, his voice trembling. He kicked himself for not following up sooner on what happened to the intruder.

"It appears so."

"Fuck…" His mind started racing, thinking about Olivia at the hospital without him. At least Carter was there with her.

Carol didn't know what to do. She thought Alexander knew that they never caught the guy. It was entirely possible that Olivia didn't know. But then there was the letter. "So, where is Olivia?"

"At the hospital," Alexander responded. "Visiting Kiera."

"Did you send Carter or anyone with her?" She tried to keep her inquiry casual, not wanting to key him in on why she was prying.

He looked up from the desk and glared at his sister, certain that she was keeping something from him. "What's going on? Why do you care? Do you know something?"

Carol returned her attention to the box in front of her, trying to avoid eye contact with her brother. "No. Of course not. It's not even my case," she said quickly.

Alexander got up from his chair and stalked across the room. He stopped in front of the desk she sat at and leaned toward her. "You know you're a terrible liar. Tell me what you know."

"Alex, please…" She raised her eyes and met his.

"Carol, we already know that there's some sort of threat against her life in regards to this evidence box that could be anywhere. Whatever you know can't be worse than that."

She took a deep breath. "The crime scene techs may have found something at Kiera's that involved Olivia, and I may have shown it to her."

"To who?! Olivia?!" Alexander raised his voice.

Carol cringed, surprised by his anger. "Don't you shout at me! Someone was bound to talk to her about it! I figured it should probably be me!"

"What was this something, Carol?" he asked through clenched teeth.

She reached down into her purse and produced her cell phone. She scrolled through it and found the photo of the evidence bag containing the letter that she had shown to Olivia the previous day.

Taking the phone, Alexander squinted his eyes to make out the scribbling on the piece of paper in the photo.

We know who you are. Your loved ones are no longer safe unless you give us what we want. Consider yourself warned, Olivia.

"Shit! What does this mean?!" he asked, his heart thumping

in his chest. His eyes searched hers for an answer.

Carol exhaled loudly, taking back her phone. "I think it means exactly what it says," she responded dejectedly. "These guys are now going after everyone close to Olivia to draw her out."

"FUCK!" Alexander shouted, running out of the room and up the stairs to his office.

"ALEX! WAIT!" Carol shouted after him, following close behind. "Don't do anything stupid!"

"Are you *listening* to yourself, Carol?! You're asking me to not do anything stupid?! The time for not doing anything stupid is so long past! Do you know what Olivia is probably thinking at this exact moment?! I was ready to tell her about everything, but now I can't!"

"What are you talking about? Why?"

"Don't you see? Once she knows what these people are after, she'll sacrifice herself to save her friends. That's who she is. I can't lose her again!"

CHAPTER TWENTY-SIX

GONE

"ALEX," MO SAID, JUMPING up when he saw him running through the glass doors of the hospital into the waiting area, his expression panicked. "Everything okay?"

"Where is she, Mo?"

"Who? Livvy?"

"Yes!" he answered frantically, his eyes scanning the hospital corridors. "Is she with Kiera?"

"Yeah. Don't worry. Carter's in there with her. She just wanted some time alone with her."

Alexander exhaled loudly, his momentary panic waning slightly as he turned to head toward the ICU.

"Alex, wait a second."

"What?" he growled, spinning around.

Mo raised his eyebrows, wondering why he was so insistent on finding Olivia. "Listen," he said calmly, hoping that he would relax. "I know things have been off lately between you and Livvy…and the rest of us, really. I'm saying this right now as her friend and not yours." He took a deep breath before continuing, meeting his eyes and giving him an icy stare. "You better get your shit together. Stop trying to protect her by keeping information from her. She's been lied to by everyone, including you, her entire life. You'd better tell her whatever you're keeping from her or you'll lose her, and I doubt you'll get her back again. She's giving you a second chance right now. Don't fuck it up. I know she said that she wasn't ready to hear what you have to say, but I'm pretty sure you weren't going to tell her the whole story anyway. You better tell her about her past. All of it."

Alexander listened to Mo's words as he spoke, torn about what to do. If he told her, he risked her remembering and sacrificing herself for the sake of her friends. If he didn't tell her, he risked her walking away again. Either way, he'd lose her, but at least in one scenario, she would still be safe. "I'm not sure I can do that, Mo. I'm sorry..." He lowered his head in defeat as he ran down the corridor toward Kiera's room.

~~~~~~~~~~

OLIVIA SAT CLUTCHING HER friend's hand, hoping that the doctors would be able to bring her out of the coma soon. "I hate not being able to talk to you, Care Bear. I hate that all of this has happened to you." A tear fell down her cheek. "I hate that this is all my fault."

A beep sounded from her phone and she looked down in her lap to see a blocked call coming through. Assuming it was Alexander calling from his office line, she picked up.

"Hello, Mr. Burnham," she said in a sultry voice. "Looking forward to oysters tonight."

"That's nice, *Libby*," a strange voice sneered. "But you may want to cancel your plans."

Her eyes grew wide in shock, the greeting she received on the other line completely unexpected. "Who is this?" she asked, standing up from her chair and backing up cautiously.

"That's not important right now. What *is* important is that I have your little friend with me." A scream sounded through the phone. "If you want her to live another day, you need to come to the new boathouse on the Charles. Alone, or she dies. In twenty minutes, or she dies. If anyone follows you, I'll kill them and the girl. Do you understand?"

Nervous energy coursed through her body and she slowly nodded her head, her voice stuck in her throat.

"I said, do...you...understand?" the voice demanded.

"Yes," she croaked out. "I understand."

"Good. Boathouse. Twenty minutes. Alone. Or she dies."

Olivia hung up, her mind racing about which one of her friends they could have now. Slowly pulling back the door to Kiera's recovery room, she scanned the hallway.

"Miss Adler," Carter said, noticing her expression. "Is everything alright?"

"Yes," she quivered. "It's just hard to see her like this. That's all."

He nodded his head in understanding. "Can I get you anything?"

She met his eyes and shook her head. "No. I just need to go powder my nose."

"Okay." He followed her down the hallway.

"I'll be fine on my own."

"I don't doubt that, but I'll lose my job if I don't escort you wherever you need to go."

Olivia opened her mouth to protest, but didn't want Carter to become suspicious. Stopping in front of the door to the ladies' room, she looked at him. "I'll just be a few minutes."

He sent her a reassuring smile. "Take your time. I'll be right outside."

A twinge of guilt washed over her for deceiving Carter when he had only been watching out for her, but she had no other option. At least in the privacy of the restroom, she could try to come up with a way to get out of the hospital unnoticed.

Taking several deep, steadying breaths, she tried to formulate a plan as she paced back and forth in frustration. A familiar voice sounded in the hallway, asking Carter where she was, and her heart sank even further into her stomach. Not only did she have to get past Carter's protective eyes, but now she also had to sneak by Alexander.

She had all but given up any hope and contemplated telling Alexander and Carter exactly what was going on when the bathroom door swung wide open, six chipper cheerleaders swarming the room.

"I can't believe that asshole dropped her!" one of them said.

"She'll be out for the season now. And at our first competition, too!"

Olivia surveyed them, her eyes settling on a girl who

appeared to be the same size as her. "Hey," she said, addressing the group before lowering her voice. "Do you all want to make a quick hundred dollars?" She raised her eyebrows. "I need your help."

~~~~~~~~~~

"WHERE IS SHE?" ALEXANDER asked Carter as he hurriedly ran up to him in the hospital corridor.

"She's using the restroom, sir. She seemed pretty upset and just needed a minute." He gestured with his head to the door of the bathroom. "Is everything okay?"

"I don't know," Alexander replied, watching as a group of cheerleaders walked past them and into the bathroom. "I don't know what the hell to think anymore."

Carter simply nodded. "Well, I'm here to keep an eye on her, sir. She's in good hands."

Alexander met his eyes. "Thank you."

"Anytime, sir."

Several anxious minutes passed as the two men waited for Olivia to emerge from the bathroom. Finally, the door swung open and they looked in its direction, their hopeful expressions falling when the group of cheerleaders filtered out.

"Oh-Em-GEE!" one of them squealed, running up to Alexander. "You're Alexander Burnham, aren't you? Macey! Look! It's really him!"

Alexander stood back in shock, Carter glancing over their heads as another girl in a cheerleading jacket walked out of the bathroom in the opposite direction, obviously completely uninterested in the local celebrity. "Ladies," he said. "This is a hospital. Please leave Mr. Burnham alone."

"Just one picture, please?" the short redhead begged, placing her hands together in a pleading manner.

Carter looked to his boss to see what he wanted to do.

Sighing, Alexander nodded his head. "Okay. One picture." He beamed his brilliant smile as the group of teenagers piled around him, and Carter snapped the photo.

"I'll never get used to that," he said a few minutes later after saying good-bye to the excited cheerleaders.

"I imagine it must be difficult. It would certainly irritate me."

Alexander shrugged. "Yeah. But my public relations rep says the more positive publicity the better. And if that means taking pictures with a few teenage cheerleaders, I'm happy to do it." He glanced at the bathroom door, wondering what was keeping Olivia. "She's been in there for a while, hasn't she?"

"She has," Carter responded, looking at his watch. "It's been over ten minutes. I know she was upset, but…"

Alexander strode over to the door, pushing it slightly ajar. "Olivia? Are you okay?"

He listened for a response. Nothing.

"Olivia, love?"

Still nothing.

Pushing the door open, his heart sank in his chest when the bathroom was empty.

"SHIT!" he screamed, running down the hallway.

"Sir!" Carter bellowed out.

"You stay here! Question everyone, including those goddamn cheerleaders!"

"Yes, sir!"

Alexander continued running frantically down the hospital corridors, looking for any sign of his Olivia. "FUCK!" he shouted when he noticed a cheerleader's jacket stuffed in the garbage canister in the lobby. Grabbing his cell phone, he tried calling her. After the fifth time that she didn't pick up, he become even more concerned.

"Marshall!" he shouted into his cell. "It's Olivia. She's missing from the hospital. Track her phone!"

"Yes, sir." Marshall hung up and returned to the desk, booting up the tracking software on her computer. She punched in Olivia's cell phone number and, within moments, found her location.

"Sir, it's me," she spoke softly into another cell phone. "Burnham called. He knows she's gone. Better tell Lucas to hurry up. He's running out of time. I'll stall as long as I can."

"Thank you, Cheryl."

"Make it quick. I can only give you a few minutes."

CHAPTER TWENTY-SEVEN

A BETTER PLACE

OLIVIA RACED TOWARD THE Charles River, her eyes searching through the torrential downpour for the enormous boathouse. Running along the riverbank, it seemed as if it got further away with each step. Finally reaching her destination, she took a deep breath and slowly opened the door, water dripping down her body.

"Hello?" she called out. "Is anyone here?"

Cautiously, she walked up an aisle of rowing boats stacked on beams, listening for some sort of clue as to where she should be headed.

A scream sounded and Olivia slowly followed the source through the warehouse-sized place, her stomach churning when she saw Melanie standing in the far corner, her wrists bound in front of her.

"Libby, don't. Please..." she cried out.

She paused, her eyes settling on someone standing behind Melanie and holding a knife to her throat. "Lucas?" She squinted, unable to believe her eyes. It was the guy they had all met and partied with in Vegas. She had never thought anything of it when he said he was from Boston. Now Olivia was starting to think it was all a set-up.

"Here's how this is going to work, *Libby*," Lucas sneered. "You scream, I cut her throat. You yell for help, I cut her throat. You do anything to draw attention *at all*, I cut her throat. Understand?"

Olivia slowly nodded her head, her eyes wide as she scanned

the boathouse for anything she could potentially use to disarm him.

"I thought we warned you what would happen if you didn't come forward, *Libby*."

"I don't know what you're talking about, Lucas," she said quietly as she took carefully measured steps toward Melanie.

"Yes you do, *Libby*." He pushed the blade even harder against Melanie's neck, tears streaming from her frightened blue eyes.

Olivia took a deep breath. "You're right. I do, Lucas. Why don't you let Melanie go and take me instead?"

"Libby, NO!" Melanie shouted.

Olivia's eyes met hers and she gave her scared friend a reassuring look.

"It doesn't work that way!" Lucas shouted, his voice showing his agitation. "I'm only supposed to encourage you to figure it out. That's all. I'm not allowed to kill you. That's someone else's job."

"Lucas, I'm the one you want. Not Melanie. Hurting her won't make me figure out whatever I'm supposed to." She took another step, closing the distance. Her heart beat frantically in her chest.

"Don't come any closer, *Libby*," Lucas demanded, digging the blade even further into Melanie's skin, blood seeping out of her neck. He pushed her hair back and leaned down, his lips only a breath away from her neck. "Remember what I told you. You make a sound, you die."

Melanie bit her lip, trying to hold in the scream that wanted to escape her mouth from the pain of the blade cutting into her throat.

Olivia stood only a few feet from Melanie and Lucas. She could try to grab the hand he was using to hold the knife, freeing Melanie, but that would only work if she could momentarily distract him. "Lucas, maybe if you gave me a hint about what I'm supposed to remember, then I can help you and we can put an end to all of this."

"Do you think they'd actually tell me that?" He threw his head back, laughing, and Olivia took the opportunity to try to disarm him.

Unfortunately, she wasn't quick enough.

~~~~~~~~~~

ALEXANDER NERVOUSLY PACED THE lobby of the hospital as he waited for Marshall to send him the location of Olivia's cell phone, hoping that she hadn't left the building. After an excruciatingly long time, a text finally came through. Dashing out the doors of the hospital, he jumped into the idling SUV. "Martin! Over to the big boathouse on the Charles!" he shouted. "Step on it!"

Martin peeled out of the hospital and drove toward the river. Several minutes later, he pulled up alongside the street. Alexander leaped out of the car, running toward the boathouse, not knowing what he would find when he got there. Quietly opening the door to the huge storage yard, he heard a scuffle echoing through the football field-sized warehouse. Turning the corner, his eyes grew wide in terror. "Olivia! No!"

Everything seemed to happen in slow motion as he ran toward her. A tall man that Alexander had never seen before had her pinned to the ground as she desperately tried to wrestle a knife from his hand. Melanie lay on the ground about ten feet away, bleeding profusely from her neck. He inhaled quickly, looking over her lifeless body. There was no way she would be able to survive a wound like that. How was he going to explain that to his brother?

He turned his attention back to the one person he could save...his Olivia. His heart dropped when he saw the man press the knife against her body, far too close to her heart.

~~~~~~~~~~

"COME ON, LIBBY. I thought you were stronger than that," Lucas breathed in her face. She was hopelessly trying to point the knife away from her chest and toward him.

"Lucas, let go of the knife. Remember, they said you couldn't hurt me."

He laughed. "Actually, they said I couldn't *kill* you. As long as you're alive, it doesn't matter what I do to you." He pushed her arms over her head, keeping her pinned to the ground and pressing the knife against her throat.

Olivia was using all her power to try to get Lucas off her. Losing strength, the knife drew a thin line of blood. "Lucas, please. Just let me go, and I promise I'll figure out whatever it is you guys are looking for." She opened her eyes and saw Alexander running toward them. *Hurry!* she thought. "Someone's coming, Lucas. You better get off me."

He turned to look, releasing the pressure on the knife just as Alexander approached.

"GET THE FUCK OFF HER!!!"

Within seconds, Lucas was thrown against the hard ground. Olivia lay perfectly still, frantically trying to calm her nerves, listening to punches being thrown. After just a few seconds that seemed like an eternity, she felt Alexander put his arms around her.

"Damn it, Olivia. Why the hell did you sneak out of the hospital?" he demanded. "You had me worried sick."

"That fucker called me! He said if I didn't come here that he'd kill…" She trailed off, her eyes settling on Melanie.

"I'm so sorry. I should have never left you alone. Are you okay?"

"No, Alex. I most certainly am *not* okay." She stood up and ran over to where Melanie lay on the ground. "NO!" she screamed upon seeing her lifeless body. She bent down, trying to find a pulse. "Come on, Mel," she begged, cradling her friend in her arms as she sat in a pool of her blood. "Don't you dare leave me here!" Tears fell down her face as she tried to save her friend. "Please!" Her hands were covered with Melanie's blood as she continued looking for a pulse, refusing to acknowledge the cold, hard truth of what she had just witnessed.

Alexander looked down while Olivia tried to save her friend. He did the only thing he could think of. He called his sister. "Carol, it's me. Have Dave get to the big boathouse on the Charles immediately. There's been an incident. Someone attacked Olivia and her friend," he said, his chin quivering as he turned away so Olivia couldn't overhear his conversation. "You should probably call Tyler, too." He took a deep breath before continuing, "Melanie's dead. Please hurry."

Alexander turned back to where Olivia sat hugging her friend in her arms. He walked up behind her, placing his hand on her shoulder as she cried, her chest heaving from her devastating sobs. "Olivia, love, please…" He didn't know what to say.

Olivia straightened her back, attempting to wipe her eyes with her hand, smudging Melanie's blood all over her face. "I need to get her to the hospital. She's been stabbed, Alex, and it's all because of me!" she cried out. She tried resuscitating her friend in a final act of desperation.

"Olivia, please," he begged her as he crouched down next to her. Placing his fingers against Melanie's neck, he shook his head dejectedly when there was no pulse to be found. "She's gone, love. I'm so sorry."

"NOOO!!!!" Olivia cried out, hugging Melanie in her arms, holding her tight, desperate for her to wake up and everything to be a bad dream. She clutched her friend as EMTs and police officers swarmed the location.

"Olivia, please, let go of her. She's in a better place," he pleaded with her, unable to hide his own tears. That very well could have been her lying there.

Alexander was right. She needed to be strong for her friend. Taking a deep breath, she stood up, leaving Melanie's body on the ground.

She was in a complete daze as she watched the paramedics check her non-existent vitals. She sank to the ground as crime scene technicians roped off the area, taking photos. She wanted to kill Lucas when she saw Carol's husband, David, place him in handcuffs and haul him off to the police station. She howled when she saw the medical examiner zip up Melanie's body bag.

"Olivia…" Alexander's voice brought her back as she watched the coroner's van drive off with her friend.

She immediately felt sick to her stomach just looking at him.

"I'm done, Alex. I can't live this way anymore." She raised herself off the ground and started to walk away, not caring that she was covered in blood.

"My sister told me about the letter left at Kiera's house!"

Olivia stopped in her tracks, spinning around, her eyes full of venom. "So you're here to tell me to not do anything stupid, am I right? Well, you're in luck because I have no idea what those fuckers are even after! Not even one clue!" She looked at him, his expression grim. "But you do, don't you?"

He remained silent as Olivia stalked over to him, standing a mere breath away. "You need to tell me everything you know, Alex. NOW! I'm done being left in the dark and letting you make all the decisions for me. I'm an adult! I need to make my own decisions! There's something going on, and these people are targeting my friends!"

"It's not about that, Olivia! I wanted to tell you everything, but you said you didn't want to talk about any of that. And now I can't, not after seeing that letter. Your life is in danger!"

She threw her head back, laughing sarcastically. "Ya' think?"

"No. You don't understand," he said, pleading with her. "If I tell you and you figure it all out, they'll kill you. As long as you remain ignorant of what they're after, you can't be touched. They're desperate for it and you're the only one who can help them. It's the only thing keeping you alive."

"But my *friends*, Alex!" she cried out, thinking about two of her closest friends and what they had to endure all because of her. "They're going after my friends." She glared at him. "They killed Mel. She's gone, and I was thinking that it's all my fault." She took a deep breath before continuing, "But it's not, Alexander. This is all *your* fault. I hope you can sleep well tonight with Melanie's blood on your hands!" She turned to walk away.

"I'm sorry, Olivia. I just can't risk losing you again. You've got to understand," he begged, running to catch up to her, desperate for her to grasp where he was coming from.

Olivia paused, looking deep into his eyes. "You can't risk losing me?" she hissed, her chin quivering. "Well, Alex, you just did." She pushed past him, bolting in the direction of the hospital.

"Olivia! PLEASE!!!" he shouted, watching as she ran away from him...again.

CHAPTER TWENTY-EIGHT

FOR MELANIE

OLIVIA RAN BACK TO the hospital, ignoring Alexander as he followed her. She was hysterical and needed her friends. They still had no idea what had happened to Melanie and she didn't know if she was strong enough to tell them. Guilt overwhelmed her when she noticed Tyler slumped in the corner of the waiting room, sobbing. Mo saw her and quickly ran over to her, wrapping his arms around her, not caring that she was covered in blood.

She bawled uncontrollably into his chest.

"It's okay, baby girl. Let it all out." He soothed her tears, rubbing her back.

Alexander looked down at Olivia in Mo's arms and felt overwhelming remorse for what had happened. Could he really have prevented it? At what cost?

Once Olivia's tears began to subside a bit, Mo pulled back, looking down at her tear-stained face. "Does Bridget know?"

Olivia shook her head. "I haven't called anyone yet. I know David was going to be notifying her parents, but no one knows yet…except for poor Tyler over there." She looked up and saw Alexander hovering just a few feet away, his eyes sad and pleading.

She turned toward him, glaring. "Please leave," she demanded.

Mo gave her a questioning look.

"I can't stand to look at you right now, Alex," she hissed. "I need my friends. Not you." She turned to walk away, wanting to be alone.

Alexander reached out and grabbed her arm. "Please. Olivia, love…"

Mo immediately shot his arm out, grabbing Alexander's. "Let her go." He glared at him and he begrudgingly released his hold on Olivia.

She darted down the hallway, hiding herself in the closest bathroom. Rushing to the sinks, she scrubbed at her skin in a feeble attempt to remove Melanie's dried blood from her body. Screaming in frustration, she collapsed on the floor. She buried her head in her lap, her tears soaking her blood-stained jeans as she thought how everything had taken such a horrible turn in the past few days.

"Olivia? Are you in there?" a gentle voice called out as her cries began to subside a short while later.

She raised her head out of her lap and wiped her eyes, pulling back the door to the bathroom and staring into Bridget's watery eyes. "I'm so sorry, Bridge." She wrapped her arms around her friend, clutching on to her.

"Hey, shut up. This is not your fault. You've got to stop thinking that," she cried out, tears flowing down her face.

Olivia hated how much everyone in her life seemed to be crying lately, including herself. She clung to Bridget, never wanting to let her out of her sight, afraid that something horrible would happen to her, as well.

"Come on, Libby. Everyone's here. We need you. We can't go through this without you. You can't go through this alone, either, okay?"

She nodded and allowed Bridget to lead her to the waiting room, hoping that Alexander had left. As soon as she entered, she couldn't keep from feeling guilty for how Tyler was feeling, his normal exuberant stature gone. All that was left was an empty shell of a man.

Giving Bridget a reassuring look, she made her way over to him. "Tyler…?" She wrapped her arms around the younger version of Alexander. "I'm so sorry. This is all my fault," she sobbed.

He looked at her through his blood-shot eyes. "It's not your fault, Libby. And it's not my brother's fault either. He told me everything," he whimpered. "If Mel was in your shoes, I'd do the same thing. I love her…" He took a steadying breath, trying to get his emotions under control. "I guess that's one of the things I learned being with her. That it's not worth it to hold grudges. Life is precious, Libby. Don't use this as an excuse to push Alex away. He loves you. He won't survive without you. Don't blame him for this. He didn't kill Mel. That fucker, Lucas, did. If there's anyone you should be angry at, it's him. Not the person who worships the ground you walk on. I've just lost the one girl I thought I could spend the rest of my life with. I wish I told her that while she was still alive."

Olivia watched in shock as he stood up and walked away. As she processed his words, she was unable to shake the thought that, had Alexander been honest with her from the beginning, Mel would still be alive.

"Miss Adler?" a voice whispered, bringing her back from her thoughts. Olivia looked up to see a couple in their late fifties standing in front of her. They had obviously just been crying.

"My name is Harold Brooks," a man with gray hair said. "This is my wife, Sandra." He gestured to the tall blonde woman standing next to him. "We're Melanie's parents."

Olivia stood up and embraced them as she tried to find the words that told them that their daughter's death was all her fault.

"We just want to thank you for everything you tried to do for our little girl today," Melanie's father said, his voice shaky as he surveyed Olivia, noticing his daughter's dried blood on her clothes.

"I'm so sorry, Mr. and Mrs. Brooks." Olivia sobbed even harder, knowing that Melanie would still be alive if it wasn't for her.

"Enough with the tears," Sandra said, releasing her hold on Olivia. "Melanie would hate to think that we were all here crying over her. She would never forgive herself if that was the case. She'd want us to only think of the happy moments we shared with her, and that's exactly what we'll do…" She trailed off, unable to follow her own words.

"She's always been a little demanding, hasn't she?" Olivia asked as she laughed through her tears.

Harold Brooks smiled. "She sure is...or was." His face became overwhelmed with emotion once more.

"It was wonderful to meet you. I'm sure you have friends and family that you want to be with, but please let me know the plans for her services whenever you know of them." Olivia gave them a compassionate look, her expression soft.

"Actually, I wanted to talk to you and your friend, Mo, about that," Sandra said, glancing at Mo standing just a few feet away. He immediately walked over.

"We were hoping that your band wouldn't mind playing a memorial show at the bar. She always loved going there to watch you perform, and it would mean a lot if we can pay our respects to her in a way that she would have wanted, with laughter instead of tears, at a place she felt at home. We both grew up in New Orleans and this is how we like to say good-bye...a celebration of her life, not a sad reminder of her death."

Olivia glanced at Mo. "What do you think?" she asked. "I mean, what about Kiera...?"

He stopped her. "Livvy, Kiera would want us to do this. For Melanie."

Olivia nodded her head in agreement. "For Melanie."

~~~~~~~~~~

AFTER LEAVING THE HOSPITAL that evening, Olivia stormed through her house, slamming doors. She knew full well that it wasn't going to fix anything, but it certainly made her feel better. She was so angry with Alexander. She gave him a choice...tell her what she wanted to know or risk losing her. She couldn't believe that he continued to keep secrets from her, not when it nearly tore them apart. She wanted to scream. Then she heard her mama's words again: *Music is the best solution to any problem.* Olivia leaned her head back and looked at the ceiling as if talking to the sky. "I sure hope you're right,

Mama. I could really use a solution to this chaotic world I've found myself in."

She ran up to the third floor of her house, sat down at the piano, and did what she did best. She lost herself in the music and, for a minute, everything was okay.

When Olivia finally came out of the music room, she had no idea what time it was or even how long she had been in there. Time always seemed to stand still when she surrounded herself with beautiful lyrics and melodies. It was the only thing that made her forget about everything. But outside the walls of her music room, the cruel reality of what had happened set in.

Reluctantly, Olivia walked down the two flights of stairs and into the living room. Her stomach growled loudly and she couldn't remember the last time she had actually eaten. After the past several days, she had no desire to cook so she ordered take-out from her and Kiera's favorite Chinese bistro.

She grabbed her purse and started to head out to pick up some wine. As she walked down her front steps, she purposely ignored the black SUV sitting outside of her house...or, at least, she ignored it for about two seconds, her hard stare softening when her eyes met Alexander's. She was furious at him but, deep down, she knew that she was still madly in love with him.

After selecting a few bottles of wine at the local liquor store, she walked back to her house, arriving just as her food was being delivered. Alexander stood on the doorstep, paying her regular delivery guy. She snatched it out of his hand before turning away from him and entering her house, slamming the door behind her.

"Not even a thank you?!" he shouted through the closed door.

"Thank you, okay?" she replied sarcastically.

"Olivia, please. Can we talk?" he asked, his voice soft and full of pain, his head resting on the door.

"You had your chance to come clean, Alex. You chose to put your own needs above mine. So no, we can't talk."

"I love you, Olivia."

She lowered herself and sat against the wall, leaning her

head on the door. "I love you, too, Alex. With all my heart, and maybe that's exactly where I should keep you. In my heart, but out of my life."

"You can't mean that," he said quietly.

"I don't know. Maybe I do. I just…"

"I'm only trying to protect you, Olivia. Keep you safe. You have to understand where I'm coming from with all of this. I thought I lost you all those years ago, and when I found out that you were alive, I promised myself that I'd never let anything bad happen to you again. So I need to keep you in the dark. For now, though…"

His heart raced when he heard the door open. He met Olivia's large brown eyes.

"Unless you're ready to tell me *everything* you know, please go." She turned and slammed the door in his face again.

Fighting back tears, she walked into the kitchen and put her food on a plate. After pouring a glass of wine, she sat in the bay window with her dinner and stared out at the black SUV into the eyes of the man she knew she would always love, no matter what.

CHAPTER TWENTY-NINE

WAIT FOR YOU

THE FOLLOWING MORNING, OLIVIA was woken up by a loud banging at her door. She stretched her neck, sore from having fallen asleep in the bay window. She looked outside and saw that the black SUV was empty. Groaning, she got up and walked over to the door, checking the peephole to see who was outside...even though she knew who it was. "Are you ready to tell me everything, Alexander?" she asked through the closed door.

"Olivia," he said with a hint of urgency in his voice. "It's Kiera. She's awake."

She swung the door open, her eyes wide. "Really?"

Alexander nodded.

She jumped into his arms. "Take me to see her. Please," she said, her voice soft as she nuzzled against his neck, inhaling his scent.

"Oh, Olivia. Do you have any idea how much I love you? You have to believe that I never meant..."

"I love you, too, Alexander," she interrupted, pulling out of his embrace and hardening her stare. "I just don't like you very much right now, and I refuse to be in a relationship with someone who keeps secrets from me. Just take me to the hospital to see my best friend."

Alexander grabbed her hand and led her down the steps toward the waiting SUV. Within minutes, he pulled up in front of the hospital and Olivia ran out of the car toward the sliding glass doors without even saying good-bye.

"Olivia, wait!" he shouted, jumping out of the car to catch up to her.

"What is it, Alex?" she asked, spinning around, an irritated expression on her face. "I need to go see Kiera."

"Do you want me to come with you?"

"It's a free country." She shrugged. "Do what you want."

"Where does this leave us?" he asked, his eyes full of hope.

Annoyed, she crossed her arms in front of her body. "In the same place we were the *last* time you decided to keep secrets from me. I can't trust you. I can't spend the rest of my life with someone never knowing if they're keeping me in the dark on matters that concern me, all in the guise of trying to protect me! I won't do it!" She spun on her heels, walking through the doors of the large brick building.

Alexander chased after her, not caring that the SUV was parked in a tow-away zone, and found her at the registration desk. "Olivia, please. Tell me how I can fix this and earn back your trust. Whatever it is, I'll do it."

She put down the pen after signing in and turned to face him, looking at his disheveled appearance. There were circles underneath his eyes and he had facial hair coming in. His clothes were wrinkled from sitting in his car all night. He looked broken, but she refused to feel guilty. It was all his fault, no matter what his brother had tried to convince her of the day before. "All I want from you is the one thing you refuse to give me. I want to know who I am...who I was. Why are these people trying to take my friends away from me? Why did they kill Mel? What is it they think I know?"

Alexander exhaled loudly and ran his hands through his hair, contemplating what he should do. He was at a crossroads. He tried to put himself in Olivia's position. How would he feel if he found out that his entire life had been a lie and that the people he had come to trust continued to keep secrets from him?

"You want to know who you are?" He took a step closer and looked in her eyes, their bodies almost touching. "Your name is Olivia Marilyn DeLuca. You were born on October sixteenth almost twenty-nine years ago, and you were the most adorable baby I had ever seen." He smiled at the memory. "Granted, I was only two the first time I held you, but I knew then that I would do everything in my power to keep you safe."

He brushed that same errant curl out of her face before continuing, "You were such a pain in the ass when you were a kid, always irritating the piss out of me. We would fight. We would argue. But then we would always apologize to each other because we both knew, deep down, that we couldn't survive without each other."

His voice began to tremble with emotion as he continued talking. He brought Olivia's body flush with his and held her face in his hands. "This is what we do, Olivia. This is who we are. Not much has changed since we were kids. We fight. We piss each other off. But at the end of the day, we realize that no matter how mad and angry we are at each other, there is something much bigger at work here. You can stay angry at me all you want, love, but you know, deep down, that you cannot live without me. You love me just as much as I love you and nothing will ever come between that." He wiped the tear that had fallen down her cheek and stared into her eyes, searching for an answer.

"I can't do this right now," she said quietly, turning away from him and heading down the long corridor to the ICU.

"I'll wait for you, Olivia. I'll always wait for you."

She continued walking, refusing to turn around to face him, knowing that his words were true.

~~~~~~~~~~~

"LIBBY!" KIERA WEAKLY CRIED out after she saw her practically run into the hospital room.

Olivia rushed to her side, hugging her friend. She looked awake, but groggy.

"Ouch. Not so hard."

"I'm sorry." Tears streamed down Olivia's face. "I'm just so glad that you're okay."

"What happened?" Kiera asked, her voice raspy. "I can't remember anything."

She clutched Kiera's hands in hers, looking down at her frail frame, not wanting to tell her anything, not knowing if she could even say the words. "Don't worry about any of that right now, Care Bear. You just worry about getting your ass out of this hospital bed, okay?"

"Okay, Libby." She squeezed Olivia's hand. "I heard about Melanie…" she quivered, tears welling in her eyes.

"I'm so sorry. It's all my fault," Olivia sobbed, looking down.

"Stop it, Libby. Mo said you were going to say that. He doesn't understand why you're blaming yourself and neither do I," she scolded her. "You couldn't have prevented any of this from happening. Okay?"

Olivia's chin trembled, wondering if she would ever be able to stop blaming herself for what had happened to Melanie and Kiera. The guilt wore her down. Looking into Kiera's green eyes, she simply nodded, not wanting to talk about it anymore. Instead, the two girls held each other and mourned the loss of their friend, reminiscing about all the good times they shared.

"Oh, good. You're here." Mo said, breaking the moment and carrying a few cups of coffee. "I tried calling your phone and you weren't answering so I called Alex. I'm assuming you got the message."

"Good assumption," she replied sarcastically, wiping her tears.

He raised his eyebrow at her, silently questioning if everything was all right.

She knew that she would have to tell him what was going on, but she wasn't ready yet. "Well, I'll give you two some privacy." She got up from her chair. "I'll be back in a little bit to check on you. Okay, Care Bear?"

Kiera smiled weakly at her. "You got it."

Olivia turned to leave.

"Oh, and Libby?"

"Yes?" she replied, facing Kiera.

"Whatever stick crawled up your ass these past few weeks, please remove it."

Olivia stared at her friend in shock. "What are you talking

about?"

"You. Being a bitch to us and everyone around you, including Alexander," she said, her voice raised. She glanced at Mo as he clutched her hand. Her expression immediately softened when she met his eyes. "This whole incident made me realize how much I appreciate what I have in my life, including the people in it." She met Olivia's gaze. "I love you, Libby. You know that. But you've got to stop shutting people out just because they fuck up and make a mistake."

Olivia looked down, feeling guilty that she had treated her friends so poorly. But, at the same time, she was the reason that Kiera had been hurt and that Melanie was dead. She could put a stop to everything if Alexander would just come clean to her, but he refused. "It's not as simple as that, Kiera." She exhaled.

"Well, humor me then." She smirked. "I've got nothing on my busy schedule today, except healing from a few bullet wounds." Her voice was heavy with sarcasm. Olivia was happy that the attack didn't seem to diminish Kiera's spirit all that much.

She retreated back into the hospital room, pulling up a chair next to Mo. "Well, I guess you both should probably hear this." She proceeded to tell Mo and Kiera about her dad being alive and running into him at MacFadden's. Then she told them about the letter that Carol had found in Kiera's house. She struggled to fight back the tears as she told them about Lucas killing Melanie to try to get Olivia to remember whatever it was they wanted her to.

"I know he's still keeping information from me, and the reason he's doing it is to protect me. He says that if I remember, he could lose me."

"Do you really blame him, Libby? Look what's happened to poor Mel. And me!" Kiera screeched. "I can't believe you're really going to stay angry at him for keeping you safe…" She trailed off, wishing she had someone looking out for her when she was attacked.

"Do you have any idea who's behind everything? Maybe that will help," Mo said calmly.

Olivia took a deep breath. "I don't see how. Nobody knows who is pulling the strings here. Carol and Alexander have apparently worked tirelessly trying to figure it all out, but no one has a clue. The only person they know of is this Mark Kiddish guy, but he's just a hired goon. Even then, there's no hard evidence that he's actually involved. At least not enough that the police can open an investigation into him. Regardless, if he's out of the picture, they'll just replace him with someone new. It won't end until they have what they want. And what they want is me...my memories. I'm the best shot at saving my friends, but only if I can remember. Alexander knows that so he's keeping my past from me. He knows what they want and he won't tell me."

"Wait a sec," Kiera said. "What about your dad? Can't you talk to him about it?"

"Carol is worried about me doing that. She said that his identity has been kept a secret for a reason and until they can figure it out, it's best that I stay as far away from him as possible so that he doesn't get hurt...or worse. I have no way of getting in touch with him anyway."

"Don't do anything stupid, Livvy," Mo said. "Don't think about that letter..."

"How can I *not* think about that letter?!" she shrieked, standing up and glaring down at her two friends. "It pretty much said that I'm the reason my friends are being targeted!" She took a deep breath before continuing, "Right now, I'm the best shot at keeping everyone safe, but the only way I can do that is by figuring out what these guys are after. And the only person who can help me with that is Alexander. His refusal to tell me what I need is putting my friends' lives in jeopardy."

Olivia spun on her heels and stormed out of the room, not wanting to listen to her friends try to talk any sense into her. She knew she sounded irrational, but she refused to admit that Alexander was doing the right thing by keeping her past from her.

CHAPTER THIRTY

COME CLEAN

AS OLIVIA WALKED THROUGH the front door of MacFadden's and up to the second floor several weeks later, she was unsure of whether she would have enough inner strength to get through that night. Waves of emotion rushed over her when she saw the swarms of people there for Melanie's memorial celebration. Huge photos of the chipper blonde adorned all the walls, people scribbling their good-byes on them through their tear-soaked eyes.

Feeling a lump form in her throat, Olivia dashed to the bar, desperately wanting to forget about everything that had happened...or at least down a few drinks to try to numb the pain that was starting to take over. After gulping back the amber liquid, she began to relax.

"Is this seat taken?"

Olivia stilled at the voice. She sighed and turned to face Alexander. "No. Have a seat."

He flagged down a bartender and placed his drink order, Olivia signaling for another drink, as well.

"Carol said that she saw you down at the station earlier." He attempted to make small talk.

"Yeah. They had more questions about Lucas and his brother, Dylan, if that really *is* his brother."

Alexander nodded, proceeding with caution now that Olivia was finally talking to him. Over the past few weeks, things had been awkward between them. She continued to live at her old brownstone on Commonwealth Avenue, but would let him in anytime he appeared at her door. She rebuked every attempt he made to help her see why he was refusing to tell her what those guys were after. Instead, they would sit on the couch together in silence, Olivia glaring at him, hoping that he would finally crack and come clean.

"How many times are they going to have you go down to answer more questions? I'll talk to Carol and have them come to your house. You shouldn't have to be inconvenienced."

Olivia took a sip of her fresh drink and turned to face him, noticing how gaunt he looked. It was obvious that he hadn't been sleeping well. Guilt overwhelmed her conscience for causing the painful appearance that he exuded. She felt the same way. She hated life without Alexander and she wanted nothing more than to go back to the way things were before, although she knew that too much had happened for that to be possible. "I don't mind," she said.

"Have they found anything?"

She shook her head in resignation. "No. They haven't been able to uncover any evidence linking Melanie's death to anyone other than Lucas, no matter what I've told them happened in the boathouse."

"They've questioned me regarding what I know about Mark Kiddish, but that's been a dead end, too. As far as they're concerned, his name change to Donovan O'Laughlin was reasonable after his father's disappearance, and he runs a legitimate consulting business with strong ties to the community. Without any actual proof that this guy is behind it, there's not much that can be done."

"They told me the same thing. The phone call was traced to Lucas' cell so they couldn't find anything there. And the asshole has refused to answer any questions, other than insisting that he was working alone. He's definitely playing the deranged psycho rather well. So, based on his answers and the fact that they've found nothing on his supposed brother, Dylan, it's not looking like this will lead back to anyone other than him."

"I'm sorry," he said, shifting nervously on his barstool. "How's Kiera doing?"

"Better. She still has no memory of what happened that night, and neither Mo nor I really want to be the one to tell her." She glanced at him and he gave her a knowing look before she returned her attention to the drink in front of her. "It's almost like her brain is trying to protect her from remembering what she probably endured those twelve hours. She's starting to perk up a bit and she doesn't appear to be in too much pain anymore. I was just there with her before I had Agent Marshall drive me here."

"Thanks for that...for having her drive you."

Olivia turned her head and gave him an icy stare before softening her expression, almost pleading with him to finally tell her the reason why he wants her to have constant protection...to tell her what those men are after.

"You need to understand where I'm coming from here, Olivia." He answered the question that was written plain as day on her face.

She sighed. "I get it, Alex. I really do. I understand your reasons, and so do the police. Unfortunately, they're on your side here. But I don't want to be left in the dark. I don't want you keeping all this information, holding it over me, saying that it's too dangerous for me to even know about my own past. Let me make those decisions." Olivia got up from her barstool, needing to distance herself from him before she broke down and jumped back into his arms.

"That house in Newport!" he shouted, getting her attention. She turned around to face him, her eyes narrowed as she crossed her arms defensively in front of her body. He lowered his voice. "The one you had me stop at when we were there for the marathon."

She glared at him. "What about it, Alex?" she hissed.

He ran his hands through his hair, looking rather vulnerable. "We used to go there a fair bit when we were kids. Your mom would take us up there from time to time. There was such a huge yard, and we would run all over playing hide-and-seek."

"Why did we go there, Alex? Who lived there?" she asked, not sure if she really wanted to know.

He took a deep breath. "Your grandparents live there."

Olivia let out a small cry. "Live?" Her lower lip trembled. "As in present tense?"

"Yes," he answered quietly. "Harris House. Your mother's maiden name was Harris." He hoped that maybe if he started to slowly feed her information about her past, she would forget about wanting to know what Mark Kiddish was after.

As she took in what he was saying, a hurt look spread across her face. She seethed with anger when she realized that he was keeping so much information from her. She had a family that she didn't even know about, but he knew. She spun on her heels, needing to get up on stage to start their performance.

"Olivia, love!" Alexander cried out. "I'm sorry. I should have told you sooner."

She refused to turn around, instead walking onto the stage, sitting down at the piano.

"Hey, Livvy," Mo greeted her as he strapped on his guitar. "Everything okay?" He nodded to where Alexander was standing, imploring her with his eyes.

She laughed. "You know what, Mo? I have no idea how to even answer that question anymore."

"Neither do I," he said before turning and stepping up to the microphone. "Good evening, friends. We'd like to start by thanking everyone for being here tonight to celebrate the life of Melanie Erica Brooks, beloved daughter and friend to all of you." Mo took a deep breath before continuing, "Mel's parents asked us to play a memorial for her here tonight, and a few people are going to get up and talk about her. After that, they're going to open the upstairs for everyone and we'll play our normal set. It's what Mel would have wanted…"

Mo was starting to crack. Olivia looked at the crowd that had gathered to pay their respects. She immediately felt the need to be the strong one that night. Many of her work friends were gathered in the audience, huddling together, shedding tears as they thought about the bubbly girl who sat at the front desk of the wellness center nearly every day. Her eyes continued scanning the room, finding Tyler standing in the corner, Alexander and Carol comforting and supporting him.

Olivia grabbed the microphone off the piano and stood up, needing to do something to try and mute the sobs that echoed through the large room. "Melanie wouldn't have wanted us to be crying for her. We need to remember the girl she was..." Olivia trailed off. She took a deep breath, trying to subdue the lump that was forming in her throat, tears threatening to fall once more. "I guess I'm one to talk." The audience laughed politely, many of them wiping their eyes.

"I remember the day Melanie came in for her interview at the wellness center. I knew right then and there that she was perfect for the job. She had so much energy. You couldn't help but smile when she greeted you at the front desk. She was always cheerful, no matter what was going on in her life. You see, that's the thing about Mel. You never really knew what was going on in her life. It was never about Mel. With her, it was always about you. She was always more concerned with *your* problems than her own. She was a psych major at Northeastern, and she would have been a fantastic therapist... I should know." The crowd laughed again as Olivia's eyes met Alexander's.

A small tear escaped before she composed herself. "So tonight we're going to remember our dear friend...a friend who was taken from us far too soon, but whose memory will go on." She turned and walked back to the piano while Mo introduced the first song they would be performing.

The next hour seemed to pass by relatively quickly with a few people getting on stage to talk about Melanie, some performing different poems and others barely managing to get through what they wanted to say. The band played between speakers, mostly upbeat songs that Melanie enjoyed and her parents had requested.

After the final speaker finished, Mo walked over and traded places with Olivia, sitting behind the piano. She grabbed a microphone, as did the rest of the band members. They stood alongside Olivia, ready to finish the song if she couldn't do it.

Taking a step forward, she addressed the audience. "This last song we'll be doing is one our good friend, Kiera, who couldn't be here tonight, requested we perform. I'm sorry if it makes some of you cry…" Olivia took another deep breath. "Hell, I'm not even sure if I'll be able to get through it. This is *Be Still* by The Fray."

Mo began to play, the simple chords of the song filling the bar. Not a sound could be heard, apart from the gentle melody coming from the piano.

Alexander listened as Olivia sang the simple haunting tune, saying good-bye to Melanie. He didn't even know the girl that well, but he couldn't help but feel Olivia's loss…and Tyler's. He glanced around the bar and everyone was breaking out tissues, crying softly for the unbearable pain of losing someone so young.

His eyes found Melanie's parents in the audience, remorse overwhelming him as he watched them clutching on to each other. Seeing their bodies shake from their tears, he wondered whether he was doing the right thing. His failure to tell Olivia everything may have caused their pain. Was their suffering really worth it? He was unsure. He knew the pain they were going through all too well. He went through the same thing when he thought he had lost Olivia all those years ago. Now that he knew where she was, was it his fault that those poor people had lost their own daughter?

There wasn't a dry eye in the place when Olivia finished the song. She took a deep breath, surprised that she had actually made it all the way through without cracking. She looked down, grabbing her glass off the barstool in front of her and raised it. "To Melanie," she said, her chin quivering as the emotion of the song overcame her.

She ran off the stage, desperately needing a friend, only to remember that two of the people she normally ran to when she was upset weren't there. Kiera was in the hospital and Melanie would never be able to smack some sense into her again. It broke Olivia's heart. She ran toward the restroom, wondering why she even cared if people saw her crying. Half the audience was still sobbing. Midway across the room, she stopped and sank to the ground, not able to take another step, her cries overtaking her entire body.

"Hey, hey," Mo said, rushing to her and sitting on the floor next to her, pulling her into his arms. He looked up to see Alexander standing over them both. Mo glared at him in warning and he took several steps back, giving them their space.

"It's not fair, Mo," Olivia sobbed, using his shirt as a tissue. "I just don't want to admit that she's gone, and this feels so final. I'm just not ready to say good-bye to her..."

"Shhhh..." Mo soothed her. "This isn't good-bye. You don't have to say good-bye to her. This is just kind of 'until we meet again'."

"I want to fucking kill them all, Mo. I'm sorry. I just can't stop crying. I wish I could, but I can't."

Olivia felt another set of arms around her and glanced to her left to see Bridget carrying a box of tissues, joining her and Mo on the floor. "I came prepared," she joked through her own tears, handing Olivia the box.

She smiled weakly. "I wish I had."

Mo rubbed her back, helping her work through her tears. As they subsided, he grabbed her chin, bringing her eyes flush with his. "Feel better now, baby girl?"

She nodded.

"Good. Because we've got a show to do," he replied, pulling both Olivia and Bridget up.

"I'll be right there," Olivia said. "Just give me a minute."

"Okay, baby girl," Mo said, hugging her and planting a chaste kiss on her forehead.

She walked over to the bar to get another drink, watching as Melanie's parents took down all the photos of their daughter. Many of the guests left the area as normal bar patrons began to flood the second floor to see the band perform their regular set.

Olivia approached Melanie's mother as she was about to remove a framed photo from the piano. "Leave that one," she said, grabbing her arm. "Please..." she implored.

Sandra smiled. "Of course. And thank you, Olivia, dear. I know you must be so confused right now, thinking that this is all Alexander's fault."

Olivia looked at her in shock.

"Tyler told us all about it and we spoke with Alexander this evening. He feels extremely guilty for what happened but, the thing is, I don't blame him. And I don't blame you. The only person I blame is sitting in a jail cell right now."

"But if he hadn't kept secrets from me, none of this would have happened."

Sandra took a deep breath. "Maybe. Maybe not. We'll never know. But what I *do* know is that it's not worth losing someone over. Haven't you already lost enough?"

Olivia looked at her and simply nodded. "Maybe I just want him to stop keeping things from me."

"Oh, dear," Sandra said, smiling. Melanie looked so much like her mother. The resemblance was remarkable. "We always tend to keep things from people we love to protect them. It's our human nature." She wrapped her arms around Olivia. "Thank you for everything."

Olivia contemplated her words for a moment as she watched her walk away. Maybe she was right. She had lost enough already. Losing Melanie was one more person than she had ever wanted to, and here she was pushing Alexander away because he was trying to protect her. But she wanted to know who she was.

Mo walked up to Olivia, a concerned look on his face. "Hey. Are you okay? You ready?"

Olivia looked over to see Alexander standing at the bar, drinking a beer.

"Yes." Olivia climbed onto the stage, helping the guys rearrange the set and pushing the baby grand piano toward the center. Dale sat behind the drum set and Mo stood off to the side with his guitar as the other band members hung back.

"How's everyone doing tonight?" she asked, her voice void of emotion. She took a deep breath and began to introduce her song. "Sorry if we're kind of out of it tonight, but we all lost a dear friend a few weeks ago. Her name was Melanie Brooks and that's her photo sitting on the piano. I hate to think her death could have been avoided if it weren't for all the fucking secrets." She looked at Alexander, his eyes growing wide in response to her words. "I don't know what else I can say to you anymore," she continued, her voice quivering. "I just want the truth." Taking a deep breath, she positioned her hands on the piano. "This is *Come Clean* by Tristan Prettyman."

Alexander listened as she began to play the opening chords of the song, her sad voice filling the bar. Her eyes met his as she begged him to tell her what she wanted to know. At that instant, he realized that Olivia deserved to know who she was, where she came from. She deserved to know her family and it was selfish for him to keep her past from her any longer, regardless of what the consequences were.

He turned away, unable to look into her cold, hard stare any longer. As he walked out of the bar, he knew the only way to hold on to her was to do what she was begging him to do. He needed to come clean.

CHAPTER THIRTY-ONE

BELONG TOGETHER

"DELIVERY FOR MISS ADLER," Olivia heard one morning several weeks later, waking her up.

She groggily dragged herself off the couch toward the front door. "Who the fuck is banging at my door on a Friday morning?" she muttered under her breath. She looked through the peephole and saw several men dressed in military fatigues with boxes stacked high.

"What is all of this?" she asked, opening the door, glancing up the street. A disappointed look crossed her face when she met Carter's eyes and not Alexander's sitting watch outside in the SUV. He had been mysteriously absent from her security detail since Melanie's memorial service. She wondered if he had decided to move on, not wanting to give her the information that she longed for.

"We're not privy to the contents, ma'am," he answered in a very matter-of-fact manner. "Mr. Burnham just asked us to safeguard the boxes as they were transported here this morning."

"Okay..." She stepped aside to allow the men to enter her house, her heart fluttering in her chest at the mention of Alexander's name.

"Where would you like everything? There are over fifty boxes."

She led them to the large guest bedroom off the living room. "Go ahead and put them in here, please." She watched as the men entered her home and stacked the boxes, rather efficiently, where she had asked them to. One person checked off the numbers on the boxes, matching them with a spreadsheet as they were brought in. Once he was able to ensure that everything was present and accounted for, Olivia signed the manifest and was left alone in her house, wondering what all the boxes contained. She spied an enveloped attached to one and decided to begin there.

My Dearest Olivia,

I've thought long and hard about what to do. I know that you're desperate for information about your past. I hope you find some answers in these boxes. My dad, apparently, kept everything that belonged to you so I'm returning it all. Maybe these will help you to remember your life before the accident.

What I don't want to tell you, but I know I have to, is what those men are after. You see, your father was a CIA analyst and he became suspicious that certain people in the agency and other governmental agencies were making deals for U.S. military equipment and intelligence with known terror organizations. He had amassed evidence to that tune. Instead of keeping it at work where anyone could have found out what he did, he brought it home. He became concerned that someone was onto him, so he wanted to hide it. He locked it in a small chest for safekeeping until he could turn it over to the right hands. Of course, you were just a little girl at the time and you didn't know, but you wanted to play your little Treasure Map game. That's why these guys are after you. You hid those documents and these people want them.

Please heed my warning. These people are dangerous, Olivia. If you do remember what happened to that chest you buried all those years ago, your usefulness is gone. They will kill you, and I cannot have that happen. We will find a way to make sure that everyone gets taken down and that you survive. I will protect you.

I will always protect you.

I love you with all my heart.

Yours forever,
   Alexander

P.S. - Please burn this letter immediately upon reading. XOXO - Your

Smiling, she grabbed a matchbook from her mantle in the living room and held the flame to the piece of paper, knowing that Alexander wouldn't want that information getting into the wrong hands. Retreating back into the guest room, she lifted the lid off the first box she saw and began sorting through all the photos she came across.

There were hundreds, spanning the first six years of her life. A tear escaped when she found one from when she was probably not even a week old. A small boy sat in a rocking chair, holding a little baby with a full head of dark hair. She turned the photo over and saw what she remembered to be her mother's handwriting.

Alex (2 years) and Olivia (5 days) – Mystic house.

She lived in Mystic. Maybe that's why everything seemed so familiar when Alexander took her there. Anxious to learn more, she spent all day sorting through hundreds of old photos. She would laugh and cry, sometimes both at the same time, as memories came flooding back.

Alexander really was an important part of her life from early on. He was in nearly every photo with her. There were pictures from birthday parties, summers on the beach, and various holidays.

The hours wore on as she continued to learn about the life that she knew nothing about. She had rummaged through a few boxes, but was beginning to feel overwhelmed by everything that still remained.

She decided to sort through one more box before calling it a night. Her heart stopped when she pulled back the lid. "Mr. Bear!" she cried out, grabbing the stuffed animal and hugging it close to her body. The large powder pink bear must have been the same size as she was as a little girl. Inhaling deeply, she snuggled with her childhood toy.

A memory came flooding back. She had gone to the boardwalk with Alexander and her mother one summer day while they were spending time at the beach. Olivia remembered what a whiny little brat she had been as a child and was surprised that Alexander would even put up with it when he could have been playing with other boys.

She had seen that bear as a prize at one of the boardwalk game stands. She begged and begged for Alexander to win it for her. He had spent nearly all afternoon trying to capture the prize she wanted. As they were about to close for the day, he finally got the ring around the bottle. Olivia remembered kissing him on the mouth.

"You got that bear the day you kissed me for the first time."

Olivia turned her head toward the doorway, surprised to see Alexander standing there, his hands sheepishly placed in his pockets. "Yeah, but I had to give myself a cooties shot after that, if I recall correctly." She smirked playfully at him.

He grinned, taking a few steps closer to where Olivia sat on the floor, clutching her bear. "Yes. You did. Do you remember what you said that day?" he asked, sitting down next to her.

She stared deep into his eyes. "I told you that you'd have to marry me to make an honest woman out of me."

Alexander erupted in laughter, the sound bringing a smile to Olivia's face. "That you did." His eyes narrowed and his laughter died down. "I still plan on marrying you, Olivia."

She sighed, looking at her bear. "I know, Alexander. You've just dropped a bomb on me and I need some time to process all of this."

"Okay," he replied, clutching her hands in his. "I'll give you all the time you need. Just please don't do anything stupid now that you know everything."

Olivia stood up, grabbing her bear. "But I don't know everything. I can't remember playing that Treasure Map game for the life of me."

He raised himself off the floor and walked over to her, placing his hands on her shoulders. "Hey, it's okay." His voice was full of compassion. "That's what all this stuff is here for…to help you remember. It's going to take more than a day to figure it all out, but I'm here to fill in the blanks if you need me to."

Olivia lifted herself onto her tiptoes and placed a soft kiss on his lips. "Thank you, Alexander." She looked at him and his eyes were still closed.

"God, your lips are so soft."

She pressed her lips to his again. He moaned before slipping his tongue in her mouth, caressing hers. Olivia giggled, pulling away from the kiss. "You better watch it, or I'm going to have to give myself another cooties shot."

He grabbed her waist and pulled her body flush with his. "I think we're far past worrying about cooties, don't you agree?" His eyes became hooded and Olivia's heart started to race.

She nodded and dropped Mr. Bear to the ground, unable to break her eyes away from Alexander's.

He gently lowered his mouth to hers.

"I still haven't forgiven you," she murmured against his lips.

"What's it going to take for you to do that?" He planted soft kisses up and down her neck.

"Tell me. Please, Alexander."

He pulled back, searching her eyes. "What, love?"

"You know what. I want to hear you say it. What you used to call me all those years ago. What I've heard you calling me in my dreams all these years."

A sly grin crossed his face. "I love you, Olibia."

Her heart swelled and she grabbed his head in her hands, forcing his lips against hers.

He picked her up and pinned her against the wall.

She wrapped her legs around his waist.

"Do you feel that, baby? You feel what you do to me?" he asked, thrusting himself against her, burying his head in her neck.

Olivia was aflame with the sensations coursing through her body from Alexander's touch.

"Tell me you feel this, Olivia," he begged. "Tell me you feel how much I love you. How much I can't live without you."

"I do, Alexander. I feel it," she said, her breathing heavy.

"Then why do you constantly keep fighting it?"

She stared into his deep green eyes and shook her head. "I don't know," she whispered.

He crushed his lips back to hers, invading her mouth. "Hold on tight, beautiful." He held on to her thighs and she tightened her grasp around his neck as he carried her up to the bedroom, slowly lowering her delicate frame onto the bed.

Olivia kept her eyes trained on him as he quickly stripped out of his clothes. Climbing on the bed, he planted soft kisses down her collarbone, slowly lifting her shirt over her head. She bucked him with her hips.

"Something I can help you with?" he asked with a hint of amusement in his voice.

"I need to feel your flesh on mine, Alex. I've missed this. Please."

"Your wish is my desire." He lowered his body down hers and swiftly helped her remove her jeans and panties before making quick work of her bra.

He raised himself back up, their eyes meeting. "Have I told you how much I've missed you?" He caressed her forehead in an affectionate manner. "I'm not talking about just these past few weeks, Olivia," he said sweetly. "When I was growing up, too. I missed you so much. I never gave up hope that I would find you. You're my heart. I love you, Olibia."

She grabbed his neck and forced her lips to his mouth, invading it with her tongue and running her fingers up and down his back. She was so overwhelmed with emotion at Alexander's passionate words.

"Alex," she said breathlessly, tearing her mouth away from his while he gently nibbled at her neck. She threw her head back, giving him easier access. Her body flamed with lust and yearning from his attentive touch.

"What is it, Olivia?" he asked between kisses.

"I need you." She wrapped her legs around his waist. "Please, Alexander," she implored, closing her eyes as millions of tremors ran through her veins. He wasn't even inside her, but she felt like she was ready to fall apart. She was experiencing the same amazing sense of excitement from his closeness as she did the very first time she set eyes on him on State Street a year ago.

"Say it, Olivia," he whispered against her neck. "Please. I

need to hear those words come out of your mouth." His voice was soft and sincere.

She opened her eyes, gazing at the boy with green eyes. "Alexander, I need you to make love to me."

He brought his hand up to her face, gently caressing her cheek. She leaned into him as he lovingly admired her. "You are so beautiful, Olivia," he whispered, brushing that one wayward curl out of her eyes. His lips met hers, their kiss delicate as he ran his hand up and down her body, savoring every inch of her silky flesh.

She moaned into his mouth, his hand leaving a trail of fire as it roamed her body. "Please, Alexander. I need to feel you."

He grinned. "You will. Let me love you, Olivia. Good things come to those who wait."

She threw her arm over her head, ready to fall apart from just a simple brush of his hand. "I'm dying here. Please."

"Patience, beautiful," he winked as he lowered his head, gently licking her collarbone, his lips traveling down to her breasts. He circled her nipple with his tongue, blowing on it. Olivia arched her back in response, savoring the warmth of his tongue and the cold air on her chest. "I love your breasts, Olivia," he said sweetly. "Just one of the many things about you that I love." He returned his mouth to her, licking and sucking as he made his way down her body.

Her breathing became ragged in anticipation when she sensed his warm breath between her legs. She was pretty sure that the second she felt his tongue on her, she would come undone. Her mind raced as she thought how one person could have such an effect on her. It was unlike anything she ever thought possible. Maybe it was because they belonged together, like Alexander had said time and time again.

"Alex," she moaned when she felt his tongue press on the most sensitive part of her body.

He slowly traced over her swollen clit, sucking gently as he worshipped her with his mouth. "I love the way you taste, Olivia. I know I say that all the time, but I just can't get enough of you." He returned his tongue to her, continuing his circular pattern. He loved being able to please her like this.

Olivia moved against him, needing some sort of release after weeks of frustration. "Please, Alex."

"What, love?" He glanced up, watching her chest heaving. A smile crossed his face when he saw how she responded to him, even after everything they had endured those past few months. "Is it too much? I'll stop."

"Don't you dare!" she screamed. "I'm close, Alex, but I don't want to come yet."

He eased a finger inside her, knowing that was going to send her to the brink and over in a matter of seconds. He knew her body, and he loved being able to give her what she needed, even if she didn't even realize what that was.

She moaned out, the sensation of Alexander's tongue and finger too much, pushing her body higher and higher before crumbling beneath his expert tongue. Her orgasm consumed every fiber of her being as she shook on the bed.

"I'll never tire of giving you what you need, Olivia," he said, raising himself and hovering over her. "That's my only mission in life. To give you everything you need. I'll never keep anything from you again. I promise, and I mean it." His face was full of sincerity.

Olivia grabbed his head, pulling it down to hers, and kissed him with more passion than she ever had. She couldn't imagine her life without Alexander in it, and she never wanted to go through another day without him by her side.

"Please, Alex. Make love to me," she begged once more. She wanted to feel the love he had for her, even though she felt it with the way he looked at her day-in and day-out.

He positioned himself between her legs and slowly entered her, filling her as he leaned down, his movement gentle. "I love you, Olibia," he said quietly as he communicated with his body exactly how special she was to him.

"I love you, too, Alex." Her nerves tingled as she met his tender pace. She grabbed his face and brought his mouth back to hers. "I just can't stop kissing you," she explained with a smile on her face before planting another passionate kiss on him. "I don't ever want to stop tasting your lips."

Alexander beamed. "Good." He slowly flexed toward her,

his breathing becoming ragged. "We've come a long way from those cootie shots then, haven't we?"

Olivia grinned, running her fingers up and down his back, savoring the feeling of his muscles beneath her hands. She felt his movements become erratic and knew he was ready to fall apart. She ran her tongue across his neck. "I've always loved you, Alex," she whispered. "Always."

Her sweet words filled Alexander's heart with more love than he thought possible and he shuddered, his orgasm taking him by surprise. "I can't survive without you, Olivia. You're my heart, and I'll die without you." He pushed into her until the last of his tremors subsided, slowly withdrawing from her and pulling her into his body. "Sleep now, beautiful Olibia."

CHAPTER THIRTY-TWO

RECOLLECTION

"DADDY! DADDY! LET'S PLAY a game!" a young Olivia exclaimed when she saw her father walk into her family's large beach estate. He had been gone for weeks and she missed him. She loved to play with her mama, but her daddy played lots of fun games with her, too.

"Hi, princess. What game did you want to play?"

Olivia spotted several small chests stacked against the bookcase in the great room. "Let's play Treasure Map, but this time, I'm hiding the treasure!" she answered excitedly, running over and grabbing one of the closed chests.

Olivia's father smiled. "Okay. Do you think you can do a good enough job at hiding it? I'm pretty good at finding things, Livvy."

She beamed. "Daddy, please. Where I hide this, you'll never find it. I can't wait to draw you a map!" She ran out of the room. "You better not cheat, Daddy!"

He chuckled. "I wouldn't dream of it, princess."

Later that night, Olivia climbed out of her bed, trying to be quiet so that she didn't wake her sleeping parents. She tip-toed down the hall and out the basement door that led to the beach. Running quickly down the private beach, she came across the old dilapidated pile of rocks. She knew she wasn't supposed to go near them, and that made it the perfect hiding spot. Plus, her daddy wasn't nearly small enough to fit in the cave-fort that she and her best friend could squeeze into. She gingerly crawled inside and buried the chest underneath the sand in the cave. She smiled to herself. Her daddy would never find the chest there.

~~~~~~~~~~

OLIVIA'S EYES FLUNG OPEN, taking in the pitch black room. *Of course*, she thought to herself. It was all starting to come back to her. Alexander was right. Seeing photos and items from her past was helping her remember. She recalled playing that Treasure Map game with her father. He wasn't around a great deal, but when he was, she loved playing games with him.

She gently pried herself from Alexander's arms and legs, sitting up in bed and staring at the beautiful man next to her.

Her stomach churned and she began to feel nauseous. Dashing from the bed, she ran down the stairs, locking herself away in the guest bathroom and vomiting up the contents of her stomach. *Shit*, she thought to herself. *Shit. Shit. Shit.* As she continued to lean over the toilet, she did the math in her head.

Flushing the remnants of her dinner down the toilet, she leaned against the wall, trying to figure out what to do. Her period was several weeks late, and she was never late. The past few days, she had been feeling slightly nauseous, but she thought that was due to stress. Now, she was starting to rethink everything.

Raising herself off the floor, she took in her appearance in the mirror. She didn't look any different. "I don't think you change overnight, Libby," she said to herself, standing on her toes and looking at a side-view of her stomach.

Shaking her head, she opened the door to the bathroom, not wanting to think about what it all meant. She wasn't ready for that yet, not until she could be sure her friends would be safe.

Making her way toward the couch, she debated what to do. After her dream, she finally had an idea about the Treasure Map game she used to play with her dad, but there was something about that memory that was telling her that those papers weren't buried where she thought. She couldn't quite put her finger on it so, for the time being, she had to trust the memory that she *did* have.

As she continued looking through the boxes, memories flooding back every time she found something else, she felt Alexander's arms slink around her. He leaned down and softly kissed her shoulder.

"Morning, love," he said. "I woke up and you were gone. I

hate that." His face was in the most adorable pout Olivia had ever seen. She wanted to bite his lower lip as it protruded out.

Her heart raced at the thought that she might be pregnant with his child. She debated whether she should say anything, but if she did and it ended up being true, he would never let her out of his sight. He couldn't know, for the time being. She wasn't even sure that she really *was* pregnant. Smiling, she raised herself off the ground, brushing her lips against his. "I'm sorry. I just couldn't sleep knowing all this stuff is down here," she lied.

"You have the rest of your life to sort through it all."

She exhaled slowly. "I know. But I've been trying to figure out who I am for years. Having all this information here at my disposal is a little overwhelming."

"I get it." He planted a kiss on her forehead, walking toward the kitchen and popping a pod in her coffee brewer. "Coffee?" he asked.

Olivia nodded, watching as Alexander made her a coffee, a warm feeling overtaking her. It felt as if she finally knew where she belonged, almost as if she finally had a family. Almost.

~~~~~~~~~~

"It feels so good to be out of that fucking house of death and disease," Kiera said Saturday afternoon as Olivia helped lead her to the couch. The hospital finally cleared her for home rest and the police had released her house so it was no longer considered a crime scene.

"K, are you sure you want to stay here?" Mo asked, his eyes full of concern.

"Jack, stop it. I'm not going to have this conversation with you every day. I need to stay here. I need to make new memories in this house…with you."

Olivia warmed at her friend's sweet words, and Mo's beaming smile in response. They were so happy together.

As she sat visiting with Kiera throughout the weekend, the location of the documents lay heavy on her mind, as did the constant bouts of nausea and headaches. She felt guilty for not telling anyone that she knew what those guys were after, but she knew that Alexander and the rest of her friends would not allow her to do what she had to do.

Monday morning, Olivia woke up before Alexander, running into her bathroom, hoping he wouldn't hear as she threw up once more. She made a mental note that it would probably be best to finally take a pregnancy test, but she wasn't sure she wanted confirmation of that fact.

Slowly opening the door and peering at the bed, she breathed a sigh of relief when she saw that Alexander hadn't moved. Gingerly walking back to the bed, she crawled in beside him, hoping he hadn't noticed she was gone. Her heart raced when he groaned, stretching, before pulling her body into his. "Morning, beautiful," he murmured into her ear. "You okay?"

She turned to face him. "Of course, I am. Why are you asking that?" She searched his face, looking for any indication that he had heard her.

A mischievous grin spread across his mouth. "Well, just making sure you're not sore after last night."

She playfully punched him, relieved that he hadn't heard her throwing up. "You're so full of yourself, aren't you?"

"Maybe a little," he replied, his eyes bright. "But you still love me."

Olivia smiled in response, snuggling against his chest. "Of course I do."

~~~~~~~~~~

ALEXANDER TURNED TO OLIVIA later that morning as they stood by her front door, saying good-bye. "I can have all those boxes brought over to the penthouse. I miss having you there. So do Runner and Nepenthe," he said.

She exhaled loudly. "I know. I miss them, too. I want to do this here. I don't know why. I just do."

He hesitated, wondering why she felt so strongly about that, but he didn't want to make her angry with him yet again. It wasn't worth it. Anyway, Marshall and Carter had agreed to sit watch outside of her house for the time being. "Okay, beautiful. Whatever you need." He leaned down and planted a gentle kiss on her lips.

"I'll see you later on," she said, brushing her lips against Alexander's.

"I love you."

"I love you, too," she replied, watching as he walked down the steps and into the waiting SUV, Martin at the wheel.

Throughout the morning, she sorted through more boxes, still trying to figure out why she didn't think the documents were buried in the chest.

Just when she was ready to give up, her phone began ringing. She was surprised to see Simon's number appear on the screen. A smile crossed her face as she thought about how he had become someone she could depend on over the last few months, someone who would give her the advice she so desperately needed. "Hey, Simon."

"Hi, Libby. I was just checking in on you to see how everything's going. I heard about Melanie. How are you holding up?"

"I'm doing better. He came clean, Simon."

His heart began racing. "What do you mean?"

"Alexander told me everything about my past. He sent over all this stuff his father had kept."

"His father?" Simon asked in confusion.

"Don't worry about that right now," she replied quickly. "That's not important. What *is* important is that all these photos, trinkets, stuff like that, have helped me remember things. I'm starting to figure it out. I know what those guys are after, Simon." Her voice was excited and pressing at the same time.

"So, where is it?" he asked urgently.

Olivia hesitated briefly. She didn't want to actually tell anyone the location. What if he found the documents and they got into the wrong hands because he was careless with them? Until Olivia could be certain they would be protected, she didn't want to divulge the location to anyone.

"Come on, Olivia. You can trust me."

"I have a pretty good idea, but I'm not entirely sure. I don't want to say anything until I'm certain about its location."

"I'll come over and we can go get it now," he said rather impatiently. "I mean, let's go where you think it could be. Might as well try, right?" He laughed nervously.

Olivia immediately became suspicious of Simon. He was acting odd…almost a little too eager to help. She recalled their conversation several months ago during her run. At one point, he had said that he was paid to date her for the sole purpose of obtaining information about her past. It was entirely possible that he *didn't* change things around in prison and was still on the payroll. Perhaps it was all a front. That would explain a lot of things. Why he was being so nice to her. Why the guy in Kiera's house had gotten away even after Simon said he was out cold.

She sank into the couch, angry at herself that she didn't see it all beforehand and now she had told him that she remembered. "Simon," she said calmly, trying to hide her nerves. "I'm still trying to figure everything out."

He exhaled loudly, his irritation apparent. "Well, you do that, Libby. I gotta go." He hung up the phone, leaving Olivia with her unsettled thoughts about what she had just divulged to him.

She thought about letting Alexander know of her suspicions, but that would mean telling him she had been speaking with Simon. She knew for a fact that he would not handle *that* information well. He would make sure that she couldn't leave the house without heavy security presence and, when the time came and she figured it all out, she needed to be able to get away without a tail following her. She had already begun to formulate a plan. But would it work?

~~~~~~~~~~

"SIMON, I HOPE YOU have some very good news for me after your phone call to Olivia today."

"She remembers. She says she thinks she knows where it is."

Donovan smiled. "That's wonderful news. So where is it?"

Simon exhaled loudly. "She won't tell me."

"Why the fuck not?!" Donovan asked angrily.

"I don't know. I don't think she really remembers it all clearly. She said she had a good idea where it was, but wasn't certain."

"Goddammit, Simon! Here's what's going to happen. You're going to *make* her remember. I want that box in my fucking hand by the end of the week or I *will* kill you."

Simon's hands began to shake. He had seen what Donovan's goons were capable of. He was not to be messed with. "Fine. I'm going to need a window where she won't have her security detail with her. Burnham's been on her ass since the attacks."

"I'll arrange it and let you know the time and place. Get it done, Simon."

"Yes, sir."

"Oh, and Simon?"

"Yes?"

"Grant will assist you. At least he gets shit done."

"Yes, sir." Simon hung up, suddenly nervous about what he was going to have to do.

CHAPTER THIRTY-THREE

PREMONITION

THURSDAY MORNING, OLIVIA WOKE with an unsettling premonition about what the day would bring. She couldn't shake the suspicion that something bad was about to happen. Ever since Simon's reaction on Monday, she was on edge about everything. For once, she embraced the protection detail that Alexander had set up for her.

As she walked back into her house after kissing Alexander good-bye, a chill came over her. The house was eerily quiet while she sorted through the last few boxes that she had been anxious to look at. She was desperate to know why the memory of the treasure map she drew for her father stuck out in her head, as if the chest wasn't buried there.

She was having trouble focusing that morning after finally taking a pregnancy test and getting confirmation of her suspicions. She grabbed her iPad and began streaming music to the surround sound speakers, hoping it would help clear her mind. After setting her playlist to shuffle, she returned to a box containing photos. She looked at the date stamped in the bottom left corner of the pictures. August twenty-fourth. Her jaw dropped when she saw the year. They must have been taken right before she and her parents left the beach house the day of the accident. Olivia wondered how there could have been any photos. Then she noticed that they were mostly of her mother. It looked like there was a small finger over the viewfinder, slightly obscuring them all.

"I guess I was some photographer back in the day," she said, joking.

As she continued sorting through the photos, Olivia felt chills again, wondering if it was just a coincidence that *Seven Devils* started blaring through her speakers. She never really believed in signs or coincidences, but something about that Florence and the Machine song playing at that moment made her think that something horrible was about to happen.

~~~~~~~~~~~

ALEXANDER SAT IN HIS office on Thursday afternoon, scouring through Olivia's parents' bank statements. There were numerous suspicious deposits. And then there was that mysterious piece of paper with his father's writing on it in some sort of code. He still didn't know what it all meant.

Nothing was making any sense to him. He was trying to figure out whether the deposits were just distributions from Marilyn's various investments, but it was difficult to ascertain the source. Apparently, it had concerned Alexander's father, but it seemed that he became paranoid the last few years of his life. Alexander didn't know what to make of it or whether he should put any faith in his father's work at all.

His mind kept wandering off, thinking about how he should have been getting married that weekend. It saddened him that things had been put on hold for a little bit, but he knew that once everything settled down, he would marry his Olivia.

"Hey, Alex?" Carol said from the sitting area in his office, looking through some of her father's old files, trying to help him put the pieces together.

"Yeah?"

"How do you think they found out that Dad was protecting Olivia?" She had a quizzical look on her face.

"Your guess is as good as mine. Why?" He glanced up from the bank statements, the numbers giving him a headache.

"I mean, do you think maybe someone inside the company…?"

"NO!" Alexander said forcefully before calming himself down. "You know how Dad operated. You know how we still

243

operate to this very day."

Carol sighed. "I know, but that would explain a few things. I'm going through some of Dad's old notes. These people found out about South Carolina. That's probably why he insisted she come to college up here…so he could keep a closer eye on her. There's no way he would let anyone know where she was. Maybe we need to start looking inside the box."

"But that would mean…"

Carol interrupted, "That if there was an inside man, that person may still be with the company."

"Shit," Alexander said, picking up his phone. "Marie, I want employment records of everyone who has worked here for the past eight years. Focus on employees who are still employed here."

Carol glanced over at her brother. "I'm probably wrong, Alex." She turned back to her father's notes.

"I hope you are," he replied, returning his tired eyes back to the financial records, kicking himself for not exploring that line of thought earlier.

~~~~~~~~~~

LATER THAT AFTERNOON, OLIVIA heard her cell phone buzz, thankful to have the momentary distraction. Everything was all a big puzzle that she desperately wanted to solve. She felt like she was close but there was one big clue missing.

Alexander: *Hey, love. Something came up here at the office and I'm going to be a little late. Do NOT, under any circumstances, leave your house, even with any of your escorts. I'll explain later. I love you.*

That's odd, Olivia thought as she glanced out her bay window and saw Agent Marshall sitting watch in the SUV. All of a sudden, she heard a deep voice speaking on a cell phone just outside of her window.

"We're in front of the bitch's house, boss," the voice said, sending shivers up Olivia's spine. She quickly lowered herself, hoping no one had seen her. The voice sounded so familiar.

"Simon will get the girl to go with him. Cheryl is turning the other way and says she'll play dumb when questioned by Burnham."

Olivia gasped, trying to muffle the sound with her hand. Agent Marshall was in on it. It all started to make sense. Every time she had seen Simon or Adele was when Marshall was on watch. No one else. Only her.

Almost instantly, there was a loud knock at the door. "Olivia, it's Simon. We need to talk."

"Shit," Olivia said under her breath, her eyes falling on the last picture she had been looking at before reading Alexander's text. A strong memory rushed back. Quickly, she grabbed the few things that would lead Alexander to the truth and, hopefully, her. She laid them on her kitchen island before propping Mr. Bear up on the barstool. It was all she could do for now.

She jumped when she heard a loud knock on the door again. "Olivia! Open up!"

With shaky hands, she texted Alexander, hoping it wouldn't be the last conversation she ever had with him. Making her way over to the door, she pulled it back, unsure of how to respond to Simon now that she knew everything.

"Hi, Simon," she said, her voice unsteady.

"Evening, Livvy," he responded, pushing her back into her house and closing the front door.

Olivia's eyes went wide at the greeting.

"Yes. The old Simon is back." He put his arm around her waist, pulling her flush with his body. "Time to go find what those guys are looking for." He started to head toward the basement, pulling her along with him.

She was right. She knew it. Her mind started racing. "Simon, wait."

"What is it?" he growled.

"This isn't you," she said softly. "You're not this guy anymore. You're better than this. I like the new Simon much better…"

He stopped in his tracks, his eyes brimming with remorse. "I have to, Olivia! They'll kill me if I don't do this!" She could feel his body start to shake. "Grant is waiting out back. There's no fucking way out. Don't you think I've tried to come up with another way? They knew I wasn't ready to go through with it, but I know too much. I don't have a choice, Olivia."

"Grant? Who's Grant?"

Simon exhaled loudly. "He's the guy who attacked Kiera."

That's why the voice out front sounded so familiar. It was him. Olivia's heart raced, her chin quivering from the memory of Kiera's lifeless body. Did the same fate await her?

"Libby, please. I don't know what else to do. If you don't come with us, I'm dead. I swear to you, I will find a way to help you, but you have to come with me. To save me and yourself. Do you understand?"

A tear fell down her cheek. "Yes. I understand." She just hoped that the clues she left were enough.

"We need to go. I'm going to have to be rough with you, but I promise I will try to find a way to help you. Okay?"

She nodded her head and Simon led her down the hallway, still grasping her waist rather roughly.

"Wait. One last thing." She released herself from Simon's hold and headed back to the kitchen. Grabbing her cell phone, she noticed that her last text never went through.

"Leave the phone, Libby," Simon said softly. "Put it down. They can track it."

Olivia nodded in defeat, placing her cell back on the kitchen island. Her eyes brimming with tears at the finality of it all, she took the engagement ring off her hand and placed it on top of a photo of her and Alexander sitting on the rocks by the house. She hoped that with those clues, he would know where she would be and the location of the hidden documents. She said a silent prayer that he would understand everything and that he would get there in time to save her.

Simon grabbed her roughly after she walked back to the hallway. Her hands shook at the thought that she was about to sit in a car for two hours with a man who probably wanted to kill her. "I'm so sorry, Libby," he whispered as he walked her through the hallway and down the stairs leading to the back door.

"Simon, wait." Olivia stopped, her voice shaking from fear. "We can run. Both of us. Right now. You don't have to do this."

His eyes searched her face, contemplating her words. A car door slammed loudly, startling them both. Simon knew it was useless. There was no way out, but he was going to do his best to help her. He put his finger up to his lips, giving Olivia a compassionate look, as if saying what words alone couldn't. "I'm so sorry. Just go along," he whispered. "I'll save you. I promise. Even if I have to put my own life on the line, I will make sure you get out of this alive."

Her entire body began to tremble as Simon picked her up, throwing her over his shoulder.

"What the fuck is the hold up, Simon?" Grant roared, banging on the back door.

"Nothing. I've got the bitch," Simon growled. "Let's get a move on." He opened the door and walked to the desolate back alley where a sole black sedan waited. He threw Olivia into the backseat before getting into the passenger seat.

Olivia looked up as the large man got in behind the wheel and turned around.

"Evening, beautiful," he said, licking his lips.

"Don't even think about touching her, Grant," Simon said forcefully before turning his attention back to Olivia. "Now, Livvy, tell me. Where to?" He pointed a gun at her head, a solemn look on his face.

"Chatham. On the Cape," she replied softly.

"That's a good girl." Grant grabbed her ankle and ran his fingers up her bare legs. The contact made Olivia sick to her stomach. She wished she had worn more than just a sundress.

Simon fished his cell phone out of his pocket, still keeping his gun trained on Olivia.

"Donovan, it's Simon. We have the girl and we're on our way to Chatham."

"Good news. Do not do anything until backup arrives. We cannot have a repeat of the last time."

"Even more backup?"

"My client is on his way. He wants to help take care of the

girl."

Shit, Simon thought.

CHAPTER THIRTY-FOUR

CHAOS

ALEXANDER POURED THROUGH EMPLOYMENT records all afternoon and into the evening. He was looking for anything that seemed out of the ordinary but, so far, he had come up empty. He had sent Olivia's parents' financial records to one of his top forensic accountants to start combing through. He hated involving anyone else in what was going on because he didn't know who he could trust, but he didn't see any alternative. He couldn't make any sense out of the records so he hoped someone else could.

"Fun way to spend a Thursday night, huh, Alex?" Carol commented several hours later, breaking the deafening silence that had occupied his office all afternoon.

"Sure is," he replied, looking up from the papers in front of him. "Thanks again for all your help, Carol. I know you'd rather be spending your time with Dave."

She smiled. "No problem. Anything to help you out. I'm certainly looking forward to collecting on this debt you owe me, though," she joked before turning back to the papers in front of her, her brow furrowing as she scanned the file in front of her.

"What? Did you find something?" Alexander asked, noticing her expression. His heart started racing as he saw Carol flip frantically through various documents.

"Shit…" she said quietly, not wanting to believe what she was reading.

Alexander rushed over to the couch, looking at the name of

the employee record she had been going through. "Carol," he looked at her, his eyes pleading. "Please, tell me…"

"I'm sorry, Alex. Random small deposits adding up to a lot of money during the months leading up to Dad's death, then nothing."

He grabbed the file out of her hands and began flipping through the pages. "No. It can't be. She was questioned about it after Dad's death, and during each of her quarterly background checks. It's right here in the file. It's part of her divorce settlement."

Carol peered at the papers in Alexander's hands, flipping through the file with him. "How do you explain the timing, though? She stopped getting that money right after Dad's death, and then the suspicious deposits started again around the same time that you met Olivia. It could just be a coincidence, but the timing is perfect."

"FUCK!" Alexander shouted, his voice panicked. "Call Dave!" he ordered Carol before bolting out of his office. "Martin! Let's go!"

~~~~~~~~~~

WITHIN A FEW MINUTES, Martin slammed on the brakes in front of Olivia's house. Alexander was furious when he saw Marshall sitting behind the wheel of her own SUV, keeping watch over the house as if nothing was wrong. He jumped out of the vehicle, running toward the driver's side, and pulled her from the seat, slamming her against the hard metal exterior. The window shattered from the force of the impact. "What the fuck did you do?!" He glared down at her, his voice full of rage.

"Sir, please, I don't know any more than you. I don't know where they're taking her. All I know is that I was ordered to look the other way today…"

Alexander's heart sank. He didn't know Olivia had actually been taken. "Who has her?" he quivered.

"I don't know," she lied.

"Where are they taking her?"

"Only Olivia knows that."

"FUCK!" Alexander screamed, handcuffing her and throwing her in the back of her own SUV. He ran inside Olivia's house, unable to make anything of the scene that greeted him. Papers and photos were all over the place. He took a deep breath, knowing that there may be a clue in the house. He slowly scanned the living room, his eyes stopping on a bunch of photos placed neatly on the kitchen island.

He quickly strode over, his heart almost stopping when he saw the picture on top...the photo of them as children playing on the rocks outside the beach house lay just beneath her engagement ring. He immediately knew where she was taking them. His eyes glanced at another photo lying on the island. It was a photo of Olivia's mom. It looked as though she was mending a tear in Mr. Bear's stitching. The date on the corner of the photo was the same day as the accident. He wondered what it all meant. Why was this photo left on the island?

It was almost as if Olivia left everything laid out perfectly, asking him to figure it all out. She was heading to the beach house, but the photo of her mom stitching up Mr. Bear? What did *that* mean? He grabbed the engagement ring and Mr. Bear off the stool, along with the rest of the photos. Bolting out of the house, he yelled for Martin to accompany him and gave him the address in Chatham where Olivia's beach estate was located.

As Martin merged onto the Mass Pike, Alexander looked out of the window, desperate to find Olivia and save her because, this time, she actually needed saving.

~~~~~~~~~~

"OKAY, THIS IS FUCKING ridiculous!" Grant shouted, pulling over on the side of the road. "Get her out of the car."

Olivia had been anything but helpful in figuring out where the evidence they needed was supposedly hidden. "No. I'm not getting out of the car." She looked around. There were no lights anywhere. It was deserted. She hadn't even seen another car for miles. "I told you where we needed to go," she begged.

"Chatham. That's all I know."

"And we're in fucking Chatham! Now where is the goddamn house?!" Simon yelled. He hated having to shout at her like that, but he couldn't let it seem as if he was going easy on her. He had to act the part.

"Simon, please... I don't remember. I only spent a few summers there when I was a little girl. Other than that, I can't remember anything, especially about how to get there. All I know is that it's a huge place right on the beach. I'd know it if I saw it."

"Fine! Let's go to the coast then." Grant put the car in drive and tore out onto the street. "If you don't find it within the next thirty minutes, I *will* put a bullet through your head."

Olivia whimpered as a tear fell down her face.

~~~~~~~~~~

AFTER ALEXANDER STORMED OUT of his office, Carol remained behind, desperate to help her brother any way she could. They had figured out that Marshall was involved, but they still had no clue as to who was pulling the strings. She sat at his desk, trying to decipher her father's coded scribblings. Something wasn't adding up. She had put in a phone call to a few of Alexander's analyst guys who were good at tracking money transfers, even from off-shore bank accounts, to see if they were able to find any suspicious connection between Kiddish and other people Olivia came into contact with, but that hadn't turned up anything yet. She had all but given up on trying to figure out who was behind everything when the phone rang.

"Hey, Jimmy," she answered, wondering if he was able to find out anything from combing through the bank records. "Wait...slow down... What are you saying?"

Carol sank into the chair, dropping her phone, as the shock of the news she had just been given overtook her entire body. She took a deep breath before making the phone call that could potentially destroy her brother's entire world.

~~~~~~~~~~

"WELL, THIS MUST BE it," Grant declared, pulling up a long driveway to an enormous shoreline estate. "It's the biggest house right on the beach in this town. I don't think they make 'em much bigger than this one. Bitch must be fucking loaded!"

Olivia looked up at the house. He was right. It was the house from her dreams and memories. "This was where I used to play with Alexander every summer," she said softly as Simon carefully helped her out of the car.

"Aw... Too bad," Grant said cruelly. "Now it's where you're going to die." He walked along the side of the car and opened the trunk, digging around for what he needed to complete the job.

Olivia began to shake nervously, protectively clutching her stomach.

Simon leaned close to her, his eyes intense. "When I tell you to...run." His voice was barely above a whisper, nearly inaudible over the crashing ocean waves. "Kick me in the stomach. Sell it. Your life depends on it."

She looked at him, her eyes wide in surprise.

Do you understand? he mouthed.

She nodded slowly just as Grant came around to the side of the car, carrying a large duffel bag. Simon dragged her up the walkway toward the front entrance.

"Don't worry," Grant laughed. "We'll keep you alive a little longer, as long as you're nice to us."

Olivia felt sick to her stomach, bile forming in her throat as her brain ran through thousands of different scenarios about what Grant had in store for her.

"Run," Simon whispered in her ear.

"I don't fucking think so!" she spat out, turning swiftly and kicking Simon in the stomach as hard as she could.

Simon keeled over, clutching his stomach in pain. "YOU FUCKING BITCH!"

Olivia spun around and started to run, thankful that Grant hadn't been smart enough to bind her arms or legs.

"Give me that fucking gun!" Grant ordered Simon. "Or shoot her yourself!"

"She's too far! I don't have a shot!" Simon shouted back, hoping to give her enough time to get away.

"You're helping her! You fucking shit! You want her to get away!"

"No way! Of course not!"

"Then go get her!"

Simon ran after Olivia, watching as she bolted up the remainder of the sandy path leading to the beach.

She desperately hoped that there would be some people out for a twilight stroll. Her eyes searched the shoreline frantically, remembering that it was a private beach, when she heard the gunshot. "AAAAGGGGHHHHH!" she screamed in pain, the bullet hitting her right shoulder. She fell to the ground, crying out.

Simon ran up and held the gun over her. "I'm so sorry. I tried to miss you without making it too obvious," he said quietly, a tear falling from his eye as he looked at Olivia's bleeding body lying on the white sand. He quickly changed his expression when Grant caught up to him and kicked Olivia hard in the stomach.

"FUCK!" she screamed, the sound of her ribs cracking making her want to vomit once more. The pain from the bullet wound and the unexpected assault to her stomach was overwhelming.

"You do *not* run away from us you fucking bitch!" Grant raised his boot and brought it down hard on her left foot, crushing the hundreds of tiny bones.

Olivia howled out in agony, her eyes growing wide when she saw him raise his boot again, intending to break her other foot, as well. "NO!" she screamed. "PLEASE STOP! I'LL DO ANYTHING!"

Grant slowed his action mid-strike and looked at her, rather turned on by the blood pouring from her body onto the beach.

"Anything?" he asked.

She took a deep breath and closed her eyes. She nodded slowly as tears began to stream down her face...no longer from being in pain, but for what she knew Grant was probably planning at that moment.

"Grant. You can't do this to her," Simon pleaded, trying to find a way to help her. He felt sick at the thought of Grant touching her. "There were very strict instructions. She is not to be harmed until you-know-who gets here."

Grant reached into the duffel bag and withdrew a gun, pointing it at Simon. "What the fuck, man?"

Simon raised his own gun, aiming it at Grant instead of Olivia.

"I'm just having a little fun, that's all. I'm not going to kill her...yet. And if you try to interfere again, I'll fucking shoot you. Step aside and I won't tell Donovan that you told her to run." Grant returned to the duffel bag and produced several long rags. Kneeling next to Olivia as she lay trembling on the beach, he gently caressed her face, making her cringe. "That's my girl," he said quietly. "Be good and we won't have to shoot you again, okay?"

Olivia opened her eyes, staring into the evil black eyes in front of her. She simply nodded, not wanting to speak.

"Good girl. But first, I need to make sure you won't try to get away from me." He quickly bound her hands together. "At least I've already made certain that you won't be able to walk," he laughed to himself.

Olivia began to cry, mourning the loss of her legs. She had no chance of running away anymore. Simon had tried to help her, but he would risk his own life if he did so again. Her only hope now was Alexander. She prayed that he would be able to figure out the clues she left for him.

"Before I forget, I know we're having a special guest. Don't want you recognizing who it is, so I better blindfold you, too."

She shook her head violently, not wanting the one sense she needed most to be taken from her.

"Sorry, beautiful. Rules are rules." Grant grabbed a rag and tied it tightly around her eyes.

Olivia's world went dark. She would have to rely solely on her ears. She was doomed and she knew it. She screamed out in pain as Grant lifted her by the waist and dragged her body through the sand and up to the palatial beach house.

After overriding the security system, he turned to Simon. "Get out of here. Stand watch out front," he growled.

"Grant. What are you going to do?" Simon asked, his voice shaking.

He raised his gun, pointing it at Simon's temple. "Leave or I pull the trigger."

Simon knew he didn't have a choice. If he had any chance of trying to save Olivia, he had to play his cards right, and that meant listening to Grant for the time being. "Fine," he huffed, spinning around and slamming the door behind him.

Grant smiled. "It will all be over soon. I promise." He carried Olivia through the foyer. "We just need to wait for our special guest to get here and then you can tell us where that box is."

Olivia willed herself to stop crying. That wasn't how she wanted to spend the last few minutes of her life. If she was going to die, she wanted to die on her own terms and not pleading for her life.

"Wow. You should see this place," he remarked as he dragged her into a large great room overlooking the coast. "Floor-to-ceiling ocean view in this room. I bet it's gorgeous during the day."

Olivia knew the exact room they were in. There was a grand piano in the center that she recalled playing as a little girl. The space was open and airy with light beige colored sofas on the far end facing the windows. The walls were wood planked and there were light drapes in front of the window. That's how she remembered it looking, at least.

"Okay, this is good enough," Grant said, his breathing heavy from dragging Olivia all that distance. He dropped her on the floor, hoping to cause her even more pain. When she had barely any reaction to being thrown down, he turned to look at her. Her face looked almost peaceful, as if she had begun to accept her fate.

That pissed Grant off. He liked it when she was scared of him. "Stand up!" he yelled.

Olivia started breathing heavy, thinking there would be no

way she could actually stand up.

He walked over to her and grabbed her ponytail. "I said STAND UP!" he shouted, pulling Olivia up by the hair.

"FUCK!" she screamed out once she was on her feet. She tried to keep most of the weight off her left foot. She had no idea what was going through Grant's head.

"On your knees!"

Olivia hesitated, unsure of how she could possibly obey the command and yet feel the least amount of pain.

"I said, ON YOUR KNEES!" He kicked her in the small of the back, causing her to topple over and fall flat on her stomach. Her reflexes were slow from her arms being bound together and she was unable to break her fall with her hands.

Olivia felt Grant kneel next to her. She began to shake, feeling his hot breath on her neck. He grabbed her arms and hoisted them over her head, readjusting her restraint, attaching it to the leg of the grand piano.

She tried to free herself, to no avail.

Grant laughed. "No use trying to run now. You're stuck."

Olivia lay there, her breathing heavy, as several minutes passed. She heard Grant walking through the house before returning and rummaging through a duffle bag. Almost immediately, she felt him by her side, pushing up her dress. Dread overwhelmed her when she heard a snipping sound, squirming at the feel of the cold metal on her skin cutting off her panties. Tears began falling even harder. She wanted to remain strong, but her entire body trembled in fear.

She felt him run a finger down the length of her torso and desperately tried to buck him off her, but he simply laughed and then brought the gun to her temple. "Stay still or I pull the fucking trigger. I don't give a shit if you're the only one who knows where the goddamn evidence is that these guys are looking for."

Olivia swallowed, crying, feeling ashamed and humiliated, wanting Grant to pull the trigger instead.

CHAPTER THIRTY-FIVE

UNDERSTANDING

"WHAT DID YOU JUST say, Carol?!" Alexander roared into the phone. "You're shitting me!"

"I know. Where are you?"

"They've got Olivia."

"Shit, Alex. Where did they take her?"

"I think to the beach house. That's where I'm heading now. Can you pull up his cell on the tracker?" he asked, typing frantically at his own laptop as Martin sped down the interstate.

"Hold on a second." Carol typed the cell number into her tracking software. "Damn it, Alex! He's in Chatham!"

"FUCK! I'm on it. Oh, and sis, I'm forwarding a bunch of documents to you. Make sure they're sent to every news outlet you can think of." Alexander hung up his cell phone. "Martin! Step on it!"

~~~~~~~~~~

OLIVIA LAY PERFECTLY STILL on the floor, blocking out everything that was happening around her. She refused to cry. She simply remained unmoving against the cold hard wood and waited for him to pull the trigger.

She heard the door open and close and immediately grew hopeful. Grant remained where he was, not moving from his position on top of her.

"What the fuck is going on here?!" a familiar voice shouted.

Grant looked up at the person who had just walked in. "Are you him?"

"Get the fuck off of her!" He swung and punched Grant out cold.

Olivia released the breath she had been holding and began to sob even harder. She felt a blanket wrap around her body. "Oh, Livvy. I'm so sorry that all this has happened to you."

"Daddy?" Olivia asked.

Her father quickly removed her restraints and took off her blindfold, wrapping his arms around her body as he tried to stop her cries. "Ssshhh... It's okay, peanut. I'm so sorry. This is all my fault. It wasn't supposed to be this way. He wasn't supposed to touch you like that."

Olivia's eyes grew wide. "I don't understand."

Her father took a deep breath. "Where is it, Livvy?"

"I'm not sure..."

"Goddammit!" he shouted, grabbing her by the shoulder, causing her to cry out in pain. He looked at her in horror, noticing the fresh blood from the apparent bullet wound that had been soaking her white sundress. "He shot you? He was told to not hurt you until..."

"Until what?" Olivia asked between sobs.

"Oh, Livvy," he exhaled. "I've made a mess of everything. I'm sorry I have to do this."

She looked at her father. "Do what?"

"This, sweetheart." He raised his hand and Olivia's world went dark.

~~~~~~~~~~

"OLIVIA, LOVE. PLEASE COME here," her mother called out.

"What is it, Mama?"

"I need to ask you a very important question. I need you to think very, very hard."

"Okay."

Olivia's mother took a deep breath. "I know you and Daddy are playing a game of Treasure Map."

"Yes!" she answered excitedly. "We are! He's letting me hide the

treasure this time. I just drew him a map!"

"Olivia, dear. You can *NOT* give him that map."

She scowled. "Why not?"

"Darling. I need you to tell me where you buried that chest."

"But that's cheating. I can't do that."

"Olivia, your father has done some very bad things, and we'll all be in very real danger if I can't turn this information over to the right people."

"But I don't have that, Mama."

"Oh, sweetheart. That's what you buried. That's why I need you to tell me where it is. And I need to get it before your daddy gets home. He can't know that we know. It has to be our little secret. Can you keep a secret and show me where you buried it?"

"Okay, Mama. I can do that. I'm real good at keeping secrets."

~~~~~~~~~~

"MAMA, WHAT ARE YOU doing to Mr. Bear?" Olivia asked, holding up her mother's heavy camera, snapping a picture.

"I'm stitching him up."

"What was wrong with him? I didn't know that he was broken."

"He wasn't, dear, but I have a bad feeling about today and if something happens to me, I need you to take this bear to your Uncle Thomas. Tell him that all the answers he needs, he can find in your bear. Do not let go of this bear, no matter what. Okay?"

"Okay, Mama…"

"All done. Now hurry, Olivia. I need you to hurry."

"Why? Daddy's not here yet."

"That's exactly why I need you to hurry. We need to get far away from Daddy."

Olivia began to cry. "I don't want to."

"Sweetheart, I don't have time to explain right now, but I will someday. I promise you."

"And what do you plan on explaining?!" a loud, booming voice yelled.

Olivia cowered in fear. It was her daddy, but he was angry. She had never seen him like that before. She was scared.

"Nothing, dear. Just packing up for the summer."

Olivia looked at her mother, who appeared very nervous.

"It doesn't look like nothing, Mary. It looks like you're running from me. Now I'm giving you one last fucking opportunity to tell me where those papers are or, I swear to God, I will kill you."

Olivia screamed, clutching her bear.

"Olivia, dear. Please. Quiet down," her mother begged nervously.

"That's right, Livvy. Stay quiet."

"How could you, Jack? Why? We have enough money!"

Jack stepped back. "You think I like it that I can't afford to pay for the lifestyle my wife is accustomed to?"

"Be reasonable. Please."

"NO! It ends now! Where are the fucking papers?!"

"I can't tell you," she said quietly.

"Let's go, Mary. You're coming with me."

"No. You're going to have to drag me kicking and screaming from this house if you expect me to go anywhere with you. You… You traitor!"

Olivia watched as her father grabbed her mother and slammed her head against the kitchen counter. She squeezed her stuffed animal tight, remembering her mama's words to never let go of the bear.

"Livvy, sweetie. Come with Daddy. We need to get out of here."

"But Mama…"

"Your mother is fine. She's just sleeping right now. She's coming with us. Don't worry."

Olivia got up from underneath the table and followed her father out of the house and into their car, her father carrying her mother and placing her in the front seat.

They left the beach house and began driving away. As they approached the turn out, Jack saw the SUV waiting and took his foot off the accelerator.

He looked at his unconscious wife as she sat lifeless in the front seat. He hated how everything ended, but she knew too much. He glanced at his daughter sitting in the back seat as she stared at her huge stuffed animal, a large SUV about to pummel into them. A crooked smile crossed his face.

"We love you, Olivia."

Olivia didn't look up. "I know."

Chapter Thirty-Six

Betrayal

"OLIVIA, SIMON WHISPERED QUIETLY. "Please, Olivia. Wake up. I'm going to get you out of here." He shook her frail body, desperately trying to wake her up. He prayed that she wasn't already dead.

Everything was his fault. He should never have agreed to help out those fuckers last summer. He had been so angry when he got arrested that he made a deal with the devil himself, agreeing to go to prison if he could be the one to kill Olivia when the time came. But during their brief encounters over the past few months, he had begun to care for her. And now here she was, shot, beaten, and raped. He would never forgive himself. He would spend the rest of his life making it up to the poor girl, provided they both survived.

Simon scanned the room, relieved to see that Grant and Jack were still off searching the house for whatever it was they were looking for. "Come on, Olivia. You have to wake up now."

She woke up with a start. Flinging her eyes open, she was happy to actually be able to see. Then she began to remember. Simon had abducted her and then tried to help her escape. He shot her in the shoulder. And then there was Grant. He assaulted and humiliated her. Her father came to intervene, but then he knocked her out.

He was in on it.

Olivia's eyes focused on the man standing in front of her. *Simon.* She tried to get up, but she couldn't. Her legs were tied to the chair. Her wrists were bound together behind her and her mouth was taped shut.

"Shhh…" Simon said. "I promise I'm going to get you out of here, but we have to be very quiet or we'll both end up dead. Do you understand?"

Olivia nodded her head in understanding, her eyes going wide in panic when she noticed a large figure moving swiftly behind Simon. She tried to warn him, but all that came out was her desperate cries.

"What the fuck do you think you're doing?!" Grant roared, hitting Simon over the head with the barrel of his gun, knocking him out.

Olivia screamed, hopelessly pulling at her restraints.

"Oh, look who's up," Grant said cruelly, walking over to where she was bound to the chair. "About time, too. Daddy is getting a little impatient to find out where you buried that chest he is so eager to find."

She tried to speak through the tape.

"What was that? Where is he? Oh, he's out searching the property. He couldn't wait for you to wake up." He hovered over her, making her flinch from his proximity. "We weren't sure if you ever would, to be honest." Grant dragged his hand up her thigh.

Olivia tried to scream out and push away from him, but it was no use.

"What the fuck did I tell you about touching her?" Jack yelled, walking into the great room.

"Come on, dude. Relax. You're the one that tied her up like this."

Jack rolled his eyes. "Grant, focus. Please. Stop thinking with your pecker and use your brain for once, if that's even possible."

"Whatever. I think that bitch daughter of yours is more scared about me touching her than killing her. My way is definitely better."

Jack exhaled loudly, turning his attention back to Olivia. "Where are the papers, Livvy? Do you remember? Or do I have to let Grant have another go?"

Olivia stared ahead in horror that the man in front of her was actually her father.

"Are they even here?"

Olivia continued to display no emotion, knowing full well what Grant was going to do if she didn't show any indication that she would disclose the location of the documents.

"Fine. Do whatever you want. If she's not going to help, may as well kill her now." Jack turned to leave and continue his search.

Olivia screamed out again, her pleas for help still muffled.

"What's with the dried blood here, Livvy?" Grant said cruelly. "Am I a bigger man than that Alexander you've been screwing?"

She closed her eyes, not wanting to keep them open to see the look on Grant's face. She heard the door open and close and became sick to her stomach that her father had returned to watch.

Her eyes grew wide when she heard a gunshot.

~~~~~~~~~~

"WHAT THE HELL WAS that?" Jack growled, walking down the hall to determine the source of the sound. "I didn't think you'd actually shoot…"

"Jack," Alexander said, an accusatory tone in his voice.

He stopped in his tracks, processing the scene in front of him, his heart racing. Grant lay dead at Olivia's feet and Alexander stood in the doorway next to Martin. They were both holding a gun aimed at him. Jack immediately raised his own weapon and pointed it at Olivia. He knew Alexander would do anything to save that girl.

Her eyes went wide and she continued to stare at Alexander, pleading with him to help her.

Trying to scan the room to determine if there were any other threats to their safety, Alexander couldn't break his eyes from Olivia's, his face flushing red with anger when he took in her bruised and beaten frame. It made him sick to his stomach, but he needed to stay strong. Surveying her body, he saw that her left foot was badly bruised. He was certain she had quite a few broken bones. There was a bullet wound that appeared to go through her right shoulder, drenching her white sundress a dark red color. She seemed to have lost quite a bit of blood and he wondered how she could still be conscious. But what made Alexander want to scream was the sight of blood trickling down her thighs. He was beside himself with anger and guilt. Once again, he failed to protect her.

"Ah, looks like you've figured it out, son, haven't you?"

Alexander took a step closer, trying to keep his composure as Olivia looked up at him, bound and gagged.

Jack closed the distance between himself and Olivia, pressing his gun against her temple, daring Alexander to come any closer. "Drop your weapons or I will fucking kill her, daughter or not," he growled. "NOW!"

Alexander immediately stopped dead in his tracks, adrenaline coursing through his veins. He turned to Martin and nodded. Slowly, they both lowered their guns to the ground, keeping their eyes trained on Jack.

"Kick them over here."

They followed his direction, holding their hands up in surrender. Alexander had been in tighter spots before, but never did he have to fight for the life of a loved one. He couldn't afford to fuck up. "How could you?" he asked quietly. "Your own daughter, Jack. How *could* you?"

"I don't have a fucking choice in the matter, son…"

"Stop!" Alexander said, raising his voice. "Do *not* call me son! You've lost that privilege."

Jack's face softened. "You need to understand."

"Understand?!" Alexander shouted, indignant. "You're holding a gun to your daughter's head! She's been beaten, shot, and assaulted. Repeatedly!" he cried out, barely holding it together. "What can you possibly say that will help me understand?"

"I fucked up, okay?!" Jack yelled. "But these people were not to be messed with! I've seen what they do if you cross them or don't follow their instructions. Not the way I want to go."

"So it was you."

"Of course. I was the brains behind the whole fucking thing," he responded, almost sounding offended that Alexander would question his ability to pull off an operation like that. "I was able to employ the help of some other people in the CIA, the FBI, the military. No one knew about anyone else who was involved, except for Kiddish, senior. We were the only ones who knew where all the bodies were buried, so to speak. I didn't want to enlist his help, but I needed someone to keep all the other players in line."

"I don't understand," Alexander said. "Why were those documents at your house to begin with? For anyone to find? Not very smart, Jack." He wanted him to keep talking.

"I couldn't keep that shit at the office, now could I? Someone would eventually catch on. Never did I think that someone at home would. So she had to be dealt with." A twisted look came across Jack's face of part remorse and part satisfaction.

"No," Alexander said quietly. "Marilyn..." He looked to Olivia, tears streaming down her face. "You killed your own wife?" he asked, unable to comprehend that the monster standing in front of him was the same man he used to build sand castles with when he was younger.

"I HAD TO! SHE KNEW TOO FUCKING MUCH!" Jack took a deep breath. "She was smarter than I gave her credit for. She was onto me. She found all the documents that we had fixed. The money transfers were there. It was all there. I was careless enough to leave it out one day. I had to lie and say that it was a case I was working on. She believed me at first, but then she started to question things. I guess the money made her suspicious. I should have been smarter about hiding the extra cash coming in.

"I made up a story about some of the people I was 'investigating' catching on to me. I had hoped to scare her off so she would stop asking questions about the details of what was going on. It worked...a little too well. Marilyn went to your father, giving him the story that I fed her before she knew of my involvement. Soon, she started digging through all my stuff and, eventually, put it all together. She knew too much. I had no choice."

"So you killed her."

"You know the answer to that."

"But the accident…"

"Well, I guess I might as well tell you everything. None of you will be walking out of this house alive." Jack shrugged, amused, almost as if he was proud of himself for what was going on. "Marilyn was dead before I even placed her in the car. I went to Kiddish, senior, to see how he thought we should deal with the potential leak. The only way was to dispose of Marilyn…and Olivia. Then I could search for the missing documents as I grieved for my deceased family. Marilyn should have kept her mouth shut. When I saw her attempting to flee with Livvy, I had to kill her. I was hoping to wait and kill her in the crash, but she was putting up a fight. I knew I was taking a risk with the car accident, as I could possibly die, too, but Kiddish said the best way would be to make it all seem natural so as to not raise suspicion. He was in on the plan. What he wasn't in on was me having to shoot him, but I wasn't expecting you and your father to show up after the crash. I had to sell it, and the only way was to kill him."

"I don't understand. Why the new identities?" Alexander asked, wanting all the information possible. He wasn't going to give up without a fight.

"It was a way to cover my involvement. Your father was helping watch out for us…at Marilyn's request. Little did I realize that she called your dad just a few hours before I got home that day, saying she was scared about something. That just shows you what your dad was like. He would drop everything to help out a friend. When you and your father stumbled across the accident, it was the perfect set-up to try and start over again. If everyone thought I died, no one would mention my involvement if there was ever a leak, which was doubtful considering I held all the documentation and the only other person who knew everything was now dead. A new identity would give me plenty of time and space to hunt for the documents, but I didn't know what Olivia would remember. Imagine my luck when the doctor explained that she suffered a rather severe brain injury and would probably have substantial memory loss.

"The best way for Olivia to forget everything was to make sure we were separated. If she never saw me, any memory about what happened at the beach house would hopefully be gone. I made sure she was given a completely new identity, totally unassociated with me. Of course, I never knew where she had been taken. During the first few years, I had quite a few of your father's security agents watching out for me, which made it difficult for me to go anywhere and search for the documents. I couldn't have planned it any better if I tried. Keeping Olivia alive was brilliant. That way, if I couldn't find the documents, I had a backup plan for finding them. Years passed and I couldn't find that damn box so I re-shifted my focus to finding Livvy. My protection detail loosened quite a bit over the years and I was able to travel more in my attempt to track her down without having to worry about anything from my former life...until your father called one day, asking too many questions. He had been going through his old files, I guess..."

"You..."

"It was the perfect opportunity to try to get Livvy's location and to dispose of another potential leak. I had to make it look like he was tortured to sell the story that he was on a protection detail. I couldn't believe Livvy was in Boston with your father, so close to where this all began. I think it worked out pretty well."

"Except for one thing..."

"What's that?"

"You weren't counting on your daughter fleeing town after you killed my dad."

"Well, that was a bit of a hiccup, and with the amount of money Marilyn left her, it was difficult to search employment records or anything for her. Right when I thought I had found her, she would disappear again. That's where Kiddish came into play. I always felt bad for having to kill his dad, but when he clocked you over the head with that gun, your dad couldn't know that I was working with him. Kiddish, junior, had been on my payroll pretty much since the accident to help me find where the box was buried. He took over the family business, after all.

"When Olivia kept disappearing, I needed the info but didn't want to get my hands dirty. I'm supposed to be dead. Kiddish would be perfect. Unfortunately, all this took a little longer than I had expected, but it's okay. I've waited twenty-two years to get my hands on this box. A little patience is expected."

"So Kiddish was just a hired goon, then?"

Jack nodded. "Pretty much. I ended up finding the girl for him last year, but after that, I didn't really know anything about what was going on. I had paid Kiddish good money to deal with everything and we maintained radio silence for months as he got the info needed. Of course, I came to Boston in February because things were moving excruciatingly slow. I didn't know what was going on, or how far Kiddish or his goons would go so I needed to keep an eye on her, too, and make sure she stayed alive...at least until she led us to the evidence box. And you thought I was playing the caring father looking out for his long-lost daughter," Jack sneered. "I do have to say that this performance may have just been my crowning achievement."

"And Simon?" Alexander asked as he looked at Simon lying on the ground. His eyes grew wide when he saw him place a finger over his mouth, slowly inching his body toward where Grant's gun lay. *I'm on your side*, he mouthed. Alexander nodded slightly, turning his eyes back to Jack.

"Kiddish thought it would be best to pay someone to date her. Maybe they'd talk about their childhoods and all that. His job was to find out the location of the box by getting close to her, but she had no memory of anything before the accident so that wasn't working. It was by pure dumb luck that she ran into you. You presented us a golden opportunity. We were able to spook both of you enough to think that she needed a constant protection detail, allowing Kiddish to use Cheryl to get close to her and see if she could find out the info. Then he was able to use Adele to split you up by telling Olivia who she really was and how you had been keeping that from her for months. And you think I'm cold-hearted…"

Olivia made a sound.

"What's that, Livvy? I can't understand you." He laughed before turning his attention back to Alexander. "After that, I knew that you'd come clean with her and that would help the memories come flooding back."

"I don't understand," Alexander said, shaking his head in confusion. "You told me that you didn't want her to know about you. Just a few months ago, you *didn't* want her to remember."

"Of course not. It was too early. I needed to approach her when she was vulnerable and needing a loving father figure. So when you screwed up your relationship with her, that was the perfect time for me to step in. I'll admit that it was risky, not knowing whether seeing me again would trigger all those memories, but it had to happen. She was the only one who could lead me to all those documents. It all worked out quite nicely."

"Except for one thing…"

"What's that?"

"That evidence isn't here."

"WHAT?!" Jack roared, pressing the gun even harder into Olivia's temple.

Alexander's heart raced. He needed to proceed cautiously. Jack was a loose cannon. Simon was so close to the gun. *Come on!* Alexander screamed in his head.

"Where is it, Livvy?" Jack demanded.

Olivia looked him in the eyes, shaking her head from side to side. Jack lifted his leg and kicked her in the stomach.

"NO!" Alexander shouted, taking a step forward as he watched Olivia keel over, screaming out in pain through her gag, tears running down her face.

Jack pushed Olivia back to a sitting position and raised his gun to her temple. "I warned you, Alex! Step the fuck back!"

Olivia's eyes met with Alexander's again, pleading for him to just end it all. She couldn't take any more pain. She was barely holding on to her consciousness as it was.

"It's not here, Jack." Alexander checked his watch. "And I'm pretty sure it's already too late to do anything."

"What are you talking about?" he asked, his mind racing.

"Olivia left plenty of clues for me, leading me straight to the evidence. Before I got here, I made sure to send all the documents to various news networks. It's over."

"You're joking," he said nervously.

"Try me. Go ahead. Check the news. I'm pretty sure they're already making arrests."

Jack walked over to the remote and turned on the large screen television, making sure to keep his gun trained on Olivia. He quickly found a national news network, his jaw dropping when he listened to a blonde anchor talk about multiple arrests of various government officials involved in acts of terrorism. "Documents we received just a short while ago indicate that these officials were responsible for selling U.S. military arms and munitions, as well as government secrets, to various terrorist organizations. These people were responsible for the downing of several flights, in addition to the bombing of multiple government buildings here and abroad. The Secretary of State made a statement saying that this is the most pervasive corruption in the government that she has ever seen. The man behind it all had apparently faked his own death over twenty years ago to cover-up his role in this operation." A photo flashed on the screen. "This is Jack DeLuca and he is wanted in connection with these acts of terrorism. He also goes by the alias Nathan Roberts."

"NO!" Jack screamed, nervously walking back to face Alexander. He pointed his gun at him, then back at Olivia, and then back at him.

Alexander looked over and saw Simon holding Grant's gun, lying flat on the ground, the gun following Jack as he paced the large room. Discreetly holding up his hand, Alexander signaled him to wait a little longer until he was certain that he'd be able to make the shot. He knew they only had one chance to take him down and he couldn't risk Simon missing. Returning his eyes to Jack, he said, "It's over."

"No, no, no, no, no...!" he cried out, shaking his head. After several intense moments, he slowly lowered his gun.

Alexander breathed a sigh of relief, taking a step toward Jack to retrieve his weapon and restrain him.

In the blink of an eye, Jack raised his gun and shot Olivia through the chest, a cruel look of fulfillment crossing his face.

"NOOO!" Alexander screamed as more shots rang out. Jack fell to the floor and Simon got up, running over to him, shooting him through the heart several more times while Alexander ran to Olivia's side.

He quickly cut her from her restraints and pulled the tape off her mouth. He lowered her lifeless body to the floor and frantically tried to find a pulse as Martin dialed 911.

"Come on, Olivia!" he cried. "You cannot die on me! Not now. Please. Stay with me." Alexander cradled her in his arms. "I can't survive without you." Tears overtook him as he wept for his Olivia lying lifeless in his arms. "I need you, love. I promise I'll always protect you from now on. Nothing bad will ever happen to you again. Just, please... Come back to me..."

CHAPTER THIRTY-SEVEN

GRIEF

ALEXANDER SAT IN A complete daze as the EMTs arrived and pried Olivia from his arms, speechless from the trauma of what he just witnessed.

After paramedics administered CPR and found a pulse, they quickly put Olivia on a gurney, continuing to give her oxygen.

"Sir, is this your wife?" Alexander heard a voice say as he stared blankly ahead, still unable to process what was happening. "Sir?"

Alexander finally snapped to. He cleared his throat, grabbing the ring from his pocket. "Yes. She is." He gently placed the ring back on her finger where it belonged, a tear falling down his cheek as he felt Olivia's cold hand.

"We're taking her to Cape Cod Hospital. Would you like to ride with us?"

Alexander slowly nodded his head, following the EMTs out of the beach house.

"I'll stay here and take care of the police," Martin said to Alexander as he walked through the doorway. Their eyes met and Martin couldn't remember ever seeing him so distraught. "She'll pull through, sir. She's a strong girl."

"I'm so sorry, Alex!" Simon called out, clutching the gun. "I never meant for this to happen." He fell to the floor, crying.

Alexander showed no emotion as he turned to catch up with the EMTs, an empty expression on his face.

The next several hours passed in a daze while Alexander sat in the waiting area at the emergency room, gazing ahead at the white walls. Every time he closed his eyes, Olivia's lifeless, blood-stained body flashed in his memory.

"Alex! Snap out of it!" his sister pleaded with him as soon as she reached the hospital in the early morning hours. "Come on. Olivia is in there fighting for her life. You need to tell us what happened...to help her. They got almost everyone involved, except Kiddish. He got away. He's still out there so you need to tell us what the fuck happened!"

To help her. Of course! "Damn it!" Alexander roared, punching the wall, startling several nurses.

Carol ran and put her arms around him, trying to calm him down. "There's my baby brother. Now, what happened?" she asked, leading him back to his chair.

A tear fell down his face. "She was shot," he quivered. "The bastard shot her in the chest." He looked past his sister. "He's dead now, though. They're both dead. Simon..."

"What about Simon?" Carol asked urgently, needing all the pieces of the puzzle.

"He was in on it. I think he's the one that abducted her...but then something must have happened. Like he intervened on her behalf because, when I got there, he was knocked out cold on the floor. Then he came to and shot Jack. Simon helped! But Grant... He fucking raped her! And her dad let him!" Alexander let out a small cry, remembering the sight of Olivia tied to the chair, blood trickling down her thighs. "If he wasn't already dead, I'd kill the motherfucker myself!"

Carol turned to face Alexander, grabbing his hands in hers. "She's going to be okay, Alex. I just know it. You didn't spend your entire life looking for this girl just for her to be taken from you again." She stared at her brother, trying to reassure him. He looked like a shell of his former self.

He had seen some heavy shit during his time abroad and had dealt with it fine, but he could not handle losing Olivia all over again. He knew that he wouldn't survive this if she didn't pull through. Olivia was the only thing that kept him going. She was his heart.

Carol stood up, knowing that the press would have questions

about what was going on. "I'm going to keep the police away from you, and I'll make sure they have a spokesman on standby to deal with the media. I'll call your publicist, as well, and tell her that she is *not* to answer any questions or make any comments on your behalf until further notice. Okay?"

He nodded and Carol turned to go make a few phone calls. "One more thing, please," he said quietly.

She stopped and faced him. "What is it, Alex? Whatever you need."

Taking a deep breath, he met her eyes. "I need you to call a Dr. Cameron Bowen out of Jacksonville. Send the plane for him. I don't know what Olivia's mental state will be when she wakes up. He needs to be here when she does. He's brought her back from the darkness before. He may need to be here to do it again."

Carol placed her hand on his shoulder, trying to comfort him. "Okay. You got it."

"Thanks, Carol. I don't know what I'd do without you."

"Anything for you. You know I love you." She gave him a quick hug. Then she left to go make all the arrangements Alexander requested.

Several minutes later, Mo came running into the waiting room. "Alex!" he exclaimed, his eyes red from crying.

"Mo! Jesus Christ!" Alexander jumped out of his chair, running to him.

Mo hugged him, trying to comfort him.

"I don't know what to do! I can't stand it!" Alexander cried out, pacing the short length of the waiting room as he ran his hands through his hair. "She's been in there for hours and no one is saying anything!"

"Sucks, doesn't it?" Mo commented, recalling how he felt when Kiera was in the same exact position just a few short weeks earlier.

"Goddammit! I just want to know what the hell is going on! All they tell me is that she is in the best hands possible. I don't care what hands she's in as long as she comes out of this alive. FUCK!" He slammed his fist into the wall again.

"Mr. Burnham?" a quiet voice interrupted, getting

Alexander and Mo's attention. He turned to see a solemn looking doctor standing in green scrubs. She was short and blonde with a sweet face.

"Yes. I'm Alexander Burnham." His heart raced.

"Can I speak with you in private please, sir?"

Alexander looked at Mo. "Anything you need to tell me, you can say in front of Mo here. He's Olivia's family."

The doctor looked at Mo before nodding her head. "My name is Dr. Hatheway. My team and I have been operating on your wife for the past several hours. It was touch-and-go for a while, and we lost her for a little bit, but we were able to bring her back. She is extremely weak. She has lost a great deal of blood, but she has stabilized for the time being. We just need to continue to monitor her vitals."

Alexander breathed a sigh of relief. "So she's going to be okay?"

"I didn't say that. We're not entirely out of the woods yet. She's suffered a great deal but, for now, she's stable."

Mo hugged Alexander, patting his back.

"Can I see her? Please?"

The doctor smiled. "Of course. Follow me."

Alexander turned to Mo, hoping he would understand if he wanted to go by himself.

"I'll let you have a moment alone with her," Mo said.

"Thanks." Alexander followed Dr. Hatheway down several hallways, finally stopping outside of the ICU.

She turned to face him. "Before you go in there, there's something else I need to tell you. Apparently, Mrs. Burnham had been kicked in the stomach multiple times. She suffered from several cracked ribs. I'm sorry, but she lost the baby."

Alexander stared wide-eyed at Dr. Hatheway. "Sh...she was pregnant?"

"Oh. You didn't know? She was about six weeks along. She hasn't miscarried yet and there's no telling when she will. There was nothing we could do to save the baby. The miscarriage may not have been a result of what happened to her. It may have occurred naturally, but I just wanted to let you know."

Alexander did the math. Of course. After seeing Kiera in the hospital when they first got back together. "Damn it..." he breathed, shaking his head. "Is she going to be okay to eventually...?"

"If she pulls through, she will be able to have lots and lots of babies. There's been no permanent damage. Don't worry." Dr. Hatheway winked as she opened the door to Olivia's recovery room. "I'll give you some privacy."

Alexander thanked her and she closed the door, leaving him alone with Olivia, the rising sun brightening the room. He walked over to where her lifeless body lay. He listened to the gentle beeping of the heart monitor and watched her chest rise and fall. Her left foot was in a cast, and her right shoulder was in a sling. He didn't want to see her other wounds, not knowing whether he could stomach seeing anything else.

He sat down in the chair next to her bed and grabbed her hand in his. "Olivia, love," he whispered through the lump in his throat. "I am so sorry. I just... I never thought in a million years that your father..."

He leaned over and brushed his lips against Olivia's cold cheek, still clutching her hand. "I should have figured it out earlier. I'm so sorry. All the clues were there. I still can't believe all those documents were sewed tight inside Mr. Bear all these years. Your mama..." He squeezed Olivia's hand as a tear fell down his cheek.

"Your mama would be so proud of what you did. *I'm* so proud of you..." He looked at her hand, toying with the ring on her finger.

"I told you not to leave the house!" he cried out, knowing that she had no control over it. "You never did like following instructions, did you?" he said, a hint of amusement in his voice. "God, even when we were kids, you never listened to me. You always played by your own rules, and I always let you get away with it because it made you happy. And when you were happy, it made me happy. I've always loved you, Olivia..."

Alexander looked around the room, a painting of a snowy scene catching his eye. He smiled at his memories of them together as children. "You HATED the snow. God, I never heard the end of it. You were such a whiny kid whenever it snowed. Then, one day, I finally dragged you out to play with me and, with your mama's help, we built our very first snowman. Every day that week, you would come out and play in the snow with me. I even let you talk me into having a tea party with that snowman. I was the only seven-year-old boy in Mystic who was whipped enough to agree to have a tea party with a girl in his own front yard!" He smiled at the memory.

"When I had to start school, you were beside yourself. You screamed and cried. You were so worried that I would go off to school and make all new friends and forget all about you." His eyes became sincere and he lowered his voice. "But I could never forget about you. That first day of grade school, all I could think about was you.

"I remember your first day, too. I held your hand as we walked to school. You didn't understand why you couldn't just skip ahead to third grade to be with me. That day, during recess, I saw two boys teasing you, pulling your cute little braids. I was so mad. Nobody messed with you after that day. You had a third-grader on your side." His eyes glistened with unshed tears at the memory. "My friends always teased me about you, but I didn't care. You were worth it. You were *always* worth it." He stared down affectionately, his chin quivering.

"The day of the accident was the day after Tyler was born. At first, I was so mad at my mom for even thinking of having a baby during the summer, taking me away from you and the beach. For the longest time, I even blamed Tyler for your death. I ignored him. I couldn't even look at him. That's when my parents put me in therapy, and I eventually got over it. But I never got over your death. When I found you last year, Olivia… I was so torn. I was thrilled you were still alive, but then I knew there must have been a reason for it all. I was scared for you. And for me because I really didn't think I could survive if I lost you all over again… I barely made it out the first time. Please, love…don't leave me here without you…"

He looked down at her stomach, gently lying his hand over

it. "You'll be an amazing mama someday. I'm so sorry, Olivia. I had no idea…" Alexander sobbed for his battered and beaten love and for the child that no longer continued to grow inside of her.

"You'll be a great dad someday, too."

Alexander swung his head around.

"Oh, Ma!" He buried his head in his hands, not wanting his mother to see him at his breaking point.

"Hey, hey…" Colleen said, walking toward her son, comforting him with her arms. "I came as soon as Carol called. Now stop with those tears. Olivia's going to survive. She's one tough cookie."

Alexander shook his head. "She was pregnant, Ma. I had no idea…" He raised his head to look his mother in the eyes.

"Was?"

Alexander nodded his head slowly, looking down at Olivia's body, placing his hand back over hers. "The doctor said she was only about six weeks along…"

Colleen stood next to Alexander, gently placing her hand on Olivia's stomach. "You better get healthy, Libby. I want some grandchildren before I'm dead."

Alexander smiled a bit. "Finally given up on Carol, then?"

"That ship sailed a long time ago, I'm afraid."

Alexander turned around and saw Carol and Tyler standing in the doorway with Mo and Bridget slightly behind them.

"Hey, guys," Alexander said, standing up to greet everyone, wiping his eyes.

"How's she doing?" Tyler asked, his face full of concern.

"She's stable, for now, but they're going to keep an eye on her." Alexander looked away, not wanting anyone to see the tears reforming in his eyes.

"Can I?" Mo asked, gesturing toward one of the chairs surrounding Olivia's bed.

Alexander nodded. "Of course."

Mo approached her, unsure of whether he would be prepared to see Olivia in the same place Kiera was just a few weeks earlier. "Oh, god…" he said quietly, a tear falling from his face as he looked over her frail body. "What happened to her?" It was so much worse than Kiera.

Alexander's eyes met Mo's, both men at their breaking point. "More than any one person should ever have to endure in their lifetime. The same fucker that did most of this to Olivia is the same person who attacked Kiera. I shot the bastard."

Mo let out a sigh of relief. "Thank god. I left Kiera with her parents, worried that this guy would still be after her."

"There's a lot more to the story, but I don't even want to think about any of that right now," he said, returning his gaze to his Olivia. "I just want to focus on doing everything I can to make sure she gets better."

"We're all here for you," Colleen said, placing her hand on Alexander's shoulder and squeezing. "And for her. She's family."

"Yes, she is."

CHAPTER THIRTY-EIGHT

ALWAYS

"CAM, DON'T ANSWER IT," a sweet voice drowsily said as the early morning Florida sun began to rise on Amelia Island.

He groaned, glancing at the beautiful brunette in bed beside him before grabbing his cell phone. It had been ringing constantly for the past five minutes. Whomever was calling wasn't about to give up.

"I have to, Taylor. It could be an emergency." He threw back the duvet and climbed out of bed, gazing at her tall, lean naked body, wishing he could just forget about Olivia. No matter how many women he dated, he just couldn't forget about those beautiful brown eyes.

"Dr. Bowen," Cam spoke into the phone.

"Dr. Bowen? My name is Detective David Wilder with the Boston Police Department. I'm sending a plane to Jacksonville Airport. We need you up in Boston."

Cam's heart began to race. *Boston? Why Boston? It must mean...* "What's going on in Boston?"

David sighed loudly. "Technically, you'll be heading to the Cape. Alexander Burnham has requested you be here. It's Olivia..."

"Olivia?" he asked quickly, nerves coursing through his body. "What's wrong with Olivia?"

"I'll go through all the details during the flight. Mr. Burnham needs you to be there for her, if and when she wakes up."

Cam let out a quiet sob. *What happened?*

281

~~~~~~~~~~

TWO HOURS LATER, CAM was sitting on a luxurious Gulfstream heading north. It took him a fair bit to process the story that the man sitting across from him had relayed. It sounded like something from a horrible movie. Yet it was Olivia's life.

"We need you to help us understand how this is going to affect her," the man named David said.

Snapping out of his shock, Cam knew he had a job to do. Olivia needed him…more than she had ever needed him in the past. All her friends and family were desperate for an explanation.

"What everyone needs to understand is this guy's mental state. I've looked at her father's file. This is someone who went into the Marines at eighteen. He did his time and then joined the agency. Hell, he had already been working on special-ops by the time he was twenty-four. He didn't meet Olivia's mother until he had already been working for the agency for quite a while. I don't want to be the one to say it but, based on everything I see in front of me here, this was someone who used his family as a cover-up for who he truly was…a person with no feelings, no emotion. He had been trained to know what people would expect and how to convince them that he was a well-adjusted member of society. That's what he was doing all those years. He put on a show, pretending to care about his wife and his daughter, but he was just using that as a front to hide his true nature, including his criminal behavior. You know how it is. You're always less likely to expect the doting husband and loving father to be capable of committing horrendous crimes."

David shook his head, having trouble understanding. "But my father-in-law, Alexander's dad…he was in the agency, too. He wasn't anything like this monster."

Cam nodded his head. "Yes, and most people can learn to turn it off. It doesn't appear Jack ever did. He couldn't separate his CIA persona with his real persona. After a while, he became the person the CIA wanted him to be. He couldn't separate it so he had no problem killing his wife. She was just another target in his mind. And Olivia…" He paused, trying to block out all the horrible things that she had endured over the past day. "Olivia…" he trembled. "She was just an asset. Nothing more. The minute she failed to be valuable to him, he had no problem disposing of her."

"But he just stepped aside while she was assaulted," David urged. "Repeatedly. I just can't understand why any father, no matter how fucked up in the head you are, could do that."

"I know," Cam agreed. "But we have compassion, something this guy never had. He never saw her as his daughter. The bond that most of us have with our own parents never existed between Olivia and her father. Olivia may have felt it, but he never did. Any happy memories she may think she had with him were simply moments that he was playing the part. When push came to shove and he became desperate enough to find that evidence, he was willing to try anything. Including…"

"Fucking bastard," David mumbled.

Cam nodded his head, all his thoughts consumed by Olivia and what kind of mental state she would be in after going through what she did those past twenty-four hours. The air was thick with silence while both men processed everything. As the plane began its final descent, Cam spoke again, "I'm not sure what we can expect when she wakes up. She's probably going to have a lot of questions that she may not like the answers to. The most important thing is that she be surrounded by people that love her. Her family."

~~~~~~~~~~

"CAM! THANK GOD YOU'RE here!" Alexander exclaimed when he heard the door open and glanced back to see him walk into Olivia's hospital room. He jumped up from his chair and hugged the one person that he knew could bring her back from whatever dark place she would be in when she finally woke up.

"How is she?" Cam asked, his face awash with concern.

Alexander shrugged, fighting back the tears. "No one knows. They don't know when she'll wake up. She was…"

"David already told me," Cam interrupted, knowing that it would be difficult for Alexander to talk about what happened. He walked over to the bed and stared down at Olivia's lifeless body, fearful of what she would have to go through when she woke up. As if suffering at the hands of the man that gave her life wasn't bad enough, she would now have to live with that every day for the rest of her existence. Cam prayed she would be strong enough to make it through. He glanced over at Alexander clutching her small hand in his own, his eyes trained lovingly on Olivia, and Cam knew that with him by her side, she could get through anything.

Sighing deeply, he turned to Alexander. "I'll let you have some time with her. I'll be here when she wakes up."

Alexander shook Cam's hand, looking him in the eyes. "Thank you for being here. For leaving your life to be here for me, and for Olivia. It seems that you're the only one who knows how to get through to her."

Cam simply nodded and left the room, heading straight to the men's room and letting all the pent-up emotions wash over him as he cried for Olivia, praying that she would wake up.

~~~~~~~~~~

"MR. BURNHAM, I'M SORRY." Dr. Hatheway made a few notes on the chart attached to Olivia's bed as she spoke to him Saturday afternoon. "I wish I could give you more information, but I just don't know. All her vital signs are good. But for now, it's just a waiting game."

"What can I do? Do you think she can hear me?" The longer she remained unconscious, the more fearful Alexander became that she was slipping further away.

"It's hard to say. Just talk to her as if she was awake. Maybe if she keeps hearing your voice, it will give her something to fight for. She's in there somewhere. Give her a reason to come back." She smiled before walking toward the door. "I'll give you some privacy."

He thanked her and turned back to face Olivia. He had never felt so helpless in his entire life. It was the worst feeling in the world, not knowing when or if she would wake up. He vowed to stay by her side until she came back to him. She *needed* to come back to him.

"It's August twenty-fourth." He sat down and grabbed her hand, toying with her ring. "Our wedding day. Well, what was *supposed* to be our wedding day." He caressed her hand, marveling at how small it looked compared to his. "I just wanted to get the horrible memories of this date out of my head. I hated what the day represented."

Alexander smiled, remembering the previous year. "Last year, when I went to Mystic to visit your grave, it was so strange. I would normally sit and tell you everything that had happened that year. That's why I always kept a journal. In fact, nearly every day since the day we buried you, I wrote you a letter, telling you about what was going on in my life."

He reached down and grabbed a journal from a large box. "See, this is from the year you were taken from me. I had Carter bring a few things to me. I'm willing to try anything to get you to wake up."

Looking over at Olivia's pale face, he opened the notebook. "This was Mom's idea, actually. She said that maybe if I wrote to you, I could keep you alive somehow…" He trailed off, trying to hide his tears. Taking a deep breath, he closed his eyes, willing himself to stay strong. It was getting more and more difficult with each passing minute.

"September first. Dear Olibia…" He looked up, smiling. "Oh, love, you should see how horrible my handwriting was back then. I can barely read it." Returning his gaze to the journal in front of him, he continued, "You were put in the ground today. I never even got to say good-bye to you. It's not fair. One day you were lying in the hospital bed. I told you to wake up. I guess you just didn't want to listen to me. Why couldn't you listen to me just once? Is it really that difficult?! I'm sorry, Olibia. I don't mean to yell at you. It's not your fault. I don't know whose fault it is. I miss you. I got back from the funeral this afternoon and I changed into my play clothes. I ran out of the house to go and play with you and then I realized that you're not there to play with me anymore..."

Alexander lowered his head, clutching Olivia's hand in his. "I'm sorry, love," he sobbed. "I don't think I can finish."

"Find a happier memory, Alex, darling..."

He turned his head around, surprised to see his mother standing in the doorway. "Ma. What are you doing here?"

"Just checking to see how you're holding up." She walked over and placed her hand on his shoulder.

"Not good, Ma. I just want her to wake up. That's all. Every minute that goes by, I feel like she's slipping further and further away." He trembled.

Colleen sat down next to her son and wrapped her arms around him. "Oh, Alex. I know it may seem so bleak right now, but you need to stay strong."

"How do I do that?" he asked, meeting her eyes.

"Think of what you would say to her if she was awake. She's probably itching to wake up and she will. She's a fighter."

Alexander clutched his mother's arms, no longer trying to hide his emotions. "I just can't lose her. Not again."

"You won't. So buck up and tell her one of your happier memories." She helped him straighten up. "Come on. I know you've got some in there."

He thought about her words for a minute. Smiling, he reached down and grabbed his journal from the previous year. He flipped through the pages, searching for a certain entry. "Ah, here it is. August nineteenth. Dear Olivia, I met someone this weekend. I can't explain it, but this is a girl I actually want to get to know, instead of just bang and then kick to the curb..." Alexander cringed, looking at his mother. "Sorry, Ma."

"Alex, darling, I am perfectly aware of all your previous sexual exploits, as is most of the country."

He blushed before returning his eyes to his journal, reading out loud once more, "She is absolutely breathtaking. If you hadn't died, I'm pretty sure you would look just like this girl. She has the deepest brown eyes I've ever seen. Her smile has probably broken many hearts, and her lips... Well, I am anxious to get a taste of them." His heart warmed at the memory as he gazed down at Olivia's cold lips, thinking how much they had both grown together since that fateful night a year ago.

"But there's something about her that reminds me of you. There are so many coincidences. Her name is Olivia, too. Well, technically, it's Sarah. Olivia is her middle name, but she goes by Olivia. She also lost her parents in a car accident. I know I shouldn't read too much into it, but what are the chances? There's something about her, though, that I just can't put my finger on. The way she carries herself is almost tragic. Her gorgeous eyes show the chaos deep within her soul, and I want her to let me in to see what's underneath her hard exterior."

Gazing over at Olivia's body, he recalled the first time he saw her beautiful brown eyes. It seemed as if there was a glimmer of recognition there. The first time he touched her, he felt an electricity and excitement that he couldn't remember experiencing with another person in all his years.

Returning his attention to the journal in his hands, he continued, "I first laid eyes on her as she was running down State Street, trying to get away from some creep who was chasing her. Turns out he was some guy she used to 'date'. Apparently, her idea of relationships is quite like mine. Fuck and then leave. But, with her, it almost seems like she does that to keep everyone away, as if she doesn't want to get close. I just can't figure it out. And there are too many coincidences. After finally giving up hope of finding you, I run into this girl. Is it you? Part of me wants it to be you. But another part of me hopes that you are safely looking over me from above because if you are still alive, why did Dad tell me you died? Why the secrets?"

His chin quivered as memories came flooding back. He wasn't ready to say good-bye yet. She had to come back to him. They hadn't even started living their lives together. Tears fell from his eyes as he buried his head against Olivia's still body, not wanting to come to terms with the idea of losing her all over again. "Please… Don't leave me…"

"Alex…"

That was his Olivia's voice, he was sure of it. His eyes went wide and he looked at his mother, hoping that she had heard it, too. Her seat was empty. He returned his gaze to Olivia. Her eyes were closed and there was no hint of movement. Maybe he was losing his mind from the lack of sleep. Still, he was certain that he heard her say his name.

"What was it that your mama always said when we were arguing? The best solution to any problem is music?" He shrugged. "Something like that anyway…"

He looked over to where his guitar case sat in the corner of the room with the other items that Carter had brought to him. "Maybe that's the answer." He walked over and grabbed his guitar out of the case. Olivia lived and breathed music. Maybe it was what she needed to wake up. He didn't care how stupid it sounded. He was desperate and willing to try anything.

Looking out the window into the darkness of the night, he checked the tuning on his guitar. He was starting to have a bad feeling about what that day would bring. It was, after all, August twenty-fourth. A day that had brought him nothing but sorrow and pain in the past.

He thought for a minute about what to play. It needed to be something Olivia would want to hear. "You've been on a bit of a Coldplay kick lately, haven't you?" he asked, looking at her, hoping she would answer. "Okay. Coldplay it is then, love."

He began playing the opening chords of *Till Kingdom Come*, looking over Olivia's beaten frame as he sang for her. Hoping to see any sign of movement as he played, he poured his heart into the song. He thought about all those hours he and Olivia would spend in the music room at their house, fooling around and playing together. It always brought back memories of their time as children. He wished that he had told her everything sooner. There were so many things he wanted to share with her. He wanted to reminisce about their past. He just hoped it wasn't too late.

As he sang the words, he knew that they were true. He would never leave Olivia's side. He would sit there and wait for her, no matter how long it took. It was fate that they had found each other again. He knew, deep down, that fate would bring her back to him once more. When she woke up, he planned on never letting her go. He vowed to be an open book and never keep anything from her again.

After finishing the song, he placed his guitar back in the case. He stood up, looking down at Olivia, silently pleading for her to wake up. He watched her for several minutes, looking for a sign of movement. Shaking his head in defeat, he walked over to the window and stared out at the night sky.

"I think a part of me has always been waiting for you…"

Alexander turned abruptly at the sound of the voice coming from the bed. Olivia's eyes were open and her one good arm was reaching for him.

"Olivia?" He rushed to her side, frantically pressing the nurse's call button.

"Alex… I'm so sorry," she whispered, tears streaming down her face.

The door to the room swung open and Dr. Hatheway ran inside. "She's awake? I don't believe it." The doctor feverishly began checking her vital signs. "My name is Dr. Hatheway. Do you know where you are?"

"In the hospital," Olivia responded, her eyes frantically scanning the room as she tried to comprehend what was going on.

Alexander stood to the side, anxious to be able to hold Olivia but couldn't with the medical staff checking and prodding her.

"Good. Do you know why you're here?"

Olivia nodded slowly, biting her bottom lip, trying to stop her chin from quivering. "Yes. I was shot, kicked, and…"

"ENOUGH!" Alexander roared, the entire room becoming eerily silent.

Everyone turned to look at him.

"Please. I beg you. Do not make her relive what she's been through. Not now…" He didn't know if he could bear hearing those words come out of her sweet mouth.

"I apologize. I was just trying to determine whether she's

suffered any memory loss," Dr. Hatheway said to him before turning back to Olivia. "Do you know the man standing over there?" she asked, gesturing toward Alexander.

A peaceful look crept across her face. "Yes. I've known him my entire life. He saved me…"

A warmth spread through Alexander's body when he saw Olivia smile. "Actually, love, Simon saved all of us. I owe him my life right now…"

"Simon? I don't understand…"

"Don't worry about it now. When you're ready, we'll talk about it. But, for now, just relax."

"Well, everything looks stable. How are you feeling?" Dr. Hatheway asked.

"I hurt all over. My shoulder and chest and foot and stomach…"

Alexander grabbed Olivia's hand, looking up at the doctor. "Olivia, there's something I need to tell you…"

She looked into Alexander's eyes and immediately became concerned when she saw them begin to water with new tears. "What is it?" she asked nervously.

"Darling, did you know you were pregnant?"

She slowly nodded, lowering her hand to her stomach, Alexander placing his over it as well. "I just took a pregnancy test the morning of…" She trailed off, her voice shaking. "Why are you talking in the past tense, Alex?" Her eyes flew from his to the doctor's, landing back on Alexander's, desperately wanting someone to tell her what was going on.

"I'm so sorry, Olivia. The baby didn't make it," Alexander said, clutching her hands.

Her entire body began to shake and tears fell down her face. "NO!" she cried out. "I never should have left the house. I should have put up more of a fight. I never did like to listen to you, did I?" she joked, smiling a little, lightening the tense atmosphere in the room.

Alexander returned her smile. "No, Olivia. You never did like to listen to me, even when we were kids."

"Well," Dr. Hatheway interrupted. "Everything is looking good. I'll give you two some privacy, but I must strongly insist that Mrs. Burnham get some rest. She's been through an awful lot and the drugs will knock her back out soon anyway."

"Yes, doctor. Thank you," Alexander said. "Really. Thank you."

"My pleasure, sir." She smiled, leaving the room.

Alexander returned his gaze to Olivia, caressing her forehead where her scar was.

"Mrs. Burnham?" She looked at him, a smirk on her face.

"It does have a nice ring to it, doesn't it?"

Olivia nodded in agreement as Alexander fed her some water. "How did you know?"

"I know cryptic, love. It wasn't too hard to figure it all out. Why didn't you just leave a note or something at your house?"

"I overheard Grant talking about how Marshall was involved. I sent you a text, but it didn't go through. I realized that right before I had to leave. Once the house was empty, she could have gotten in, so I needed it to look normal, as if I wasn't sending you a message."

"Why the beach house? That's not where all the evidence even was."

Olivia smiled. "I needed to lead them on a wild goose chase. I needed to be as far away from the evidence, but also close enough so you could get to me quickly if things went wrong. I thought of the first place I could. The beach house...where I fell in the rocks and got the scar. To be honest, that's where I thought the chest was buried right up until I left my house. As I was sorting through the last box of photos, I remembered something...how my mama asked me to tell her where I buried the box and then how she sewed all those papers inside Mr. Bear. I had to lead *them* away from the evidence, but lead *you* to it. It was the only way. Never in a million years did I think I would..." Her chin quivered, the memories of everything she had endured those past several days fresh in her mind.

Alexander gently wrapped his arms around her. "Hey. None of this is your fault."

Olivia took a few deep breaths as she tried to control her tears. "Like I said, I wasn't sure what Simon's game was. He said he wanted to help, but I just didn't know. I had to make him believe that I would be taking him and Grant to where the documents were buried, but I needed you to figure out where they really were so if anything happened to me, it wouldn't be for nothing. I just never would have thought my father..."

Alexander gently rubbed Olivia's arms. "Let's not talk about it anymore. You get some sleep."

Olivia yawned, clutching Alexander's hand in her own. "Please stay..."

Alexander pressed his mouth to hers. "I'll stay forever."

A smile spread across her lips as she closed her eyes. "Good, because now that you knocked me up, you need to make an honest woman out of me."

Alexander laughed. "I'd make an honest woman out of you even if I *didn't* knock you up. You better rest up and get healthy so we can get back to practicing making babies."

"Hey, Alex?" Olivia asked sleepily.

"Yes?"

"What day is it?"

"It's Saturday."

She opened her eyes, heavy with exhaustion. "Happy birthday. I'm sorry. I forgot to get you a present."

"Oh, doll, you're the best present. Now rest up so you can get better."

Olivia closed her eyes. "I love you, Alexander Burnham."

"And I love you, Olivia DeLuca. Always have. Always will."

CHAPTER THIRTY-NINE

COMPLETE

"WHERE IS SHE? I want to see her!" Alexander heard, waking him from his sleep. He looked around the hospital room where Olivia rested, a look of peace finally on her face. He hoped the nightmares were gone once and for all.

"Goddammit! That's our granddaughter in there!" a muffled voice sounded from down the hallway.

"Shit!" Alexander exclaimed, jumping from his chair and heading out the door to speak to Rose and Donald Harris.

"Alex!" Rose exclaimed. "What is going on? We got a phone call saying that Olivia's alive. Please say it's…"

"Yes," he replied. "It's true. She's alive, but she's in pretty bad shape right now." He lowered his voice. "Please. Let's go somewhere we can talk, and then I'll check with her to make sure she's strong enough to see you. She's had a rough go of it lately."

"Okay," Donald agreed, sighing, trying to comfort his emotional wife. Alexander led them down the hallway and into the hospital cafeteria. After grabbing a few coffees, he sat down with Olivia's grandparents and told them everything. How she never died in that crash. How his father changed her identity to protect her, making everyone believe that she actually *did* die. How Alexander found her in August and realized it was her, but kept her true identity a secret…at first for selfish reasons, and then to protect her. How Olivia's father led a corruption ring, selling government secrets to known terror organizations. How their daughter died trying to expose him.

And how Olivia almost died doing the same thing.

"I just want to meet her," Rose cried out, clutching her husband's hand.

Alexander looked up. "Rose, you already have. That girl you ran into in the bathroom back in October the night before the Newport Marathon…"

A quiet sob left Rose's mouth. "That was…?"

"That's Olivia."

"Oh!" Rose cried out, burying her face in her husband's chest. "She looks so much like her mother."

"Yes," Alexander said, a twinkle in his eye. "She certainly does."

~~~~~~~~~~

"CAM? IS THAT YOU?" Olivia sobbed out later that day when detectives wanted to begin questioning her about what had happened at the beach house.

"Hey, Libby," he said softly, rushing to her side and wrapping his arms around her. Alexander nodded and retreated from her recovery room, giving them some privacy.

"I just don't understand," she cried into his chest.

"Hush. It's all okay. You're going to be okay. You're stronger than this. I'm going to stay by your side as long as you need me to. I'll explain everything, and make you understand that nothing you could have done would have stopped what happened, okay?"

Olivia pulled her head out of Cam's chest and looked into his brilliant silver eyes that were full of compassion. Wiping her tears, she nodded, thankful that he was there for her.

He stayed by her side throughout the week, helping her understand exactly how her father could do what he did and feel no remorse for his actions. It was difficult to process but, in the end, Olivia was grateful he was there. She didn't know how she would have dealt with everything had Cam not been there to shed light on her father's mentality.

Once Cam deemed her strong enough toward the end of the week, a detective arrived, wanting her statement. Glancing around the hospital room, she was thankful to have Carol and Alexander there alongside Cam to help her answer all the questions the police were asking.

"So, let's go back to Simon," the detective asked after hours of questioning regarding what she knew about her father. "What was his involvement?"

"Leave Simon out of it," Olivia vehemently replied. "If it wasn't for him, I'd probably be dead right now. He tried to help me escape, as much as he could."

"I understand. You've said that over and over again, but he *was* involved. He's admitted as much. He has been extremely valuable to our investigation and told us about everyone who was involved that he was aware of, but he is going to have to do some prison time. We're just trying to understand everything that happened."

Olivia sighed. "He's a good man, a changed man. And that's all you need to know about Simon. Like I said, he's probably the only reason that I'm alive right now. I'm done talking about him so you can move on to something else, or you can leave." She glared at the detective. Carol chuckled a little bit, glad to see the old strong-willed Olivia returning.

"Okay. I'll move on from Simon." He glanced around the room. "I apologize, but I need to ask about Grant."

Her chin quivered from the memory and Alexander clutched her hand in his, giving her a reassuring nod.

"I'm sorry, Miss Adler, but it's imperative to the investigation that we know exactly what happened."

She took a deep, steadying breath, looking for the inner strength to relay everything that Grant did to her at the beach house. She broke down several times and Alexander didn't do much better. He wanted to kill Grant all over again. He wanted him alive so he could torture him just as he tortured his Olivia. Thinking about it made him wild with rage, but he tried to control his emotions and remain calm.

"We'll stop here for today," the detective said as the sun began to set after several hours of questioning about Grant. "Thank you for all your help, Miss Adler. It's been very useful."

She nodded, watching as he began to retreat from the room. "Did they catch everyone?" she asked. "And not just everyone incriminated in the documents. Did they catch everyone that was involved?"

He nodded. "Yes. Everyone that was named in the documents and who was involved in the plot has been apprehended, except for Mark Kiddish."

Olivia perked up. "Does that include Adele Peters?"

"Yes. She is currently in police custody as they try to determine the extent of her involvement."

Olivia grinned, trying to hide her delight at the thought of Adele being led away in handcuffs for her role in everything, wishing she could have been there to witness it. "Thank you."

"My pleasure." The detective left the room, Carol close on his heels.

"Libby," Cam said, looking down at her. "I need to get back to Florida, but I can stay if you need me to. Are you going to be okay?"

She glanced at the two men at her side and she smiled, squeezing both his and Alexander's hands. "For the first time in my life, I know that I will be. Thanks for being here."

"Anything for you." He planted a kiss on her forehead. "The next time I see you, you better be out of this hospital bed, okay?"

She nodded, watching as Cam left her room.

"Olivia, love," Alexander said once they were finally alone. "There's something I need to talk to you about. I want you to know that no one is pressuring you to do anything that you're not ready for yet. Do you understand?"

"What is it, Alexander?"

He took a deep breath. "Olivia, darling, your grandparents are here. They've been here every day this week but we wanted to wait until you were ready. They would really like to see you, but they understand if you need more time to process everything."

Her bottom lip quivered. "I can't believe that I finally have a family!" she cried out, a tear escaping from her eye.

"Oh, love," he said, cradling her in his arms. "You always

had a family."

"I used to think I was all alone in this world," she explained through her tears.

"You were never alone. I always knew you were out there." He planted a kiss on her head.

She turned and looked into Alexander's eyes. "Can I see them?"

"Of course. When do you want to see them?"

"Now?"

Alexander smiled. "Okay." He got up to go find Rose and Donald Harris. When he approached the doorway, he glanced back. "Hey, Olibia?"

"Yeah?"

"I love you."

Her heart swelled. The green-eyed boy loved her, and she had a family. She finally felt complete. "I love you, too."

Chapter Forty

A New Beginning

"ARE YOU SURE ABOUT this, Olivia?" Alexander asked as he drove down the familiar streets of Mystic, the barren trees beginning to bud.

"Yes. I need to see it," she responded firmly.

"Okay," he exhaled, steering through the gates of the cemetery. Helping her out of the car, he wrapped his arms around her. "You're a strong girl, you know that?"

Olivia blushed.

"And that's why I love you so fucking much. Now, come." He held her hand and led her to the three gravestones he had become so accustomed to seeing once a year for the past twenty-two years. They trekked through the dew on the grass on an early March morning and stopped in front of the three marble headstones.

"Wow," she said under her breath almost in disbelief at the sight in front of her. A tear escaped.

Alexander squeezed her hand. "We can leave if it's too much."

She shook her head. "No. I need to do this so that I can move on with my life." She turned to stare into the green eyes that she had loved since the day she was born, even if she didn't know it. "My life with you."

Alexander smiled. "Okay. But the minute it becomes too much, you let me know and we'll go."

Olivia nodded before breaking away from him. Clutching the stuffed animal that held all the answers in her hand, she walked over to her mother's grave. She gently ran her hand across the headstone and set Mr. Bear in front of it. "Thank you, Mama. I did what you said. I held on to Mr. Bear. All those people are finally behind bars. At least, now, your death wasn't for nothing." She looked up and saw several butterflies flutter from behind the grave. She was caught by surprise and immediately thought of her mother's words about how she would know when she was in love.

"Tomorrow's my wedding day. Alexander and I are finally getting married...a real wedding this time, instead of one of our make-believe ones." She smiled at the memory of all the games she used to make Alexander play with her. "He found me even after I was taken away from everyone when you died. He never gave up hope that I was still alive. He never forgot about me. All those years, I thought that I had no family, but I did...one that was searching for me. One that is about to celebrate the biggest day of my life with me tomorrow. I wish you could be here for it." Her chin quivered as she looked at the vibrant red roses lying in front of her mother's grave. "I love you, Mama. Thank you for loving me." She pressed her lips to her hand before leaving a kiss on her mother's headstone.

Taking a deep breath and trying to find the inner strength to get through what she needed to, she walked to where her father had supposedly been buried for all those years...his fake grave. Memories of that night back in August flashed through her mind. Her knees gave out and she sank to the ground, unable to hold back the tears.

"Olivia!" Alexander exclaimed, rushing to her side and wrapping his arms around her. "Come on, let's go. You don't have to do this." He brought her head into his chest, soothing her sobs. "This is too much. I'll have that fucking gravestone removed. You shouldn't have to be reminded..."

Olivia vehemently shook her head. "No! It stays. The man I knew as my father *did* die that day. The man I met last summer was *not* my father. I need it to stay, as a reminder."

He sighed. "Okay. If you're sure."

She nodded, bringing her head out of his chest, and looked

at her father's gravestone. "Can I just have a minute, please?"

"Of course." Alexander planted a soft kiss on her forehead before leaving her.

She turned her head, staring at the grave belonging to the man that, at one point, ruined her life. But the more she thought about it, the less that seemed true. He didn't ruin her life. If one thing differed, she may not be where she was at that moment. If she wasn't ripped from her friends and family, she may have grown apart from them eventually, Alexander included. She didn't even want to think about not being with him. He was her life. He was her world so, for that, she held no grudges.

"Hi, Daddy," Olivia said. "I know you're not buried here, but the memories of the man I knew and loved are. I just wanted to say that I forgive you. I *need* to forgive you so I can move on. You will never be able to ruin my life again. For the longest time after I got out of the hospital this past August, that's what I thought. I was so angry at you for ripping me away from my friends and family. But that anger won't change anything. For me to move on, I need to bury that anger. And the only way I know how is to forgive you for what you did to me...this past August *and* that August all those years ago. You don't deserve my forgiveness, but I need to be the bigger person. So I forgive you. After today, I'll never have to think about you again...at least not the man you turned into." She slowly stood up. "Good-bye, Daddy." She gently caressed the headstone. "Your Livvy will always love you, but Olivia will not." She turned away, tears streaming down her face.

"Olivia, angel. We can come back later..." Alexander pulled her body into his, hating to see how upset she was.

"No. I need to see it. I'm stronger than this."

"I know you are, but it's okay if you want to go."

Olivia shook her head. "No. I only need one more minute. I just want to see it." She turned away and walked to a smaller headstone, yellow sunflowers lying in front. She glanced over her shoulder, grinning. "Been here recently, Mr. Burnham?"

He shrugged. "It's a standing order. You always loved sunflowers. You called them..."

"Giant daffodils," she recalled. "You were right. They look nothing like daffodils."

"Yeah." A tear fell down Alexander's face, weeping for the loss of his best friend all those years ago. He took a step toward Olivia, brushing a wayward curl away from her eye. "I wish I could have known you all those years. I think that's what hurts the most."

"But if one thing was different, we wouldn't be where we are now…about to get married." She stood on her toes, brushing her lips against his, savoring the feeling of his mouth on her cold skin. "Now please. Take me home and make love to me before Kiera gets here and banishes you to your house until tomorrow afternoon."

His eyes grew wide, forgetting that he wouldn't be able to see Olivia that night. "Yes, ma'am!" He scooped her up in his arms and gingerly placed her in the front seat of the car. He drove rather carelessly through the streets of downtown Mystic before pulling up in front of Olivia's childhood home.

"This place brings back some great memories," he commented after Olivia opened the front door, granting them both entry.

"You can reminisce later, Alexander." She took off her coat and walked up to him. Unbuttoning his jacket, she stood mere breaths away. "Right now, I need you inside of me." She looked into his vibrant green eyes and felt shivers run through her body.

He crushed his lips to hers and pushed her against the wall of the kitchen. "God, Olivia. Just a simple kiss and I'm ready to ravage you."

She leaned her head back, giving him access to her neck. He nipped her earlobe, planting rough kisses on her skin. She moaned out in response.

"You like that?" he asked coyly.

"Yes," she exhaled. "I need to feel your lips on me. Don't stop."

"We'll make love tomorrow night," he growled. "I plan on fucking you right now, right here against this wall. Now take off your clothes," he demanded.

Olivia's heart started to race. She loved the two very different sides of Alexander. It was one of the many things she loved about him. She stood staring into his green eyes, overwhelmed with love.

"What did I say, Olivia?" Alexander asked, snapping her back from her thoughts.

"Sorry."

"Sorry, what?" he said, grabbing her nipple through her shirt and pinching.

Olivia moaned. "Sorry, Mr. Burnham."

"That's better. Clothes. Off. Now."

"Yes." She quickly rid herself of her sweater and bra, followed by her jeans and panties while Alexander stood watching.

"Turn around," he said quietly.

Olivia obeyed, spinning around, and looked straight ahead at the kitchen wall in front of her, listening to the sound of Alexander's clothes hitting the floor. She could feel him approach behind her. The anticipation was killing her.

"Put your hands up on the wall. Brace yourself, love." His voice was demanding but, at the same time, soft and sensual.

She did as she was told, tremors coursing through her entire body. Out of nowhere, she felt his tongue between her legs as she stood bracing herself against the wall. "Fuck!" she exclaimed.

"You like that, Olivia?" Alexander breathed.

"God, yes," she replied, his tongue continuing its torturous journey around her clit.

"You are delicious, Olivia. I just needed a little taste before I have to wait an entire day."

She felt him raise himself and, within seconds, he gradually pushed into her, both of them moaning in pleasure. He moved slowly at first, filling her.

She held her arms against the wall as he picked up the tempo, flexing in a steady rhythm.

"I love this view. You have the cutest butt," he said, bringing his hand back and smacking her cheek.

She yelped out in surprise before he grabbed on to her hips, his movements still gentle and deliberate.

"Faster, Alex," she exhaled. She was so close. She needed her release.

"Already, Olivia?"

"Yes," she exhaled.

"Damn." He picked up his pace, driving into her, reaching around and tugging on her nipple.

Olivia squealed, the feeling of him moving inside of her and pulling her nipple sending her over the edge. She screamed out his name and came undone, the aftershocks of her orgasm lasting several minutes as Alexander found his own release, coming inside of her.

He reached around, resting his hand on Olivia's stomach, helping to support her as he gently nipped on her shoulder. "I know I say this all the time, but I just love being inside of you."

Olivia smiled. "And I love it when you're inside of me. Now move it so I can clean your come off me."

"Nah. Keep it there."

"Alex..."

He laughed, withdrawing from her and gently picking her up in his arms.

"I love you, Olibia."

"And I love you, Alexander. I can't wait to be your wife."

"I've been waiting all my life for you to come back to me. And you were so worth it."

CHAPTER FORTY-ONE

SURPRISE

"KIERA," OLIVIA SAID THE following day as she got ready in her childhood bedroom. "Can you go down the street and give this to Tyler, please? Tell him to give it to Alexander right before he enters the church." She handed her a small envelope. "It's his wedding present from me."

"What did you get him? This is just a card."

"The present is *in* the card," Olivia replied, nervous energy coursing through her entire body as she contemplated Alexander's reaction.

"Okay. I'll be back in a few."

Kiera left and Olivia returned to stare at the girl in the mirror. She looked the same as she did over a year-and-a-half ago, but she felt so different, like a huge weight had been lifted. She was no longer just going through the motions, trying to survive. She had something to fight for. She had Alexander. She had a family. Finally.

~~~~~~~~~~~

"KNOCK, KNOCK," KIERA CALLED out, walking into Alexander's house. Hordes of people were milling about in the large living and dining areas, waiting to head to the historic church down the street.

"Hey, baby," Mo said, wrapping his arms around her. "It's our turn next, ya' know."

Kiera grinned, excited about marrying him the following

304

year. "Where's Tyler?"

Mo gestured with his head toward the dining room. "He's in there, talking with Olivia's grandparents."

"How's Alex doing?"

"Good. Excited. He just wants the wedding over. He wants to marry that girl something fierce."

Kiera laughed. "And I want to marry you something fierce."

"Then let's go to Vegas next weekend! Come on, baby…"

"Jack, both of our families would kill us. It'll be the crime of the century anyway, an Italian marrying an Irish woman in Boston."

"You're right about that," he laughed.

"I gotta run. I'll see you at the church." She planted an affectionate kiss on his lips and went in search of the best man. "Tyler!" she yelled, half of the house turning to look at her. "Whoops."

Tyler simply shook his head and walked over to Kiera in her deep green tea-length bridesmaid dress. "You sure do know how to make an entrance."

She laughed. "I know." She handed him the envelope. "I've been instructed by the bride to give this to you. You are to give it to the groom right before he goes into the church and not a second before. Do you understand?"

He scrunched his eyebrows in confusion. "What is it? It just looks like a card."

Kiera shrugged. "Hell if I know. Bitch hasn't told me anything."

"Okay. Well, here." He picked up a shirt-sized box from the dining room table. "Give this to the bride. She can open it before she leaves."

"Got it." Kiera grabbed the gift and left just as people began filing out to make their way to the church. She hurried back to Olivia's house to finish getting ready.

"It's about time you got back," Bridget remarked when Kiera walked through the front door.

"Sorry. I got held up. Is she ready?"

"Yeah. I helped her into the dress. I had to hook all those buttons by myself, thank you very much!"

"Sorry."

"It wasn't that bad. I'm just giving you shit."

Kiera laughed. "Bitch." She ran up the stairs, busting through the door to where Olivia was getting ready. She looked at her best friend and tears began to well up in her eyes. "Oh, Libby. You look beautiful."

Olivia met Kiera's eyes, becoming rather emotional all of a sudden. "Stop it, Care Bear, or I'm going to cry and smudge my eye makeup."

"It's okay. I used waterproof."

"Good, because I'm so going to need it." She eyed the box Kiera had clutched in her hands. "What's that?"

"Oh. This is from Alexander. He said you can open it now. Do you want some privacy?"

"No. You can stay." She grabbed the box and slowly unwrapped it, gasping when she pulled back the tissue paper, exposing her gift.

"What is it?"

"I can't believe he still had this…" Olivia looked down into the box. There was a frame around the picture she drew for Alexander on his first day of school. "I was so mad at him for leaving me and starting school," she explained to Kiera. "I cried and cried that day. Then my mama told me that Alex wouldn't be very happy if he came over after school and I was still crying. She told me to draw a picture to give to him. I drew this." She looked at the old drawing of stick figure versions of Alexander and Olivia eating ice cream. Her heart swelled and she desperately wanted to get to that church and marry her best friend.

~~~~~~~~~~

"NERVOUS?" TYLER ASKED AS he drove Alexander to the church.

"No. I've never been so sure of anything in my life."

"You're not leaving this one at the altar, are you?"

"Ha, ha. Very funny."

Tyler pulled the car into the parking lot and the two

brothers got out, heading toward the front door of the church. "Wait. Before you go in, Olivia wanted you to have this." He handed him the envelope.

"Alex, dear!" his mother called from the front steps. "We need to start! Olivia's here and the girls are all ready. We just need the groom. Tyler, you're on my shit list for taking him to a bar on the way here, young man!"

"Coming, Ma." Alexander laughed, opening the envelope as he walked into the church. He stopped dead in his tracks when he looked at the fuzzy black-and-white picture mounted on a piece of card stock.

"What is it?"

Alexander's heart started racing. He couldn't believe it. "I'll tell you later. Let's get this show started." He was so excited that his hands were shaking. He wanted nothing more than to see Olivia at that moment. He wanted to wrap his arms around her and kiss her and never let her go again.

He took his place at the altar and the processional began. The guests laughed when Runner emerged onto the aisle, trotting toward his master with two shining rings attached to his green collar. "Good boy," Alexander said, grabbing the dog's collar and handing the rings to Tyler.

It seemed to take forever for Bridget and Kiera to walk down the aisle of the church. Alexander just wanted to see his bride. Finally, he heard the music change to the familiar strains of The Beatles' *I Will*, and he knew Olivia was about to walk down that aisle. His heart started to beat madly in his chest. Finally, she appeared in the doorway carrying a bouquet of sunflowers with Mo standing next to her. He thought it was sweet that she asked him to give her away. She looked amazing, wearing a champagne-colored gown. It was simple, yet elegant. It was very Olivia. That's what she was. Simple, yet elegant. Finally, she took a step, but Alexander couldn't wait any longer.

Stepping into the aisle, he rushed to her, wrapping his arms around her, and kissed her. "It's true?" he asked through his tears.

Olivia looked at him through her own tears. She nodded, a

grin on her face. "Yeah. We're having a baby, Alex. September."

He crushed his lips to hers once more, not caring that everyone was watching.

"Hey, man. I haven't given her away yet," Mo said.

Olivia laughed as Alexander pulled back, staring deep into her big brown eyes. "You better get up there, Mr. Burnham. You knocked me up. You've got to make an honest woman out of me now."

"Oh, love. I've been waiting my entire life for this moment."

"Me, too." She tilted her head and brushed her lips against his.

CHAPTER FORTY-TWO

LOVELY

AUGUST TWENTY-FOURTH. A DAY that he used to hate, no longer lay heavy over Alexander's heart. The sun woke him up early that Sunday and he lovingly admired his wife, her belly protruding from her slim frame, before hopping in the shower. When he was finally ready to start his day, he returned to the bed where his Olivia was still resting peacefully, and gingerly placed a kiss on her forehead.

Olivia stirred, rubbing her eyes. "Hey," she said sleepily.

"Good morning, love. How are my two best girls this morning?"

She smiled. "One of us is tired. The other one is running a marathon. Take a guess which is which."

Alexander laughed. "She's definitely taking after her mama then." He leaned down and planted an affectionate kiss on her lips. "I need to head into the office for a quick meeting. I'll be back in a few hours. Will you be okay?"

"Go. I'll be fine. I'll probably be in the same exact position when you get back."

Alexander raised himself off the bed. "Okay. I'll see you soon, Mrs. Burnham."

"I can't wait, Mr. Burnham."

He turned to leave.

"Oh, and Mr. Burnham?"

"Yes?" Alexander said, spinning around.

"Happy birthday, Daddy."

Alexander smiled, leaving Olivia resting in their bed. She

soon drifted back off to sleep for a bit before the excruciating pain set in. She raised herself into a sitting position, feeling something sticky between her legs. Looking down, she saw blood.

~~~~~~~~~~~

AFTER HIS MEETING, ALEXANDER decided to stop and get sunflowers for Olivia. It was August twenty-fourth, after all. Why break with tradition? Instead of having Martin cart him around, he let him have the day off, hating to ask someone to work on a Sunday when he could easily walk to the office. After the meeting, he strolled through the city streets of Boston, love overwhelming his heart when the vision of Olivia's pregnant frame flashed through his mind. Stopping at a flower market, he grabbed a beautiful sunflower bouquet before making his way back to his penthouse.

As he approached the front door of his apartment building, he reached into his pocket, suddenly realizing that he had left his cellphone on the nightstand. "Crap," he said, running to the bank of elevators and pressing his code for the penthouse. He hoped Olivia hadn't needed anything while he was gone.

When the doors opened, he ran out of the elevator and up the stairs to the bedroom. Olivia was nowhere to be found.

And on her side of the bed was a pool of blood.

"Shit!" he exclaimed, grabbing his cell phone, seeing several missed calls, mostly from Kiera. "FUCK!"

With shaking hands, he called her.

"Alex!" she shouted, answering the call. "You left your phone at home!"

"Don't you think I know that?! Where's Olivia?"

"She's here at M.G.H. Her placenta ruptured. They had to knock her out. You need to get here. They're getting the baby out."

"Fuck! I'll be right there."

He ran down the stairs and scrambled into an elevator, willing it to move faster. Within thirty minutes, he pulled up out front of M.G.H., rushing to the labor and delivery floor to find out what was going on, the entire time thinking about how nothing good had ever come out of August twenty-fourth.

"Alex!" Kiera shouted when she saw him run through the doors leading to the registration area.

"Kiera! Mo! What's going on?" he asked nervously, his expression changing when he saw their calm, smiling faces.

She beamed. "You're a daddy, Alex. Come on." She grabbed his hand, walking him down a long corridor as he tried to process the fact that he was a father. "Olivia is still knocked out. They had to give her general anesthesia and perform a C-section. She's a little small considering she *was* born about three weeks early, but baby and mommy are fine."

"Damn it. I missed it."

Kiera laughed. "We all did. No one could be in the room with her. They kicked me out, too." She stopped in front of a door and gently pushed it open. A nurse sat feeding a bottle to a tiny pink bundle, looking up when she heard the door open.

"Are you the daddy?" she asked.

Alexander's heart beat faster. *Holy crap. I'm a daddy.* He simply nodded his head, speechless for the first time in recent history.

"Good. Then I'll let you do this so she can start to bond with you while Mrs. Burnham sleeps it off." She got out of the rocking chair and Alexander sat down. "Everyone is okay. It was scary for a minute, but Mommy and baby pulled through wonderfully. May I introduce your daughter." She placed a small bundle in Alexander's arms and he held his daughter for the first time, rocking her as she drank from the bottle.

"Am I doing this right?" he asked.

The nurse smiled. "You're a natural."

He looked down at his daughter. She wasn't even an hour old and she already had a full head of dark hair. She kept her eyes closed as she nursed. He rocked back and forth, feeling overwhelmed with love for his Olivia and the little person that they created through their love.

~~~~~~~~~~

OLIVIA WAS DREAMING THE most wonderful dream when she started to hear soft singing. She fluttered her eyes open, staring at comforting pink walls. She gazed over at the far corner of the room where the green-eyed boy sat rocking a little pink bundle, singing a slow version of *Isn't She Lovely*. She smiled at how perfect everything was.

"Hi, Daddy," she said after Alexander finished singing to their daughter.

He shot his head up, smiling when his eyes met Olivia's gaze. Slowly raising himself off the rocking chair, he walked over to the bed. "Hi, Mama. Want to meet our daughter?"

She nodded and he helped her sit up before placing the newborn in her arms. "She's perfect," she commented, looking at her adorable little nose.

"What do we want to name her?" Alexander asked, kissing Olivia's forehead.

"Melanie," she replied, not even having to think about it.

Alexander smiled. "Melanie. It's perfect."

Olivia held her baby, gently kissing her head, thankful for everything she had. It was truly fitting that little Melanie made her appearance on August twenty-fourth. The day that had represented loss and pain for so long now represented something entirely different. It represented second chances. It represented life. It represented love. And, above all, it represented family.

PROLOGUE

"WHAT TIME ARE YOU off tonight?" Kiera asked as she wiped down the bar.

"I'm cut at midnight. You?"

"Closing."

"It's kind of dead, except for that group of guys over there. They're throwing 'em back something fierce, too! It's a Tuesday night, for crying out loud! Who gets that hammered on a Tuesday night?" Olivia remarked.

"You have to remember that you're in Boston now, sweetheart. There's a college every three feet. It's a little different than Charleston, isn't it?"

Olivia sighed. "Yeah. But that's a good thing."

"Finally!" Kiera laughed. "Took you long enough to realize this city is far better than Charleston."

"I've only been here a year, Care Bear. It took me a little bit to get used to the faster pace of everything."

"I know. I'm just teasing," she said, playfully pushing her friend. "That guy over there is kind of hot, don't ya' think? He looks like he's your age," Kiera commented, gesturing with her head to where a group of eight college-aged guys sat guzzling back beers, apparently celebrating something.

"I guess," Olivia replied, shrugging her shoulders.

"Come on, Libs. I know you. He's so your type. Go talk to him. I'm going to take my break before you leave, anyway. What do you have to lose?"

She sighed. "How many times do I have to tell you? I don't date. I…"

"Yeah, yeah," Kiera interrupted. "You fuck and that's it. I got it. But, one of these days, you're going to find someone that sweeps you off your feet, and you'll want something more meaningful. Too bad it's not with the hottie over there," Kiera replied cheerily before climbing over the bar and down a long corridor into the staff room, leaving Olivia alone behind the bar with just her thoughts to consume her time.

~~~~~~~~~~

"TO ALEX!" A RATHER drunk kid shouted, his voice ringing through the relatively empty bar. "I can't believe you're crazy enough to go through SEAL training. You are one bad ass motherfucker!"

"Damn straight!" Alex slurred, slinging back his beer. He had lost track of how many he had drank that night. He was trying to get his fill while he could. In two days, he would be heading back to Norfolk before having to report for training, and he needed to get through. Failing was not an option. He needed this. He needed something that could finally take his mind off *her*. She still haunted his dreams. He saw her everywhere. Hell, she was even his bartender that night.

"That hottie bartender is looking over here," one of Alexander's old Harvard friends said, interrupting his thoughts. "Dude, go talk to her. Get one last piece of ass before *your* ass is back in the Navy. Come on, Alex. Looks like she's about to go home for the night. It's now or never."

Alexander grinned and chugged the rest of his beer. He had been enjoying the last month that he was home on leave. He had been screwing girls left and right because that's what he did. He needed to. It was the only way to get *her* out of his head. The guilt of what happened that day still lay heavy on his heart.

"You're right!" Alexander shouted, slamming his empty beer bottle on the table. "It's one of my last nights here! Why waste it hanging out with you fuckers?!" He stumbled off his barstool and made his way toward the front door, catching up with the bartender he had his eye on. "Excuse me," he said, trying to get her attention.

This is why I hate bartending, Olivia thought to herself as she spun around, crossing her arms protectively in front of her chest and glaring at the drunk guy who called out to her. Her gaze softened when she saw his brilliant green eyes. He looked so familiar, but she would have remembered meeting someone that devastatingly handsome before.

He stood there with a dumbfounded look on his face, remaining silent while Olivia stared.

"Well, are you going to talk or are you fucking mute?" she spat out, rebuilding her wall.

Alexander ran his fingers through his hair, trying to compose his thoughts. There was something about her that made him nervous. That was a new thing for him. He was *never* jittery around women. And those eyes… "I just wanted to thank you for taking care of me and my friends tonight," he said, finally finding his voice. He reached into his wallet and took out several large bills. "You made most of our drinks and I didn't want you to get shortchanged on your tips." He handed Olivia the cash.

She looked down. "This is two hundred dollars. I think that's a little much. Anyway, we pool tips."

Alexander shrugged. "I know. But I thought you should have it."

Olivia stared at him. "I don't need it."

"Neither do I. I'm in the Navy. I'm heading for SEAL training in two days. This is one of my last nights in Boston," he explained.

"Maybe you should donate this money to charity then."

"Well, if you won't take my money, let me take you out to breakfast tomorrow."

"Why?"

"Because." He shrugged. "You're the most beautiful woman I've ever laid eyes on and I want a good memory of this city before I leave."

"I don't think so." Olivia handed the cash back before she pushed past him and out the front door.

"Wait!" Alexander shouted, following her onto Boylston

315

Street.

Olivia huffed, but turned around. There was something about him that made her want to obey him. "What?"

Alexander shuffled his feet a little, looking into her big brown eyes, wondering why he felt as if he knew her from somewhere. "At least tell me your name."

Olivia sighed. "Sarah. My name is Sarah." She looked across the street and noticed her uncle sitting in his car, keeping an eye on her. He would not be happy if he saw her talking to anyone he didn't know. "I have to go," she said quickly before turning and practically running away.

Alexander turned his head to where she was looking before she got spooked. *What the…?*

He stormed across the street to the car where the reason why he wanted to leave Boston so quickly sat. He threw open the driver's side door. *Sarah must have noticed someone looking at us,* Alexander thought.

"Son," Thomas said. "What…?" His eyes went wide, wondering if he realized who he was just speaking with.

"Come to spy on me, Dad?"

"Alex, calm down," he said cautiously, debating whether to tell him about everything. He had been keeping such an enormous secret from him for years, and he was about to go for SEAL training. If he made it through and was sent overseas to work special-ops, he may never see his son again. No. It was time to tell him. He needed to know. "That girl…"

"No. You know what?" Alexander interrupted. "I'm done listening to you! What I do on my own time is my fucking business! If I wanted to go out with the guys for some beers or take home a hot girl, I'm damn well going to do it! If you really cared about me, maybe you should have been around more when I was growing up instead of putting your fucking job ahead of me! I'm done with you. Tell Ma if she wants to see me before I leave, I'll be at Charley's tomorrow around eleven for breakfast."

He spun around and hailed a cab.

"Alex, wait!" Thomas yelled.

Alexander flipped off his father as the yellow cab sped away, driving him to Adele's apartment by Wellesly.

"That's your Olivia. I'm so sorry, Alex," he said to no one at all.

The End.

PLAYLIST

Contact High - Allen Stone
Beneath Your Beautiful - Labrinth
I Won't Give Up - Jason Mraz
Out Of My Hands - Dave Matthews Band
Some Devil - Dave Matthews
I Was Gonna Marry You - Tristan Prettyman
Before it Breaks - Brandi Carlile
Elephant - Damien Rice
L'il Darlin - ZZ Ward
Last Love Song - ZZ Ward
Landed - Ben Folds Five
Been A Long Day - Rosi Golan
Nine Crimes - Damien Rice
Time Bomb - Dave Matthews Band
Cold Hearted - Zac Brown Band
Mess I Made - Parachute
Be Still - The Fray
Come Clean - Tristan Prettyman
Seven Devils - Florence & The Machine
Bottom Of The River - Delta Rae
A Thousand Years - Christina Perri
A Beautiful Mess - Jason Mraz
My Baby Blue - Dave Matthews Band
Till Kingdom Come - Coldplay
February Seven - Avett Brothers
I Will - The Beatles
Isn't She Lovely - Livingston Taylor
                    (Original by Stevie Wonder)

ACKNOWLEDGEMENTS

I have no idea where to even begin with acknowledgements. With each book, these are getting more and more difficult to write, and I couldn't be happier.

March 29, 2013 is a day that I will always remember. It was the day that I wrote the very first lines of my *Beautiful Mess* series. Those lines actually appear in this book. The first scene I ever wrote was when Olivia found out that Alexander had been keeping her identity from her. Of course, at that time, her name was Taylor and Alexander was Gregory. It sounded a bit too presidential to me, so I switched up the names, mainly because I heard Alexander yelling at her and screaming the name, Olivia, instead of Taylor. It's amazing how much inspiration you can find when you shut off for a minute and go for a run.

Now, over a year later, I feel overwhelmed with the positive response to these books. These are my babies, and I'm not ready to say good-bye to these characters. I've lived and breathed the story of Alexander, Olivia, Kiera, Mo, and Cam over the past fourteen months. They've woken me up in the middle of the night, telling me that I had to change something. I've laughed with them. I've cried with them. I've felt every emotion that they faced, and because of that I hate to say good-bye.

This has been an incredible journey… A journey that I hope is just starting as there are so many more stories that need to be told, battling for attention in my head. None of this wouldn't have been possible without the love and support of my parents and my two sisters - Donald and Linda Martin, Melissa Morgera, and Amy Perras. Thank you for encouraging this crazy dream of mine since I told you about the books back in July. To my best friend, Kerri Deschaine, thanks for being crazy enough for me to base a character on you. Everyone needs a little Kiera in their lives and I'm sure glad I have you in mine... (Sorry for what happened to Kiera. I still love you, Care Bear!)

To my wonderful editor, Kim Young. Thank you for being able to read my mind when it couldn't function because too many thoughts were swimming in my head. I am so grateful that I found you and can't wait for you to work on Cam's story for me... (I know... You're so #TeamCam!)

To my fantastic Head of Social Media, Lea James, my own Fierce & Fabulous Book Diva, I love you hard. And next signing event, all drinks will be in a sippy cup.

I also need to mention my incredible street team. Without them, I'm fairly certain that no one would have heard about my books. You all rock my world and words seem to be so inadequate to relay how much your time and effort means to me. Alexis Brodie, Anna Kesy, Brenda Mcleod, Cecilia Ugas, Cheryl Tuggle, Christine Davison, Chrissy Fletcher, Cindy Gibson, Claire Pengelly, Crystal Casquero, Crystal Solis, Crystal Swarmer, Danielle Estes, Donna Montville, Eann Goodwin-Giddings, Ebony McMillan, Erin Thompson, Estella Robinson, Jamie Kimok, Janie Beaton, Jennifer Goncalves, Jennifer Maikis, Jennifer Patton, Jessica Green, Johnnie-Marie Howard, Kathryn Adair, Kathy Arguelles, Kathy Coopmans, Kayla Hines, Karrie Puskas, Keesha Murray, Kim King, Kimberly Kazawic, Kimberly Twedt, Lea James, Lindsey Armstrong, Lori Garside, Lori Moore, Marianna Nichols, Meg Faulkner, Megan Galt, Melissa Miller-Mattern, Natasha Rochon, Nicola Horner, Nicole Chronister, Pamela McGuire, Rachel Hill, Shane Zajac, Shannon Baker-Ferguson, Shannon Palmer, Shayna Snyder, Stefani Tabakovska, Stefanie Lewis, Suzie Cairney, Tabitha Stokes, Tiffany Tyler, Tracey Williams, Victoria Stolte, Yamara Martinez... Much love and #BurnhamBitchesForLife.

A special thanks to the lovely Liz Lovelock from *Magic Within the Pages* Blog, and Amy McGlone and Tonya Nagle from *Turn The Pages*. I could never repay you for all your amazing support and words of encouragement. Without bloggers like you, this indie world would be hard. You make it fun… So thank you.

To my amazing husband, Stan Kellam, thank you for supporting this crazy notion of mine to actually be a writer full time. I'm truly blessed to have run into you in the parking lot of a Jimmy Buffett concert all those years ago.

To my incredible group of Beta readers: Lynne Ayling, Karen Emery, Natalie Naranjo, Stacy Stoops… This is not the end… It's only the beginning. I can't wait to share with you what I have next!

And last but not least, thank you to all my amazing fans. Thank you for taking the chance on a no-name indie author. Without all of you, I would never have experienced the success that I have. Much love and now it's Cam's turn!

ABOUT THE AUTHOR

T.K. Leigh, otherwise known as Tracy Leigh Kellam, is a producer/attorney by trade. Originally from New England, she now resides in sunny Southern California with her husband, dog and three cats, all of which she has rescued (including the husband). She always had a knack for writing, but mostly in the legal field. It wasn't until recently that she decided to try her hand at creative writing and is now addicted to creating different characters and new and unique story lines in the Contemporary Romantic Suspense genre.

Her debut novel, *A Beautiful Mess*, has garnered relative praise, having been an Amazon Best Seller, as well a Number One Best Seller in Romantic Suspense, Women's Action and Adventure Fiction, Women's Crime Fiction, and Women's Psychological Fiction. Recently, the book was named by The Guardian as a top reader-recommended self-published book of 2013 as well as a 2013 Reader's Favorite in Publisher's Weekly in addition to being named an Amazon Romance Editor's Fan Favorite for Top Debut Author and Best Page Turner.

The sequel to *A Beautiful Mess*, entitled *A Tragic Wreck*, became an Amazon Top-50 Best Selling Book on the day of its release. It is also an Amazon Number One Best Seller in Women's Sagas, Women's Psychological Fiction, Women's Action and Adventure Fiction, and Women's Crime Fiction.

When she's not planted in front of her computer, writing away, she can be found running and training for her next marathon (of which she has run over fifteen fulls and far too many halfs to recall). Unlike Olivia, the main character in her Beautiful Mess series, she has yet to qualify for the Boston Marathon.